Book One

JENNIFER HARTMANN

This book is for you, Mom.
You kept a poem I wrote when I was just a little girl in your bedside drawer, saying I was going to be a writer one day. You're not here to see that day, but I think you'd be really proud of me.

AUTHOR NOTE

This duet was originally published in April and May of 2020, being my debut series as an author. These two books have since been remastered into first person point of view to match the voice of my other works, and to stay consistent with the more conventional writing style of the contemporary romance genre. While major plotlines and character arcs remain the same, many areas of the story have been fleshed out, and a few bonus scenes have been added. This is not a full rewrite. It's more like a polishing of a preexisting story. This romance has always remained close to my heart, so I wanted to give it a second chance to shine. ♡

PROLOGUE
CHELSIE

FIVE YEARS EARLIER

His hands were around my throat.

I couldn't breathe.

I couldn't breathe.

"Sweet Chelly Belly," he sing-songed, his eyes long past dead. "You look so pretty when you struggle."

"I-Ian... pl-please..."

"Even prettier when you beg."

My lungs burned for air as I kicked at him, my legs flailing wildly. Ian's hulking frame caged me in, my body trapped between his knees as he loomed above me with amusement dancing across his lips. Peppermint shampoo tickled my nose, fusing with the gin on his breath.

I couldn't breathe.

Gasping and choking, I squeaked out more desperate pleas. "Let... let me g-go..."

"Don't you want to know, Chelly Bean?" His fingers curled harder around my fragile neck, bruising and punishing.

"Wh-what?"

I kept kicking, kept fighting, kept begging for mercy.

Ian grinned with malice. "Don't you want to know what it feels like to take your last breath?"

My eyes popped. Fear swam through my veins, potent and palpable.

This was it.

I was going to die at the hands of someone I once called my lover.

But Ian was no lover—he was always a monster, and monsters couldn't love. I'd been a fool to think there was a man hiding inside all of that ugliness.

I clawed at his face, adrenaline and survival giving me a second wind. Thrashing beneath him, I shot my knee up until it connected with his groin, but I was too weak. Too frail.

He just laughed.

"I... I don't want to die..." I rasped.

Ian's smirk seemed to freeze in place for a moment before he finally let go. Jumping off me, he rose to his feet and scratched at the coarse bristles on his chin. "I s'pose you're more fun to play with when you're alive."

It took a long heartbeat for me to realize I could finally breathe.

I sucked in a giant mouthful of air, my hands trembling as my fingertips touched my throat. Pain radiated through me, my lungs wheezing, still fighting for breaths.

He always got like this when he drank—nasty and violent. Ian loved playing games with me. He got off on my fear.

Finding a jolt of strength, I scooted myself backward until I was pressed up against the far wall with a heavy chest and glistening eyes. Tears fell as I whispered, "Stay away from me, Ian. I- It's over."

He barked a cold laugh. "It'll never be over, Chelsie."

"It is," I insisted, nodding emphatically through my tears. Two gray-blue eyes stared back at me, twinkling with steel and frost. "I'm done. I'm done being scared and weak and—"

Ian moved forward so fast, like an animal; a skilled predator closing in on its prey. "You'll always be scared and weak," he murmured, crouching down until we were face-to-face. His hand extended, knuckles grazing over a slow-healing bruise along my cheekbone. "That's 'cause I'll always be with you, little girl. I'll be hiding in every shadow, every creaky footstep in the hallway. I'll be lurking inside every man you think you can fix."

A gasp escaped, leaving me rattled.

"You can run, Chelly Bean, but I'll be right behind you, breathing down your neck." He brushed a finger down the side of my throat, his eyes dipping to where his hands had choked me. A smile slipped. "Besides, who's going to take care of you? You think you'll find someone who'll put up with your bullshit? Someone who will... what?" The smile stretched, laced with cruelty. "Love you?"

My head swung back and forth while stringy, unwashed hair smacked me in the face. "Stop... I'm going to make it on my own. I-I'm leaving you for good."

"Where would a lost little girl like you go?" he pondered. Leaning in, Ian's hot breath whispered along my lips, dripping with liquor and venom. "You're nothing but a disease—a leach. No house, no car, no job. Even Mommy and Daddy left you behind. They knew you were beyond repair."

My eyes narrowed.

"I only tolerate your stupid ass. That's the best you're ever gonna get."

I shoved him away, planting my palms against his shoulders until he teetered back with a chuckle. Scrambling to my feet, my legs were still shaking as I tried to find my balance. "If you come after me, I'm calling the police."

"Scary," he mocked.

Newfound purpose bubbled in my blood.

I didn't want to live like this anymore.

And I didn't want to die.

Sparing him a final glance, I whipped around, darting out of his living room and heading for the door. It was time to start over.

It was time to truly live.

"You'll be crawlin' back in no time, Chelly Belly," Ian called out, his words prickling my skin as I escaped into the afternoon sun. Before the door slammed shut, laughter mingled with his final send-off. "After all, there ain't no place like home."

My feet pounded the pavement as I raced through the grass, down the sidewalk, and into a frightening unknown.

Home.

He was right—there *was* no place like home.

I just hadn't found it yet...

CHAPTER ONE

CHELSIE

NOW

I t was Beatlemania all over again.

Fans were crying, screaming, fainting, undressing, and pulling each other's hair just to get closer to the four men on stage. The crowd consisted of hormonal college girls, soccer moms, grandmothers, men, and a pair of disabled women using their wheelchairs as weapons as they weaved through the masses. It was pure hysteria, and I couldn't wait until the night was over.

I inched down the skirt of my waitress uniform as I made my way over to a corner table, holding a tray of refreshments high above my head. The noise level at The Pit Stop bordered on painful, and I adjusted my handy ear plugs when I passed by a table of twenty-somethings.

A girl in a scandalous pink tube top squealed over the music. "*Oh. My. God.* He looked at me. Devon Sawyer just looked at me. You saw that, right?"

Her friend nodded with excitement. "He totally looked at you! Scratch that—he *totally* checked you out."

Both girls shared in a girl-bonding-giggle-fest, and I held my tongue as I walked by the Scandalous Twins. My fake smile was firmly in place, my pleasantries—well, pleasant—while I passed out drinks to another table of college girls. They handed me a tip, so I upped my smile to an award-winning flash of teeth.

It twisted into a sour scowl as soon as I pivoted and headed toward the kitchen.

I hated my job. I hated the crowds, the loud music. I hated everything from my four-inch stiletto heels to the crooked nametag pinned to my collared shirt.

"Hey, sweet cheeks!"

I hated even more that nobody bothered to read said nametag.

Pushing through the maze of sweaty bodies, I trudged over to a pot-bellied man standing against the wall.

"What can I get for you, sir?" I asked, my voice barely penetrating Devon Sawyer's guitar solo.

"A kiss," he slurred, then puckered his lips.

Gross. I visibly cringed before storming away. Just another reason why I hated my job.

When I reached the kitchen, I set down my empty tray and leaned against the counter with an embittered sigh.

"It's nuts out there, huh?"

I looked up at my friend and co-worker, Lisa, forcing a smile. "It's brutal. Can I go home yet?"

"Fat chance. Freeze Frame is only on their third song. And why would you want to? You're making bank in tips, and these guys are amazing."

"Yeah, they're super. What is it with this band, anyway?" My nose crinkled with disdain. "We've never had anyone this famous play here before."

Lisa pulled her scarlet curls back into a loose ponytail. "Jerry is friends with the band's manager. He did him a solid. We're just fortunate we were put on the schedule tonight."

"Ah, yes. I'm so privileged to be a part of this history in the making," I said with a theatrical eyeroll, piling my tray high with beer and cheese fries.

Lisa whisked her trays through the double doors with a laugh. "You'll see. You'll be telling your grandkids all about this one day."

I couldn't help the snort from breaking through. Okay, so, these guys had a fanbase. Any decent-looking guy with a TikTok had a fanbase these days. Huffing out a sigh, I picked up my tray of orders and followed Lisa out the door.

Before I could exit, Jerry made a beeline in my direction.

Great. What did I do wrong this time? I smoothed out my pencil skirt and checked to make sure my blouse was tucked in.

"Get those kids some more water, will you?" Jerry ordered.

My heart galloped. "Huh? Me?" I glanced at the stage, then back to my boss. I was certain the phrase "deer in headlights" did not begin to accurately convey the stunned look on my face. "The band?"

"Yes, you. Yes, the band. Get them water. Did I stutter?" Jerry snapped.

Gulping, I shook my head. "No, sir. Just making sure."

I took a deep breath and spun back around toward the kitchen, collecting four water bottles from the refrigerator and tucking them under both arms.

"Lucky bitch!"

The familiar voice prompted a glance over my shoulder, and I discovered my other co-worker, Julia, sticking out her tongue. "It is what it is," I breezed with mock importance. "I'm just that cool."

"I would kill to get that close to those gorgeous boys," Julia sighed. "Every girl here would."

"Oh, please. It's just water. And you know I don't care."

Julia yanked her ponytail tighter and peered down at her ticket order. "Duh, that's why Scary Jerry chose you. You're not some swoony fangirl who's going to faint at the sight of them."

I chuckled at the thought. "God, could you picture that? *Me* —actually showing interest in a man."

"You know you have to jump back into the dating pool eventually, Chels. Not every guy out there is like—"

"Chelsie!"

The water bottles nearly slipped from my arms when I spun around to find Jerry glaring daggers at me. "S-Sorry, I'm coming," I called back.

I turned to Julia and held up a water bottle in playful victory.

She flipped me the bird in response. "I hope you fall on your ass up there," she said with a laugh.

"Chelsie!"

I jolted into action. "I'm coming!"

"You're really starting to piss me off," Jerry said, shaking his head with disapproval.

My chin dipped to my chest, cheeks heating as I rushed past him, my eyes fixed straight ahead. I resituated my grip on the water bottles when I sauntered toward the staircase leading up to the stage. The security guards moved aside to let me pass, and I couldn't help but succumb to the faint buzz that shot through me, while my sweaty palms betrayed my proclaimed indifference. I could feel the crowd's eyes on me as I neared the band, and I knew every person in that room wanted to be me.

Don't fall on your ass. Don't fall on your ass.

What I didn't expect were the eyes of one incredibly good-looking lead singer to be boring holes into me as I approached. My stomach fluttered in response.

What was that all about?

Swallowing, I held out a bottle of water to the shaggy-haired rock star and offered him a warm smile. "Here you go," I said. I was trying to ooze confidence, but my trembling hand portrayed otherwise.

He smiled back.

And *oh*, did he smile back. I could almost feel my eyeballs turn into animated cartoon hearts, and hey, was that a cupid flying over my head with an arrow pointing at one unsuspecting Devon Sawyer?

Get a grip! I pried my eyes away from the lead singer and passed out the remaining water bottles. The drummer and bassist nodded their thanks, but the guitarist snatched the water out of my hand with a sneer, refusing to look at me. I frowned but said nothing, then turned to walk off the stage. That's when a silky, strangely titillating voice made me stop in my tracks.

"Hey... thanks again, uh..."

I twisted around, my heart beating comically out of my chest. Lead Singer Guy was staring right at me, another melt-worthy smile on his face. "M-My name's Chelsie," I replied, cursing myself for stuttering like a lovestruck fool.

"Thanks, Chelsie."

Another smile, then a wink.

A wink.

Tucking a piece of hair behind my ear, I returned Devon's smile with far less charm and bewitchery and almost tripped on one of the steps leading off the stage. I could practically hear Julia laughing at my plight as I pulled myself together and continued the trek back down to the lounge.

Sure enough, Julia was peering through the kitchen doors with a smirk on her face.

"You slut!" Julia shouted when I approached.

"What? How am I a slut?"

"You were totally eye-fucking Devon up there. Look, you're even blushing."

My cheeks burned hotter than Death Valley in the middle of July. I raised my hands to my face to hide the evidence. "I was not. He's not even my type."

Julia laughed, her raven ponytail swaying back and forth as she shook her head with pity. "Chels, you just found your type, and apparently it's the most lusted-after male in the country."

Crap. I bowed my head with equal parts mortification and infatuation. "He was... attractive, maybe, but it takes a lot more for me to—"

"Melt into a pile of girly-goo and almost trip over your own two feet in front of hundreds of people?"

"So, you *did* see that?" I asked with dismay, lifting a hand to my neck as the heat from my cheeks traveled south.

"Every minute of your wanton flirting," Julia admitted.

"Okay, first of all, that was not flirting. That was—"

"Eye-fucking. We established this."

"No." My voice was laced with playful teasing. "Please stop incorrectly finishing my sentences."

Julia sighed in resignation. "Fine, whatever. You were completely unaffected by his charms."

My eyes lowered as a small smile slipped out. "I never said *unaffected.*"

Well, I supposed I was a little more than unaffected.

Perhaps, maybe... I was utterly and completely under the spell of Devon Sawyer.

Damnit.

Lisa came barreling into the kitchen, tossing her empty tray onto the counter with a clatter. "Chelsie, I hate you!" she squealed. "Oh, but I love you. Tell me everything!"

Our giggles intermingled as I began to speak, but I was cut short when Jerry stormed through the doors.

"What the hell is this?" he blared. All three of us flinched. "There are customers out there waiting. This is our busiest goddamn day, and you three are having a hormone-infused pow-wow in the kitchen? I should fire you all on the spot."

We shuffled to collect our orders.

"Sorry, sir," I muttered.

Lisa and Julia squeaked out an apology and hurried out of the kitchen.

"Hey." Jerry blocked my path before I could make a swift exit. "I expect a little more professionalism in the future," he said before storming away and pushing through the kitchen doors, muttering profanities under his breath.

I loathed the sting of tears threatening my eyes. Jerry was never lacking in the insult department, but he had never once called me unprofessional. In fact, I prided myself on my responsible nature, and everyone around me knew it. They respected me for it.

Taking in a deep breath, I lifted my head and went back out there to do my job.

It wasn't long before ten o'clock rolled around and Freeze Frame was on their final song. I'd never worked so hard in my life. My swollen ankles throbbed, and my ears were ringing with reverb from the bass guitar. I had spent the evening carrying heavy trays over my head and cleaning spilled drinks and barbecue drippings, while simultaneously trying to dodge the lusty looks Devon Sawyer had been throwing in my direction. The first time our eyes had locked, I thought my knees would give out and my drink orders would topple onto table number four. Why had this superstar set his sights on me when the room was filled with glamorous women? What made *me* so special?

Once upon a time, I might have considered myself special. Pretty, desirable. Unfortunately, Ian Masterson had successfully crushed my spirit and self-esteem a long time ago.

Glancing at my silver watch, I passed out a round of martinis to a crowded table and handed them the bill. When I turned around, I almost collided with a beefy security guard.

"Oh! I'm sorry, sir," I apologized.

"Miss Chelsie?"

I crossed my arms over my chest with a quizzical frown. "Am I in trouble?"

The guard let out a hearty laugh, his authoritative demeanor quickly dissolving. "Quite the contrary. Mr. Sawyer sent me over here to give you a private invitation to a V.I.P. event tonight with the band."

Um... *what?*

My eyes widened. "Mr. Sawyer? As in..." The words trailed off as I looked over at the stage. Devon's t-shirt was currently plastered to his sweaty torso, his well-defined abs undoubtedly taunting me.

I gulped.

"Yes, ma'am—*that* Mr. Sawyer. They'll be at Marley's tonight after the show. He'd like you to be there."

I was speechless. How was I supposed to respond?

"We'll be there!"

Julia had snuck up behind me, wrapping her arm around my shoulder and inciting my drawn-out groan. "Julia, I don't want to go."

She ignored me, grinning brightly at the security guard. "Tell him we'll be there. Our shift is up at eleven."

Julia's hand snatched mine, dragging me away before I could protest further.

"Jules, that wasn't cool. I have zero interest in being a musician's one-night stand," I huffed, yanking my arm away.

"You'll thank me for it one day," Julia said with a shrug.

Julia was one of those fortunate females who could reel any guy in with her long, obsidian hair, bedroom eyes, and ample cleavage. I was perfectly willing to pass off Devon Sawyer to my more experienced friend.

I think.

Exhaling the doubt, I held firm.

Yes... Devon would only find disappointment and bloody battle wounds beneath the layers of Chelsie Combs.

I was headed home for the night.

CHAPTER TWO

CHELSIE

I wasn't headed home for the night.

"You are such a mirror hog, Lis," Julia snapped, pushing the redhead out of the way with her hip.

"Hey, straightening this mop takes time. Not all of us were blessed with shampoo-commercial hair."

"Are you two almost ready?" I tapped my foot against the laminate flooring as we freshened up in the lounge bathroom. "I'm exhausted."

Marley's was not my scene. I was the kind of girl who liked to curl up with my cat and a good book after a long night of work, and then call it a night. Julia and Lisa were constantly trying to get me to party more often, but I'd always decline, the nightlife far from enticing. What was so appealing about getting drunk and trying to impress unworthy men?

Sure, I enjoyed a cocktail every now and then, but overall, booze and bad boys were not my thing.

"Ready," Julia said, popping the cap back on her cherry lipstick. "How do I look?"

"You know how you look," I smiled sincerely.

Five minutes later, we were piled into Lisa's Jeep, on our way to Marley's. It was a popular bar in New York City, down the street from The Pit Stop with a dance floor and a V.I.P. lounge upstairs. It was often occupied with beautiful and recognizable people.

I wouldn't know from experience, though—I'd only been there once for Lisa's mandatory twenty-fourth birthday party two years ago, and I'd been wildly unimpressed.

"This is unbelievable," Julia said. She bounced up and down in the backseat. "We're seriously going to hang out with Freeze Frame!"

Lisa nudged me in the ribcage as she drove through town. "And hopefully do more than hang out with them. Right, Chelsie?"

I scoffed at Lisa's statement from the passenger's seat. "We all know that's not happening. I'm sure the moment Devon sees you two, I'll be a blip on his ever-growing radar."

Julia leaned forward with a melodramatic roll of her onyx eyes. "Stop selling yourself short, Chelsie. You're gorgeous. Men are completely enamored with you, and you refuse to believe it."

The compliment made me itchy as I shifted in my seat. I'd believed that once. "You're sweet, Jules, but it's usually just the scary ones who hit on me."

"Or... hot lead singers," Lisa said.

Julia threw her hands up. "Thank you!"

I buried my insecurities as Lisa pulled the car into a parking garage, slinging my purse over my shoulder and gripping the strap with a tinge of nervous excitement. My heart was lub-dubbing against its normally peaceful confinements, pulling my expression into a frown.

Knock it off, heart!

I wasn't sure why my heart was acting so out of character, but maybe it was because Devon Sawyer was a legend in the making, and I was merely a down-on-my-luck cocktail waitress with a tormented past.

Or maybe it was the look he had given me when I'd traipsed up the stage steps with water bottles in my hands and forced indifference in my eyes. Or maybe it was the look he'd given me when I was re-filling cups of ice water and had accidentally zoned out, pouring a pint of it into a furious customer's lap. Or *maybe* it was the look he'd given me when I was handing out plates of jalapeño poppers to the group of envious fraternity girls who had, in turn, stiffed me.

I took a moment to scold myself for documenting all of Devon's provocative looks like a meticulously maintained Excel spreadsheet.

My sigh was weary as I strolled out of the parking garage with my two best friends.

It was a short walk over to the upscale lounge. The entry line had to be a few blocks long. We pinned on our badges and marched our way up the sidewalk to the front of the building, where we were greeted by a bouncer who offered us a blank stare.

"Badges," he deadpanned.

We flashed our badges with pride and were swiftly let into the bar, the sounds of booing trailing behind us as we breezed through the entrance.

"Suckers!" Julia shouted back. She inched down the neckline of her very revealing silver blouse. "Now, where are those yummy boys?"

My heart continued to race as I scanned the crowd. The loud music reverberated right through me, my arms linked with Lisa's and Julia's, and it wasn't long before we were smashed between dancing bodies and blinded by colorful DJ lights.

Yay. So much fun.

Julia's eyes lit up as she pointed to a staircase leading up to a private room. "Bingo," she grinned.

Before I was hauled away to the elusive staircase, the guitarist of Freeze Frame ambled down the steps, exuding an equal amount of sex appeal and surly nonchalance.

"Holy gorgeous," Julia swooned.

A look of disdain swept across my face, and I puckered my lips. "Don't get all excited. That guy is a dick."

"Uh-huh... sure..." Julia trailed off, pushing through the masses to approach him.

"Julia!" I called out, but was promptly ignored. "Shit."

Julia didn't hold back in flirting with the cocky guitar player, and I watched as she flipped her hair over one shoulder with a bright grin, leaning into him as far as she could. He seemed to be charmed by her advances, but that was no surprise. Julia was a next-level babe.

They both looked over in my direction, causing me to stiffen in place. The guitarist nodded, his eyes dancing between me and Julia. I maintained my look of disinterest and sipped my cocktail through a tiny straw, unable to hear the conversation over the deafening music.

Julia hadn't been lying when she'd called him gorgeous. He *was* good-looking, but in a different way from Devon—Devon's hair was light and shaggy, where the guitarist had dark, sable hair, mussed with gel. He was tall and well-muscled with a distinct edge about him, evident by the stubble across his jawline and a tattoo on his right forearm.

And the asshole persona.

A few more moments passed before Julia began waving me over. *Great.* I swallowed my drink with a clunky gulp and grabbed Lisa's hand, pushing our way through dozens of women who had started noticing the musician's presence.

Julia beamed as we joined them at the base of the private staircase. "Hey, guys! This is Noah Hayes," she introduced, her eyes glowing with enthusiasm. "As we all know, he's the guitarist for Freeze Frame."

Blinking, I slapped on my most noteworthy "unimpressed" face and eyed Noah with guarded apprehension. I wasn't going to give him the satisfaction of a greeting—much like he had unkindly done to me earlier that evening.

Then I felt Julia's elbow ram into my ribcage. "Ouch!" I hissed.

Noah crossed his arms over his faded green t-shirt, clearing his throat. "Right. You were the one who brought us the water," he said, holding up a finger in remembrance. The muscles in his forearms twitched, his eyes glimmering by way of DJ strobe lights.

"You're welcome, by the way," I quipped.

Noah quirked an eyebrow at my boldness. "Well, you're not shy."

"You were disrespectful. I just thought you should know."

"You walked up there all googly-eyed. What was I supposed to do?"

A feisty comeback teased the tip of my tongue.

Julia noticed, quickly maneuvering herself between us. "Ooo-kay! How about we meet the rest of the guys?"

Lisa gave an enthusiastic nod in agreement.

Noah narrowed his eyes in my direction. "Sure," he said flatly.

I trailed behind the group, indignation swimming through me. I wasn't even sure what had gotten me so fired up—Noah Hayes was a stranger. He didn't owe me anything... even respect. And yet, my veins were pumping hot with adrenaline.

"Don't worry, Chelsie. I'm sure that guy's just a bad egg. Devon will be great, I promise," Lisa said, squeezing my hand. "Don't let this ruin your night. You're the luckiest girl in the room right now."

My smile felt forced. "Thanks, Lis."

We traipsed up the staircase and entered the private lounge—a spacious room, illuminated with multi-colored lights. My eyes scanned the plush red couches and a minibar against the far wall as soft music filtered through a speaker.

My sour mood scattered when I spotted Devon sitting in the corner of the suite, chatting with the two other band members. I swallowed, my gaze traveling back to the bar where two buxom blondes were giggling over martinis.

"Hello, boys," Julia purred. It was no surprise she was the first to speak. "I'm Julia."

Noah cleared his throat. "And this is Water Girl," he said, making an animated hand gesture toward me.

Annoyance squeezed my chest. I jerked my head in his direction, glaring at him with impassioned eyes. His own eyes sparkled in reply, and my stomach pitched at the realization that he was getting off on tormenting me.

"Chelsie has a better ring to it." Devon appeared at my side, holding out his hand in greeting, a slow smile curling at his Cheshire lips. "It *is* Chelsie, right?"

I nodded, my anger dissipating. "Yeah. I mean... yes. I'm Chelsie." When our hands met, a spark shot through me, and that anger dissolved into ash.

"I'm Devon," he replied, our palms still clinched together. "I'm glad you could make it out tonight."

I tried to keep my flush of excitement in check and swallowed back my nerves, but my heart rate increased to a concerning pace as we maintained eye contact.

Oh, boy.

"So," Devon continued. "I see you and Noah have already met."

"Unfortunately." I spared Noah a side-eye, clearing my throat. "But I'm confident I got the worst out of the way."

The room broke out into laughter.

"Ouch," Noah said, holding a hand to his heart like an invisible dagger. "You're just all sorts of sassy, aren't you, Water Girl?" He sauntered over to the minibar and threw his arms around the two model-wannabes. "At least Sadie and Sophie are nice to me."

The blondes nuzzled in closer, and I looked away in disgust, trying not to outwardly gag.

Devon rolled his eyes. "Just ignore him. I know I do. Here, let me introduce you to the rest of the band."

I followed him to the other side of the room.

"This is Miles, our bassist," Devon said, pointing to the wiry man with a mop of dirty blonde hair. Then he turned his attention to the beefier bandmate with dark hair and a goatee. "And this is our drummer, Tad."

The two men smiled and raised their beers, and I was relieved to find that my assumption had been correct—I'd indeed gotten the worst out of the way.

Devon made me a cocktail at the minibar and handed it over, his enchanting smile still firmly in place, causing my insides to stir with both attraction and alcohol buzz. He wasn't what I'd envisioned him to be. He seemed to be down-to-earth, personable, and kind—unlike the egotistical womanizer I had assumed all rock stars were.

I glanced in Noah's direction. He was sprawled out on the couch with Julia, his hand running up and down her exposed thigh.

Well, at least Noah was out there doing his part to feed the stereotype.

"I can tell him to get lost if you think your friend is uncomfortable."

My gaze redirected toward Devon, and I shook my head. "Julia can take care of herself," I noted, before pausing to add, "She just prefers when good-looking musicians do it for her."

Devon chuckled and popped open his beer. He held it up, clinking the bottle against my glass. "Well, here's to being dependent on good-looking musicians."

A warm flush seeped into the apples of my cheeks, and I ducked my head. Devon's eyes twinkled back at me as a swarm of butterflies invaded my nether regions.

I chugged my drink to drown them.

"Here. Do a shot with me," Devon offered, handing me a tiny glass of clear liquid.

"Oh... I'm not much of a drinker." Hesitant fingers curled around the glass. "But what the hell." Tipping my head back, I was unable to hide my grimace when the tequila slid down my throat. "Wow, that's terrible."

Devon laughed as he swallowed down his own shot, guiding me over to one of the red loveseats and taking his place beside me. "Sorry, I probably shouldn't have started with Patrón. Tequila can be a little intense."

I heard him speak, but his words didn't quite register. Devon Sawyer was sitting so close, I could feel the heat of his body radiating into my blushing skin. I could feel the rough denim of his jeans pressed up against my bare leg. His presence was jarring to my senses, but in a sinfully delicious sort of way. When he spoke, his sultry voice sent tiny shivers up my spine, prompting the butterflies in my stomach to do the Mambo.

"I'm not very good at this." The words were clumsy and unplanned as they escaped my lips. I didn't dare glance in Devon's direction, instead concentrating on the colorful carpet fibers beneath my feet.

"Not very good at what?" Devon asked.

Life in general.

"You know... this. Us," I replied, wagging my finger back and forth between us. "I haven't had a conversation with a man that went beyond "would you like some ketchup with those fries?" in years. So, I just wanted to warn you that I suck at this."

Devon didn't answer right away. His sapphire eyes regarded me carefully, and I was convinced he was deciding on how to send me on my way with as much grace as possible. He surprised me by reaching over my lap and taking one of my hands in his. "Chelsie, you don't have to warn me about anything. And you don't have to explain yourself," he reassured. "I'll admit that I'm a little surprised. I figured a girl as pretty as yourself had the men lining up."

I couldn't hide my sheepish smile at the compliment. "That's sweet of you to say, but that's more of Julia's scene. I'm kind of the loner in our social circle."

You're doing a great job of selling yourself here, Chels.

"So, you're not the kind of girl someone might find cozied up to an international superstar in a private V.I.P. lounge, huh?" Devon teased.

My smile brightened. "Not exactly." I glanced over at him, braving his steely blue eyes, feeling naked and vulnerable beneath his gaze. "Why... me?" I asked.

I had to know why Devon Sawyer had fixated on me when he could have had any woman he wanted.

"Why *not* you?" he countered. He didn't even hesitate. "Maybe there's just something about you I had to get to know."

Of course, I considered the fact that he could have been feeding me a bunch of pretty lines to get into my pants, but the sincerity in his voice had me questioning everything I had ever believed about men. His lines were either superbly well-rehearsed, or they were genuine.

And if they were genuine... well, I was in for a world of trouble.

Devon raised his hand to my face and ran a finger along my jawline. I had to remind myself to keep breathing—such an easy thing to do on an ordinary occasion. But with Devon Sawyer melting into me, smelling like leather and tequila, the normally effortless task was becoming increasingly problematic. Feeling compelled to raise my own hand, I allowed my fingers to comb through his caramel locks... a bold move. "Devon..." I whispered. It was supposed to be a question, but all it sounded like was, *"take me now."*

Devon responded by leaning in and pressing his lips against mine. It was a sensation I hadn't felt in years. Up until now, I'd had no desire to kiss another man... no, not after Ian. Not after his poisonous kisses that had led to a broken heart and broken bones.

This was different. This was tender and beautiful and positively *exquisite*. The kiss deepened, and I had to push against his chest to catch my breath.

A magnetic smile stretched across Devon's face—the kind only lead singers and movies stars could effectively pull off. "You okay?"

I nodded. Our mouths entangled again, and I positioned myself on his lap like it was the most natural thing in the world. "I don't... usually..." *Oof*, it was hard keeping my lips off of him. "... do this kind of thing."

Devon pulled back, his hands gripping my thighs. "You don't have to explain yourself, remember? Just live in the moment."

We moved in to continue the kiss when a persistent finger began tapping me on the shoulder. My neck craned to locate the source of the interruption, and I shouldn't have been surprised to find a smug Noah standing behind us with merriment dancing in his dark green eyes.

"That didn't take long," he bemused. "I had a feeling Water Girl wasn't the innocent maiden she portrayed."

I was climbing off Devon's lap in a flash, running the back of my hand across my mouth, as if to hide what we were so obviously doing.

"Dude, don't be an ass," Devon said, his tone teetering between playful and aggravated.

I took a moment to glance around the room, finding Lisa and Julia standing against the far wall, chatting with Miles, Tad, and the two blondes. I wondered how much of our public display of affection had been witnessed. My cheeks heated in response. "You know, it's fine," I said, rising to my feet and running my fingers through knotted hair. "I should get going."

Devon stood up in protest, pulling me back to him with a flirty grin. "It's still early."

I untangled myself from his arms, despite my body screaming at me otherwise. It was difficult to get back in the mood with Noah the Asshole standing there glowering. "That's kind of the issue," I apologized. "It's, like, three in the morning."

Noah rolled back on his heels. "Let her go, Dev. Water Girl clearly has better things to do than hang out with the likes of you."

My teeth clenched. He was really getting under my skin. "It's Chelsie," I corrected.

Noah shrugged, amused. "Sure. Whatever you say, Charley."

I stepped over to him, arms crossed and eyes spitting fire. "My *name* is Chelsie."

Noah leaned in closer until I felt his hot breath skimming my face. My resolve almost broke from his proximity—he was seriously invading my personal space and loving every minute of it. Refusing to back down, I glared up at him, daring him to say something.

"You're right. I'm sorry," Noah said, humor flickering in his eyes. "Charley was last night's conquest. You know... Devon's girls all start bleeding together after a while."

His implication had barely processed when Devon grabbed Noah by the shirt collar and pushed him up against the wall.

"What the fuck is up with you, man?" Devon demanded.

I could only watch the scene unfold in silence because Noah's comment had rendered me speechless. His words had sucker-punched me right in the gut. Did I have the word "insecure" scrawled across my forehead in bold, red letters?

What did he have against me in the first place? Why would he want to *hurt* me?

The room was closing in on me and I had to get out of there. Storming over to the exit, I signaled Lisa and Julia to follow. We exited the lounge, just as Tad and Miles ran to break up the ensuing fight.

"What the hell happened in there?" Julia wondered. Her voice was shrill over the hip-hop song pulsating through the DJ's speakers.

I tried to hide the sting of tears in my eyes as the we navigated our way out of the bar. I'd been naïve to think I was *special*.

Maybe Noah was right. Maybe Devon was just a stereotypical rock star, after all.

Maybe I was doomed.

Lifting my chin, I forced a smile. "Nothing. Just guys being guys."

CHAPTER THREE

CHELSIE

I strolled through my cozy apartment, humming to myself as I wandered into the kitchen to make a sandwich. Natural light filtered in through the lace drapes, a welcome contrast to my dismal mood. It had been a long week, and I hadn't had a Saturday to myself in a long time. I loved days when I had all the time in the world to relax and not have to worry about unsatisfied customers or my skeevy boss—honestly, I was content spending the afternoon with my cat, Misty, and catching up on reading.

It had taken years to get to this point after many brutal years of co-dependency. My life wasn't always the picture of serenity and independence people saw now... I had a lot of skeletons in my closet. But I'd pulled myself together and crawled out of that dark hole.

It was a good life; a simple life. A tiny studio apartment was all I could afford on a waitress' salary, but it was enough. I surrounded myself with positive people, a steady job, and absolutely *no* men.

That was important—I refused to regress back into the damaged and dependent girl I had once been.

"You'll always be scared and weak, little girl."

I shuddered, forcing away the memories of my past life.

It was probably for the best things had ended the way they had with Devon Sawyer. He would not have been a good influence on my life, considering rock stars were known for their excessive drinking, drug habits, and multiple women. I'd had enough experience with toxic men to last several lifetimes.

Devon was also a rock *god*. He wasn't just an average, struggling musician playing at coffee houses and music festivals. Devon Sawyer was a household name. He toured the world and enticed women to throw their underwear at him on stage.

I had no desire to go down that complicated road.

So, why did his indigo eyes and kissable lips continue to plague my thoughts day-in and day-out?

A curse, obviously. The Devon Sawyer Curse.

I let out a half-hearted sigh as I dipped a knife into the mayonnaise jar, startling when my cell phone rang. Skipping into the living room, I snatched it off the couch. "Hello?"

"Chelsie?"

The familiar voice caught me off guard. My heart raced. "Yes. Who's calling, please?"

"Look, don't hang up, okay? It's Devon. Devon Sawyer, remember?"

Remember? I'd only thought about him every day for the past week.

Because of the curse.

"Sure, of course, I remember. How did you get my number?"

"I got it from Noah... who got it from Julia. Sorry to call you out of the blue like this, but you've been on my mind a lot since the other night."

Noah. That was a name I'd been looking forward to never hearing again. "Oh?"

"Yeah. I was hoping we could maybe meet up some time. For coffee, or dinner... anything. I'd like to see you again."

My body lowered to the couch because my quivering legs were moments away from failing me. "I see."

There was a pause before he continued. "You don't sound very excited."

"I am! I – I mean... I'm sorry. It's great to hear from you, Devon." I had no idea how to take it all in. It was too abrupt; too mind-boggling. I was just getting comfortable with the idea of never speaking to him again.

"Hey, I'm really sorry about how crazy things got that night," Devon explained. "Noah pulled a total dick move, and I apologize on his behalf. He just gets that way sometimes. I'm sure he was only jealous I'd managed to score the prettiest girl in the room."

An enchanted smile crept across my lips, but I forced it away, clearing my throat. I needed to be smart about this... so, why was logic was the furthest thing from my mind? "It's okay. No harm done."

"What Noah said was complete bullshit, by the way," Devon added. "I may be a musician, but I'm not the sleazy kind. I'm just a regular guy once you get to know me. And I'm hoping you will... you know, get to know me."

There he was, being all charming again. Stupid curse. "Devon, I—"

I have no idea what I'm doing. I'm a hot mess express on wheels.

"It's just a cup of coffee," he persisted. "I enjoyed talking with you, and I regret the way things went down. I didn't even get to say goodbye."

I hesitated. It was just a cup of coffee... no expectations. No commitments. No pressure. "I suppose I could do coffee," I finally answered.

Devon's sigh of relief was evident. "Awesome. I mean, that's great. Thanks for giving me another chance."

I picked at my fingernails. Devon Sawyer was thanking *me* for giving *him* another chance? Swallowing, I wondered, "Are you still in New York?"

"No, I'm in Los Angeles right now. We've got a gig tonight. How about tomorrow?"

My heart rate quickened. "You can make it back here that fast?"

"For you? Absolutely."

Oh.

Devon certainly wasn't lacking any charisma. "Well, it was good to hear from you again, Devon. Call me tomorrow when you get back into town, and we can decide on a place to meet."

"Sounds like a plan. I'll see you soon."

I continued to hold the phone to my ear, well after our goodbyes had been said, paralyzed with shock. I pinched my arm to make sure I wasn't dreaming. Devon Sawyer, lead singer of Freeze Frame, was going to travel across the country in less than twenty-four hours to have coffee with me.

With *me*.

A surge of dizzy adrenaline coursed through me, and I jumped off the couch, dancing around my living room while Misty glared at me in a way only a judgmental cat could pull off. My reservations had been set aside for the time being.

I was going to sit back and enjoy the ride.

My fingertips danced across the high-top table. I sat there awaiting Devon's arrival, deciding that this was the most nerve-wracking cup of coffee I'd ever had. We had decided on a quaint café called Luca's in the heart of New York City, and the aroma of cappuccino and pastries was the only thing calming my jitters. While my eyes stayed fixed on the main entrance, my foot tapped against the burnt orange tiles as I checked the time on my phone once again. He was almost a half-hour late.

I was about ready to leave when Devon breezed in through a side door.

"Man, I'm so sorry," Devon apologized, maneuvering himself around the tables and approaching me with a sheepish grin. "My flight was delayed, and then there were these fans at the airport..."

"Hey, it's no biggie." My smile brightened as I let my eyes fall over him. "You're a popular guy."

Devon reached for my hand and placed a chaste kiss along my knuckles. "And you're an incredibly beautiful girl. Have I told you that?"

"You might have let it slip," I grinned, feeling almost hypno-tized. With any other man, I would have laughed at such a cheesy line. But Devon's words felt sincere and the look in his eyes was tickling my insides.

When we were both seated at the table, we ordered our beverages and regarded one another with nervous smiles. I folded my hands in my lap, chewing on my bottom lip—an awful habit. "You know, this was the last thing I expected to do today," I said. "I never thought I'd see you again."

Devon's gaze was electrifying. "I couldn't let you get away that easily," he smiled. "I felt shitty about what happened that night. I needed to apologize, even if you never agreed to see me in person."

"I should probably apologize, too," I told him. "I didn't mean to leave in such a hurry. I'm sorry I freaked out."

"Hey, it's totally fine. Noah was being an ass. He knows that, and he's sorry."

I couldn't hold back my snort of laughter. "Right. I'm sure he's really broken-up about it."

"No, he is. I mean, sure, Noah's kind of a dick sometimes, but he's a good guy. We've known each other since the first grade."

My eyebrow lifted with curiosity as I leaned forward on my elbows. "I guess I just don't understand why he had such a problem with me."

"You know... Noah is a mystery, even to me. It's nothing you said or did. He tends to go on the defense when a girl enters the picture that may pose a threat to the band. He's serious about what we do, and he doesn't want a pretty face to jeopardize that," Devon explained.

I frowned. "A threat?"

"Well, he could sense that I liked you. More than just a one-night stand sort of thing."

Oh.

Oh.

"Oh," I said through a slow blink.

Devon ducked his head with a timid smile. "Yeah."

I was certain my cheeks were more crimson than my red romper—I was officially under the love spell of Devon Sawyer and there was nothing I could do about it. Before I could speak, a barista came by with two macchiatos and placed them down on tiny square napkins.

"So," Devon began. "Tell me about yourself." He brought the

coffee to his lips, his eyes still fixated on me over his khaki-colored mug.

Raising my wrist, I glanced down at my invisible watch. "There's only twenty-four hours in a day. You want the cliff-note version?"

Devon laughed. "We'll start with the easy stuff. Have you always lived in New York?"

I bobbed my head, wrapping my hands around my mug and taking a quick sip. "Born and raised. My parents moved down to Florida to retire, but my home is here."

"Do you have any siblings?" he inquired.

"Nope, only child. It's certainly had its pros and cons."

"I've got four brothers. Consider yourself lucky."

My lips pursed with thought. "Sometimes I do, sometimes I don't. It would be nice to have that special bond with someone. I mean, I had friends, but they came and went. Lisa, the redhead you met last week, has known me most of my life." I lowered my eyes as a wave of guilt passed through me. "And my parents and I haven't spoken for a long time."

Devon's expression softened. "Do you ever get lonely?"

Lonely was the perfect word to sum up my life. "Nah," I lied. "My cat keeps me company and my job keeps me busy. I have no complaints." I wondered if Devon could see the wounded girl beneath the cheerful façade. Was I transparent, or did I hide my demons well? All I knew for certain was that I wasn't ready to confess how depressing my life truly was.

"Well, that's good to hear," Devon replied. "As long as you're happy."

I was quick to turn the conversation off myself, clearing my throat. "What about you?" I asked. "What's it like to be a rock god?"

He smirked. "I really can't complain. I'm getting paid to do what I love, and I'm traveling the world with my best friends. Not to mention... I've discovered quite the compelling young woman."

I dismissed him with a good-natured shake of my head. "Smooth."

Devon leaned back in his seat, folding his hands behind the nape of his neck. "You know, I was hoping to take you and your friends out for drinks tonight. Something fun and casual. Miles and Tad are still in Los Angeles, but Noah's back in town if you think you can stomach his presence. Maybe we can all get to know each other better."

My grip tightened around my cup. Just the sound of Noah's name made my claws want to come out. "Absolutely," I forced out. "That sounds great."

Devon clapped his hands together and sat up straight in his chair. "Awesome. It's a date, then."

I smiled brightly, and we continued our conversation for the next two hours.

We spoke of Devon's career, his friendship with his band members, and his life before the spotlight—he was an auto mechanic who played Nirvana covers in his garage. I listened with interest. Devon had a charismatic way of making something as mundane as tire pressure sound exciting.

I, in turn, shared small details about my life in the big city— my hobbies and aspirations, my dreams of making a difference someday. I had always wanted to go back to school to become a guidance counselor, but rent and bills forced me to work long hours at the lounge. Being a cocktail waitress had not been my life goal. I'd always wanted to help people, not carry around heavy trays of junk food and clean up spilled drinks.

Devon didn't look down on me, though, nor make me feel ashamed of my hampered ambitions. He reminded me that everyone starts somewhere, and that it's not where we begin, but where we end up that truly matters. Everyone has the ability to change their path.

When we left to go our separate ways, I felt a yearning in the pit of my stomach. I was enamored with Devon, and he seemed to reciprocate my feelings. It felt like I was in some kind of alternate reality.

As he sauntered out the door with his J. Crew blazer, luxury sunglasses, and endless amounts of modest swagger, I sighed dreamily. It had only been thirty seconds and I already missed his company.

Later that evening, Julia barged into my apartment, attacking me with a monster hug as Lisa strolled in behind her. "Girl, you are my hero. I can't believe you scored me a date with Noah tonight," Julia squealed.

I steadied my balance as I recovered from the hug. "He's a douche, remember?"

"Yeah, he's a total douche," Julia agreed. "But he's fine as hell, and I am *so* getting me some action tonight. Finally!"

I cringed at the mental imagery. "Gross. Just keep him away from me, okay?"

"That will not be a problem."

A few hours passed by, and we were putting the finishing touches on our makeup and wardrobe accessories when the doorbell buzzed. I could hear Lisa and Julia giggling with excitement from the bathroom.

Running a nervous hand through my freshly straightened hair, I opened the door. I'd expected to see some sort of bodyguard or personal assistant, but both Devon and Noah stood before me in the entryway looking more handsome than I'd remembered. Devon wore a white collared shirt with fitted blue jeans and a chain around his neck, while Noah was dressed more casually in a snug black t-shirt with a band logo I didn't recognize. The scent of masculine cologne infiltrated my senses as I stepped back to let them enter.

"Hey," I greeted, flashing a bright smile in Devon's direction before shifting my gaze to the man on his left. "Hi, Noah."

My tone was noticeably less enthusiastic.

"Hey, Chelsie," Noah replied.

I could have sworn he sounded sincere, so I forced a smile. "You remembered my name."

"Did you prefer Water Girl?" he quipped.

The gleam in his eyes was playful. I softened.

"Oh, boys," Julia sing-songed as she strolled out of the bathroom. Her hips sashayed in a way only professional flirts could pull off. "Are you ready for me?" She struck a sexy pose, then ran over to the two men, giving them each a hug.

Lisa followed behind, looking slightly more intimidated, so I rushed over to my friend and linked an arm with hers. "We're going to have a blast tonight, yeah?"

Lisa nodded. "Damn straight."

Devon approached me, his eyes alight with prospect. "Long time, no see. You look... unbelievable."

I blushed at the compliment. For the first time in years, I *did* feel sexy tonight. An ivory spaghetti-strap dress was cut right above my knees. My blonde hair laid perfectly in place over my bare shoulders, and two sparkly heels matched the champagne shimmer in my eyeshadow. I didn't make a habit of dressing up, but I figured the occasion called for a little extra mirror time.

"You do clean up nice," Noah murmured, shoving his hands into his pockets.

I wasn't expecting the flattery. A small smile sprouted on my lips. "Thanks," I replied before returning my attention to Devon. "Are we ready to go?"

"Ready when you are. The limo's outside waiting," Devon said. He held out his arm and I took it with pride.

When Lisa and Julia spotted the stretch limo, they gasped.

"This is what I'm talking about!" Julia exclaimed as she jumped inside. Devon slid in next to her, followed by me, then Noah and Lisa. "Why does Chelsie get to be sandwiched between the two hotties?" Julia pouted. "Some girls have all the luck."

I instinctively scooted closer to the hottie on my left. Devon put his arm around me as I nuzzled in next to him with a fluttering heart.

As the limo took off, Noah snatched up the bottle of whiskey and took a big swig. "I'm ready to be intoxicated," he declared. "Anyone want to join me?" He held the bottle out as an offering, pointing it specifically in my direction.

My nose turned up at the sight of it. "No, thanks." I waved my hand in dismissal. "I actually want to remember tonight."

Noah shrugged and put the mouth of the bottle to his lips. "Suit yourself."

"Hey, let's play *I've Never*," Julia suggested. She grabbed a handful of beers and passed them down the row. "It's a great way to break the ice."

"You've never what?" I wondered, my brows pinching together. I crinkled my nose with confusion as I attempted to twist off my beer cap.

"Here, let me," Devon offered. "And *I've Never* is a drinking game." He popped off the cap with his teeth, then handed the drink back to me. "One person makes a statement beginning with "I've never..." and if the other players have done said statement, they have to drink. The statements are generally laced with debauchery."

"That means you'll be forced to spill all your dirty, little secrets, Chels," Julia said with a wicked grin. "My money's on Chelsie being drunk first. I bet she's not as innocent as she looks."

My insides pitched with panic. My dirty, little secrets did not need to be addressed in the backseat of a limo with two super-stars. Julia knew little about my relationship history—all she knew was that Ian was a jerk and he inspired my long-term ban on rela-tionships. As much as I adored my friend, Julia was the queen of gossip, and I didn't feel comfortable spilling the beans about my very tortured past.

Lisa, on the contrary, had first-hand knowledge of my secrets... which was why she was currently shooting sympathetic glances in my direction.

"I don't know," Lisa shrugged. "The game sounds kind of childish."

"Oh, please," Julia argued. "No one's ever too old for drinking games. Chelsie, why don't you go first?"

My clammy hands clutched the beer as I silently begged for it to open into a big, black hole I could crawl into. It did no such thing —instead, its contents splashed around inside the bottle as the limo drove over dips and bumps. I took a moment to gather my courage before clearing my throat. "All right, fine," I said. "I've never..." Fidgeting in my seat, I tried to conjure up something sinful. "Okay, I've got one. I've never gotten a speeding ticket." Everyone stared at me, prompting my cheeks to flush. "What? Was that lame?"

Lisa took a swig. "I've gotten two," she admitted. Devon, Noah, and Julia followed suit.

"Okay, Chelsie is fired. My turn," Julia said. "I've never had sex in a public place."

"That's more like it." Noah offered a mischievous grin and leaned over to clink Julia's drink with his own. "Cheers." He gulped down a swig, and Devon joined him.

Julia took a sip as well. "Just kidding," she laughed.

I slunk down into my seat, embarrassed, while Devon gave me a reassuring squeeze.

"I'll go," Lisa announced. She sat up straight, her eyes twinkling. "I've never had a threesome."

"Boring," Julia dismissed, taking an extra big swig. Noah followed.

To everyone's surprise, I took a quick sip.

Noah choked and sputtered on his beer. "Are you serious?" He gazed at me with stunned curiosity. Julia also looked astounded.

"My ex was very persuasive," I explained, my tone low and unreadable. I didn't go into further detail—they didn't need to know that *persuasive* was code for *forced*. "Who's next?"

"Shit, I'll go," Noah said. "I've never been pregnant."

The group laughed and nobody drank.

"I've never done hard drugs," Devon said.

Noah drank.

"I've never cheated," Lisa stated.

Julia drank, then said, "I've never been in love."

Both Noah and I took a sip.

I raised an eyebrow at the man on my right. "You? In love?" I was incredulous with my query, as if he'd just announced he was a nuclear physicist at NASA. Acknowledging the rudeness of my implication, I softened the blow. "I mean... you just don't seem like the romantic type."

Or tried to, anyway.

Noah scoffed at me. "Love isn't always rainbows and roses, Water Girl." He chugged down the rest of his beer with vigor and tossed the empty bottle into the trash. "And, what, you don't think I look lovable?"

I pretended to think hard about the question, my lips thinning. "You probably don't want me to answer that."

"Touché," he said flatly.

"Noah is just a big, giant teddy bear," Devon said, reaching behind me and smacking his friend on the back. "Aren't you, Hayes?"

Noah looked less than amused. "I've never killed anyone," he muttered, reaching for another beer. "Yet."

Laughter filled the limo. I noticed that Noah was not sharing in the mirth, and I wondered if I'd hit a nerve with my comment about love. It was true, though—I couldn't picture Noah in love with another human being. He was crude and arrogant, and even his friendship with Devon surprised me. They were so... *different*.

As the limo pulled up to the bar, I glanced up at Devon, my heart racing at the thought of being Devon Sawyer's date for the evening. My eyes shifted to Noah who was nursing another beer, his foot tapping against the floor of the limo. I squinted my eyes.

I knew that look.

Noah had the look of someone who'd suffered a broken heart.

CHAPTER FOUR

NOAH

I trailed behind the group as they entered the bar through the back entrance, sucking on my cigarette and blowing the smoke out into the early spring air. My eyes assessed the three women in front of me, landing on the blonde-haired nuisance who'd stolen my bandmate's heart.

Chelsie was an obnoxiously beautiful girl—she must have known that fact, as it was apparent to anyone who had eyes. Yet she carried herself in a modest, humble way with troves of nervous energy and mysterious secrets hiding behind her pretty features. I decided that what she lacked in confidence, she made up for in fire and sass. I couldn't believe it when the petite waitress had come at me with her defenses up, claws sharpened, looking for a fight. The girl had been burned before, that much was obvious.

I recognized a broken heart when I saw one.

And being the asshole that I was, I had no problem playing into her insecurities.

When I'd first laid eyes on her, I was convinced she was just another bubble-headed fangirl who was pissing herself with joy from being on stage with us. I'd been surprised to discover that she was merely a woman who'd fallen under the love spell of my lusted-after lead singer. Devon had a way with the ladies—I'd seen plenty come and go, never to be heard from again.

But this was different. There was a light in Devon's eyes I hadn't seen before.

The girl was getting to him, and I didn't fucking like it. Freeze Frame was the priority; the band came first, and I'd be damned if a pretty piece of tail got in the way of that.

My eyes fixated on her ass as she breezed through the bar's double doors before traveling down her long, milky white legs.

I supposed I wasn't completely immune to her appeal.

Chelsie turned around at that moment, and I quickly cut my eyes away.

Caught.

"Don't worry, I'll just be a minute," I said, exhaling a puff of smoke out through my nostrils.

"I wasn't worrying."

My lips pursed together as I gave her a tight smile.

Her appeal was fading fast.

Taking a final drag on the cigarette, I joined the group inside on the second floor and collapsed onto the plush couch, throwing my arms behind my head. I glanced around the room, my gaze settling on Devon, who was deep in conversation with the pesky blonde. They were cozied up on an obnoxious neon orange loveseat with Lisa sitting quietly beside them. Lisa was a pretty young woman with a mop of red curls and doe-like features. She was shy and reserved, but I decided that I'd probably sleep with her if given the opportunity.

Julia was headed down to the bar, her gold sequin minidress traveling dangerously high up on her bronzed thighs. Julia was also a gorgeous woman with sultry lips, raven hair and eyes, and a rack that could make any head turn. I was certainly looking forward to some fun between the sheets, but nothing more. I didn't do relationships... not anymore.

Blowing out a long breath, I returned my attention to Devon and Chelsie. What exactly were the lovebirds discussing? I decided to do what I did best—interrupt their conversation with a tasteless comment and piss Chelsie off. I couldn't risk the band being compromised with talk of marriage and children or whatever "white picket fence" garbage they were yapping about.

Before I could speak, Chelsie noticed me eyeing her and got

the barb in first. "Seriously, Noah, is there something you want to say to me?"

Challenge accepted.

"Easy there, killer," I breezed, throwing my hands up in surrender. "I didn't say a thing."

Thinking about saying something didn't count.

Her gaze was icy. "All you've done since we got here is eye me down. I know the insult is just waiting on the tip of your tongue."

"You say *insult* as if I only had one," I shot back. Adrenaline was coursing through me at the prospect of a fight. "You underestimate me."

"You're unbelievable."

"Guys," Devon interrupted. "Can't you try to get along? Call a truce or something? I wanted this to be a chill night."

I stood from the couch and stepped over to her, plucking her empty glass from the table. "Rum and Coke, right?"

The look on her face was priceless. I figured a sparring match was only going to dampen the mood, so I needed to find a new tactic to get Water Girl out of the picture. Maybe getting her so hammered she ends up puking all over herself by midnight would do the trick.

Bonus points for puking on Devon.

Chelsie narrowed her eyes at me. "Why would you buy me a drink?"

I realized the honest version wouldn't be in my best interest, so I tried to be as charming as possible—my second best trait, following my proficiency in scathing sarcasm. "Look, Devon is right. Let's make a truce."

"Why the change of heart?"

"Why question it? Do you want your drink or not?"

She bit her lip, as if physically holding back a fiery retort. "Okay. Fine."

"Perfect. I'll be right back." I couldn't hide the knowing smile on my lips. Nothing was a bigger turn-off than a girl who couldn't hold her liquor. She'd be back to waiting tables in no time. And it wasn't that I *hated* the girl—I was sort of enjoying our heated banter. But Chelsie was a threat, and the threat needed to be eliminated.

Simple facts.

Heading down the V.I.P. steps, I called over a waitress. She came by with the drink orders a few minutes later.

"One rum and Coke, and one shot of whiskey, coming right up," I declared, waving the alcohol in front of Chelsie's face.

Julia glared at me. "Where's my drink?" She crossed her arms over her chest with a pout. "I thought I was your date for the night."

"It's a white-flag drink," Lisa explained.

Chelsie took her drinks with hesitant hands, wrinkling her nose at the shot. "What is this?"

There was revulsion in her tone, like I'd just handed her a severed limb on a plate. "It's my good friend, Jack. Drink up— you'll like it."

Chelsie sat there for a moment in silence before her wary expression faded into casual acceptance, and she tipped her head back, chugging down the shot in one swallow.

She gagged.

"*Yuck* does not give justice to what I'm feeling right now," Chelsie balked. She covered her mouth with her hand in an effort to keep the liquor down and physically shuddered.

I laughed, downing my own shot with ease. A devious smile lingered on my lips. "You'll get used to it."

"As if I'm going to have more?"

"Damn right, you are." I spotted the waitress coming up the staircase again, so I waved her over. "Five Jägerbombs," I told her. "And keep the liquor coming."

CHELSIE

I eyed the peculiar cocktail. It resembled liquified tar that had been placed into a larger glass of pee water. I'd served these drinks as a waitress, but never dared try them. Glancing around the room, I noticed everyone had already chugged down their own respective glasses of pee water. "Here goes nothing."

"'Atta girl," Noah said.

The beverage tasted like licorice and seltzer water. It wasn't quite as heinous as the shot of whiskey, but I would die happy if I never had to drink it again.

It wasn't long before a solid buzz settled in.

"You're holding your own over there," Devon said with a smile pulling at his lips. He patted my knee with a wink.

I flashed him a radiant grin. "Are you impressed?"

"Maybe a little."

When I squeezed in closer to Devon, the aroma of his bourbon cologne made my head feel dizzy. Or... was that the *actual* bourbon?

"Ready for another?" Noah had set his sights on me again after putting equal effort into flirting with both Julia and our blue-haired waitress.

My already dizzy head started to spin at the thought of another drink. "No, thanks... I'm already starting to feel those last few."

"So, why stop now?" Noah ordered another round of bombs.

My eyes narrowed at the mischievous glint in his gaze—he was up to something.

"Shit, man," Devon said as he slipped his arm around my shoulders. "Take it easy on the girl. She's not an alcoholic like you are."

Heavy silence infiltrated our small group, and I could sense the tension lingering just beneath the repartee. The look in Noah's eyes said it all.

Lisa tapped me on the shoulder, leaning into my ear. "Bathroom break," she said, standing up and throwing her purse over her shoulder. Julia followed suit.

"I'll join you," I replied. When I stood from the loveseat, stars began to flicker behind my eyes, and it took a few seconds for my balance to steady. I squinted at Noah. "You totally spiked my drinks, didn't you?"

Noah snorted. "Yeah, with a little ingredient called low alcohol tolerance."

I grumbled through a frown. I was certain I must have consumed twice the amount of alcohol I thought I had. Lisa and Julia appeared on both sides of me, linking their arms with mine. "Thanks," I murmured, carefully making my way down the squeaky steps, petrified of tripping over my own feet and breaking my neck.

Then again, if I tripped down a flight of stairs in front of Devon Sawyer, breaking my neck would be a welcome alternative to the abject humiliation of it all.

"What do you think they're talking about?" Lisa wondered. All three of us glanced up to the second-floor balcony. Devon and Noah were engaged in man-to-man conversation.

Julia shrugged. "Probably band stuff. Or sex."

"Speaking of sex..." Lisa nudged me playfully in the ribcage. "You and Devon?"

"Oh, no," I said with a shake of my head. "It's going to be a while before I go there with any guy. If he's truly interested in me, he can wait."

"Good for you," Julia said. "I wish I had that kind of willpower."

"You do?"

She nibbled her thumbnail with consideration. "No."

"Does that mean you and Noah will be at it like rabbits tonight?" I teased.

Julia's smile faded from her perfectly lined lips. "Honestly, Noah seems more interested in you than me."

Objection teased my tongue. I knew Noah was only trying to make amends for the sake of Devon... that, or he was trying to kill me by way of alcohol poisoning.

The latter seemed more believable.

"Personally, I think Noah is a douche and you can do better, Julia," Lisa chimed in. "I know he's famous and all, but you're just going to get your heart broken."

Julia snickered. "Sweetie, this heart is immune to pain. I'm all about having fun and moving on to the next sucker. Besides, there's no way in hell I'm passing on a Freeze Frame member. You really can't do better than that... except for maybe raising John Lennon from the dead."

Laughing, I stumbled into the bathroom, squeaking out an apology when I accidentally slammed the door into an annoyed patron.

The woman sneered. "Drink some water."

"You okay there, Chelsie?" Lisa asked.

"I'm fine. Where's the bathroom?"

Julia shot me a concerned glance. "We're in the bathroom, babe. The stall is to your right."

Oops.

"I knew that." I wobbled over to the stall and took a moment to gather my composure. There was no way I could go back out there stumbling over my own two feet in front of Devon. He would never speak to me again. I sucked in a deep breath and tried to stop my head from spiraling before joining Julia and Lisa outside the doors. "Sorry, I just needed a minute. I'm okay now."

"Are you sure?" Lisa put a gentle hand on my shoulder. "We can take you home, you know."

"No, absolutely not. I'll just... suck it up. Let's go." Gathering my crumbling wits, I staggered over to the private staircase. It resembled Mount Olympus, and it looked to be swaying back and forth. I headed up, my hand gripping the railing.

"Sorry about that," I apologized when I noticed Devon staring at me.

"Here, sit down. You're going to fall and hurt yourself," Devon said.

As I went to sit down, I missed the couch and toppled to the floor instead. I couldn't help but find the situation incredibly funny, bursting into a fit of giggles.

"God, Chels, are you okay?" Julia asked, rushing to my side.

I couldn't stop laughing. "I fell. It's... so funny."

"I think it's going to be a long night," Lisa sighed, sitting down beside me and rubbing my back.

Noah watched with an amused grin from the other side of the room. "Or an incredibly short one."

CHAPTER FIVE

NOAH

"Let's dance!" Chelsie rose to her feet with dramatic enthusiasm, almost losing her balance. "Wait, no. Let's drink. More drinks, please."

Devon shot me a death glare when I snickered in reply.

"You're an asshole," he said, trying to stop Chelsie from waving down the waitress. "This is your fault."

I shrugged, willing to accept full credit for my participation. "Looks like you're going to have your hands full tonight," I acknowledged, taking a sip of my beer and enjoying the entertainment for the evening. Drunk girls always put on a good show.

"Hey... hey now, mister," Chelsie stammered. She pushed at Devon's chest when he tried to sit her back down. "Jus' lemme go. We need more drinks."

"We definitely don't need more drinks," Devon said.

Chelsie pushed him away and stumbled over to me.

"You." She pointed an unsteady finger in my direction. "Get me beer."

Devon shot me a look that clearly implied, *"I will kill you if you get her beer."*

Figuring I'd done enough damage for the night, I shook my head. "The beer is gone," I told her, then chuckled at the horrified look on her face.

"Gone?" she whimpered. "Why would they do that?"

"Don't worry about it. I think you just need to sit down."

"No... no." She dodged me, crossing her arms. "I'm perfectly good."

I skated my gaze over to Lisa and Julia, who looked like they'd gone into shock from humiliation.

"Right," Lisa piped up, springing into action. "Come on, Chelsie. Let's take you home."

"But I wanna dance!" she exclaimed. Chelsie bolted toward the staircase. "Dancing is a fun and exiblerating experience." She hesitated through a frown. "Ex-hil-her-ate-ing..."

Julia caught her just in time. "Dancing is for sober people, babe."

"You know, I don't mind taking her home," Devon offered, clearing his throat. "You guys can stay."

"Nonsense." Julia waved her hand with dismissal. "We've got her back. You guys try to enjoy the rest of your night."

When the girls approached Chelsie, she had already managed to sneak down the staircase and was halfway onto the dance floor.

"Shit," Julia cursed.

I leaned over the balcony, watching as the two friends went in search of Chelsie.

Devon appeared by my side, venom radiating off of him. "I knew you were up to something."

I guess I felt mildly guilty about putting a damper on what could have been a fun night—I'd even screwed myself over in the process because now Julia was leaving, and I was out of a perfectly good hook-up. "Yeah, well... it's not like you were going to marry the girl."

Devon moved in dangerously close. "Fuck you, Hayes. I like her. But what would you know about that? It's all about the chase for you."

"It's all about the music," I corrected him, choosing to ignore the barb despite the way my hackles rose. "I thought we were on the same page. The band comes first."

"*I* say what comes first. *I* make the rules. And if you fuck with my personal life again, you're out."

My jaw clenched as Devon stormed off down the stairs with

his cell phone to his ear. I gripped the balcony rail, my knuckles turning white. Arguments with Devon were nothing new—I knew I was playing with fire tonight. But I also knew Devon's threats were always empty. We'd been through far worse together and had still managed to maintain a cordial working relationship and friendship.

Scratching at the base of my neck, I made my way down to the dance floor to find the girls, quickly spotting them dancing their hearts out to an upbeat song. Chelsie looked drunk, but she was keeping her balance as she jumped up and down to the music. It was obvious what Devon saw in the woman—she had a perfect mix of sweetness and sass. I decided that the sass only came out when I was around, and I was okay with that.

And as far as looks went, Chelsie was hard to beat with her slender physique, ivory skin, and emerald eyes.

I shook my head, not liking where my train of thought was going, before eyeing the room for any sign of Devon. Not seeing him anywhere, I sighed in defeat and pulled up a bar stool, signaling the bartender for another drink.

An hour went by and not much had changed.

"I'm not going anywhere!"

I turned to see Chelsie putting up a fight with Julia. Lisa approached me then, groaning with dismay. "She's been doing this all night. We can't seem to get her off the dance floor."

"Yeah, I sure as hell thought she'd be passed out by now," I shrugged. "The girl's got spunk—I'll give her that."

Lisa's features contorted with worry. "I'm not sure what to do. I don't want to make a scene."

My jaw ticked as I glanced up at Devon, who was now sitting alone on the balcony, texting furiously. "You know, Devon and I can take her home. I was the one who got you guys into this mess." Apprehension settled in the red-head's eyes, so I smiled warmly. "Seriously, she'll be okay. We'll get you and Julia a limo, then take Chelsie home when she's ready."

Lisa gave a nervous nibble to her lip. "Are you sure? I don't want to inconvenience you guys. You've been so good to us already."

"It's not a problem," I said.

I planned on giving full "Chelsie Duty" to Devon.

"Okay," she relented. "I'll go get Julia."

I watched as the two friends discussed the plan before veering back in my direction.

Julia stormed at me with her hands on her hips. "If I turn on the news tomorrow morning and find that Chelsie was left for dead in a ditch somewhere, I'm hunting you down. I'm only trusting you because you're rich and famous. And hot."

"I appreciate the sentiment," I chuckled. "The limo is outside." My shoulders sagged as I watched my evening of sin walk out the door and sighed wearily, knowing I only had myself to blame. "All right, Water Girl, let's get you to your babysitter for the night..." I mumbled. When I turned to collect Chelsie, she had disappeared back into the crowd. "Damnit."

My eyes perused the dance floor, trying to pick her out from the rest of the petite blondes packed into the room, coming up unsuccessful. Panic crept up inside me, knowing I was a dead man if I didn't find her fast. I pushed my way through the dancing bodies, my eyes on high alert. The music was loud. Fog and bright lights were making me dizzy, and the beers I'd just downed were creeping up on me. "I am so fucked," I muttered to myself.

Five minutes later, I was right back where I started after being roped into scribbling seven autographs onto cleavage after a crowd of women spotted me—only, I was missing the one woman I'd offered to take responsibility for.

"Sir?"

I spun around to find a bouncer standing in front of me. "Yeah?"

"Sir, I think your friend is in the bathroom. We really need her to leave. She's passed out in a stall."

My teeth ground together. "Blonde hair, white dress? About 'yay' high?" I gestured just over five feet.

"That's the one."

Releasing a bitter chuckle, I headed toward the bathrooms. All eyes were on me as I entered. I pushed open each stall door until I found Chelsie lying sprawled out over one of the toilet seats.

Awesome.

"Jesus, woman, you're really making my life a living hell." Chelsie was motionless and I was running out of options, so I picked her up and carried her out of the bathroom, having every intention on handing her off to Devon.

I tried to ignore the giggles and pitiful looks I received while I traipsed through the club, as the unconscious blonde in my arms was catching everyone's attention. Had they never witnessed a passed-out drunk before?

I made my way up the staircase, relieved there was almost an end in sight. But I froze when Devon had seemingly vanished. Setting Chelsie down on the nearby couch, I pulled out my cell phone to call my bandmate.

That's when I noticed an unread text message from ten minutes earlier.

It was from Devon.

Devon: *Gotta bail. Meeting Sean at the studio to work on somethin major. Make sure the girls get home safe. You're still an asshole.*

My stomach soured. I glanced over at a comatose Chelsie, then back at my phone. Realization hit me that my plan had completely backfired, and now I was the one left solely in charge of taking care of this woman.

Deep breath. Stay calm. You can do this.

To make matters worse, I had no idea where Chelsie even lived. I hadn't paid attention during the drive over to her apartment.

I called Devon, but it went straight to voicemail.

Ah, fuck.

I only had Julia's number written on a gum wrapper in my car, which was miles away from the bar. I cursed myself for not saving it into my phone. My only other option was to take Chelsie back to the hotel with me—it sounded like the worst possible idea, but I couldn't think of anything else through my own foggy alcohol buzz.

Stepping over to Chelsie, I leaned down to scoop her up. She looked so peaceful, so content. So unaware she was about to be whisked away to a strange hotel room with a man she loathed.

I was certain she was going to castrate me come sunrise, so I made a mental note to remove all sharp objects from the room.

"Here goes nothing," I said, lifting the petite blonde into my arms. "At least you don't weigh anything."

Chelsie stirred, her eyes fluttering open. "I want French fries," she muttered. Then she wrapped her arms around my neck and nestled her head against my shoulder.

I tensed, trying to ignore her soft hair tickling my neck and the scent of citrus on her skin. "French fries sound great."

CHAPTER SIX

CHELSIE

Something startled me awake.

It could have been the pounding headache, or it could have been the blinding sunlight that pooled across my face. Or maybe it was the unknown bed I was sleeping in while still wearing last night's clothes.

My mouth was dry, my stomach hollow, and my entire body was painfully sore. I blinked a few times as my eyes adjusted to the light before sitting up and massaging my temples, looking around the room for some sense of familiarity. It appeared to be an upscale hotel room.

Had I been date-raped? Kidnapped? A willing participant in a one-night stand? All three scenarios made me cringe.

I set my sights on an adjacent nightstand where I spotted a black leather wallet. Curious as to who my company was, I snatched it up and began to look through its contents.

Oh... *crap.*

According to the driver's license, the wallet belonged to none other than my very best friend, Noah Hayes. My stomach twisted into knots. Why would I be in a hotel room with Noah?

Oh my God, I drunk-slept with Noah!

Panic sluiced me, but I forced it down to keep digging.

I continued to browse through the wallet, discovering a large wad of cash, some credit cards, stale pieces of gum, and a photograph. I pulled the small picture out and studied it—it was a photo of a young boy, maybe three or four years old. He had adorable chubby cheeks and light brown hair. A nephew, perhaps.

Not finding anything else of interest, I discarded the wallet and threw my legs over the side of the bed. I squeaked in surprise when my toes tickled a sleeping male body lying on the floor next to me. My legs popped back up as if I'd stepped on hot coals, and it didn't take long for me to realize that the man was Noah.

The whole situation was confusing. Where was Devon? Where were Lisa and Julia? Why did it feel like I'd been run over by a semi-truck?

Weighing my options, I decided to climb out of bed from the opposite side and tiptoe to the bathroom. My full bladder was bordering on painful. When I returned, Noah was sitting up and watching me with interest.

I froze. Not giving him a chance to say anything, I balled my fists and began the interrogation. "Where the hell am I? Where are my friends? Did I have sex with you? Did I puke?"

Did I puke while having sex with you?

Horror bubbled inside me at the possible scenarios.

"Easy there, tiger," he said, holding his hands up. "What do you remember?"

My mind raced.

What *did* I remember? I recalled going to the club, having some drinks, arguing with Noah, talking with Devon. Maybe... dancing? "I – I don't remember much. Just the usual stuff. Nothing that explains why I'm alone with you in your hotel room."

Noah stood, stretching out his arms with a yawn and scratching his chest. "Well, the short story is that you couldn't resist me. I had no choice but to take you back to my room and make sweet love to you."

The color drained from my face.

"Don't worry, it was amazing. I promise," he smiled. "I was very attentive."

I couldn't speak. I'd gone into shock.

Noah finally released a light laugh, shaking his head. "I'm kidding."

I blinked. "I hate you so much."

"Yeah, well, you got completely wasted and I was left in charge of you, so you're not exactly my favorite person either."

My mouth was still agape as I stared at him, his words trickling through my stupor. I finally stuttered, "Wh-what? That doesn't make any sense."

"It makes perfect sense. You drank a lot of alcohol and you got intoxicated."

Flustered, I racked my brain for some sort of trigger. I vaguely recalled a tipsy walk to the bathroom with my girlfriends... and well, that was the *last* thing I remembered. "So, it's pretty much all your fault," I concluded. My eyebrow arched with incrimination. "You bought me all those drinks."

Noah sniffed at the accusation. "Whatever you say. Just keep in mind, I'm the one who took care of you when everyone else bailed."

A haunting memory seized me like an electrical current.

"Besides, who's going to take care of you?"

My expression wilted. I had no idea why Ian's words decided to puncture me in that moment.

Swallowing, I tried to remember something. Anything.

Why would my friends leave me alone with Noah? And what kind of guy did that make Devon for ditching me like that?

Better yet... what kind of guy did that make *Noah* for sticking around?

My stance softened as I unclenched my hands. "Well, thanks, I guess. Why didn't you just take me home?"

"Trust me, I would have loved to have avoided this exact moment," he said. "I didn't know where you lived. I didn't have your friends' numbers and Devon turned his phone off. What other choice did I have? Should I have left you at the club?"

"No," I said quickly. "I appreciate that you didn't leave me at the club. I'm just having a hard time processing everything." Inhaling a deep breath, I made my way over to the bed and sat down, running my fingers through tangled hair. "I don't understand why everyone left me there."

Noah perched himself beside me on the bed as the mattress squeaked beneath his weight. "Honestly... it was a misunderstanding. Your friends needed to leave, but you insisted on staying. I offered to take you home with Devon, but by the time they left, Devon had taken off to the studio, thinking you were going home with your friends. That left me," he explained.

I ducked my head in embarrassment. "Wow. I must have made a fool of myself. I don't usually drink like that."

I could only imagine what Devon thought of me now. Would he ever want to see me again?

"If it makes you feel any better, I can tell Devon likes you. Don't beat yourself up over it."

My teeth gnawed at the inside of my cheek as I looked up at Noah. I would have thought he'd do anything to get me out of the picture—but here he was, giving me a little bit of hope.

"That does make me feel better," I replied softly. "Thanks." We sat in silence for a beat before I asked the inevitable question every blacked-out drunk girl asked. "Did I do anything... um, embarrassing?"

His eyes flashed with something.

Something I couldn't pinpoint.

What was he hiding?

I buried my blushing face into my palms, coming to the only logical conclusion. "I totally puked, didn't I?"

Noah laughed, the mysterious look melting into familiar teasing. "No, you danced for most of the night," he shrugged. "I mean... there was the occasional falling on your ass. And we can't forget the passing out in a bathroom stall."

I cringed. "Oh God."

"Yeah, I had to carry you out. You were basically unconscious."

"You carried me?" My tone was incredulous. I was appalled by my behavior.

"Well, yeah. Unconscious people can't walk. Don't worry, though... you'll probably see pictures of it in the tabloids tomorrow."

More whimpers of humiliation escaped me. "I'm such an idiot. Noah... that's not me, I swear. I didn't even drink in college."

His lips curled into a half-smile. "Hey, we've all been there. No need to apologize."

Noah's change in attitude was alarming. He'd taken care of me at the club, carried me out, slept on the floor, and now he was engaging in pleasant conversation. Was he up to something? I was reluctant to let my guard down, but the new Noah was one I hoped would stick around.

If *I* managed to stick around, anyway.

"Thank you... really." I couldn't hide the sincerity in my tone as I spared him a look of gratitude. "I know we haven't been on the best of terms, but I do appreciate you having my back."

Noah shifted on the bed and scratched the collar of his neck. "It's cool," he mumbled, clearing his throat. "So, should I have the limo take you home? I have some family stuff to do today."

I stood up, rummaging for my shoes and purse. "Sure, yeah. I'll get out of your hair." As I searched around the room for my personal belongings, I tried to make idle conversation. "Does your family live around here? Did you grow up in New York?"

Noah glanced at me, his green gaze flickering with surprise at my interest. "Um... yeah, actually. I have a house not ten miles from here."

"A house? Why did you get a hotel room, then?"

"I assumed Julia was leaving the club with me last night."

"Oh." My cheeks heated. "Why not just take her to your own place?"

Noah blinked, glancing away, and I could sense that he wasn't used to talking about his personal life.

"Sorry," I said, slipping back into my shimmery heels and wincing. My ankles were sore and swollen from the previous night's adventures. "I didn't mean to pry."

He didn't answer right away, taking his time lighting a cigarette before returning his attention to me. "I have family staying with me."

I watched as he blew smoke toward the ceiling, running a hand through his tousled hair. I could tell he wasn't revealing everything. There was something mysterious about Noah that intrigued me.

And what had that look been all about when I'd inquired about my embarrassing behavior?

What was he not telling me?

NOAH

I drove into the studio parking lot, killing the engine of my Corvette and pulling off my sunglasses. It had been a few hours since Chelsie had left my hotel room, and I'd yet to speak with Devon since the club. I was more than curious about this "major thing" Devon had referred to in his last text message.

Stuffing my keys into my pocket, I climbed out of the car and entered the studio, spotting Devon chatting with our manager and agent, Sean Pierce.

"Yo," I called out, garnering the two men's attention.

Devon had an enthusiastic look on his face, which was a welcome contrast to our previous interaction together. I'd been expecting a well-deserved punch to the jaw.

"I figured you'd be here hours ago. Sorry I bailed, but you're going to shit yourself when you hear the news." Devon took a sip of his soda as he approached me. "What the hell took you so long?"

"I told you, I had family stuff to do today. Plus, I had to take care of your girlfriend this morning."

Devon stalled in his tracks. "What are you talking about?"

I bristled at the memories from the night before. "Chelsie. I was stuck with her last night. I sent Lisa and Julia home, thinking you would take care of her, but then you left, so I had no choice but to bring her back to my hotel room with me." I had to take a step back when Devon advanced on me with murderous intent in his clear-blue eyes. "Whoa, nothing happened, all right? I wouldn't do that."

"You had *no choice?* Why didn't you call Julia or Lisa to come back and get her?"

"I didn't have their numbers."

"And you didn't think to check Chelsie's phone for their numbers? Or look at her driver's license for her address?"

"I..." I paused, realizing I didn't have an answer. Why *didn't* I do that?

All I could do was blame it on the alcohol.

"Awesome." Devon let out a caustic laugh. "As if you haven't traumatized her enough, she had to wake up to your fuckin' face this morning. Real nice."

My defenses flared as I took a step forward. "Hey, I took care of the girl last night. I had to physically carry her ass out of the club after she passed out in the bathroom. Where the hell were you?"

"You know, I have no sympathy for you. You made the mess, and you deserved to clean it up," Devon shot back.

It was true. I rubbed my hands over my face and sighed. "Fine. You're right. I was an asshole. But I don't want you losing sight of the big picture because of some pretty face."

"Losing sight? Dude, I just booked us the gig of the century."

I froze, my mind racing. "What?"

Devon's smile returned as he pulled a contract out of his back pocket. "The fuckin' Grammy's, man."

CHAPTER SEVEN

CHELSIE

It was a cloudy Sunday afternoon, and I had yet to hear from Devon after my embarrassing spectacle on Friday night. I was certain I'd scared him away for good. In fact, he was probably touring China just to get as far away from me as possible. What kind of idiot epically botches her first date with Devon Sawyer?

This girl.

I was lying on the couch, reading the latest Tarryn Fisher novel and wallowing in my own pathetic misery, when there was a knock at the door. I glanced at the clock, not expecting Lisa to arrive for our lunch date for another hour.

"Coming," I muttered. I gave a sharp tug to the messy bun on top of my head, still in my pajamas. The dreary day complemented my mood quite nicely.

Stepping over to the front door, I swung it open, prepared to tease my best friend about her early arrival. Lisa had always been the overly punctual type.

But I was unprepared when I discovered that the person standing on the other side of the door was... Noah Hayes.

"Hey," he said.

I was so taken aback by his presence, I could only gawk at him.

"Uh, can I come in?"

"No. I – I mean, sure. Um... what are you doing here?" Finding my footing, I stepped aside, allowing the musician to enter my apartment. "You're the last person I expected to show up on my doorstep. Especially considering you had no idea where I lived."

He spared me a sheepish grin. "Devon had your address."

"Why are you here?"

Noah shoved a hand into his back pocket and pulled out a familiar silver chain. "I found this in the hotel bed yesterday before I checked out. Since you were, unfortunately, the only girl I had in my room that night, I figured it might be yours."

I couldn't help the rosy stain from flooding my cheeks. "Uh, right. Yes, that's mine... thank you."

When I held out my hand, Noah dropped the delicate necklace into my palm. He fidgeted in the doorway, looking uncharacteristically nervous.

"So, what do you remember about that night?" he asked.

Confusion washed over me as I blinked at him. "I told you... I remember taking a bathroom break with the girls, dancing a little, um..." I trailed off when I noticed him shaking his head. "What? Is there something I should know?"

Noah scratched his jaw as he regarded me before pacing around the apartment. "I just meant... well, what do you remember after we got back to the hotel?"

It took a moment for his words to sink in.

And then my stomach coiled with dread.

My mind spun with different scenarios, none of them pretty, all of them humiliating. Most of them involving puke. *Did I even want to know?*

"I thought we already had this conversation. I don't remember anything," I admitted, swallowing back the lump in my throat and monitoring his expression carefully.

Noah's face remained unreadable at first. Then the corner of his mouth curled into a familiar, taunting grin. "I could really have fun with this, you know."

"Noah, please. Just tell me." I paused to add, "And then shoot me."

He sighed, folding his arms. "Okay, look. You told me things you probably wouldn't have told me if you were sober. Some pretty heavy stuff."

My blood swam with ice. My knees quivered as I lowered myself to the sofa. "Wh-what?"

"Well, we were having a rare bonding moment over French fries. They were great... you know, McDonalds. The best. You were doodling these little animal designs in the ketchup—cats, I think, or maybe hamsters. You said you had a cat, but you always wanted a hamster, so I can't remember—"

"Noah," I warned, waving him on to get to the point.

"And then you told me about your ex."

I paled.

This wasn't happening. This couldn't be happening.

Noah continued, the levity leaving him. "I'm, uh, not trying to make you uncomfortable. I just wanted to apologize for being a dick to you and let you know your secrets are safe with me."

I tried to speak, but it felt as if all the air had been sucked out of my lungs. I was sick to my stomach, and all I could do was bow my head and try to hold back the tears.

Lisa had been the only person I'd trusted with my past. How could I have told *Noah*? He was completely unworthy of knowing my dark secrets.

And *oh*, were they dark.

"I – I don't know what to say."

Noah appeared out of his element, fidgeting and rubbing the back of his neck. "We can... talk about it... if you want."

"God, I don't even want to know what I said," I whimpered. I hated that Noah was seeing me so vulnerable. So exposed.

"I mean, it's not a big deal. Like I said, I won't tell anyone. Not even Devon."

I swallowed and looked up at him, my eyes stormy and glistening. "It *is* a big deal. It's a huge deal." My voice caught as I drew in a deep, shaky breath. "My past is something I try to forget every day."

"I get that," he said, his tone oddly sympathetic. "But your past is something that happened to you. It's not who you are."

I blinked back tears, nodding in agreement. "Look at you... being all insightful."

"What, you think I made it this far on just my looks?"

"No, I figured it was a toss-up between your charming personality and your uncanny ability to make a girl feel special. I know I was swept off my feet."

"That's true." His shoulders shrugged with modesty, a smirk hinting. "I'm basically a triple threat."

"How am I not falling in love with you right now?"

"I don't know," he laughed. "Where did I go wrong?"

I couldn't help the smile that broke free.

I never expected to be sitting in my living room, exchanging quips with Noah Hayes. Regaining my composure, I cleared my throat. "Can I get you anything? Something to drink?"

Noah cocked his head, following me as I stood and trekked into the kitchen. "Sure, why not? But I'm going to watch you make it. I don't want you slipping any rat poison in there."

"You would deserve it." I gave him the side-eye as I opened the refrigerator. My lips puckered with disappointment when I realized I hadn't gone shopping in two weeks. There was a half-gallon of Sunny Delight, an assortment of odd condiments, a package of hot dogs, and month-old string cheese. "Uh, my tips were kind of bad this month. Sorry."

"Yikes. Sunny D, it is."

I pulled a glass out of the cabinet and poured the drink. "Not exactly a celebrity-worthy cocktail," I said, offering him an embarrassed glance. "Want to sit down?"

Noah followed my lead as I made my way back to the living room sofa, a silence settling between us. The last thing I wanted to talk about was my unexpected confession, but I needed to find out what Noah knew about my past. "So," I began, watching as Noah took a swig of his juice. Wringing my hands together, I took a deep breath. "What exactly do you know?"

NOAH

I found it hard to believe I was sitting on Chelsie's couch, sipping on Sunny Delight, when a few days ago she was just another one of Devon's conquests I'd aimed to annihilate.

Today I was her confidante; an unlikely companion. I knew all about her dark past—more than Devon may ever know—and for some peculiar reason, I felt inclined to give her solace. Maybe it was the wounded, forsaken look in her eyes, or maybe it was the troubled way she'd spilled her guts to me. Her strong and fiery spirit had been reduced to a lost and lonely young woman who'd experienced more than her fair share of trauma.

I would never forget the way she had climbed into my lap, taking my face between her shaking hands and *begging* me to never speak a word of it to anyone.

"Noah, this... this is serious," she'd rasped, holding me tight.

I'd stared at her as she'd straddled me, my arms instinctively wrapping around her to keep her steady as we sat on the floor, my back to the hotel bed. "What is?"

We weren't talking about French fries anymore, that much I knew. Her eyes had glazed over with more than just alcohol, dark shadows lurking inside the smoky green of her irises.

Chelsie's breath had all but stopped as she licked her lips. "The monster. The monster I thought I loved."

I'd been confused, frowning as she'd clenched her thighs around me. I'd also been getting hard, but was too distracted by the desolate look in her eyes to focus on the effects of her squirming on me. "I'm not following. What monster?"

"Ian. He beat me. Raped me. He said I was a disease, and no one would ever love me." She'd dipped her eyes to my mouth before glancing back up. "Devon could love me, right?"

My own breath had caught as my skin prickled with alarm. "What?" I'd questioned, searching her face for answers. "Are you in danger?"

Our drunken, inconvenient rendezvous had shifted into something far more dire.

She'd nodded. "I'll always be in danger. He follows me."

Swallowing, she'd swayed on my lap before tapping a finger to her temple. "In here."

"Listen, are you actually in danger? Is this a cry for help?"

"He... he tried to kill me, Noah." Chelsie had leaned in close, whispering the next words right against my ear. "He wrapped his fingers around my throat like the Grim Reaper and asked if I wanted to know what it felt like to take my last breath."

We'd locked eyes when she'd inched back. My chest had hummed with warning, with genuine concern as we stared at each other. I'd swallowed. "Are you okay?"

"No. I'm a disease, remember? That's not okay at all..." She'd nearly toppled over before I caught her, forcing her fluttering eyes back on mine. "I'm sleepy..."

"Chelsie, hey," I'd urged, cupping the side of her face with my palm. It was an intimate gesture, but it was an intimate moment—it had felt like a *pivotal* moment. "Where is this Ian guy? Does he live nearby?"

She'd lazily shaken her head. "He's in jail. He raped some poor girl because the police never took me seriously and refused to arrest him." Sighing, she'd clung to me, her forehead falling forward and knocking with mine. "He was a monster, but I thought I loved him... I guess that makes me a monster, too."

"You're not a monster."

"You don't like me because you can see the truth. I'm broken. Unlovable."

Shit—I really had been a dick to her, and for what?

Guilt washed over me as I'd chewed on my cheek. "I didn't know you. I didn't know any of this, and I'm sorry for being an ass when you clearly didn't deserve it."

It had been as candid as I'd ever been, and Chelsie must have sensed it, even in her inebriated state. She'd let a smile slip, her head swiveling side to side, her long hair curtaining us. Her breath had grazed my lips as she'd whispered, "You smell good."

I'd stiffened in more ways than one.

"I think I might puke."

Blinking though the rapid subject changes, I'd reached for a water bottle on the little nightstand. "Here, drink some water."

Chelsie had chuckled. "Water Girl."

And then she'd passed out cold, falling limp and weightless against my chest, until I'd placed her into the bed and snagged an extra blanket for my accommodations on the floor.

I didn't think I'd ever forget that moment.

Luckily for Chelsie, she would never remember it.

I sat beside her now, repeating the horror stories she had confessed to me, noting that same damaged look in her eyes. When I noticed her picking at a sofa pillow, I stopped to ask if she was okay. "We don't have to talk anymore." I set my glass down on the coffee table, finding her eyes. "That's basically all I know."

Chelsie forced a small smile, clutching the pillow to her chest. "Thanks for being so cool about this, Noah. I feel like I've come a long way, but I'll never truly be... you know, *free*. It will always be this black cloud hovering over me."

"It'll always be a part of you," I acknowledged. "But use it to shape you into an even stronger person." I wasn't any good at this pep-talk shit, but I tried to be thoughtful with my words.

Chelsie's gaze lowered to her lap. "I'm afraid if Devon even gives me another chance, I'm just going to keep screwing up. Who would want to date a nutjob like me? Nobody wants to deal with that kind of baggage. Especially a guy who could get any girl he wanted."

"Stop undermining yourself. That's your first problem," I said, firm in my delivery. "From what I see, you're an amazing girl with a lot of great qualities. And I won't lie... I noticed you waiting tables long before Devon set his sights on you."

Yikes. Had I gone too far?

Her head popped up, her nose crinkling at the confession. "Huh? I thought you hated me from the beginning."

"I never *hated* you. I was just being an asshole because that's what I do. You're smoking hot, even sitting here in your sweatpants."

Double yikes. I needed to stop talking.

Chelsie inched the pillow up to her chin, trying to hide her pink cheeks. "Um... thanks."

The doorbell rang, breaking through the tension that had developed between us.

"Oh my God... Lisa." Chelsie jumped to her feet and raced

over to the front door. "I completely forgot about our lunch date."

"I need to get going, myself." Standing from the couch, I followed her lead before halting in my tracks when Chelsie whipped around to face me. Her eyes were sparkling with genuine candor.

"Thank you," she said. "Really."

My heart stuttered. I was about to reply, but the knocking persisted.

"I'm coming!" Chelsie shouted, running the rest of the way to greet her friend in the doorway. "Sorry, Lisa, I lost track of time. Noah was just leaving."

Lisa had a perplexed look on her face as she glanced over at me, so I offered a wave.

"Uh, hey." Lisa looked back and forth between Chelsie and me. "Am I interrupting something? Should we reschedule?"

I cleared my throat. "Like she said, I was on my way out. It's nice to see you, though."

"I'm a hot mess, Lis." Chelsie looked frazzled. "Let me freshen up. Ten minutes?"

"Of course," Lisa nodded. As I brushed past her to walk out the door, she placed a firm hand on my arm. Her voice turned low and ominous as she told me, "Don't go there."

My jaw tensed at the warning. I had to suppress my man-pride from saying something scathing. I pulled my arm back, deciding to play dumb. "I'm not following."

"Please, just leave it alone. She's been through a lot."

I was aware of the "Best Friend's Duty"—it was an unsaid rule to protect said best friend from the scum of the Earth at all costs. Therefore, I forgave Lisa's assumption that I was on a mission to get into Chelsie's pants and break her heart. She had every right to jump to conclusions, considering I hadn't been on my best behavior.

Shoving my defenses aside, I shook my head. "It's not what it looks like," I forced a smile. Issuing Lisa a friendly salute, I stepped past her and out into the hallway before heading outside to my car.

I needed to clear my head because I, too, had a date that afternoon.

CHAPTER EIGHT

CHELSIE

It was Friday night, and a week had passed since my mortification occurred in the presence of Devon Sawyer.

Again.

It had been almost a week with no contact. No follow-up phone call begging for a coffee date. No text message forgiving me for making a giant ass out of myself.

Nothing.

It was a tough truth to swallow: I had epically blundered any chance I may have had with the famous musician. And now, I was drowning my sorrows in a fruity cocktail with Julia and Lisa.

"You know," Julia began, taking a sip of her giant frozen daiquiri. "You can always contact Devon yourself, Chelsie. You did immediately save his number to your phone, right?"

"Yes, Julia. I'm not a complete idiot," I replied... though, I didn't entirely believe that statement. "I just don't feel comfortable bugging him. I feel like he would contact me if he really wanted to."

"True," Julia shrugged.

My shoulders sagged with defeat. "I'm doomed."

"Don't be such a Debbie-downer," Julia said. "You'll find the right guy. No one nearly as good-looking or successful, but somebody will come along."

Lisa rolled her eyes. "Really not helping, Jules." She turned to me then. "Hey, do you want to get out of here? Depression and alcohol rarely lead to good things."

I shook my head. "Thanks, but I'm okay. I just need to forget about Devon and enjoy myself. I've been harboring guilt and self-loathing all week. I have to move on from this." My cell phone buzzed as I brought the little plastic straw to my lips. Glancing at it, I did a double-take—then a triple-take. Just to make sure. "Um, guys... ?" I trailed off.

"What?" both girls asked in unison.

"Devon just texted me to meet him at Marley's."

"Fuck yeah!" Julia exclaimed, chugging down her daiquiri and flinging her purse over her shoulder. "Let's get out of here. I am totally having sex with Noah tonight."

"Whoa, whoa, whoa," Lisa said. She grabbed Julia's hand to hold her back. "Are we even invited, Chelsie? Is this just a *you* thing?"

My face beamed with excitement as I turned the phone around to my friends, Devon's text message in full view:

Devon: *I miss u. Bring your friends and meet us at Marley's.*

Thirty minutes later, my arms were linked with Lisa's and Julia's as we strolled into Marley's. The last time I'd been there, the night had ended in heated words and a swift, embarrassing exit. Luckily, I was feeling optimistic tonight—I had smoothed over my volatile relationship with Noah, and Devon sounded eager to see me.

It was going to be a good night.

When we made our way inside, I heard my name echo through the crowd. I looked up to find Devon waving at me from atop the balcony, so I waved back with a schoolgirl grin and marched up the stairs to the V.I.P. room.

"Hey," Devon said. His handsome face broke out into a genuine smile. "I'm so glad you could make it. I've been meaning to get in touch with you all week."

I reached over and gave him a hug, a delicious shiver creeping up my spine as his body pressed against me. He smelled of musky cologne and expensive liquor, and I couldn't help but nuzzle my face into the crevice of his neck and breathe in the intoxicating scent of him. Devon responded by running his hands up and down my back.

"Hey, how come you never greet *me* like that?" said a familiar voice to my left. I pulled myself away from Devon and smiled at Noah, who was leaning against the wall with a beer in his hand. Our eyes met, and Noah shot me a playful wink.

"I see you two are finally getting along?" Devon glanced back and forth between us, hesitant but hopeful.

"For now," I shrugged, turning my attention back to Devon. I took him by the hand and led him over to our customary corner of the room. "We should probably talk about how things unfolded last week. I want to explain myself."

Devon held his hand up, stopping me before I could continue. "No need. I know exactly what happened. My bandmate is a dick."

A chuckle slipped out. "I won't argue that. But I want you to know that the person you witnessed that night wasn't me. I'll have a drink every now and then, but I don't get... blackout drunk. You know?"

"Chelsie, I know this," Devon reassured me. He lifted his hand and tucked a strand of rebellious hair behind my ear.

My heart rate quickened, my eyelids fluttering at Devon's touch. I inhaled sharply as his fingers swept through my long locks. "I didn't freak you out?"

He shook his head. "It takes a lot to freak me out. The reason I didn't call you was because the band got a pretty amazing opportunity and it took up a lot of my time. I wanted to contact you when my mind was clear."

I hardly heard him because his hand was stroking my cheek, causing my legs to quiver. I pulled him over to the adjacent couch with a flirtatious grin. "Sorry, standing is becoming problematic."

Devon's blue eyes sparkled as he studied my face. "God, you're beautiful."

Swallowing, I lowered my gaze to escape his intense stare.

"Hey, look at me," he said, taking my chin between his thumb and finger and raising my head until we were face-to-face. "I mean it."

When our eyes locked, I knew he'd meant it. I hadn't heard

anyone say it with such sincerity before. The only time Ian ever told me I was beautiful was after a beating, or a rape—it was his way of "apologizing" to me; of reeling me back into his powerful, destructive hold. Those words had fallen on deaf ears ever since.

I responded in the only way that felt right, leaning into Devon and kissing him hard. He kissed back with an equal amount of fire, wrapping his arms around my waist and pulling my body against his. In that moment, I decided...

I wanted this.

I'd been running from men for too many years, and it was time to gain back control of my life. My power.

Men were not the enemy. *Devon* was not the enemy.

"Where do you want to go from here?" Devon asked, pulling back slightly to speak. His voice was husky and full of promise.

I sat up and swept the hair back from my face, not entirely prepared to answer that question. "I don't know. All I know is that I want to keep seeing you. I've never dated a famous person before... so I'm sure there's more to it."

"Famous or not, I'm still just a guy who likes a girl. We don't have to complicate this."

I mulled over his words, still hesitant to believe that Devon Sawyer wanted to be with me. *Me.* Granted, he wasn't aware of my tremendous baggage and relationship history—no, Noah, of all people, was the one privy to that—but it was still something I was having a hard time coming to grips with.

I'd never felt like I was destined for great things. I was just a shattered, sheltered twenty-six-year old from a small town.

"You're just a lost little girl," Ian would always say to me.

Banishing the words from my mind, my mother's voice replaced them.

"Leap or retreat," she would tell me. "There is strength in both."

I thought about my mother before the years-worth of wreckage unfolded. Before I'd pushed my parents away, thinking Ian was all that mattered. Before I'd allowed him to sabotage my family dynamic and infiltrate my mind with wicked thoughts and notions.

Now, it was too late. I hadn't spoken to my parents in years, dodging their calls and attempts for reconciliation. I was a coward.

I didn't want to be a coward anymore... and Devon was a start.

"I want this," I whispered on a shaky breath, cupping Devon's face between nervous palms and watching his face morph into authentic relief. "Let's try to make this work."

Leap.

I was going to leap.

We made our relationship official, and soon, four weeks had passed us by.

Four weeks of touring and paparazzi. Four weeks of traveling, crazed fans, and after-parties. The entire month had been a blur, and I was loving every minute of it.

I'd cut back my hours at the lounge, so I was able to travel with the band when they played out of state. I had a good nest egg in my savings account that my parents had given me when I'd turned eighteen—I'd barely touched it until now. And it wasn't as if I was never picking up a full-time schedule again—of course, I would. I refused to regress into old patterns of co-dependency.

But I was grateful for the extra savings because it helped me keep up on my rent payments. Freeze Frame played a lot of local shows, but it was always a treat when I was flown to San Diego or Chicago on a first-class ticket, seated beside my celebrity boyfriend.

That took getting used to.

Devon Sawyer was my... *boyfriend.*

Lisa and Julia were incredibly supportive, albeit a tiny bit jealous of my newfound fame. It wasn't just Freeze Frame making headlines—it was Devon's mysterious new girlfriend. The tabloids had been having a hay-day with our story, and Julia made sure to text me covers of the latest gossip magazines whenever I was out of town.

It was thrilling to be a household name... yet, it was also intimidating that every woman in America wanted to burn me at the stake. Devon did his best to shield me from the spotlight, but technology made it impossible.

Taking a sip from my water bottle, my eyes skated around the small room as I fidgeted on both feet. I was standing backstage at the United Center in Chicago—*no big deal.* I placed my earbuds into each ear to drown out the deafening screams from the audience as fans waited for Freeze Frame to take the stage. Devon was sipping from his own water bottle while Noah tuned his guitar. Tad, the drummer, twirled two sticks between his fingers as he paced the room.

"This shit never gets any less nerve-wracking," Tad said, grabbing a Red Bull from the mini-fridge and popping off the tab.

"Don't be a pussy," Noah shot back. His words were muffled by the cigarette dangling between his lips.

I studied Noah as he fiddled with his guitar strings. My blossoming friendship with the snappy guitarist had been one of the stranger things to unfold throughout this crazy journey. No one seemed to question it, so I figured that our friendly alliance was preferable to our initial lethal banter.

"Want me to grab one of the techs?" I offered, watching as Noah struggled with the strings. He huffed through his cigarette in reply.

Well... *mostly* friendly.

Miles breezed past me, phone to his ear, and I could tell by his tone of voice who he was talking to. A smile bloomed.

Lisa and the Freeze Frame bassist had become quite cozy with each other during the past month. While nothing was official, they talked and texted constantly, and it was apparent they were enjoying each other's company—Lisa's face lit up whenever she spoke of the skinny, long-haired musician. I was eager for Lisa to join me in the spotlight as a "Freeze Frame Girlfriend."

"All right, boys, it's showtime." The band manager, Sean, bustled around the room, making the rounds to all four men. Noah had finally gotten his guitar in tune, and it was time to make some music.

I could hear the screams of every woman in the Chicagoland

area from where I stood, watching with anticipation from the side of the stage as the four band members disappeared to woo the crowd.

It was always a rush watching them play.

While Devon was my main attraction, I couldn't help but fixate on Noah from time to time. He played his instrument with such passion—almost as if it were more of an erotic experience than a musical one. It was incredible to watch him hone his talent in front of the crowds. I stared at him, eyeing the sweat that escaped down his bronzed neck, soaking the collar of his t-shirt.

I swallowed. Then I shook my head and refocused my gaze on Devon who was riling up the crowd. The audience was eating it up, making my insides tingle with adrenaline.

Devon could *sing*. He wasn't a synthesized pop artist in a boy band—no, Devon Sawyer was the real deal. His voice was raw, his range incredible. Goosebumps puckered my skin every time he opened his mouth.

Much to the disappointment of the cheering crowd, the show wrapped up two hours later, and the four men skipped off the stage.

"We're Freeze Frame! Goodnight!" Devon shouted, lifting his guitar into the air. The applause was resounding.

Pure magic.

When the men returned backstage, Devon grabbed me by the back of the head and planted a heated kiss on my lips. I pulled away, breathless. "You nailed it out there."

Noah came sweeping in then, scooping me off my feet and crushing me in a tight hug. "That's why they pay us the big bucks," he murmured against my ear.

"Yuck, put me down... you're all slimy," I grimaced, hugging him back with a playful squeeze despite my protests.

Devon draped a towel over his shoulder and took me by the hand, tugging me away from the sweat-soaked guitarist. "We're gonna hit the bars, babe. I'm feeling celebratory tonight. Want to join us?"

I shook my head. Late-night drinking shenanigans with Freeze Frame were always entertaining, but I was exhausted from all the traveling. "I'm pretty tired. Mind if I call it an early night?"

Noah approached us, snatching Devon's towel to wipe his face. "Me too, Dev. I got no sleep last night."

Devon's eyes danced back and forth between us before he shrugged. "Knock yourselves out. You're just going back to the hotel, then?"

Nodding, I cut my gaze to Noah. I was surprised he didn't want to join the rest of the band, as Noah was usually the first to suggest a night of alcohol after a grueling show.

Noah flung the towel over his shoulder. "It's better if you're not on your own, anyway, Combs. I'll call our driver and make sure you get back to your room in one piece."

Combs. Noah had been calling me by my last name for the last few weeks, and it was sort of... endearing.

Devon gave my hand a gentle squeeze. "You sure you won't change your mind? I can't imagine spending any time with this asshole is going to be all that fulfilling."

I leaned in, playfully. "I'll make a clean break," I said, planting a quick peck on his lips.

Devon kissed my nose, then my mouth, before letting go of my hand. "Get some sleep. I'll see you in the morning."

"Goodnight."

I sighed, certain my eyes were full of dreamy adoration as I watched him go.

Noah snuck up beside me, holding out my jacket. "I'm beat. Let's head out."

NOAH

Moments after we'd stepped out of the limo, a torrential rain poured down on us. I pulled off my leather coat and held it over Chelsie's head as we sprinted toward the hotel entrance.

"Thanks," she said, shaking the rain droplets from her hair while we hurried through the revolving doors.

Running my hands through my own drenched hair, I paused, taking a moment to catch my breath in the hotel lobby. "Is this weather bi-polar or what?"

"Good ol' Chicago for you," Chelsie smiled, then began walking ahead of me to a nearby elevator. "Well, thanks again for the makeshift umbrella. I'm going to turn in for the night."

I followed. "I'll walk you to your room," I offered, pushing the button for the eighth floor. I wasn't sure why I wasn't ready to say goodnight just yet, but maybe it was the two beers I'd just washed down during the limo ride over.

Or maybe it was the buzz from the show we'd just performed.

Or... maybe I was lonely, and Chelsie was looking rather enticing in her miniskirt and knee-high, leather boots.

Nope. Bad maybe.

Chelsie chuckled, shooting me a questioning glance. "I appreciate the sentiment, but I think I'll be okay. We're at the Ritz-Carlton."

The elevator doors opened. My jaw tensed as I tore my gaze away from the sheen of her skin that was still glistening from the freshly fallen rain. Clearing my throat, I stepped into the elevator with her. "Can't be too careful these days. Besides, I promised Devon I'd get you to your room in one piece. Can't have any pieces left behind."

Chelsie crinkled her nose, her look furling into a frown. "Are you drunk?"

"Not yet, but the night is young." A thought came over me—a bad one, probably, but a thought, nonetheless. I turned to Chelsie. "Hey, I do have a fridge full of beer in my room. Care to join me?"

"Well, *now...*" she quipped with a smile. After a moment of consideration flickered by, Chelsie shrugged her shoulders. "Actually, I wouldn't mind the company. As much as I love coming to these shows, I can't deny getting a little homesick."

Homesick. Chelsie had no idea how homesick I felt every time I stepped onto an airplane or drove off in a tour bus. A sigh escaped me as we rode up the elevator in silence. Devon was lucky to have Chelsie in his life—*the bastard*. I yearned for that connection, that bond.

I'd had it once. With Ruby.

But she'd broken my goddamn heart.

"Is this one your room?"

Chelsie's voice pierced through my hopeless daydreams, and I realized we were already standing in front of my hotel room.

"Uh, yeah. This is the one." I scrambled for the room key, stuffing my hands into every pocket before sifting through my wallet, still coming up empty. "Shit. Tad or Miles must have it," I groaned. "I'll run down to the front desk."

Chelsie shook her head. "Don't bother. We can hang out in my room. Devon won't be back for a few hours, and I want to change out of these wet clothes, anyway."

A mental image of Chelsie changing out of her wet clothes popped into my mind, and I had to wonder if this was a good idea...

"Yeah, okay."

Yep. Good idea.

"We only have a couple bottles of wine, though. No beer. You know Devon isn't much of a drinker," Chelsie muttered as we strolled down the hallway to her room.

I didn't respond right away because I was still thinking about her changing out of her wet clothes. An elbow nudged me in the arm, causing me to glance up. "Huh?"

"Wine. No beer. Comprendo?" she repeated, as if I were a preschooler—a Hispanic, alcoholic preschooler.

"Sure, yeah. Fine."

Chelsie casted me a worried glance as she popped her room key into the door and opened it. She flipped on the lights, then set her purse down on a nearby table. I threw myself on the bed with a long sigh.

"Hey! No wet shoes on the bed. Devon will flip," Chelsie scolded.

Humming contentedly, I leaned back with my hands behind my head, eyes closed. "Devon is out enjoying his night. He is blissfully unaware that my wet shoes are on his bed."

She didn't share in the amusement, storming over and

smacking my legs off the bed with an irritated swat. "Don't be an ass."

When she ambled into the adjoining bathroom to change, I sat up and craned my neck to steal a peep of her through the cracked door. Almost instantly, she shut the door all the way, and I cursed my disappointment under my breath.

After a few minutes of debating whether or not I should fall asleep or pop open that bottle of wine, Chelsie emerged from the bathroom in a pink tank top and sweatpants. She pulled her hair into a high ponytail, yanking it tightly as she breezed past me. A whiff of lavender and rainwater trailed her as she reached into the mini-fridge and pulled out the wine.

"Cheers to Freeze Frame," Chelsie said, handing me a glass. She filled her own glass with the sparkling Moscato and held it up.

"I'll drink to that," I nodded. I brought the wine to my lips, studying her over the rim. "Also... cheers to us."

Chelsie swallowed abruptly. "Us? What about us?"

"You know... us," I repeated. "From mortal enemies, to a kindred fellowship."

"A kindred... what? Are you sure you're not drunk?" Chelsie pressed, her features pinching with concern.

"Hey, I'm trying to have a moment here."

"Yeah, an awkward moment. You're being weird."

I grumbled, leaning back on one arm and chugging the rest of the wine. "Fine, whatever. I'm just glad we were able to get past our differences, you know? You're pretty okay, Water Girl."

Chelsie's expression softened as she sipped her Moscato. "You're okay, yourself." Her eyes glimmered like emeralds over her wine glass. She sat down beside me, holding her beverage primly in her lap as she cleared her throat and shot me a sideways glance. "Can I ask you a question?"

"I suppose." I poured myself another glass of wine and promptly chugged that one, too—just in case I didn't like the question.

She tapped her perfectly painted toenails against the carpet. "What happened to the girl you were in love with?"

Chelsie's question felt like a punch to the gut.

I generally avoided questions about my personal life, and I *especially* avoided questions about Ruby. I knew something sinister must have flashed in my eyes because Chelsie recoiled and started to backpedal.

"I – I mean, I'm not trying to pry. You mentioned you were in love before. I was just wondering what came of it. You don't have to talk about her if you don't want to."

"I don't want to."

The look in Chelsie's eyes shifted from sympathy to annoyance at my hardened tone. "Okay. Sorry I asked."

I stood up and began pacing the room. "You know, it's not really customary to bring up ex-girlfriends out of the blue. In fact, it's a terrible fucking idea."

Chelsie rose to her feet, accepting my invitation for a fight. "*You know* I didn't mean any harm by it. I said you didn't have to talk about it if you didn't want to." Her hands were firmly planted on her waist.

"I said I didn't want to. Then you got all... pissy-eyed." Two fingers waggled in front of her face for emphasis.

"*Pissy-eyed?*" Her tone turned incredulous. "Excuse me for wanting to learn more about you. Pardon me for caring. In fact... I *think* it was you I spilled my guts to not that long ago."

My defenses flared as I leaned in close, her hot breath skimming my face. "You think I wanted to know all about your tortured past?"

The look in Chelsie's eyes morphed again, this time from aggravation to something along the lines of "you killed my puppy."

Shit. I'm a dick.

"Really," she spat back through gritted teeth. "I confide in you, and you throw it in my face? Here I thought maybe I had misjudged you. Maybe you were just... *misunderstood*. But no." Chelsie pursed her lips, crossing her arms over her chest. "You really are an asshole."

My shoulders sagged, the fight long gone. I didn't want to hurt her. "Look—"

"Get out." She pointed a sharp finger toward the door. "Just go."

"Listen to me, Combs." Chelsie stiffened, her eyes brimming with tears. I ran a hand over my face, letting out a hard breath. "The girl I loved? Her name was Ruby. She broke my heart into a million fucking pieces, and I've never really recovered from it. And it doesn't help that Ruby gave me something that reminds me of her every day."

Chelsie's features softened, but her stance remained rigid. "Yeah, well, Ian gave me scars and bruises that will never heal. What did Ruby give you? Herpes?"

I ignored the well-deserved barb and reached into my back pocket. Hesitating briefly, I pulled out my wallet and fished through the contents, removing a small photo. I handed it to her. "No," I said, meeting her eyes. My heart squeezed as the next words spilled out: "She gave me Sam."

CHAPTER NINE

CHELSIE

Noah Hayes had a son.

Noah. The tattooed, foul-mouthed, cigarette-smoking Freeze Frame guitarist. He had a child. By all accounts, an adorable, well-adjusted child.

After only having a week to digest this information, I was on my way to Samuel Hayes' fourth birthday party.

Devon tapped his hands against the steering wheel of his black Jaguar. The top was rolled down, yet the wind hardly disturbed a hair on his slicked-back, gelled-up head.

"I can't believe no one mentioned Noah was a single dad," I mused, pushing my sunglasses up over my hair to tame the fly-aways.

"Yeah, he's private about Sam so we're used to not talking about it. I guess it never came up."

"Understandable. What's his house like?" My voice was shrill over the howling winds and The Rolling Stones. I smiled to myself, envisioning the bad-boy rocker planting perennials and hosting martini mixers.

Devon shrugged, not missing a beat of his amateur drum solo on the wheel. "It's a normal house. It's just him and Sammy. And Rosa, the caretaker."

I'd learned about Rosa over the past week. She took care of

little Sam when Noah was off touring or playing shows. I couldn't help but feel bad for the poor kid... he had no mother in his life, and his father was hardly home.

"What is Noah's relationship like with Sam?" I wondered, curiously.

Devon switched off the radio and placed his hand atop my bare knee. "They're close," he said. "It was hard being a single dad in the beginning, but they make a great team."

I bobbed my head with a thoughtful smile. Noah hadn't provided any details into why he'd become a single father, but I knew better than to press his buttons on that subject.

Twenty more minutes passed as we pulled into the driveway of the Hayes household. I twisted in my seat to get a good look at the place Noah called home, noting that Devon had been right—it *was* normal. A picture of suburbia. I could almost see the soccer moms through the walls of the cookie-cutter houses lined up along the picturesque street.

We stepped out of the car, my eyes twinkling when I spotted three balloons tied to the mailbox, swaying gently with the spring breeze.

"Hi, Uncle Devon!"

My chin lifted when I heard a small voice coming from the front of the house. The voice was accompanied by an excited young boy running full force into Devon's welcoming arms. Devon raised him high off the ground, as all good uncles should, spinning him around until tiny giggles emerged from the brown-haired child.

"Put me down, Uncle Devon! I just had cake."

The boy's face was beaming with blue frosting. Devon chuckled. "I can see that. You got into the cake already?"

"Yes. Miss Rosa let me have some." Sam leaned in, whispering into Devon's ear, "Shh. Don't tell my dad."

He laughed again before standing to reach for me. "Sam, I'd like you to meet a very good friend of mine and your dad's. Her name is Chelsie."

I expected Sam to cower behind Devon's legs or give me the silent treatment, but I was almost knocked off my feet when forty pounds of sugar-infused four-year-old attacked me with a giant hug, instead. I patted the boy's head, laughing out loud. "That was quite the hug," I giggled, squatting down until I was at eye-level with him. "In fact, that was the best hug I've ever had. Do you practice that a lot?"

Sam nodded with pride. "I give my Daddy *all* the hugs in the world." He held out his arms to emphasize the greatness of this feat.

My smile broadened. Sam was adorable.

"Come on, squirt. Let's get you back inside. You're the star of the show, after all," Devon said, tousling Sam's hair and leading him toward the house. I rose to my feet and put my arm around Devon as we traipsed up the pathway to the front door.

"Hey, who invited this guy?" Noah greeted us in the threshold with a smirk, eyeing Devon with mock distaste. When his eyes shifted to me, his smirk softened into a tender smile. "You, on the other hand, are more than welcome."

I stuck my tongue out at him. "Not without my date," I teased.

"Daddy, this is Miss Chelsie." Sam poked my arm with an eager finger. "She's here to eat cake with me."

"I do love cake," I shrugged.

Noah scooped up his son, and the little boy rested his head against his father's shoulder. "This little monster could eat cake all day long. Isn't that right?"

My eyes misted. I had never seen Noah so stripped down, and so... *happy*. There was a sweetness in him reserved only for Sam.

"Can I open presents now?"

Noah returned Sam to his feet. "Who said anything about presents? I haven't seen any presents."

Sam's eyes grew wide and fearful. "But it's my birfday!"

"Oh, right." Noah pressed his index finger to his chin. "I guess there are presents, then. But not until later. Why don't you go find your friends and show them the fort you made downstairs?"

Sam ran off as my gaze settled on Noah. I was surprised to see him in something other than his signature t-shirt and ripped jeans. He was wearing a crisp white button-down and khaki pants. The stubble along his jawline had grown out over the last week, and the tattoo on his arm was even more striking against his snowy, rolled-up sleeves. Most noticeably, his green eyes held an extra sparkle in them today.

Devon and I made our way through the living room, dodging a sea of children chasing each other with plastic spoons.

"Hey!" Noah snatched the make-believe weapons away and ushered the kids back into the kitchen. "The spoons are for ice cream, not mayhem."

Giggles poured out of me at the sight of Noah playing an authoritative figure. "You've really nailed the Stern Dad Voice," I joked.

Noah grinned. "Yeah, well, Sam has given me exceptional practice."

I jumped when I felt a tugging at my sundress, glancing down to see two large green eyes beaming up at me—eyes that looked remarkably like his father's.

"Will you color with me?"

I brightened at the request. Sam's chocolate curls were stuck to his forehead, so I swiped them back, nodding, "I would love to. I thought you'd never ask."

"Here, I'll show you to the playroom," Noah offered.

I gave Devon's hand a friendly squeeze as we stepped away. "Your house is really nice," I observed, making conversation while we headed up the stairs. I eyed the picture frames along the walls leading up to the second floor. A black-and-white photo of Noah and a mystery woman holding Sam as a newborn caught my eye. It was the only photo the woman was featured in.

"Thanks. My decorator did most of the work. I know that sounds pretentious, but I don't really have time for interior design with my schedule." When we reached the top of the staircase, Noah pointed to a room on the left.

Gasping, I couldn't help but marvel at Sam's playroom. The walls were a spectacular shade of tangerine. A huge elephant-shaped clock hung on the far wall, surrounded by canvases of animal paintings and a large portrait of Sam. The room was filled to the brim with toys. It was every child's dream playroom.

Sam clapped and danced around the room. "Here's my coloring table!" He pointed to a miniature table with two wooden chairs. "Do you love it?"

I shared an affectionate smile with Noah. "I do love it," I replied. "I bet you spend a lot of time in here."

"Yep." Sam pulled out a giant stack of construction paper and Crayola markers. "Now you can play with me, too. I like having friends over."

My mind raced, wondering if Sam's "friends" were primarily adults. He seemed to distance himself from the other children at the party.

"Daddy, will you and my new friend draw pictures with me?" He held up a crumpled piece of purple paper, his eyes wide and innocent.

"Your new friend is Miss Chelsie," Noah reminded. He sat down on the colorful rug and glanced my way.

I joined him, taking a seat beside him until our knees touched, sending a curious tingle up my spine. Frowning, I inched away.

Sam sat down at his coloring table which was much too small for the adults. "Miss Chelsie is really pretty, Daddy. I like her."

My cheeks heated as I ducked my head, refusing to make eye contact with the man beside me. I already knew there was a smirk dancing across his face.

"You're right, Sammy. She's very pretty. Your Uncle Devon is a lucky man."

"Oh... thank you," I managed to squeak out. The blush was climbing my neck, so I raised a hand to hide it.

"Why, Daddy?"

"Because Chelsie is your uncle's girlfriend," Noah explained.

"Are they married?" Sam inquired.

"No, Sam. They're dating."

"What is dating?" Sam asked. His tongue poked out between his lips as he began to draw stick-figures on the violet-colored paper.

Noah leaned back on his hands. "That's what people do when they like each other."

I could tell that Noah was trying to simplify the situation as much as possible.

Sam looked to be deep in thought while his marker traced uneven lines along the construction paper. "So, are you and Miss Chelsie dating, too, because you like each other?"

I cleared my throat. "No... no, sweetie. Your Daddy and I are just friends."

"Like you and me?"

"Yes," I smiled. "Like you and me."

This seemed to please Sam, and he continued drawing, concentrating hard on his masterpiece. "Done!" He held up his artwork with pride.

Noah sat up and took the paper from his son's hands. He held it toward me, so I could see it as well.

"This is lovely," I murmured, watching as Sam grinned at his accomplishment. "You're a great artist."

"You sure are, tiger," Noah agreed. "What is it a picture of?"

We leaned into each other, shoulder to shoulder, studying the picture. Sam rocked in his chair as he explained his vision. "It's me and Daddy and Miss Chelsie. We're a family, and we live together in a big tree high in the sky with birds and baby squirrels. Do you like it?"

My heart galloped as I glanced at Noah. His eyes were focused on the picture, but the sparkle in them had dulled. Raising a tentative hand, I placed it on Noah's shoulder to let him know he was doing a good job—because he was. Sam was smart and full of life. He was a breath of fresh air. Just because Sam didn't have the stereotypical childhood, didn't mean Noah was failing him. I wondered if the gesture conveyed all the things I wanted to say.

If it did, Noah didn't show it. He cleared his throat and handed the picture back to Sam. "It's great, Sam. How about we get back to your party?"

"Okay!"

I watched as Noah stood and followed his son out into the hallway, maintaining my place on the rug for a minute longer. My eyes panned to Sam's drawing, imagining the grand schemes that had crept through his vivid imagination when he'd detailed his thoughts onto paper. Two stick-figures were standing beside a smaller stick-figure while the two "adults" held hands.

I let out a wistful breath as I set the picture back down, wishing I could be the stick-figure in the drawing for Sam's sake...

But my heart was with someone else.

CHAPTER TEN

NOAH

Picking up piles of shredded wrapping paper, I stuffed it all into a garbage bag as partygoers began to disperse. My living room was filled with new toys, a neon green bicycle, *Toy Story* bedding, action figures, and *Hot Wheels* accessories. A vision of birthday party dreams.

But the man of the hour wasn't interested in his hoard of birthday treasures—no, he was sitting on the lap of Chelsie Combs, completely captivated by every word that came out of her mouth. She was telling him a story about how she and a group of grade school friends had gotten lost in a cave when she was on a Girl Scouts trip. It was a run-of-the-mill childhood story, but the way Chelsie told it made it that much more compelling.

I found myself straining my ear to find out how it ended.

"Great party, Noah. Take care." I smiled at the father of one of Sam's friends, shaking his hand before he left.

"Wow! Cool story, Miss Chelsie."

Crap. I missed it.

My eyes lingered on Chelsie as I continued cleaning the room. Her baby blue, polka-dotted sundress was a mix of sexy and sophisticated. Her hair was swept back into a loose ponytail, though a few rogue strands graced each side of her pretty face. Her strappy heels showed off her slender legs, and I had to remind myself that this was *Chelsie* I was checking out. This was my bandmate's girlfriend.

The reminder sunk in when Devon reached over and pulled Chelsie to him, his fingers tracing mini designs along her bare shoulder—her shoulder that was spattered in tiny, sun-kissed freckles.

I mentally slapped myself. What kind of guy notices shoulder freckles?

Fuck.

Shaking my head pathetically, I carried on with the mundane task of picking up wrapping paper. I'd been so focused on my efforts, I hadn't noticed when Chelsie slid up next to me, tossing her own wadded clumps of paper into the bag. She gifted me a smile, her rose-tinted lips one of the many distractions keeping me from successfully cleaning the damn living room.

"I thought it would go faster if I helped you." She followed me around the room, helping me collect the discarded tissue paper.

I huffed in response, uninterested in her help. I was still reeling from Sam's picture, and Chelsie's presence was only making it worse. "I got it. And whatever I don't get, Rosa will." My tone was gruff, causing her to wince, and I wondered if I should apologize or tell her to get lost. It was a decision I struggled with on a regular basis when it came to Chelsie Combs.

"I'll take the hint." She dropped the paper, then turned her back to me and strolled over to the couch. Chelsie leaned over Devon, whispering something into his ear.

Meanwhile, I tried to ignore the perfect curve of her ass as she bent over the sofa.

"We're going to head out," Chelsie said. Devon rose to his feet beside her and stretched his arms. "You're probably stressed out with the post-party chores, so we'll get out of your hair."

I felt a little bad about the way I'd reacted to her, so I was about to ask them to stay, but Sam beat me to it.

"No, don't leave yet! I didn't show you my race cars."

I shrugged. "He didn't show you his race cars."

Devon pulled out his phone to check the time. "I don't know, man, we should probably get going. I have a meeting with Sean tonight to finalize details about the Grammy's."

Chelsie's head popped up. She gave her boyfriend a pointed glare. "What do you mean? I thought you made reservations for dinner?"

I crossed my arms over my chest, watching the budding lover's quarrel as I reached for my invisible popcorn. I knew they'd had dinner plans because Devon had mentioned it the day before. Devon was about to be in the doghouse.

"Jeez, Chelsie, I'm sorry. I completely forgot. I can take you out tomorrow, instead."

Chelsie's features crumpled with disappointment. "I work the next three nights."

Sam piped in with his own thoughts on the matter. "Oh, I know! Miss Chelsie can stay here and watch *Toy Story 3* with us while we eat popcorn and have tickle fights."

Ooh, real popcorn. I'm sold.

It was a brilliant idea, but I concealed my true feelings with a dismissive shrug. "You're welcome to stay," I offered.

Chelsie looked as though she were about to laugh it off, but then she hesitated, biting at her lip. "I guess I don't have anything else going on now." The trace of resentment in her tone did not go unnoticed.

Devon leaned back on the balls of his feet, stuffing his hands into his pockets. "Babe, I'm really sorry. This is important business. It's the *Grammy's.*"

"I know, Devon. It's fine," Chelsie relented. "You're right, it's important. Dinner can wait." She reached up on her tiptoes to plant a chaste kiss on his lips. "I'll hang out here and take an Uber home."

Sam danced around in circles. "Yay!"

I resisted the urge to dance around in circles and say, *"Yay!"*

Instead, I said goodbye as the final group of guests left for the evening, including Devon. "Let me know how it goes, Dev," I told Devon as he stepped out onto the porch. "Text me later."

Devon gave me a mock salute in reply. "Will do."

My caretaker, Rosa, strolled into the living room, draping a shawl around her shoulders as she tucked a purse under her arm.

Her face was round and kind, her hair black with silver threads. Mauve lipstick was smeared along her chin, more noticeable when she sent a smile my way. "You behave now, Noah," Rosa said, placing a motherly hand against my cheek. "She's a nice *muchacha* and doesn't need any corrupting from the likes of you."

I rolled my eyes and pulled Rosa in for a hug. "Thanks, Rosa. You know very well she's a taken *muchacha*. She's with Devon."

"Oh, I know that. But I also saw the way you were looking at her today. I know you're lonely, *cariño*, but you'll find the one."

My jaw tightened, but I chose to ignore the insinuation as I walked her to the door. Rosa was full of wise words and unsolicited advice. "Thanks for all your help, Rosa. Today and always."

The older woman blew a kiss as she stepped outside, and I shut the door, turning around to find Sam and Chelsie cuddled up on the couch together.

Damn. It was a sight that tugged at my jaded heart strings. I was realizing more and more how much Sam needed a maternal figure in his life. Before Chelsie had come into the picture, a woman was the last thing on my mind—it was all about the band, non-committal flings, and providing a cushioned life for my son. But seeing how well a woman could fit into our lives was making me reconsider everything.

"Dad, we're waiting for you," Sam called out, beckoning me toward the couch.

I realized I'd been lost in thought, standing in the entryway looking like a deer in headlights.

"I think he's in a cake trance," Chelsie teased. She winked at Sam before directing her twinkling eyes at me.

I hesitated.

Then I sprinted to the sofa, catching my son off guard. "I was just waiting to make my move," I said, picking Sam up and hurling him under my arm. I tickled him with my opposite hand while my little boy flailed helplessly under the attack.

"Put me down!" Sam pleaded. He kicked his feet, trying to escape the tickle onslaught. His laughter betrayed his request, so I only tickled harder.

"I'm going to laugh so hard when he throws up all over your socks," Chelsie grinned, wiggling her eyebrows at me.

"All right, all right," I conceded, flipping Sam back around and plopping him down on the couch. I collapsed beside him. "Please don't throw up on my socks."

We settled down as *Toy Story 3* lit up the television screen.

Five minutes later, Sam was snoring in Chelsie's lap.

She stroked my son's hair with a languid smile. "And... he's out," she whispered.

The nurturing gesture was not lost on me, and I knew I could easily get used to moments like this. Pulling a blanket off the back of the couch, I laid it on top of my sleeping boy. "That didn't take long. I guess the busy day took its toll on him."

Chelsie had a look of contentment on her face. "It was a really great party. You outdid yourself."

"I can't take all the credit. Rosa did most of the work."

Sam began to snore, and I chuckled under my breath. "I'm going to get the little monster to bed. I'll be right back." I felt Chelsie's eyes on me as I picked up my son and left the room, entering Sam's bedroom and placing him in his bed. "Goodnight, Sammy," I whispered, leaning over and giving him a kiss on his forehead. "Love you, buddy." I turned on his Buzz Lightyear nightlight, closed the blinds, and pivoted to leave the room—stopping short when I saw Chelsie standing outside Sam's doorway.

She ducked her head with a smile. "Sorry," she said, wringing her hands together. "You're just so sweet with him. It's a side of you I don't see very often."

My jaw ticked as I studied her beneath the soft glow of the hallway light, watching as she fidgeted with her ponytail. She was waiting for me to say something, but I'd been rendered speechless by how natural she looked standing at the top of my staircase, observing me tuck my son into bed. Forcing my voice to stay level, I finally replied, "You better not tell anyone. I have an image to maintain."

Chelsie relaxed. "Your secret is safe with me."

I held her eyes for another heartbeat before making my way down the staircase, catching a whiff of lavender and lemons as I passed her. She trailed behind me. "Hey, I have some popcorn if you want to watch a movie that doesn't involve talking potato heads," I suggested on a whim.

When we reached the living room, I spun around to gauge her reaction. Chelsie glanced at the doorway, then back at the couch, confliction marring her features.

I decided to make it easier on her. "I also have ice cream."

"Sold."

CHELSIE

I licked chocolate ice cream off the back of my spoon, watching the credits roll on the screen. We'd decided on a movie called *Kill List*. "I didn't see that coming," I said, breaking the post-movie silence and glancing up at Noah, who had been highly engrossed in the film.

His eyebrows pulled together as he leaned back against the sofa cushions. "What the hell did I just watch?"

The bewildered look on his face had me chuckling as I yanked the blanket up to my shoulders and set the empty ice cream container down on the table. "I don't know about you, but I loved it." I lifted my feet up onto the couch, accidentally tickling his leg with my toes.

Noah flinched, but didn't pull away. He turned to me with a nod of approval. "Me, too. Good choice. I didn't peg you for liking that sort of stuff."

"What, you thought I only watched Disney movies and romantic comedies?" I placed a hand over my heart, appalled. "I'll have you know, I'm a cinematic wonder."

Noah perked up at my declaration. "Favorite movie."

"Easy. *Citizen Kane*."

Noah shook his head with disapproval. "Overhyped."

"Are you kidding me? It's a classic. Name something better," I challenged, feigning horror.

"*Fight Club. Apocalypse Now. American Psycho.* I could go on."

"Wow, could you be any more of a stereotypical guy?" I shot back, a playful smile tugging at my lips.

Noah's smile mirrored my own. "Those are great films. You can't deny it."

"Fine, but *Citizen Kane* is better."

"Please. It's contrived and highly overrated," he argued.

I threw a pillow at him in response.

"See?" Noah tossed it back at me. "You have no argument to support your claims, so you have to resort to violence."

Laughing, I was about to pick up another pillow when a small figure appeared in front of us. We jumped up as if we were two teenagers who'd been caught making out on our parent's couch.

"Daddy, I can't sleep. There's a monster in my room."

Noah pulled Sam in for a big hug. "Monsters, huh?"

"Just one monster, Dad. He's—"

"Let me guess," Noah interrupted. "Under your bed."

"No, that's silly. He's in my closet."

My heart fluttered as I watched father and son interact. I approached them both, running a hand through Sam's hair. "I can get him back to bed if you want."

"I want Miss Chelsie to tuck me in," Sam pleaded. "Please, Daddy? She can scare the monster away."

Noah raised an eyebrow at this assessment. "I don't know, Sammy. She's not very threatening," he teased.

Sam looked confused. "What does that mean?"

We both chuckled, and Noah nodded his head toward the staircase. "Never mind, Sam. Chelsie can tuck you in if that's what you want."

"Yay! Let's go," he squealed, grabbing my hand and pulling me to the stairs.

I noticed a fleeting look in Noah's eyes as I followed Sam, but I didn't know how to describe it. My chest tightened.

"My closet is super, *super* scary, Miss Chelsie," Sam warned as he leaped onto his bed at full speed and hid under the covers. "The monster has yellow eyes and sharp teeth. He might eat you."

"Don't worry, Sam. I'm very brave. I'll go talk to him and tell him to find another closet."

Sam peeked over the edge of his blanket. "What if he eats you before you can talk?"

"I promise he won't eat me." I stepped over to the closet door and reached for the knob, then swung the door open and let out a theatrical sigh of relief. "Your closet is monster-free, Sammy," I said, holding the door wide open so the young boy could investigate.

Sam climbed out of bed and tiptoed my way. His eyes lit up. "Wow, you did scare him away! Thanks, Miss Chelsie." Two tiny arms enveloped me in a tight hug.

I returned the hug and guided Sam back to his bed. "Now, it's time to get tucked in," I told him, watching as he scurried under his bedsheets and snuggled a raggedy brown bear close to his chest.

"This is my teddy bear," he announced, holding up the floppy animal friend. "His name is Bear, and he sleeps with me every night."

I offered my hand to Bear in greeting. "Hi, there. You'll watch over Sam tonight and make sure no more monsters get in, right?"

Sam nodded the teddy bear's head.

"Good." I leaned over and pulled the blankets up over Sam's small frame. "It was very nice meeting you today, Sam. I hope we can see each other again soon."

"Maybe next time we can read books together and you can tell me more stories."

A warm smile tipped my lips. "I'd like that. Goodnight." I clicked off his lamp and watched as he turned over, already dozing off into a peaceful sleep.

When I headed back into the living room, I noticed Noah was still sitting on the couch where I'd left him. A reflective silence welcomed me as I approached.

"You made a big impression on him today," Noah said. His eyes never left me as I returned to my place beside him on the couch.

Plopping down, I pulled a pillow into my lap. "You have a special little boy, Noah. I mean that."

Samuel Hayes was a smart, funny, and compassionate kid. He hadn't been traumatized by his father's travels or lack of a maternal figure like I'd originally feared. Noah was doing a good job.

Noah propped his feet up onto the black leather ottoman and inched closer to me. "I worry about him sometimes."

I held my breath, waiting for him to continue. Was Noah finally going to share some insight into his mysterious past?

"I wonder if I'm doing the right thing, you know?" he continued. "Raising him as a single parent—a parent who's gone all the time. I mean, I've sabotaged numerous relationships because I'm afraid of someone getting too close to Sam. But seeing you with him today..." Noah trailed off, looking up and catching my gaze. He was both tense and soft; a contradiction. "Seeing you with him makes me wonder if Sam really does need a woman in his life."

Conflict radiated off him. I reached over, giving Noah's knee a reassuring squeeze. "Look, I'm no life expert... as I'm sure you're well aware," I said, dipping my chin. "But I can tell you this— you're his father. You know what's best for him. If something told you to break off those other relationships, then there was a reason for that. Trust your instincts because your instincts have served you well. He's an amazing little boy."

Something changed in Noah's expression... a wall came tumbling down. He was staring at me with such intensity, I felt bare and vulnerable beneath his gaze. Had I said too much? I was about to pull away from him when his own hand came down on top of mine, sending an odd charge between us. My heart stuttered, and I froze when Noah's thumb flicked across my knuckles.

"Thanks," he said. "I needed to hear that."

I nodded slowly before gently pulling my hand out from under his grasp. "Y-Yeah, of course. That's what friends are for," I stammered, massaging my hand to cease the strange tingling. "Hey, I should probably get going. It's getting late." Forcing a smile, I pulled out my phone to search for an Uber.

"Right," Noah said, rising to his feet.

I felt his eyes on me, like he wanted to say something. My head popped up, almost afraid of what his words might be.

"Thank you... really." He tucked his hands into his khaki pockets and began rocking on the balls of his feet. It was clear Noah Hayes didn't make a habit of being the sentimental type. "I know I said that already, but it meant a lot... what you said. I don't have many people to talk to about this stuff, so it's nice to have someone who will lend an ear."

I softened, happy to see that my words had made an impact on Noah. "Maybe we can do it again sometime."

"I'd like that."

An hour later, I was back at my apartment with a fat cat in my lap. Misty purred as I ran my fingers through her soft gray fur, and I jolted when my cell phone buzzed beside me on the nightstand.

I was expecting to see a "goodnight" text from Devon, but was surprised when Noah's name flashed across the screen, instead. Tapping on his name, I couldn't help but smile when his message popped up.

Noah: *Citizen Kane still sucks.*

CHAPTER ELEVEN

CHELSIE

I awoke to the sensation of a strong arm around my waist and a warm body pressed up against my back, absorbing the rhythmic motions of his chest.

Rolling over, I let my eyes settle on the handsome face of Devon Sawyer.

My boyfriend.

Even though months had gone by, it still took getting used to. I pushed aside a strand of hair that had fallen over his forehead and pressed a kiss to his lips. Devon stirred, but didn't wake, so I increased my efforts by running my hand down his bare chest and into his boxers, grinning when his eyes fluttered open.

Devon shuddered and pulled me close. "Mornin', sunshine," he said, his voice gruff with sleep.

"Morning," I replied.

Breaking away, he gave my backside a playful pat. "So, what are your plans for the day?" He sat up, throwing his legs over the side of the bed.

"I thought we were doing them." I couldn't help but jut my lip out with a petulant pout. I'd been looking forward to an early morning roll in the hay.

Making love with Devon was nothing like the caustic sex I'd experienced with Ian. Devon was patient and kind. He never left me feeling empty or used. Our first time together had felt like it was straight out of a romance novel, even though I'd been full of nerves and insecurities. Devon went above and beyond to make me feel comfortable.

Offering an apologetic smile, he pulled a shirt over his head. "Sorry, babe. I have a meeting in an hour. Lots to do before our flight. What are you up to today?"

My shoulders deflated. The boys were flying across the country to play a gig in Los Angeles, and I had been taking too much time off work, so I was staying behind. "Well, I told Noah I'd meet him and Sam for ice cream later before you guys leave. Then I was going to go shopping with Lisa."

"Ah, I see." He paused for a moment. "I, uh... noticed you've been spending a lot of time together."

"With Lisa?" My nose crinkled.

Devon scratched his head before standing up to look for his pants. "No, with Noah. You guys hated each other, and now you're going on ice cream dates."

I bristled at the implication, pulling the bedsheet up over my chest. "It's not like that. It's more for Sam's sake, anyway... he's really taken a liking to me."

He made a humming sound as he tightened his belt buckle. "He's not the only one, it seems."

"What?"

"Nothing... nothing." Rummaging through a pile of clothes, he settled on a previously worn pair of socks. His stance softened as he regarded me, a smile stretching. "Sorry. I'm glad you two are finally getting along."

I didn't reply. The truth was, I *did* enjoy spending time with Noah—he was a good listener, he was funny, and he seemed to really "get" me. I looked forward to our talks and get-togethers. And Sam was such a joy to be around.

But my relationship with Noah was strictly platonic, so I was surprised to hear suspicion in Devon's tone. Nodding lightly, I decided to change the subject. "You'll be back in time for my birthday on Saturday, right?"

"Of course, babe. I'm looking forward to it." Devon must have noticed the melancholy in my voice because a renewed twinkle danced in his eyes. He climbed onto the bed and army-crawled over to me, pressing his mouth against mine. "On second thought... maybe I have a few extra minutes to spare."

I giggled, kissing him back with fervor while removing the clothes he had just changed into. When we finished, spent and satisfied, Devon gave me a wink and kissed my nose. "I'm going to shower and get going."

Watching him disappear into the bathroom, I took a moment to revel in the afterglow before rolling out of bed and slipping into sweatpants and a baggy t-shirt. As the shower jets turned on from the hall bath, my mind wandered to the upcoming weekend.

I couldn't believe my twenty-seventh birthday was around the corner. I had never looked forward to my birthdays in the past, but this one was different.

I had a reason to celebrate this year.

NOAH

"I want chocolate. No, Superman.   No... Superman with chocolate sprinkles!"

Standing in line for an ice cream cone with a four-year-old was everything one would expect it to be. I held my son back from charging through the other customers and throwing himself head-first into the tubs of frozen delights.

"Hey! Sorry I'm late."

My head perked up at the sound of a familiar voice.

"Miss Chelsie!"

Sam ran into Chelsie's outstretched arms and wrapped his tiny legs around her waist. Chelsie managed to maintain her balance as Sam clung to her like a monkey.

"Only you could pry him away from Superman," I grinned.

Truthfully, I was also excited to see her, but I wasn't quite as obvious about it. Sam didn't realize how lucky he was—everything he did was socially acceptable.

"Yeah, well, I'm sure it was a tough decision." Chelsie carried Sam back to the never-ending stream of ice cream patrons, joining me in line.

"I don't know," I shrugged, hooking my thumbs into my belt loops. "I think I've taught him well. Pretty blondes always win out over ice cream." I reveled in the way a rosy blush crept up her neck and into her cheeks.

Chelsie slapped me on the arm, refusing to look me in the eye. "Don't be a pig."

"A charming pig." I studied her as her skin continued to flush pink. My eyes traveled down the length of her petite frame, settling on her denim shorts. They were short enough to make me grateful that I'd fathered a son.

After we finally placed our orders, the three of us sat down at a nearby table with our midday desserts. I smiled as I wiped Sam's face, the ice cream dribbling down his sticky chin.

"So, I actually wanted to discuss something with you," Chelsie said. She placed her arms on the glass table and clasped her hands together.

My interest piqued as I swallowed back a bite of mint chocolate chip. "Shoot."

"Okay, I don't want to step on anyone's toes... well, Rosa's toes. I mean, you can certainly say no, and I would totally understand. But... you see, I was wondering if you'd let me watch Sam sometimes when you and the band travel for your shows. Or... for any reason, really."

Her nerves were evident as she stumbled over her words and refrained from eye contact. Pretty fucking cute. I grinned, nodding. "Of course. Just tell me when."

Chelsie opened her mouth to speak, but faltered as if she hadn't heard me correctly. "Really?"

"Yeah, sure," I shrugged. "Why do you look so surprised? You're great with Sam and he adores you. I think it's a good idea."

"Oh." Chelsie relaxed, exhaling the breath she was holding in. "Thanks, Noah. Are you sure Rosa won't mind?"

"Rosa needs a break. I work that poor woman to the bone. I'm sure she'd be thrilled to have some nights off."

Chelsie nodded with a thoughtful expression. "I always wanted younger siblings when I was growing up," she explained. "When that didn't happen, I yearned to be a teacher or a counselor. And when... well, when my life fell apart, that dream fell apart with it. So, now I'm just a waitress dating a musician." Chelsie sighed and tipped her head, making light of her life choices. "But spending time with Sam has sort of rekindled that passion. It feels good to make a difference, even if it's a small one."

I wondered why she felt the need to explain herself—I was more than happy to have the help, and I knew my son would be thrilled.

I couldn't lie, though. There was something incredibly endearing about the way she cared.

Clearing my throat, my gaze softened as I took another bite of ice cream. "Hey, making a difference is no small feat. That means something." There I was, getting all mushy again. I didn't know why this girl brought out such a sappy side to me.

Chelsie beamed from ear to ear. "Thank you," she whispered before turning her attention to Sam, who was oblivious to the conversation. He was far more concerned with how much ice cream he could fit into his mouth without getting a brain freeze. "What do you say, kiddo? Do you think I can hang out with you more often?"

Sam shot up in his seat, his eyes popping with excitement. "Oh, yes! We'll have so much fun. Can Miss Chelsie sleep over, Daddy? Can we have a sleepover party for her birfday? She can sleep in my dinosaur sleeping bag."

My heart clenched. I relished in the look on my son's face as Sam bounced in his chair. "I think Miss Chelsie has other plans, Sammy, but maybe another time." I glanced at Chelsie, watching as she sucked a bite of ice cream off her spoon. "You excited for your birthday?"

"Yep, can't wait." She plunged the spoon back into her dish. "You'll be there, right?"

"Wouldn't miss it. You're practically my BFF now," I winked.

Chelsie snorted under her breath. "Yeah, okay. We're twelve, I see."

"Where's the party happening, anyway? I vote Marley's... where it all began."

"You mean our loathing introduction and hostile banter?" she quipped. "I hope you know I almost punched you."

A chuckle escaped me as I leaned back in my seat. "I was more referring to your sickeningly sweet romance with Devon, and our... well, I suppose loathing introduction sums it up. Thanks for not punching me, by the way." I offered her a smile that she instantly returned. "But I gotta say, I do miss our hostile banter. Good times."

Chelsie raised an eyebrow. "You did seem to enjoy it in an unhealthy way."

"I know. You're cute when you get all fired up." I observed the way the blush returned to her cheeks as she pulled her bottom lip between her teeth, and I idly wondered if I'd taken our friendly chit-chat into the dreaded "flirting territory."

"Daddy, look, that man wants to take our picture. Cheese!"

Sam's announcement pulled my attention away from Chelsie, and we both looked around to find the intruder.

"Damn paparazzi," I muttered with disdain. I stood up just in time to see a man running away with a camera. "What happened to privacy and common courtesy?"

"I'm pretty sure fame and fortune happened," Chelsie said. She glanced at her cell phone and began collecting her empty bowl and napkins. "Shoot, I'm supposed to meet Lisa at the mall in fifteen minutes. I should get going."

I took the items from her. "I got it. Go enjoy your girly day of retail therapy, pedicures, and chocolate."

Chelsie let out an amused chuckle. "Is that what you think all girls do?"

"Well, yeah. And go to the bathroom in large groups."

"That's true," Chelsie smirked. She stepped over to Sam, kneeling in front of him. "I have to go now, but maybe I can come see you tomorrow after your Daddy leaves. Would that be okay?"

Sam jumped in her arms with another bone-crushing hug. "Yes! Thanks for having ice cream with me."

"My pleasure." Chelsie turned to me then, leaning in for a hug and catching me off guard.

I hesitated briefly before pulling her close, resting my hand along the small of her back. "Good to see you, Combs," I murmured into her ear. "Can't wait to buy you a birthday shot on Saturday."

Chelsie pulled back to flash me her teeth. "Looking forward to it. Have a safe trip."

With a lingering smile, she collected her purse and disappeared into the parking lot. I watched her go as I carried the discarded items to the trash and wiped down the table. Reaching for Sam's hand, I tried to ignore the way her warm body felt pressed against me. "Let's go, buddy. It's time for a Candyland rematch."

Chelsie

There was something special about the anticipation of meeting your best friend at the mall for retail therapy and girly gossip, and I wondered if it was a feeling that would ever go away.

I recalled how excited I was when my thirteen-year-old self would walk to the shopping center downtown, eagerly awaiting window browsing and Chinese cuisine from the food court with my besties, Lisa and Riley. Years later, I still felt that same buzz I had when I was a preteen. Fifty years from now, I could see myself parking in the handicapped spot and riding into the mall on a motorized scooter. The gossip may change from love and sex to dentures and Depends, but by God, that Chinese food would still taste just as good.

A shock of bouncing scarlet curls came into view, and I couldn't resist the squeal that escaped my lips when I spotted Lisa. The thirteen-year-old in me came out as I skipped through the mall and threw my arms around my friend. "Oh, Lis, it's so good to see you!"

"Uh, yeah... I can tell. Gosh, Chelsie, it's as if we didn't see each other a week ago," Lisa laughed. She returned the hug with a tight squeeze.

"I know. Can't a girl just be excited to shop, talk, and stuff her face with highly caloric meat by-product?"

Lisa chuckled, adjusting her purse strap over her shoulder. "You're right. What's a better excuse for calories than a shopping date with your bestie?"

We glided through the mall, hardly noticing the window displays as we idly chatted.

"I'm so happy for you, Chelsie," Lisa said. "I knew your guy was out there. Devon is amazing. You're so lucky."

My grin was glowing. "I know. Things finally seem to be going my way. And did I tell you about Noah?" I continued. "We've become such good friends. It's crazy. Who would have thought?"

Lisa's smile waned. "I'm glad you two are on better terms... but be careful, Chels. I don't trust him as much as you do."

I stiffened, even though I understood Lisa's concerns. I'd had a lot of toxic people in my past—Ian, his brother, Brad, my old friend, Riley, and everyone else who went along with that social circle. Lisa was no stranger to any of them, and Noah hadn't made the best first impression. But Lisa didn't know him the way I did. She didn't see the other side of him he was too proud to share with most people. She didn't see how nurturing he was with his son, or the way he smiled when something made him genuinely happy. It wasn't the smile that came out when he signed autographs or gave interviews—it was different.

I frowned, shaking the thoughts away. "Noah is a good guy, Lis," I said. "Once you get to know him better, you'll understand. Besides, spending time with Noah means spending time with Sam. That little guy has been a huge highlight in my life."

"I concur. I'll give Noah credit in that department... he must be doing something right," she acknowledged.

I was about to respond when something in an approaching store window caught my eye, stopping me short. I strolled up to the display, almost like I was being pulled by an invisible force.

"What is it?" Lisa wondered, trailing my heels.

My eyes landed on a gold watch with a striking emerald green face. "This one," I murmured, pointing at the watch.

"The green one?" She pursed her lips together. "It's nice, I guess. What's so special about it?"

"I don't know. I think it just reminds me of him." I lifted my fingertips to the glass, entranced. "It reminds me of his eyes."

There was a pause before Lisa replied. "Chelsie... Devon has blue eyes."

When the words sunk in, I yanked my hand back as if I had touched a flame. I stepped back from the window and looked down at my strappy, brown sandals, nibbling my bottom lip. "Yeah, I know," I said, clutching my purse in a tight grip before popping my head back up with a smile. "Never mind. Let's go get a Frappuccino."

We resumed our pace and the conversation picked up where it had left off. I filled Lisa in on my travels, the celebrity life, all of Devon's cute quirks, and just how happy I finally felt.

But when the day wound down and we hugged our goodbyes, I couldn't seem to shake an odd sensation. My mind wandered back to that damn watch. What was so special about it? It was just a watch. It meant nothing.

Only, it did—for when I'd spotted it, another man's eyes had flashed through my mind.

Noah.

I refused to make any sense of it as I jumped in an Uber, popping in my earbuds and drowning out my thoughts with my favorite playlist.

I knew that when I got home, I would climb into bed, snuggle my cat, and fall right to sleep. When I dreamed that night, Devon would surely be there.

And when I woke up the next morning, that watch would just be a watch.

CHAPTER TWELVE

CHELSIE

"Y ou're on the front cover of *US Weekly*. Happy birthday!"

That was the voicemail I'd woken up to on the morning of my twenty-seventh birthday, and I had Julia to thank for bringing the ordeal to light. I was used to being tabloid fodder, but the fodder had turned to scandal with one innocent picture.

Crawling out of bed, I was careful not to wake the snoring man beside me. I locked myself in the bathroom and called Julia, anxious to hear the juicy details.

"Me and Noah? A scandalous fling? Huh?" I whisper-screeched into my cell phone. "You've got to be kidding me."

"I believe the word used was *salacious*," Julia corrected. "It has a little more flavor. And yeah, apparently you guys are totally fucking and you're the bitch-queen of the universe for cheating on an unsuspecting Devon Sawyer."

My tiny apartment bathroom shrank half its size. The walls were closing in, the air becoming scarce. This was not the way the morning was supposed to go—I was supposed to wake up slowly to Devon's adoring arms around me and then gorge myself on birthday cake for breakfast. Instead, I was holding back hot tears, cursing the paparazzi for trying to ruin my life.

"Julia, what is the picture? I mean, it can't be horrible. There is absolutely nothing going on between Noah and me."

"Oh, it's nothing too obscene. The cover is an adorable family photo of the three of you eating ice cream together, while you and Noah make moon-eyes at each other. It's more the implication and corresponding story that really packs the punch. Here, I'll text you the cover."

I pulled up the photo and studied it through squinted eyes. "This is ridiculous. Did you see this headline? *Girlfriend of Freeze Frame Front Man Gets Cozy With Sexy Bandmate*— it's obviously all lies." Fury boiled my blood, the pitch of my voice rising with every heated word.

"Yeah, I read it," Julia replied. "I know it's lies, and *you* know it's lies, but the rest of America is surely going to jump headfirst onto that bandwagon. I feel for ya, Chels."

"Ugh..." I was about to continue my rant when a new text notification came through.

It was from Noah.

Noah: *Apparently we're front cover material on the gossip mags. I had no idea we were sleeping together, did you?*

My sigh was long and weary. "Julia, I'll call you back. I have unnecessary damage control to take care of."

"Don't worry about it, babe. I'll see you tonight. Happy birthday!"

"Thanks." I clicked off the call and dialed Noah.

His gruff, sleep-ridden voice answered on the first ring. "Hey, baby. I can call you that now since we're in a salacious relationship."

Normally, I'd laugh, but I was in no mood this morning. "This isn't funny, Noah. This could ruin Devon and me. I have no idea what to do." Sliding down the bathroom wall, I crumpled to the ground with a groan.

"Well, first off, good morning. Second, happy birthday. And third, get used to it," Noah said. "Your name is going to be smeared all over the media whenever a promising story comes to light. You're the girl dating America's favorite rock star. You're going to be the villain no matter what."

"But we didn't do anything wrong," I insisted. "I would never cheat on Devon... especially with you. No offense."

A brief silence followed, and I wondered if I'd offended him. *Oops.*

"Cute," Noah sniffed. "The feeling is mutual, of course. And don't worry about Devon. He's used to being in the public eye, so he knows what he's getting himself into. He trusts you. You two will be fine."

"Maybe you're right." I worried my bottom lip between my teeth, wiggling my pastel pink toenails. "This whole thing just sucks. Happy birthday to me."

"We can commiserate over birthday drinks later. Until then, try not to think about it and just enjoy yourself," Noah said.

Exhaling a calming breath, I let a smile slip. "Thanks, Noah. I'll try." I paused, tapping my finger against the phone. "Are you coming tonight? Is Rosa going to watch Sam?"

"Yeah, the little monster is all taken care of. I wouldn't miss your birthday party... especially now. Since we're dating."

My eyes rolled as I tried to hold back a grin. "Funny. You know how much I enjoy your unsolicited attempt at humor."

"Attempt?" Noah huffed in reply. "I'm hilarious. Don't try to deny it. I can practically see your smile through my cell phone right now. Hold on, we're going to video chat so I can actually see it and prove how damn funny I am."

A burst of laughter betrayed me. "Okay, okay, I'm smiling. Happy? No need for visual conversation. I just got out of bed and I'm a hot mess."

"I'm sure you're pretty as a picture, as usual. See you later?"

"I'll be there with bells on. Thanks, Noah."

"Happy birthday, Combs."

I clicked off the call, the ghost of a smile on my lips. Noah always had an eerie tendency of cheering me up. It was odd, considering how good he used to be at pissing me off.

Well... he *was* still pretty good at that. Noah was a man of many talents.

A knock sounded at the bathroom door, so I rose to my feet and pulled it open, greeted by my sleepy-eyed boyfriend. I threw my arms around his neck and leaned up for a kiss. "Good morning!"

Devon gave me a gentle squeeze in return. "Mornin', babe. Who were you talking to?"

"Oh, just Julia. She called to wish me a happy birthday." I shoved my cell phone into my back pocket, knowing I should probably mention the tabloid cover to Devon, but not wanting to start my birthday morning off on a bad note. I'd bring it up later. "You're up early, huh? Did I wake you?"

He yawned, scratching his chest. "Nah, I just wanted to be the first to tell you happy birthday. Guess I was too late," he said with a pout.

"You're so sweet. Don't worry, you can still make it up to me." The wink I sent was full of implication.

"Oh, really?" Without another word, Devon scooped me up and carried me back to the bedroom, then tossed me onto the bed and climbed over me, his eyes full of mischief. "Happy birthday."

I wrapped my fingers around his neck and pulled his forehead against mine. "Thank you," I whispered. I let the rough start to the morning dissipate as I lost myself to the handsome man above me. Devon peppered kisses down my neck, collarbone, shoulder, and chest, while I arched my back and ran my fingers through his messy bedhead. Closing my eyes, I savored the moment. Maybe it would be a memorable birthday, after all.

The rest of the morning passed by uneventfully, which I was duly grateful for. Devon had left to run errands, and I was getting ready to visit Sam, having promised that I would stop by to eat birthday cake with the littlest Hayes. I wondered if going to Noah's house was the brightest idea, considering we were currently the paparazzi's golden couple, but I knew our relationship was completely innocent. People were going to believe what they wanted, regardless of the truth.

I reached for my phone to message Noah I'd be leaving shortly, only to find a missed text message from Devon. My insides twisted with anxiety when I read his text.

Devon: *Thanks for the heads up about your other relationship. I really wanted to find that out from a bunch of reporters with cameras in my face.*

Wincing, I cursed myself for not being upfront with Devon.

He must have talked to Noah. I hesitated briefly before dialing his number.

No answer.

Tossing my cell phone onto the couch cushions, I buried my face into my lap before letting out a miserable sigh and standing up, heading to the bedroom to throw on fresh clothes. I needed to visit Noah—Sam was always a good distraction when my spirits were down.

Twenty minutes later, I was sitting in Noah's kitchen, licking frosting off the back of a fork. "I feel like sugar is becoming a recurring theme here," I mused. "Are you trying to make me fat?"

Sam giggled as Noah plopped another piece of chocolate cake onto my plate.

"Ooh, *Curious George* is on, Daddy!" Sam jumped down from his seat and dashed into the adjoining living room. Only cartoons could pull that kid away from cake.

I watched him with a peaceful expression. "I knew your little guy would make me feel better," I said, setting down my fork and pushing the remaining dessert away.

Noah sat beside me and snatched my plate, digging into the cake. "Tell me what happened," he pressed. "Devon just freaked out on you?"

"He sent me this accusatory text message, then dodged my calls. I don't know what to do. Did you talk to him?"

"Well, yeah," Noah admitted. "Sorry. I assumed you'd told him about it."

I released a deep breath. "No, I know. It's not your fault. It's only natural to assume I was a responsible girlfriend and told Devon the truth right away. I just... wanted to enjoy the day. I was afraid he wouldn't take it very well and think the worst of me. I wanted a memorable birthday for once. I guess that totally backfired." I ran my hands through my uncombed hair and rested my forehead on the kitchen table. Moments later, I felt a comforting hand rubbing my back. I let out a slow breath, my body relaxing to his touch.

"Hey, listen," Noah said. "You're going to party like a fucking rock star tonight. I'm going to see to that. If Devon wants to get his panties in a twist, let him. But don't let him ruin your day. You deserve a celebration."

My head lifted. "You know, you're right," I nodded with renewed optimism. "I'm sure this thing will blow over soon and I'll regret being grouchy on my birthday."

"That's the spirit."

Noah's hand left my back, causing a chill to sweep through me at the loss of contact. "Thanks, Noah. You've really been there for me lately, and I can't tell you how much I appreciate it."

"You don't need to thank me." Noah dismissed me with the wave of his hand. "That's what friends are for, right?"

"Come watch, everybody!" Sam shouted from the other room. "This is the part where he makes a *really* big mess and it's super funny."

I shared a grin with Noah, and we abandoned our cake to join the *Curious George* viewing party.

NOAH

I was hesitant to move, let alone breathe too hard, as I didn't want to wake the sleeping woman in my lap. Sam was sprawled out in the recliner, sound asleep for his midday nap, and Chelsie... well, she was also sleeping, only her head was resting on a small pillow between my legs. Some may think it was odd that my friend's girl-friend was passed out in my lap, but the oddest thing about it was how natural it felt. We'd been discussing a new television series when Chelsie decided to curl up next to me and lie against my shoulder.

"Here, get comfy," I'd told her, plopping a pillow on my thighs with all the nonchalance in the world. I'd been expecting a death glare, an elbow jab, or even a fit of hysterical giggles—I had not expected Chelsie to accept the invitation. She hadn't even hesitated to situate herself on my legs with a content smile on her face.

I, on the other hand, was far from content. There was a gorgeous, off-limits blonde snuggled far too close to my groin.

When I shifted slightly, Chelsie stirred, her head slipping off the pillow and settling centimeters away from my dick—which was *also* beginning to stir.

I sucked in a deep breath. I had to admit, I was thrilled Chelsie was becoming so comfortable with me and my son. We had a unique friendship that couldn't be explained. There were times when I would literally crave her company because Chelsie had the type of aura that made people gravitate toward her. Sam spoke of her daily, always asking when she would return for a play date or a sleepover. No one fit into our lives quite like Chelsie Combs. It was both refreshing and... alarming.

"Mmm..."

I froze when a soft murmur escaped her lips. She moved her head closer to my neither regions, and the pillow fell forward off my lap. Chelsie lifted her head and glanced up at me. "Sorry," she croaked out.

I was surprised she hadn't jumped off me instantly and run for the door. "Sorry?" I wondered.

"Sorry for falling asleep on you." Chelsie rolled onto her back, resting her hands on her stomach, making herself even more comfortable as she peered up at me with sleepy green eyes.

My body hummed from her proximity, and I resisted the urge to remove a rebellious strand of hair off her forehead. I opted for being offensive instead—I was better at that. "Hey, no complaints here. I welcome pretty females to make themselves at home between my legs."

Chelsie flew off my lap. I couldn't contain my laughter as she scurried away.

"Charming," she said, picking up the pillow off the floor and flinging it straight at my head.

"Ouch," I protested. "I resent that."

She couldn't mask the ghost of a smile on her lips. "And I resent you being a pig."

I tossed the pillow back at her. "A charming pig."

Chelsie huffed, catching the pillow and tucking it under her arms. She glanced at me through timid eyelids, her smile waning. "Seriously, though... I hope I didn't make you uncomfortable."

Not in the way you're thinking.

"Not even a little," I opted for. "And that's what I like about us. You can pass out on my lap and there's nothing weird about it."

Chelsie nodded. "I know what you mean. I feel the same way." She paused, pulling her brows together in contemplation. "Do you think it's weird that it's not weird?"

My eyes narrowed as I debated the question, then I shook my head. "I think it's awesome. I can honestly say I feel more comfortable with you than I have with any other woman in my life."

Her eyes widened, her wheels spinning. She approached with caution. "Even... Ruby?"

The sound of Ruby's name procured a physical reaction from me, causing my jaw to tense. Normally, I would try to change the subject right about now, but I decided it was time to tell Chelsie about the mother of my child.

Hell, I knew all of Chelsie's darkest secrets... it was only fair.

"Especially Ruby," I admitted, averting my gaze to the opposite side of the room. My mind swam with dark memories. "I held that woman up on a pedestal since I met her eight years ago. It was a toxic fucking relationship, and I don't think I was myself with her for even a single second. I always felt this need to play a part—to show her I was this perfect guy she couldn't live without." My heart was pumping with nervous beats as I released my ghosts. Chelsie sat still and silent, clutching the pillow to her chest. Her eyes roamed my face with curiosity. "Our relationship was... unhealthy," I continued. "Ruby was beautiful and exotic. She would walk into a room and all eyes would be on her, and she ate that shit up; she loved it. At first, I felt pretty damn good having the most beautiful woman in the room on my arm, but then it became... a burden. Ruby paid more attention to the men falling at her feet than she did to me. It felt like a competition every time we'd go out. And then she just started going out without me. We fought all the time, there were secrets and lies... it was ugly. But I was a lovestruck fool. I thought I needed her."

Chelsie held eye contact with me, her voice quivering as she asked, "What happened?"

"She cheated on me. All the time," I answered bitterly. "The last straw was the pregnancy, especially after a test confirmed it was my baby. She continued to party. She continued to drink. I couldn't be with someone who had such disregard for our child." My teeth ground together, my blood swimming hot through my veins. "It's a miracle Sam is such a healthy kid. She could've killed him."

Chelsie's eyes were wide with disbelief as she soaked it all in. "Did she even want Sam?"

"Ruby only cared about herself. I don't think she wanted anything that took away from her freedom," I said. "She signed off on custody when Sam was only two weeks old, and I never saw her again. I figured she'd come crawling back once my name hit the spotlight, but she never did."

Chelsie absorbed everything in silence, sliding over next to me on the couch. Her mouth parted to speak. Words touched at her lips, but they dissipated as she rested her head against my shoulder, her warmth giving me comfort. Calming me.

Her unspoken words hovered between us, and that was enough.

It was all I needed.

CHAPTER THIRTEEN

CHELSIE

The rest of the day dragged by until it was finally time to partake in my birthday festivities. I paced back and forth near the bar, fidgeting with the straw in my watered-down rum and Coke. I found myself more interested in chewing the piece of plastic to calm my growing anxiety than the cocktail itself.

My cell phone buzzed from inside my purse, and I snatched it up so quickly, it toppled to the bar floor. Groaning in frustration, I bent over to grab it—but when I stood back up, I collided with a waitress who had unsuccessfully tried to dodge me. All three lemon drops fell off her tray.

"Oh, my gosh! I'm so sorry," I apologized, crouching down to help pick up the mess.

"Don't bother," the waitress barked.

"I'm really, really sorry." I held back tears as the woman stepped away from the scene. Sighing, I remembered the notification on my phone and glanced at it. More disappointment.

Still no word from Devon.

It had been six hours of radio silence, and I was beginning to wonder if Devon would ever contact me.

"Anything?" Julia returned from the bathroom, sensing my increased panic. "Still no Devon?"

I stuffed the phone back into my purse. "Nothing. And to top it all off, I just pissed off our waitress and she's probably going to spit in our next round of drinks."

"Oh, Chels," Julia commiserated. "He'll be here. Don't worry."

"I'm honestly getting mad now," I huffed. "I know I should have told him about the article, but nothing happened with Noah. He should know that. It's not fair to ignore me on my birthday." The tears threatened to reemerge, so I chugged my drink to distract myself.

"He's being a total man-child. Forget about him and enjoy yourself."

"Hey, birthday girl." Noah appeared in the crowd, a smile lighting up his face. "Long time, no see."

I perked up when I spotted him. Noah had cleaned up nicely in a pair of jeans that probably cost more than my rent and a navy-blue button down over a black band tee. When he leaned in to hug me, his Usher cologne tickled my nose. "You smell good," I stated softly.

"Uh, thanks," he chuckled as he pulled back, shooting me a curious glance. "It sure beats the smell of Dad Life from thirty minutes ago. Sam thought it would be hilarious to make me a spaghetti hat. So, tonight we are thankful for hot showers and Usher. Also, that's why I'm late."

A grin spread wide despite my sour mood. Noah had a sneaky way of doing that, no matter how miserable I might feel. "Cheers to that," I said, holding up my empty glass. "Oh, um... any word from Devon?" I was almost too scared to hear the answer.

Noah looked confused. "He's not here?"

"Nope. And zero contact since his text this afternoon."

Noah pulled out his phone to call Devon, but the moment it started to ring, Devon entered the bar.

"Wait, he's here. I see him." My eyes rounded. Butterflies fluttered in my belly as I braced myself for the potential confrontation.

"Hey."

"Hi," I replied.

"Can we talk?" Devon slipped his hands into his pockets as he approached our group, his gaze fixed on me.

"Of course."

My gaze darted to Noah for just a moment as I followed my boyfriend out of the bar. Noah offered the faintest smile in reply.

"Devon, what's going on? You've been dodging my calls and ignoring me all day. On my *birthday*. It... hurts." Tears rimmed my eyes despite my efforts to hold them back.

He pulled out a pack of cigarettes, even though he wasn't a smoker. "I care about you. A whole fucking lot. And I get that we're going to be in the public eye—there's no escaping that."

I frowned. "You can't seriously be upset about that article," I insisted. "It's a dramatic fabrication. You know that. You know *me*."

"Do I?"

The insinuation caught me off guard. "What?"

"Do I really know you?" Devon repeated. "We've only been dating a few months and I feel like you spend more time with my guitarist than me. I feel like I'm in a competition with Noah... and it's starting to piss me off. Yeah, the tabloids are bullshit. But it also opened my eyes to what's been going on between you two."

My heart stuttered, taken aback by the accusation. "Devon, there's nothing going on. Noah and I are friends. Good friends. I adore his son... that's all." Panic swept over me. Was he about to end things? *Was this it?*

He blew out a puff of smoke, his eyes focused away from me. "Do you love me?"

My breath caught in my throat.

Love.

We had never used that word before. My only experience with "love" had been dependence, isolation, abuse, and control. Devon was none of those things. He celebrated my independence. He was nurturing and kind. He appreciated me for everything I was—flaws and all.

Devon took care of me.

Maybe I did love him...

"I think so," I whispered, stepping forward and closing the gap between us. I took his face between my hands and forced him to look at me. "I mean... I do. I love you, Devon."

His features softened, posture relaxing. He tossed his

cigarette to the cement and wrapped his arms around me in a fierce hold. "Shit, Chelsie, I'm sorry. I'm fucking sorry, babe."

When he hugged me tight, I let out a sigh of relief. "I understand why you were upset, but please... just talk to me. I need you to talk to me," I pleaded, tilting my head to place a soft kiss on his lips.

Devon deepened the kiss and pulled me tighter. "I will. I'm sorry this happened on your birthday," he apologized. "I just needed time to cool off, gather my thoughts. I'm not the jealous type, I swear. This just triggered me for some reason."

"Is it because of Noah specifically? Is there something between you two that I don't know about?"

Inching back, he plucked out another cigarette. "I guess you could say that," he shrugged, lighting up and leaning against the brick wall. "I mean, there's always been some friendly competition between us for as long as I can remember. But things shifted a bit during his relationship with Ruby."

I was really beginning to hate that woman. "What did she do?"

"What *didn't* she do? She was a viper. Noah was a complete idiot for staying with her for so long."

I flinched, slightly offended. What would Devon think of me if he knew about Ian and all the things I'd put up with? "People do crazy things when they think they're in love," I offered in defense.

"Yeah," he sniffed. "I guess they do."

Stretching a small smile, I closed the gap between us once more and rested my head on his chest. "Can we forget all this ever happened? I'd really like to make this a good birthday."

He relaxed a little, letting out a sigh into my hair before stepping back. Devon sifted through his pockets again, pulling out a small, badly-wrapped package. "I got you something."

I reached for the present with a grin. "Reindeer in August. Nice."

"Sorry, it was all I had," he said, chuckling at the festive wrapping paper. "And don't freak out. It's not exactly what you think."

My fingers hurried to open the gift, revealing a jewelry box beneath the paper—and inside the box was a ring. "Um, Devon?"

I studied the treasure. It was a claddagh ring with a turquoise stone in the middle.

"It's a promise ring," he explained. "And it has your birthstone in it."

My heart warmed, touched by the gift—a promise ring from Devon Sawyer. My *boyfriend*. There was only one problem... my birthstone was a peridot.

Deciding to ignore the oversight, I jumped into his arms with a commanding hug. "I absolutely love it. Thank you so much."

He returned the hug and kissed the top of my head. "You're welcome, babe. Now, let's go celebrate."

The night had taken a turn for the better as the hours progressed. I swallowed down my third Sex on the Beach shot with Julia and Lisa and had a nice buzz going on, thankful I was back in Devon's good graces. Even the bartender I'd knocked over was full of smiles and free drinks, likely due to the famous people at my party.

"Another round for the birthday girl," Noah ordered, pointing at me and waving down the waitress.

"Are you trying to get me drunk again?"

"I'm honestly just trying to see those awesome dance moves again," he winked, taking a big swig of his whiskey. "So, if that's what it takes."

Everyone laughed as a new round of drinks were set in front of us.

"To Chelsie," Lisa proclaimed, holding up her cocktail. "The sweetest girl I know."

"The *luckiest* girl I know," Julia chimed in, gesturing toward Devon.

My chin dipped to my chest. "You guys are too much. I do feel lucky. Thanks for making my birthday so special."

"To Chelsie," Devon said. "My amazing girlfriend. My biggest cheerleader. My number one fan."

I gave him a big kiss before turning my attention to Noah. "Okay, okay, let me hear it," I joked, wiggling my fingers at him with anticipation.

"Is this where I give you a shining tribute?"

"Obviously. Birthday girl, here. I'm needy and buzzing, and I need to feel the love." I gave him a playful punch on the shoulder as I sipped my newly-made drink. Then I nearly heaved with disgust. "God, what is this? Motor oil?"

"Whiskey sour," Noah corrected. "It's delicious. Drink up."

"I don't think I like whiskey..."

"You'll learn to. As for a toast, I actually did get you a little something."

My spine straightened in my chair, intrigued. "Really? You didn't have to get me a gift." I fiddled with the promise ring on my finger as Noah reached over to the chair behind him.

"It's not much. It's actually terrible," he said. "Sorry."

I frowned with curious apprehension. "Thanks?"

He handed me something wrapped in construction paper. "Try not to rip the wrapping. That part is from Sam."

My smile was organic as I ran the pads of my fingertips over the orange paper. "Sam is the best." I carefully pulled the paper apart to reveal a picture drawn in colored markers—it looked to be a drawing of a stick-figure standing with a smaller stick-figure.

"That's you and Sam," Noah explained. He pointed out a scribble in the corner. "And that's *Curious George*. Not sure how he got in there."

Tears nearly seized me. I looked down at the other gift in my hand, shrouded in a thin layer of tissue paper, and tore it open. It was a DVD copy of the film *Citizen Kane*.

"See? Terrible," Noah said, shaking his head. "I don't think people watch DVDs anymore, but I had to get you something."

Reaching out, I squeezed his arm, more tears threatening to spill. I was beyond grateful for the gift. It was thoughtful... it meant something. "I love it," I told him. "Thanks, Noah."

Devon cleared his throat. "Let's hear it for the birthday girl. Happy twenty-seventh, Chelsie."

Everyone raised their glass as I looked around at my tribe. The day had gotten off to a rocky start, but deep down, I felt more blessed than ever. I recalled a time when my birthdays had consisted of violent sex, mental abuse, and a feeling of hopelessness and despair. Ian always made sure he brought his *A* game on my birthday. The only celebration was that I'd survived another day.

It was hard to believe *this* was my life now. My abuser was behind bars and a rock god was by my side.

I only wished my parents were here to see my happiness.

Maybe someday...

As the hours rolled by, I decided to call it a night, stumbling into my apartment at almost three A.M. and grabbing the mail on the way in.

"Hey, Misty." The cat purred, curling around my ankles as I yawned and sifted through the assortment of bills in my hand. "Happy birthday to me," I grumbled to the credit card statements and utility notices. As I was about to toss the pile onto the table, a return address caught my eye.

Auburn Correctional Facility

I recognized the handwriting on the envelope.

My stomach dropped. My throat squeezed. My chest tightened.

With shaking fingers, I opened the small envelope, discovering a simple birthday card with a cartoon picture of a teddy bear holding a red balloon. Sucking in a shaky breath, I flipped open the card.

"I hope your birthday is full of surprises. – Ian"

Car headlights flashed in my open window, momentarily blinding me. My apartment faced the building's parking lot, so it was nothing out of the ordinary, but it was enough for a deep-seated feeling of dread to seep into my bones. I rushed over to the window and pulled the drapes closed before wringing my hands together and closing my eyes, trying to calm my nerves.

I reached for my cell phone and automatically began to call Devon...

But I paused when I remembered that Devon knew nothing about my grim past and convicted felon of an ex-boyfriend.

Swallowing back the lump in my throat, I scrolled farther down my contact list until I landed on Noah. A pang of guilt coursed through me.

I should be confiding in my boyfriend. I should be giving Devon the opportunity to soothe my fears.

I couldn't, though. What if he saw me in a completely

different light after learning about my past? What if he didn't want me anymore once he knew how broken I was?

Ian's voice cackled in my mind: *"You're pathetic. Weak. A nobody. No one will ever love you the way I love you."*

Insecurities drenched me.

No... I couldn't risk that. Noah only knew because of a technicality—a drunken, embarrassing technicality. My darkness needed to stay hidden away from Devon Sawyer.

I clicked Noah's name, sighing with relief when he picked up on the first ring. "Combs? Did you get home okay?"

My hand trembled as I held the phone to my ear. "Noah, I think he's back," I said in a quick, fearful breath. I squeezed my eyes shut to hold back the wave of tears. "I think Ian's back."

CHAPTER FOURTEEN

NOAH

S unday morning began with a much needed band meeting. The smell of freshly-brewed coffee filled the studio as the rest of the Freeze Frame members filtered in. Everyone looked tired and hungover.

Tad and Miles had joined the birthday party festivities a little after midnight, and they were looking rough—a sure sign of a successful Saturday night. Tad had a box of donuts under his arm as he approached the meeting table, and the group flocked like vultures to the sweet treats.

"Mornin'," Miles said with a giant yawn.

I snatched the only cream-filled donut, stuffing it into my mouth. "Hey," I replied, my greeting muffled by the pastry. I was exhausted and restless, having been up until sunrise talking on the phone with a paranoid Chelsie.

"You need to move in with Devon," I'd told her. "You'll be safer there."

Chelsie had refused. She was too "independent" and had worked too hard to recreate herself to give it up. She never wanted to depend on a man for anything.

"My apartment is like my trophy," she had said. "It means I did it. It means I survived."

I couldn't really argue with that, so... I listened. I did what I could to lessen her nerves until she drifted off to sleep as the sun came up.

"Hey there, sunshines," Sean said as he entered the room. "No rest for the wicked. Hope you boys put on your business pants this morning."

"Dude, you're lucky I managed to put on any pants at all," Tad grumbled.

Devon slid into the seat next to me looking disheveled and smelling like alcohol. "How late did you stay out?" I asked, reaching for another donut. I had left shortly after Chelsie and the girls took off, probably around two o'clock.

Devon ran a hand over his weary face. "Late." He didn't elaborate.

I was surprised Devon had continued to party with the other band members. He'd never been a big drinker, especially if we had band-related business the next morning.

"All right, my friends." Sean perked up as he took a seat at the round table. "Let's talk Grammy's. I want to discuss the game plan, as we're only a few months out. I know you boys think you're untouchable, but you're not even close to being ready."

"Sean's right, man," Miles agreed. "We totally botched *Super Sonic* at the Cherrywood show. No excuse for that."

"That was a fluke," Devon argued. "No one noticed. You know we can play that song in our sleep."

"That was my bad," Tad acknowledged. "I was sloppy."

Sean nodded. "I'll be honest... it hasn't been the first time in recent months. Everything okay, Tad?"

I glanced over at the beefy drummer. I'd been so preoccupied with my own shit, I hadn't even noticed my friend's sunken-in eyes and blank stare. "Yeah, man," I added. "You know we're here if there's something going on. There's no going down that road again."

Tad winced at the insinuation. "I'm fine. Ain't nothing to worry about in that department." He crossed his arms over his barreling chest and leaned back on the legs of his chair. "What about the Aberdeen lawsuit? Any word on that?"

Sean dismissed him. "Jackson is taking care of that. That's what the suits are for."

"Hey, when's my endorsement shoot for Gibson happening?" I wondered, chewing on my cheek, feeling seriously out of the loop. I skimmed through the calendar on my phone. "Shit."

"Yeah, that would be tomorrow," Sean said. "Hope you've got it covered."

"And my charity event for the school is Friday, right?" Devon confirmed, scribbling down notes. "Then we've got the show at El Rey on Saturday night."

"I fucking hate Los Angeles." Miles tossed his half-eaten donut back in the box.

"Suck it up, princess," Sean replied. "The fans eat you up there. I'm working on the set list for El Rey. I'll e-mail it over tonight."

I sighed, depleted, glancing up at our manager as he typed away on his device. Sean was a good guy. He was the one who had taken a chance on us when we were struggling artists playing at dive bars and local clubs. With an alarmingly tall stature, Sean was a big guy—slightly overweight with black-rimmed glasses and a crew cut, always chipper and happy-go-lucky. Above all, he treated us right.

"Back to the Grammy's," Sean said, looking up from his screen. "I'll admit, I'm nervous."

Devon scoffed. "We're all nervous. It's the goddamn Grammy's. I'm probably going to piss myself in front of Beyonce."

The group chuckled.

"I'm serious, kids," Sean scolded. "You're not ready. I'm noticing a seriously lack of professionalism and dedication lately. You're sloppy, you're preoccupied, and you haven't even mastered the new song yet." He shook his head with a flicker of disappointment. "I believe in you, boys. But it's time to get your shit together."

With another long sigh, I gulped down my coffee and stood from the chair. The new song was called *Hometown Girl* and it was about Chelsie Combs. Devon wrote it while on tour the month prior, and it was about to hit the radio. "Let's practice tomorrow after my Gibson shoot," I suggested. "We'll get it done. We need to nail down a few others, too."

Everyone nodded.

I pushed my chair in and tossed my empty cup in the trash can. "I'm off. I need to spend some time with my kiddo before diving into this crazy ass week. Later."

It was true. I desperately needed bonding time with my son. I also needed to make childcare arrangements for my hectic traveling schedule. These were the moments I resented Ruby the most—Sam didn't have a mother to take care of him when I was gone.

Strolling to my car, I pulled my phone out of my pocket to call Chelsie.

Her voice was low and raspy when she answered. "Hello?"

"Sounds like you finally got some sleep," I said with a smile. "I was calling to see if you wanted to keep an eye on Sam tomorrow. I totally forgot about this guitar photoshoot I have downtown."

I heard Chelsie rustling around the room. "Oh, sure. Yes, of course," she replied. "Sorry, I don't even know what year it is right now."

Chuckling, I confirmed, "Eight o'clock?"

"I'll be there."

CHELSIE

I tossed the phone onto my bed covers and plopped down with an exaggerated yawn—but my plan to go back to sleep was interrupted when my phone began to buzz again. Snatching it back up, I opened the text message, letting a gasp slip when I recognized the name. It was the name of a woman I hadn't spoken to in five years.

Riley Hoffman.

Riley: *Hey girl, I hope this is still your number. It's been a while. Please call me.*

It had certainly been a while. Our friendship promptly ended when Riley took my ex-boyfriend's side when I had needed her most. Riley was dating Ian's brother, Brad, at the time, and it was an equally volatile relationship.

What could Riley possibly want after all these years?

Memories of my old life came rushing back. Memories of a completely different Chelsie Combs. It was hard to believe that life had even existed—it all felt like a bad dream.

I gathered my wits and pressed the call button. If Riley was reaching out, it had to be important.

"Chelsie?"

The familiar voice sent a shiver down my spine. Visions of double dates, drive-in movie theaters, and epic sleepovers sluiced me in nostalgia.

But those visions quickly evaporated into haunting memories of coerced threesomes, raves, and abuse. Riley was there through it all.

And then she wasn't.

Riley and Brad had been the equivalent to me and Ian. Both men were victims of childhood abuse by their mother, and in turn, became abusers themselves. Both had done jail time. Both enjoyed tearing women down until there was nothing left; it was some sort of sick transferred aggression brought on by their own mother's violent temperament. Ian's tragic past was the driving force behind my decision to stay with him for so long. I always said that Ian was *made* into a monster... he wasn't born one. So, I always thought I could rehabilitate him somehow and help him conquer his demons. I'd always had a soft spot for broken souls.

The problem was that Ian didn't want any help. He enjoyed what he'd become.

Riley and I had both wanted to fix our damaged men—but the difference between us was that I had gotten out. I had chosen to make a better life for myself.

Riley had stayed. Riley had chosen Brad.

And when I'd gone to the police station covered in bruises with Riley as my witness to Ian's crimes, she'd choked. She'd told the cops that I'd been in a fender-bender, and that Ian was innocent. She'd lied, saying he had never laid a hand on me.

I'd never felt more blindsided, and the lingering residue of betrayal still left a sour taste in my mouth.

"Yeah. It's me." My tone remained flat and indifferent. "Why are you contacting me?"

"It's been a while," Riley said. A silence settled in before she sighed. "Listen, I know you hate me. But there's someone you hate more than me, and I have some information."

My blood ran cold.

Were my fears from the night before completely justified?

I had fallen asleep to Noah's comforting reassurance that I was overreacting. The headlights in my window were a coincidence. The shadows on my wall were my imagination. The terrifying theory that Ian was out of jail and hunting me down was only something that happened in television crime shows.

"Is it Ian?" I finally choked out.

A pause.

A long, painful pause.

And then...

"Yeah, Chels. He's out."

NOAH

I didn't expect to find Chelsie on my doorstep a few hours after speaking to her that day. And I certainly didn't expect the petite blonde to be tear-stained, frantic, and hell-bent on making an immediate escape over the Canadian border.

My peanut butter-and-jelly making afternoon was cut short when I discovered Chelsie standing on my front porch, white as a ghost. I'd sent Sam up to his room to watch a movie while I tried to calm my terrified friend.

"Whoa, whoa, whoa... breathe," I said, taking Chelsie by the shoulders and guiding her to the couch. Her eyes were wild. Her mascara left dark stains across her flushed cheeks. "What's going on?"

Chelsie removed herself from my grip and began to pace the living room. "It's Ian. I knew it. I just *knew* it," she rushed out. She sat down on the couch, then stood back up again. "I have a target on my back, Noah. He's coming for me."

I ran my hands over my face as I tried to process everything. "Okay, slow down. How do you know he's coming for you? How do you even know he's out of jail?" I wondered. "In fact, why the hell is he out of jail in the first place?"

Chelsie shook her head. "Good behavior, I guess. Riley called me."

"Riley?"

"An old acquaintance."

"Did this acquaintance tell you he was going to hurt you? If that's the case, we're going to the police right now," I told her firmly.

"Screw the police," she shot back. "They didn't listen to me the first time. My bruises didn't mean anything. It took the rape of an innocent woman for them to take Ian seriously. And now... they let him out."

Thinning my lips, I studied the girl in front of me. She was panic-stricken, and I could only imagine what she was going through. She'd overcome so much, only to have the skeletons in her closet reemerge. Her slender frame was trembling, her eyes glazed over. Chelsie had noticeably left her apartment in a hurry, as she was wearing mismatched socks and a t-shirt that was two sizes too big over pajama shorts.

I idly wondered why she had come to me. Why not run to Lisa? Why not confide in her boyfriend?

Why did she trust *me* so much?

"Chelsie, you need to take a deep breath and focus," I encouraged, approaching cautiously and reaching for her shoulders again. She tried to dodge me in an attempt to continue her unproductive pacing, but I caught her before forcing her to look at me. "I'm serious, Combs," I whispered. "Breathe."

Her body relaxed beneath my gaze, lips parting with a soft breath. "You don't understand, Noah."

"You're right... I don't. I could never possibly understand how you're feeling." I squeezed her shoulders when she stepped in closer to me. "But I need to know if you're in real danger right now. What did your friend say?"

"Acquaintance," she corrected. "She called me because she felt like she owed it to me after we had a huge falling-out years ago. I guess no threats were made, but she heard from the crowd we used to hang out with that he was out on good behavior, and he was asking about me. Someone told him I was dating a famous musician and he said, "I know." Then, he took off. This was yesterday morning, and they hadn't seen him since."

My brows pinched into a frown. I nodded, taking in the information. "And you got that birthday card yesterday?"

"Yes. He probably mailed it right before he was released."

"So, he knows where you live," I concluded. Ice trickled through my veins. "And he's obviously been keeping tabs on you while locked up."

"Don't you see why I'm so freaked out?" she pleaded. Her eyes glimmered with fresh tears as she stared up at me, begging for me to *understand*.

I couldn't deny there was cause for concern... but Chelsie wasn't going to like my suggestions. "Honestly? You need to go to the police. And you need to tell Devon everything."

She pulled away, crossing her arms over her chest like a defiant child. "I'm telling you, Noah, the police won't help until it's too late. And if you want me out of the picture for good, fine— I'll tell Devon. That will be a surefire way to get rid of me."

"First of all, have more faith in Devon. You think he's going to dump you because of your past? That's ridiculous," I insisted. "Second... you might be "out of the picture for good" if you *don't* go to the police. You can show them the birthday card and get an order of protection."

A caustic laugh left her. "Excellent," she snapped. "I'll hand them my birthday card with a damn teddy bear on it and say *help*. That'll solve everything."

My defenses flared. "Fine," I bit back. "Do nothing, then. Just call me crying every time you get scared until you eventually wind up in a ditch somewhere with a bullet in your head. Sounds like a plan."

Chelsie's body tensed up, the prospect of a fight looming in the air. I could see the familiar spark of anger in her green eyes. She bit down on her bottom lip as if she were trying to keep her smart comeback at bay. It seemed to do the trick—instead of slinging an insult, she stormed past me and headed for the door.

"Where are you going?" I called to her.

She reached for the door handle. "Don't worry about me. I can figure this out myself."

"I'm just trying to help you," I said. "This could be life-threatening. You think I want your blood on my hands? You confided in me, and now I'm involved whether you like it or not."

As she swung around, her long mop of hair flew over her shoulder. Her eyes flashed with anger before morphing into wounded surprise. "Is that all I am to you? You don't want... *my blood on your hands?*"

My chest tightened with regret. I backpedaled, realizing how crass that had sounded. "I didn't mean it like that, Combs. You know that."

"I thought maybe I meant a little more to you than a sense of responsibility," she said, her voice cracking. "But I guess I'm just a burden."

You are so much fucking more than that.

"Wait," I said, trying to catch her as the front door flew open. "There might be one more thing you can do."

Chelsie paused but didn't turn around.

This was a bad idea. A *terrible* idea. But... it was the only idea I had left.

"I have a gun. Take it."

CHAPTER FIFTEEN

CHELSIE

Almost a month had gone by since I received the news that my psychopathic ex-lover was on the loose and potentially plotting my elaborate death. It had been a month filled with anxiety, paranoia, and many sleepless nights.

There had also been a lot of big changes.

Devon had finally convinced me to move in with him.

While I was fiercely opposed to the idea at first, my new predicament didn't exactly put me in a position to say no... plus, our relationship had been getting stronger. It felt wrong to head home to my small apartment when a high-rise condominium could be mine. I was the only one holding myself back from living the good life.

For a long time, the "good life" had been simply existing. I had made it out alive. I had my own place, a small group of friends, and my beloved fat cat. That was all I ever wanted. But now that I was getting a taste for more, I wanted to truly *live*—not just exist. Devon could give me that. He *wanted* to give me that.

He wanted to give me the world.

He even bought me a car, so I didn't have to take an Uber everywhere. I'd grown independent over the years, but not having to struggle with bills, rent, and transportation was a nice change.

"I think I got the last of the boxes," Devon said. I watched as he carried the rest of my life out of the apartment, wondering again why he hadn't hired professional movers. Devon insisted on doing it himself. He claimed it gave him a taste of real life, which kept his ego from getting too big.

"Today I'm just a regular guy moving my girlfriend out of her apartment and into my place," he had told me with a smile.

I supposed that made sense.

"Just one more thing," I called out as Devon placed the box down in the bed of the truck. Misty purred from the front seat. "Be right back."

Jogging back into my apartment building, I headed toward the bathroom and peeked behind my shoulder, just to make sure Devon wasn't following, before shutting the door. I stood on top of the toilet seat and popped one of the ceiling tiles out of place, revealing a hidden treasure.

Noah's firearm.

Climbing off the toilet, I carefully placed the gun inside my purse, zipping it shut. Devon still didn't know about the gun. Or Ian. Or any sordid details about my past. He had tried to learn more about my past relationships, but I'd been vague, as usual.

"You seriously don't have any good ex stories for me? That seems impossible," Devon had prodded me over Chinese takeout one night.

"Oh, you know me. I've always been a wallflower. There was this one guy who I was kind of serious with, but he cheated on me. All men were the Devil from that point forward," I had laughed lightly. "Until there was you."

Devon had seemed to accept my boring relationship history. It felt too late to tell him the truth.

"Okay, we're good!" I said, skipping over to Devon and giving his hand a gentle squeeze.

"What did you need to get?"

"What? Oh... nothing," I replied. "I just wanted to take it all in one last time. Lots of big life changes happened in that apartment." My eyes averted away from his. I hated keeping things from Devon, but the truth was too risky.

Devon flung his arm over my shoulder and pulled me close. "I get it," he said. "On to bigger and better things."

Hugging him tight, I murmured, "Thanks to you."

We hopped into the truck and drove off. I closed my eyes, taking in the moment as I stroked Misty's fur.

Life was good. Ian hadn't made his presence known—there had been no sightings, letters, or suspicious phone calls since my birthday. I wasn't sure if he was waiting in the shadows to strike, or if I'd blown everything out of proportion.

Maybe Riley had only called to scare me; after all, she was hardly a trustworthy source.

Maybe the birthday card was a one-time scare tactic.

Maybe everything was going to be just fine.

Unfortunately, my friendship with Noah had been strained since our argument, but I was trying to grow content with that. Distancing myself was probably for the best.

Devon had every right to feel bothered by our peculiar relationship. Looking back... we *had* become too close.

I still watched Sam on a regular basis, but my interaction with Noah was all business. There were no more movie nights, pillow fights, or late-night talks. And while I couldn't deny missing the way things used to be, I knew it was for the best.

I was Devon's girl.

"Hey, what are your thoughts on a triple date tonight?" Devon asked, breaking through my musings.

"Triple date? With whom?"

"I was thinking with Lisa and Miles, and Julia and Noah. It's been forever since we've all gotten together for some laughs and drinks, you know? Practices have been grueling with the Grammy's coming up, and this past week has been all about moving you in. I could use a little R&R. You up for it?"

My muscles tensed. "Julia and Noah?" Somehow, that was the one thing that had stuck out. "Are they dating or something?"

Devon turned on the radio and began tapping his hands against the steering wheel. "Oh, you know how it is. Their version of dating, I guess."

I hadn't spoken to Julia or Lisa in weeks, our only correspondence being the occasional text or a tag in a Facebook meme. I realized I'd been isolating myself to avoid conversations about Ian. "That works for me," I shrugged.

A night out sounded fun. The Ian drama seemed to have blown over, and my apartment was officially cleared out.

I had a lot of catching up to do with my friends.

NOAH

"Thanks for coming on such short notice, Rosa."

Rosa smiled as she placed her sweater on a nearby coat hook. "Oh, it's my honor, señor Noah. Mi chico dulce loves spending time with his abuelita."

Nodding my appreciation, I guided her to the kitchen where Sam was coloring in his notepad. "One of these days I'll learn Spanish."

"Miss Rosa! I missed you." Sam bolted out of his chair and gave his caretaker a hug. "Come color with me."

Rosa followed Sam to the kitchen island where he was eager to show her his artwork. "Muy bonita," she declared, kissing the hair on Sam's head. Her gold necklaces tickled his nose as she leaned over him.

I grabbed my keys and wallet from the counter, then stuffed them into my pockets. Checking my reflection in the microwave, I made a mental note to get a haircut. "I'll be back in a few hours, Rosa. Sam's dinner is in the fridge. You'll just need to warm it up."

Rosa shooed her hand at me. "Disparates! You know this chico will only get a home-cooked meal from Rosa."

"Yay!" Sam squealed. "I love when Rosa cooks."

A grin slipped. "If you insist. Don't make anything too hard on yourself. I'll check in later."

"Enjoy, mi querido. Have a wonderful night with señorita Chelsie." Her statement was followed by a knowing wink.

I ignored the inuendo. "Goodnight," I said, making my way

out the door and to my electric blue Corvette Stingray. Immense satisfaction whipped through me as the engine growled to life.

The only thing missing was a female counterpart in the passenger's seat.

My mind wandered to Julia. We'd been "seeing each other" over the past two weeks, but it wasn't anything serious. Nothing ever felt serious when it came to my sexual partners, and I wasn't sure if it was because Ruby had ruined me, or because a certain blonde had set the bar too high. There was always something missing with everyone else... no one compared to Chelsie Combs and how perfectly she had fit into my life.

And fuck—I was aware of how ridiculous that sounded. Chelsie was a walking headache, *and* she was dating my bandmate. But somehow, every woman lately had paled in comparison to her. I was trying my best to get past the inconvenient feeling, so that's why I'd called Julia up one night for a sushi date... maybe I would see something in her I hadn't noticed before.

I hadn't found it yet.

Pulling up to the valet service, I noticed Devon and Chelsie approaching from the opposite side of the parking lot. Chelsie spotted me instantly, our eyes locking.

She was wearing a yellow sundress with a high side-slit, showing off one long leg. She swept a hand through her halo of golden hair, revealing dangly, bohemian earrings.

Christ, she was fucking pretty.

A smile pulled up from the corner of her mouth, but it disappeared as quickly as it came. She looked away as they approached me, and I pulled out a cigarette, fumbling with the lighter.

"Be right in," I mumbled.

Devon nodded before he and Chelsie entered the upscale restaurant. After a couple of deep drags, I ground out the cigarette and joined my friends at a private rooftop table. Julia had already been seated, and she pounced on me with a commanding hug when I entered. I was quickly enveloped in a heady cloud of designer perfume and top-shelf champagne.

"Hey, stud." She wrapped both hands around my arm and pulled me over to a chair.

My eyes met with Chelsie's again, and she arched an

eyebrow. I responded by swinging Julia back around and planting a kiss on her crimson lips.

"I didn't know you two were a thing," Chelsie muttered as she sipped her sparkling wine, her eyes fixed on the display.

I pulled away with a shrug.

"I think it's great," Devon added. "You guys make a sexy couple."

Julia beamed, taking a seat and flipping her dark hair over one shoulder. "We know," she quipped. "Can someone pass the champagne?"

I sat down next to Julia, which was across from Chelsie. Her gaze was still pinned on me, so I shot her a smirk and clapped my hands together. "You know I don't do that bubbly shit. Let's get some whiskey over here."

Miles raised his empty glass in agreement. "Shit, yeah. Bottle of Blue Label would be nice."

I gave the server a quick nod, beckoning her to our table. When she approached, Miles leered at her half-exposed breasts as she pulled out a notepad.

I kicked him.

Lisa shifted in her chair. "I'm so happy we could all get together tonight. Chelsie, I feel like it's been forever since we spent quality time together. How did the move go?"

Chelsie sipped her champagne, her feathery earrings fluttering against her face as she addressed her friend. "Devon was amazing. We cleared out the apartment in less than two hours. I can't wait to get settled and start this new chapter."

New chapter built on lies by omission.

I was feeling on edge, and I wasn't sure why. Maybe it was the growing resentment that Chelsie had barely spoken to me in weeks. Or maybe I was envious of the fact that Devon seemed to have his shit together, while I had never felt more lost. Or maybe it was simply that I saw my whiskey coming, and whiskey always brought out the grit and vigor in me.

My gaze trailed back to the woman across from me as the amber liquid was poured into my glass. Chelsie was illuminated by the rooftop string lights and a subtle glow from the moon. Her bracelets jangled as she laughed at something Lisa said, tucking her hair behind her ear.

It was difficult not to stare, just as it was difficult not to regret being such a dick to her at the start of it all.

Maybe things would be different.

Maybe she would be more than my imaginary tabloid girlfriend.

Wait.

I couldn't possibly have *feelings* for Chelsie Combs. I was incapable of feelings ever since Ruby. I was fractured; an empty shell. A single dad with a chip on his shoulder.

And Chelsie was my front man's girl.

But, *goddammit*, when she looked at me—I felt it. That *thing.* That thing people felt when they realized they'd met their match. I felt it when she read bedtime stories to my son, and when she argued with me over movies. I felt it when her eyes glowed bright with unwavering affection whenever she engaged with me. I felt it when she called me up out of the blue to get ice cream.

And I felt it the fucking most when she didn't call me at all.

Here she was... sitting two feet in front of me, oblivious to my fucked-up revelation. She was smiling—*again*—because she did that. She was always smiling with her sparkling white teeth, dimples, and rosy lips, unaware of the effect she had on men.

Maybe that was part of it: her complete and utter ignorance to her own perfection. And now she was looking at me—*again*— because she fucking did that, too.

I didn't look away this time.

No, I continued to drink her in, from her furrowed brow, to her eyes twinkling with confusion, to her bottom lip caught between her teeth.

She was the opposite of Ruby in every way.

And maybe...

Maybe that was why I was falling for her.

CHAPTER SIXTEEN

CHELSIE

What the hell was that?

My hand gripped the champagne flute as I chugged it down, tearing my eyes away from Noah. Why was he looking at me like that? And why was there a sudden swarm of butterflies in the pit of my stomach? No one had ever looked at me like that before... not even Devon.

"I gotta take a piss," Noah said, breaking into the conversation.

"Me, too... actually," I blurted. I did not have to take a piss, but I was suddenly very interested in finding out why Noah needed to. Noticing Devon's curious frown as I rose from the chair, I placed a reassuring hand on his shoulder. "Be right back."

I caught up to Noah just as he was pulling his cigarettes out of his pocket. "Noah, wait." My feet slowed until I matched his pace.

He plucked out a cigarette and popped it between his lips. "What is it, Combs?"

"That's what I want to know. What was that all about?"

"What?"

I blew a few careless strands of hair out of my face with a huff. "Can you stop walking and talk to me?"

Noah stalled in resignation, eyeing me over the rolled paper and nicotine. "What do you want?"

When he finally made eye contact, I saw it again.

That look.

"That," I said pointedly, jabbing a manicured finger in his face. "That thing you're doing with your eyes. At me."

He shook his head with a dry chuckle. "I've got something better," he scoffed. "What's with the radio silence for the past three weeks? Shit, Chelsie, I gave you my *gun*. If Devon didn't talk about you all the time, I probably would have thought you were dead."

I stiffened in defense, my hands planting on my hips. "I mean, you basically told me I was nothing more than blood on your hands, remember? Honestly, I didn't think you cared."

That was only part of it, of course.

The other part was that I'd been spending far more time with Noah than I had with my own boyfriend, and I'd enjoyed our time together... a lot.

More than I should have.

But Noah's ego didn't need to hear that.

"Didn't care?" Noah asked in disbelief. He tossed his cigarette to the ground and snuffed it out with the toe of his shoe. "Are you insane? You know I didn't mean it like that. I think it's pretty obvious that I care."

As much as I wanted to shoot back a spiteful retort, it wouldn't be deserved. The truth was, I *did* know Noah cared. I had dodged his calls and texts for weeks. I'd avoided him at practices.

I had pushed away my trusted friend.

A breath escaped me that sounded a lot like apologetic defeat. "You're right," I conceded. "I'm sorry."

"I guess that's something." Noah stuffed his hands into his pockets.

Swallowing down a lump in my throat, I let the champagne finish the talking. "I've missed you, Noah. You're kind of my best friend." He blinked through a slight frown but didn't respond. *Had I said too much? Was it weird?* "Listen... we were spending a lot of time together. It wasn't fair to Devon. I was just trying to... distance myself. You know?"

Noah scratched the back of his neck, causing his t-shirt to

inch upward, revealing the hemline of his boxers. I refocused my gaze while I awaited his reply.

Was he ever going to reply?

"It's cool," he finally said.

Eyes narrowing, I waited another moment, assuming he had more to say.

More silence.

"Damnit, Noah... is that all? I'm trying here."

Noah dipped his head and let a smile slip. "It's cool. We're cool," he said, shaking his finger between us. "We don't need to hug it out or braid each other's hair."

"I mean, your hair *is* getting kind of long," I teased, reaching out and fiddling with a strand of his hair. It was almost beginning to curl at its ends. Hints of gold had been sprinkled into his dark locks, thanks to the autumn sun, and his eyes held flecks of gold as well.

Had they always been there?

Suddenly, I felt his hand wrap gently around my wrist to lower my arm. Color flooded my cheeks when I realized how intimate the moment had become. "Sorry," I said softly. I expected him to release me then, but he lingered.

And that damn look was back in his eyes.

I inhaled a sharp breath when his thumb brushed delicately along my wrist, as if tracing the intricate pattern of my veins. Tiny goosebumps scattered across my skin.

"You two look cozy."

Noah dropped my arm, and I jolted in place, clutching my wrist with my opposite hand and massaging away the tingling sensation. I looked up in time to see Devon breeze by us, heading toward the bathroom and deliberately bumping shoulders with Noah as he passed.

Neither of them said a word, and Noah was already on his way back to the table when Devon disappeared into the restrooms.

Faltering, I glanced down at my wrist.

What the hell was that?

The rest of the evening passed by uneventfully, filled with band talk, Devon on his phone, and Julia all over Noah like she was trying to earn herself a damn rose on *The Bachelor*.

My alcohol buzz escalated as I finished my champagne.

"It was so great hanging out with you, Chelsie," Lisa said, sliding her chair closer. "I know you've been busy, but I've missed you. We're not even on the same shifts at work anymore."

I pursed my lips with disappointment. "I swear Jerry does it on purpose. He's such an asshole."

"I know. I'm surprised you still work there since you're basically a celebrity now."

"Should I come out with my own line of lip gloss or something?" I teased. "Or better yet... nametags! I hate those damn things. I can bedazzle them."

We giggled as we finished picking at our dessert.

"Please tell me I'm coming home with you tonight," Julia whispered to Noah. One of her hands was resting on his thigh as the other trailed up the front of his chest.

My stomach soured for unknown reasons, so I drew my eyes away.

"I've got Sam."

Devon interrupted with a brittle laugh, his eyes lowered to his cell phone. "Please take her up on it. You need to get laid, man."

Lifting an eyebrow, I glanced at Noah as he downed the rest of his whiskey.

"Thanks for the vote of encouragement, but I think I do okay for myself."

"I mean, you clearly need a distraction," Devon muttered. "Something to redirect you from my girlfriend."

A chill encompassed the table, and I almost spit my drink as I turned to face my boyfriend. "Devon, please. That was completely unnecessary—not to mention, untrue."

"More importantly, what do you mean I'm a distraction?" Julia demanded. She sat up straight and crossed her arms over her chest. "I'll have you know I rock his world, buddy. I guarantee you he's not thinking about your girlfriend."

Devon shrugged, then leaned back in his chair as if nothing had happened.

"You know, this is rich coming from you," Noah continued. He twirled his whiskey glass between his fingers, seemingly unfazed by the accusation. "If we're on the topic of boundaries, I have an interesting story I could share."

Devon's eyes finally reflected something other than apathy. He set his phone on the table and scratched his head. "I think I'm ready for the check. You guys good?" He looked pointedly my way.

"Uh... yeah. I'm ready when you are," I said, turning my gaze toward Lisa. Lisa looked equally confused, but Miles had a smirk on face as if he knew exactly what Noah had implied.

"Sure." Noah reached into his pocket and pulled out his wallet. He tossed several one-hundred-dollar bills onto the table as he rose to his feet, holding his hand out to Julia. "You coming?"

Julia jumped out of her seat while she adjusted the straps of her cocktail dress. She reached for her designer purse, blowing a kiss to the table. "Goodnight, everyone. I'm off to have mind-blowing sex."

Eww. I wasn't sure why, but the thought of Noah and Julia together made my insides coil with unease. "Have fun," I forced out.

I guess I couldn't shake the feeling that Noah deserved... better?

Shitty.

I was a shitty person for thinking that. What kind of a friend was I? Why did I even *care* who Noah slept with?

When my friends began to disperse, I gathered my leftovers and followed Devon out to his car. The drive home was made in silence, and it was the kind of silence I didn't dare break—the kind that penetrates the air, thick with tension and unanswered questions. If I were to speak, the sound of my own voice would be so jarring, it would fracture my entire essence.

It was *that* kind of silence.

So, I just sat there with my thoughts and questions, bubbling with anxiety, addled with impatience. Every minute felt like a lifetime, and every mile felt like an eternity.

Luckily, that eternity came to an end when we were finally standing face-to-face in Devon's luxury condominium. The sound of his keys clanking against the glass entry table had been kind enough to break the harrowing silence.

"Well, that was—" Before I could finish my sentence, he was on me. He was pulling at my dress as he backed me down the hallway and into the bedroom. "Devon, what…"

My words were cut short again by his lips. His tongue dove into my mouth, tasting my questions, worries, and doubts. Devon was never aggressive with me—our lovemaking was gentle. Unhurried. This was… *different.*

Devon flipped me around, tossing me face-first onto the bed. He yanked up my dress and a sense of panic crept in.

This felt too familiar.

"Do you like it rough?"

His voice was alarming. He didn't sound like himself. I tried to pull myself back up, but Devon pressed me onto the bed with a firm hand while the other unlatched his belt buckle.

I gathered my strength, twisting my body until I was lying on my back. "Get off me, Devon. I don't want it like this." My heart was pounding. Beads of sweat were trickling down my forehead. Visions of Ian flashed through my mind as my breathing became more labored, more desperate.

It felt like I couldn't breathe at all.

I drew into a sitting position as Devon backed away. My chest heaved. I was clawing at my throat with shaky hands, attempting to get my breathing under control.

It had been years since I'd had a panic attack.

"Shit, are you okay?" Devon asked, his eyes gleaming with worry. He zipped his pants back up and sat beside me on the bed, wrapping a strong arm around me. "God, I'm so fucking sorry."

I closed my eyes. I needed to compose myself. Devon had no idea his aggressive sexual advances would trigger deep-seated memories. He *couldn't* know.

I hadn't told him any of that.

"I – I'm fine. I'm sorry," I croaked out as my breaths began to steady.

"*You're* sorry? Fuck, I'm a total asshole. Jesus Christ." Devon stood up and paced around the room, running his hands through his hair. "I guess I had too much to drink, and I was... pissed. Jealous. You probably think I'm a psychopath."

My eyes fluttered open. "No, I..." I trailed off as I tried to center myself and gain control of my racing thoughts. Then, I forced my eyes on his and spit the words out: "I was raped before."

It was time to tell the truth.

Devon stared at me in bewilderment—or shock. Perhaps both. "Are you serious?"

I nodded, pulling my knees to my chest. "I haven't been entirely honest with you, Devon. I didn't want you to think I was screwed up."

"Why would you think that? You don't trust me?" He was pacing the room again, shaking his head back and forth. "Well, now... I guess you have little reason to trust me."

"I do trust you, Devon," I said, and it was the truth. Despite his actions, I knew he would never hurt me. *He wasn't Ian.* "I'm sorry I never told you the truth about my past. I should have. There's no excuse."

"Does anyone else know about this?"

I paused, hesitating. This was another relationship-defining moment—*would I pass or fail?*

"Just Lisa. No one else besides my family."

Fail.

There was no point in opening that can of worms. Devon was already feeling jealous and paranoid over my friendship with his bandmate. If he knew I'd confided in Noah over him... well, that would be the end of our relationship.

I could kiss my future with Devon Sawyer goodbye.

Devon sat down beside me and placed a gentle hand atop my knee. His smile was warm and kind. *He was Devon again.* "Tell me everything."

CHAPTER SEVENTEEN

NOAH

"That's a wrap," Tad said, spinning two drumsticks between his fingers.

I reached for a towel to wipe the perspiration off my face. We had just finished a grueling practice, gearing up for the Grammy's.

"That was a fuckin' doozy." Miles clapped his hands together with satisfaction. "I think we nailed it, my friends."

"I'm with you there," Tad agreed.

Devon cracked open a beer and held it above his head. "Here's to Freeze Frame going to the Grammy's," he said. He chugged down the beer and crushed the can in his hand. "Want to celebrate at Ernie's? Drinks on me, assholes."

"I'm game," I shrugged.

The accompanying wince from Devon did not go unnoticed.

"Sweet," Miles said. "I think that foxy bartender works Thursday nights."

"Don't be a shithead," I scolded, packing up my guitar. "Lisa's an awesome girl."

Miles held up his hands. "I didn't do nothin'. A guy can appreciate is all I'm saying."

Sighing, I checked the time on my cell phone. I'd told Chelsie I would be home by eight, and it was getting close, so I sent her a text to see if she would be okay staying a little longer. Getting drinks with the guys wasn't the most honorable excuse, but I could really use the distraction.

Not that I was hankering to spend more time with Devon, exactly. We hadn't been friendly with each other since our dinner date the week before, keeping things all "business." No chit-chat, no humorous banter, and certainly no mention of our blonde common interest.

Chelsie had been withdrawn the past week. Mopey and melancholy. I had tried to pick her brain, but she wasn't budging.

"You know I appreciate your concern, but nothing is wrong, Noah," she had told me that afternoon after arriving for Sam duty.

"I also know you're great at withholding information, so you're not off the hook that easily," I'd replied.

She'd offered a smile that hadn't quite reached her eyes, but I'd decided not to probe any further. I knew that Chelsie might be able to keep secrets from her boyfriend... but she always came around with me.

"Imma head out," Miles said, throwing his bass over his shoulder. "See you fuckers there."

I nodded as my phone vibrated in my pocket. Unlocking the screen, I was greeted with a selfie of Chelsie and Sam. My son was holding up a piece of paper that said, *"Have fun, Dad!"* and Chelsie was giving a thumbs-up. A grin stretched as I stared at the photo.

Damn. She fit into our lives so perfectly.

It was a short drive to the local dive bar called Ernie's, where our celebrity status generally went unnoticed by fellow patrons. There was the occasional swooning fan, and plenty of "they look familiar" whispers—but, for the most part, we could enjoy our drinks in peace.

"Four shots of Blue Label, honey," Miles said to the bleached blonde server as he leaned over the bar. I scowled at my band member's complete lack of respect toward his girlfriend. Miles was a dog, and he wasn't very good at hiding it. I was surprised Lisa even tolerated his antics, considering what a straight-edged woman she was.

"Noah Hayes?"

Ah, shit. I was in no mood to cater to the fans tonight. All I wanted to do was drink my whiskey, share a few laughs, and get the hell out. Pivoting toward the bubbly voice, I came face-to-face with a posse of young girls in low-cut blouses.

"I'll do a quick autograph," I said as politely as I could. The girls danced around while they pulled out their cell phones and tried to capture selfies.

"Have a good night, girls. Don't drink and drive."

"Thanks, Noah!"

"Marry me!"

With a jaded sigh, I joined my friends at one of the high-top tables. "Jesus, Dev, are you trying to out-drink the whiskey master?" I teased, noting three empty shot glasses in front of Devon.

Devon looked up with surprise. It was the first amiable thing I had said to him all week. His eyes narrowed before he looked back down at his beer. "I didn't know it was a competition," he said stiffly.

The subtle parallel did not go unnoticed. What also did not go unnoticed was Devon's sudden interest in alcohol. He had always been the "professional" one in the band—he'd been rigorous about doing things by the book and not letting any vices get in the way of our music.

Drugs and alcohol were two things Devon had stayed away from over the years. He was the one *we* looked up to.

Now, Devon was drinking heavily almost every night. He was getting stoned on a regular basis. He was forgetting lines, singing out of key, and losing his temper with the guys at every practice. "What the hell is going on with you lately?" I couldn't help the question from spilling out of me. I wanted answers.

"What the fuck do you mean?" Devon leaned back in his chair, rocking on its rear legs.

"The drinking. The pot. The shit attitude."

Devon scoffed at the accusations. "I've spent my whole life being a do-gooder. It's time to stop being a pussy and actually enjoy myself."

"That's ridiculous," I argued. "You can enjoy yourself without getting inebriated every night and treating us like crap."

I knew enough about Devon to know he had always felt the need to stand out. Growing up with four brothers had given him a competitive drive unlike the average person. When we'd been in sports together, Devon needed to be the one to score the most goals and rack up the most points. When his older brother became an auto mechanic, Devon needed to become a *better* auto mechanic. When we had started the band, simply playing local shows wasn't good enough. Devon needed his name in lights.

He had gotten his way, as he always had. He had fame, money, and the perfect woman on his arm. He had it all.

Where does someone go when they're already at the top?

They fall.

Devon ran a hand through his mess of sandy hair. "Get off my back, Hayes."

"I'm just trying to help you."

"Don't need your help," Devon said. "If you want to help, you can stop sniffing after my girl."

My hackles rose.

Luckily, Tad's voice broke through the budding argument. "Hey, who the fuck is that guy?"

Deciding to let the barb go, I leaned back in my seat and surveyed the crowded room. "What guy?"

"That dude over there keeps staring at us. I'm used to the women, but that motherfucker is creeping me out."

My eyes landed on a twenty-something man with light blonde hair. He was wearing a red and black plaid shirt with scuffed jeans and a menacing scowl. He had a chiseled jawline, prominent nose, and there was an icy look in his dark eyes. He was perched against the bar with a beer in his hand, staring right at us.

"Just some fan, my man." Devon burst out laughing. "Shit, that rhymed."

I rolled my eyes, hoping I wouldn't be on lead singer duty tonight. Devon was already intoxicated.

"He doesn't look like a fan," Miles observed. "He looks like he wants a piece of us. Should we kick his ass?"

"Maybe he wants a *piece* of us," Devon snickered. "It's not just women who want to get in our pants."

Frowning, I looked back over at the mystery man. He still hadn't taken his eyes off our group, specifically Devon.

"Fuck, he's coming over here," Tad said.

The stranger approached our table, his group of brutish minions trailing behind. With a weary sigh, I resigned myself to the fact that I wasn't going to have a peaceful night, after all.

"Look at these fucking jokesters," the man said, folding his arms over his puffed-out chest.

"Who the hell are you talking to?" Miles stood up from his seat, ready for a fight.

I extended my arm in an attempt to block Miles from pouncing. "Can we help you?"

"Well, well, well... Devon Sawyer in the flesh," the ringleader sneered. "I've been dying to meet you."

One of the man's cronies stepped forward with a grin. "He looks a lot smaller in person, huh, Ian?"

Devon jumped from his seat as my skin prickled.

Ian.

The name sent a shiver down my spine.

The notion of him being *the* Ian seemed impossible, but the charge in the air reeked of bad intentions. This Ian character looked to be the right age, and his eyes shimmered with cruelty. "Your name is Ian?"

"Why the fuck do you care?" Ian spit to his left. "Unless you're Devon Sawyer, get the fuck out of my way."

I stepped forward, getting right in the man's face.

I had to know.

"Dude, who is this asshole?" Devon wondered, moving in beside me. "You know him?"

Ignoring him, I continued to bore holes into the man. "Answer me."

"Yeah, so what? My name is Ian." He looked back at Devon with a smirk. "Your buddy has something of mine. I want it back."

My chest hummed with awareness; I felt it in my bones.

This was the man who'd destroyed, abused, and demoralized Chelsie Combs. This was the man who'd stolen her innocence— who'd beaten, raped, and terrorized her.

A surge of red-hot adrenaline coursed through my veins.

Instinct and vindication for Chelsie took over, and I lunged, tackling Ian to the bar floor and pummeling him with my fists.

"Fucking hell!" Devon shouted.

Hands pulled at me, but I pushed them away. I was too zoned-out, running on rage and retribution. I wasn't thinking about consequences. I wasn't worried about the cameras in my face, or the flock of stunned bystanders. I had no concern for the fact that my bandmates were yelling and swearing, begging me to stop.

The only thing on my mind was making this man suffer.

Blood spurted from Ian's nose as I continued my furious blows, but it wasn't long before he managed to gain the upper hand. He landed a hard fist square in my jaw, rendering me momentarily dazed. I tasted the salty trickle of blood in my mouth as Ian flipped us both over, mounting me. I heard a ringing in my ears when another blow connected with my face, my skull striking against the tile floor. I was about to throw another punch when Ian was peeled off of me, his arms flailing, his face unrecognizable from the blood spatter.

"You're a fucking *dead* man!" Ian threatened. "You are done. Fucking finished. I swear to *God!*"

"Your ass is going to jail," one of the men in Ian's group added with contempt. "My brother will make sure you rot."

Drawing up on my elbows, I wiped the blood from my mouth. Miles and Tad were by my side, helping me to me feet as I bit out raggedly to Ian, "Stay away from Chelsie."

Police cars flew by outside the window, lights flashing and sirens blaring. I glanced at Devon, who seemed to be in his own daze. He was looking back and forth between Ian and me with a mask of confusion... or was it some kind of realization?

"Dude... what the hell, man," Miles said in frustration. "Do you have any idea the steaming pile of shit you just brought on all of us? What was that?" He tossed a napkin at me, and I held it to my bleeding lip.

Reality sunk its teeth into me. I cursed under my breath, knowing I'd royally fucked up.

As I tried to regain my composure, a group of police officers approached our group.

"I'm pressing charges!" Ian bellowed, pointing right at me. "This asshole jumped me unprovoked. I want his punk ass thrown in jail."

My body was riddled with aches and pains from the fight as I stepped through my front door. Devon and I had sent multiple texts to Chelsie with no response, so I assumed she'd fallen asleep.

It was a little after three A.M. and the house was completely dark, save for a dim light glowing from the kitchen. I wasn't surprised to find Chelsie sound asleep on the couch with a blanket pulled up to her chest... however, I *was* both startled and charmed to find my son passed out on top of her.

Stepping over to the couch, I studied my favorite people with a slow-blooming smile. Sam rose and fell with each one of Chelsie's breaths, his little arm dangling over the side of the sofa. A dribble of drool stained the blanket beneath his face. Chelsie was on her back with her head tilted to the side, her palm still resting protectively along his spine.

A feeling of peace swept through me, the evening's arduous events leaving my mind. My body didn't hurt, my jaw wasn't swollen. Ian was a distant memory—or perhaps, he didn't even exist.

I wasn't sure. All I could see was Chelsie and Sam, and I allowed myself to imagine a life where this was what I came home to every night.

"Noah?"

I'd been so lost in thought, I hadn't noticed Chelsie's eyes flutter open. She lifted her head to see me better in the dark.

"Hey," I replied softly.

"You're home..." She tried to sit up, then remembered the extra weight sprawled across her chest. I could make out her small smile through the shadows. "I guess we passed out reading *Clifford* books."

I leaned over, scooping Sam up as carefully as possible, until he collapsed like a rag doll against me. "Hey, buddy. Off to bed."

Sam muttered something unintelligible, his eyes never opening.

"Be right back. Sorry I'm so late," I said to Chelsie, turning to carry Sam to his bedroom. When I returned, Chelsie was sitting up on the couch, wrapped in a fleece blanket. A lamp had been switched on, illuminating the room and casting attention to the wounds decorating my face.

Chelsie leaped up when she noticed. "Noah? Oh my God..." She ran to me, her hands reaching for my swollen jaw. "Let me see you."

My eyes closed tight with regret, knowing this could be the last time I felt her touch. Her concern. "Combs, I fucked up," I whispered in a rushed breath.

I studied her face as curiosity, worry, and confusion flickered in her eyes. She grazed her thumb across my inflamed bottom lip, sending a tremor right through me. It was supposed to be a gesture of tenderness, but it made my dick twitch instead. It took all my willpower not to tug her to my chest and kiss her senseless in the middle of my living room. It took all my strength not to bend her over my couch and ride her hard.

Swallowing, I shooed the intoxicating images away and went against everything my body was telling me. I lowered her hands from my face.

Chelsie chewed her bottom lip, confusion marring her delicate features. "Did I hurt you?"

I shook my head. "No... but you're going to want to be as far away from me as possible when I tell you about my night."

She didn't step away from me like I'd assumed. The concern didn't fade from her green gaze. She stood her ground, our bodies inches apart. "Noah, tell me what happened."

CHAPTER EIGHTEEN

CHELSIE

I wondered if I'd invaded Noah's personal space, but I couldn't help it—my nurturing instincts had kicked in, and I couldn't contain the rush of empathy I felt when my eyes landed on his wounds. Now, a million scenarios raced through my mind as his words digested.

Noah let out a heavy breath and looked up at the ceiling, as if silently asking it for courage. "Shit, I don't even know where to begin. I guess I should tell you that I just spent the last few hours at the county jail."

I inhaled sharply. "What? Are you serious?"

"I'm serious. I got into a bar fight. I..." His voice trailed off, his gaze fixed away from mine. "I beat the shit out of your ex."

My knees went weak. It felt like I was holding the weight of a thousand men. Stumbling backward as his confession processed, my ankles collided with the couch, and I fell back onto the cushions.

I was speechless.

Ian?

Noah... *beat him up?*

"I – I don't even know what to say," I finally said. My skin grew hot. Bile was creeping up my throat.

"I feel like you might be in danger now," Noah told me, his face pinched with remorse as he approached my slack-jawed stance on the couch. He didn't sit beside me. He kneeled in front of me, right between my legs, until we were face-to-face. "I screwed up, Combs. When I put the pieces together and realized it was him, I just snapped. I thought of everything he put you through and I wanted to fucking *kill* him."

A mix of emotions flooded me, and I didn't know what to think or feel. Ian was clearly keeping tabs on me and my personal life; there was no doubt about that anymore. Not only did he have a vendetta against me... but now with Noah, too.

And where was Devon during all of this? Was he in danger?

So many questions—and yet, Noah was between my knees, his bruised face a mask of frenzy and guilt. All I wanted to do was tell him it was okay. Reaching out my hand, I placed it against his cheek. Dried blood crusted along his jawline, and I wiped at it with my trembling thumb.

Noah had taken punches for me. He'd defended my honor.

No one had ever done that for me before.

"Thank you," I whispered, leaning forward and pressing a light kiss to his forehead. "I'm not used to having someone care so much."

The guilt in Noah's eyes flashed to bewilderment as he studied me. "Chelsie, you shouldn't be thanking me. I put your life in danger. I compromised the band. I may have ruined Devon's reputation. I'm an idiot," he said. "I acted on impulse, and I did a lot of damage."

"But you did it all for *me*," I countered, as if that were undoubtedly the only thing that mattered.

"Exactly. I did it all for my bandmate's girlfriend, which is also dubious." Noah shook his head, sitting back on his heels and running a hand through his mess of hair. "I risked a lot of shit for you, Combs, and I don't know why."

My belly tickled at the admission. I didn't know why either. I didn't know how our relationship had evolved from loathing enemies, to reluctant allies, to trusted friends, and now to... whatever this was. It felt like a new category in our ever-changing story.

Regrouping, I fiddled with the string on my sweatpants and wondered, "Noah, what did he say to you?"

Noah stood, taking a seat beside me on the couch and exhaling a deep breath. "Nothing. He was there to size-up Devon, and I interceded," he told me. "Devon had no idea who he was... but he does now."

My stomach dropped. *Shit.* I had told Devon that no one else knew about my history with Ian. Now, he was well-aware I had confided in Noah. "Did you just... attack him?" I gulped.

Noah's jaw tensed through a nod. "Pretty much. He said Devon *had something of his*—meaning you. I just flew off the fucking handle."

Vindication swam through me at the thought of Ian getting pulverized. He was a monster, after all; he'd deserved every blow. He'd deserved to know that I had moved on without him. I had survived and was stronger than ever. He wasn't "it" for me, like he had tried so hard to drill into me for all those years. He wasn't the best I'd ever have, and he sure as hell didn't hold a candle to the men in my life now. I hoped every strike was a crude reminder of that.

"I really gave it to him," Noah continued. "There was blood everywhere. He's *lucky* if all he got was a broken nose."

I pivoted, fully facing Noah. "And you were arrested?"

"Yeah, the cops and paparazzi swarmed the place. Ian said he's pressing charges and all that shit. Lawsuit, I'm sure. Devon bailed me out, but I've got a court date next month. I'm sure you'll see it on the news tomorrow morning."

"Did he threaten you at all? Or any of us?"

Noah nodded again. "He said I'm a dead man... but I can take care of myself. It's you I'm worried about."

"At least I'm staying with Devon now," I sighed, folding my arms across my body. "I'll admit, I'd be a little freaked out all alone in my apartment."

"We'll need to up security on you. The guy is out for blood."

As freaked out as I was, my concern for Noah trumped that. He had a target on his back. "Noah... are you going to be okay?" I asked gently. "I have your gun. You should take it. You're the one he's going to want to get revenge on."

"Absolutely not." Noah straightened, hardened. "You need

protection. I kicked his ass because of *you,* and he knows that. You're still the most vulnerable target."

A chill encompassed me because I knew what Ian was capable of. I also knew that I didn't stand a chance against him without a weapon. "What about Sam? What if you need to protect him?"

"I'll get another gun, Chelsie. I'll make sure Sam is safe."

My phone vibrated before I could respond, flashing with Devon's name. I swiped to answer. "Hey, Devon. I'm about to head out."

Devon's tone was pure ice. "Don't bother."

"What?" Anxiety settled in my gut as my grip tightened on the phone. "Why?"

"Look, I'm not ready to talk to you yet. You told Noah every-thing—*before* you told me. And you lied about it. I need a night to think."

Tears rimmed my eyes as I pressed my lips together. "I can explain, Devon." *Could I, though?* What was there to say? The truth was, I *did* lie... there was no getting out of that. "I'm sorry."

"Stay the night with your other boyfriend. Maybe I'll be ready to talk tomorrow," Devon said, his tone clipped.

"That's not fair. It's not like that at all."

"Tomorrow," Devon repeated. "Goodnight."

The call disconnected, and I stared at my phone blankly, trying to register what had just happened. A tear slipped down my cheek. "Devon doesn't want me to come home," I sniffed.

Noah offered a look of sympathy. "I heard. You're obviously more than welcome to stay. You can take my room."

My chin lifted, gaze darting up to Noah. "What have I done? I ruined everything. I was too scared to tell him the truth."

"Try not to think about it tonight," Noah said, his words laced with reassurance. "I'm sure he just needs to sleep on it. He'd be a fool to lose you."

My stomach did a little whirl. He'd said it so flippantly—yet, his words moved me to the core.

He'd be a fool to lose you.

"I'm the fool," I muttered as self-loathing wormed its way

inside of me. "I'm honestly not sure why you think so highly of me."

Noah's face was unreadable, but he had that look in his eyes again. The look that made my belly flutter. The look that made me question things; things I didn't even understand. "I see what Sam sees," he said firmly. "And Devon. And probably every person you cross paths with. I'll never understand how you don't see it, too."

I gaped at him, stunned into silence by a man who had once been a master of slinging insults at me. Now, his words were the only ones I wanted to hear. "Thank you." It was an inadequate bestowal for such a high acclaim, but it was all I could muster.

"Come on." Noah tapped my knee and stood from the couch. A playful kindling danced in his green eyes. "I'll show you to your quarters, m'lady."

I always stayed out of Noah's room when I watched Sam. I'd only been in there once after Sam had jammed his *Hot Wheels* car underneath the door. As I stepped through the threshold, I noted that it looked the same as it had that day—charcoal gray walls and similar bedding. It was stark and unfitting for a man like Noah, who was full of personality and humor. The bed was unmade, and a small dresser was the only other piece of furniture in the room.

"This space could use the touch of a Gaines," I teased, glancing around.

"A what now?" Noah wondered. He poked his head in the closet for an extra pillow.

"Never mind. You're clearly not the HGTV type."

"No, I'm not," Noah agreed with an amused chuckle. "But you're welcome to decorate whenever you're over. I suppose some color pops wouldn't hurt in here. Maybe a ficus in the corner."

"Definitely a ficus," I smiled. "Those trees are so... happy."

"Okay, Bob Ross."

My grin stretched as I stepped over to the edge of the bed. "So, this is it, huh? My arrangements for the night? You know I don't mind the couch."

"Only a total douche would put a woman on the couch," Noah said.

The king-sized bed did look appealing, and I didn't have any fight in me to argue. With a reluctant shrug, I spun around to say goodnight, my smile still lingering.

But it dissolved when I discovered Noah standing much closer than I'd anticipated. A breath caught in my throat. A glimmer of moonlight shone through the cracked curtains, lighting up his silhouette. For one profound and disarming second, I thought that maybe... *maybe*... he was going to kiss me.

A strange tension burned low inside me as I stood there frozen, the back of my legs grazing the foot of the bed. Our eyes locked through the shadows, and I could see his own glinting with a sentiment I couldn't place. Something heavy.

"Goodnight." Noah handed me a fresh pillow, his voice cracking slightly.

Then, he was gone.

I released a breath, tightening my grip on the pillow. I didn't know what that was, or what I wanted it to be. The air around me still felt charged. I placed a hand over my heart, as if that would somehow slow its hurried beats.

"Goodnight," I finally whispered to the room. Turning around, I climbed onto the mattress, the cool sheets a welcome contrast to my feverish skin. I was about to place the pillow under my head, but changed my mind, tossing it to the floor, instead. Reaching beside me, I pulled one of Noah's pillows underneath my cheek, breathing in deep. The scent of tobacco and sandalwood consumed me.

Purely Noah.

Closing my eyes, I smiled and tugged the comforter up to my chin. Despite my confrontation with Devon looming on the horizon, I felt content.

I fell asleep with a smile on my face, the anxiety and fear washing away.

CHAPTER NINETEEN

CHELSIE

"Wake up, seepy head!"

I startled awake, my eyes glazed with sleep. I tried to focus on the source of the disturbance, but was distracted by a familiar smell in the air. "Is that... pancakes?"

"Yes, Miss Chelsie! Daddy made us pancakes."

My gaze landed on Sam, who was bouncing with excitement on the bed. Rubbing my eyes with a yawn, I smiled, "Hi, Sam."

Sam bounced harder. "Are you excited for pancakes? I helped crack the eggs," he said with pride.

It had been a long time since I'd awoken to the smell of pancakes. Devon was not the culinary type. Ancient memories danced through my mind of my father making Sunday morning pancakes and U2 playing through the speakers. I'd always lived for Sunday mornings.

"Come *on*," Sam begged, pulling at my arm. "They're getting cold."

My smile widened as I threw off the covers and followed Sam down the stairs, checking my appearance in the hallway mirror. I cringed at the knots in my hair, the smeared mascara, and yesterday's clothing. I looked like a walking one-night stand, only I had no fun stories to go along with it. Running my fingers through my tangled mane, I frantically wiped at my raccoon eyes and straightened my shirt. Not much else I could do.

"Mornin'." A familiar voice greeted me in the kitchen where Noah was plopping a stack of pancakes onto each plate. "Syrup is on the table. I kind of overdid it on the butter, but when it comes to pancakes, go big or go home, right?"

"I completely agree," I grinned, my stomach growling. "It smells wonderful."

"Old family recipe," Noah explained with a wink, setting the plates down at each chair. "Cinnamon is the secret ingredient."

I took my seat and eyed the steaming pile of flapjacks. A bowl of fresh fruit was set in the center of the table, so I snatched a grape and popped it into my mouth. "Such service," I quipped to Noah, watching as he made his way around the kitchen like he was trying out for a competitive cooking show. "I had no idea you enjoyed cooking."

Noah glanced my way while he lit up a skillet and tossed bacon slices into the pan. "Enjoy, yes. Do I have time for it? Almost never," he admitted. "My schedule is insane. I'm lucky if I have time to make a sandwich. Rosa usually takes over in the cooking department."

I decided that was a shame because he had made some top-notch pancakes. Bobbing my head with approval, I shoveled another forkful into my mouth. "These are so good. Thank you."

"Did I do a good job?" Sam looked between us, searching for praise.

"You sure did, buddy," Noah said. He strolled over to the table, carrying a platter of sizzling bacon, and took a seat beside me.

"Miss Chelsie? Why did you have a sleepover in Daddy's room?"

I almost choked on my food. Sam was using his fork to make designs in the syrup on his plate, having no concept of what his innocent query implied. I cleared my throat. "Well, your dad got home a little late last night and I was really tired. It was safer for me to stay here and sleep, instead of drive home."

"Because you might crash in your car?" he wondered.

"Sure, it was possible. It's always better to be safe."

"Can you have a sleepover with me in my room next time? I have a sleeping bag you can use."

My cheeks stretched with a smile. "That would be really fun."

"Miss Chelsie?"

"Yes, Sam?"

Sam set his fork down with a clumsy clatter and began to swing his legs back and forth. "Can you be my mom?"

The question sucked the air from my lungs. I glanced at Noah, but I couldn't read him. I hated when I couldn't read him. "Oh, um, well..." Stuttering, I didn't know what to say. I swallowed back an assortment of explanations and excuses because nothing felt right. How could I respond without breaking his precious heart?

No matter how I phrased it, the answer was still... *no.*

"Sammy," Noah cut in. "Chelsie can't be your mom."

"Because she's already someone else's mom?" Sam asked, unaware of the tension mounting in the room.

"She just can't. Now, eat your food."

Setting my fork down, I folded my hands on the table and forced a smile of reassurance. "Sam, it means so much that you would ask me to be your mom. I care about you and your dad a lot. Being your mom would be very special," I explained. "But I can only be your friend."

Sam picked at a dollop of dried food that was stuck to the table. "Is it because I'm bad sometimes?"

Tears prickled my eyes. My heart ached. "Oh, honey, that's not it at all. You're a good boy." I reached out a hand to comfort him, but Sam pushed his chair back and hopped down.

"Nobody wants me," he said tearfully before jogging out of the room.

I cupped a hand over my mouth, gutted, spinning to my right to look at Noah. He was leaning back in his seat, his eyes closed, stance taut and rigid. "I – I'm sorry if I butchered that. I didn't know what to say."

A muscle in his cheek ticked. "It's fine. There's nothing else you could have said."

When Noah opened his eyes, the sorrow on his face was unmistakable. I bit down on my tongue, wringing my hands together in my lap. "I had no idea he had been thinking about that," I choked out.

Noah let out a heavy sigh. "Maybe *I* need to start thinking about that..." he considered. "Settling down. Laying roots. Maybe that's what he needs." Noah zoned out momentarily. "Sometimes I just wish..."

I braced myself for the rest of his words, but they never came. There was only silence. I reached out my hand and placed it on his knee. "You're doing a good job, Noah. A great job. He's going to be okay." Noah's face turned stoic. The sadness left his eyes as quickly as it had appeared.

He drew his lips into a tight line, pushing his tongue against his cheek. "You should probably go."

With a small frown, I glanced down at my plate of half-eaten breakfast. I could tell his suggestion was a kindly disguised order, and I supposed I understood.

The only problem was, I had nowhere to go.

"Thank you for the pancakes," I told him, pushing myself away from the table. My shift at The Pit Stop didn't start for another four hours, but maybe I could clock-in early, considering my leisurely morning plan of playing dinosaurs and board games with Sam had just disintegrated.

I debated going to the condo in hopes of a joyful reunion with Devon, but I couldn't stomach the thought of his possible rejection—not yet.

"I didn't mean to be rude," Noah interjected as I stood from the chair. "You didn't finish eating. Please sit."

My palms were sticky with syrup. I rubbed them against the front of my jeans and massaged the tiny balls of fibers that had transferred over between my fingertips. I considered it. More time with Sam and Noah was never time I regretted.

However, I knew my lingering presence was only confusing little Sam. Distance might be for the best.

"Thanks," I replied. "But you're right... I should go." I watched as Noah rose from his seat, either in protest or to walk me to the door, but I held out a hand to halt his efforts. "I can let myself out. I appreciate everything you did for me."

Turning away, I walked through the kitchen to the living

room, snatching up my purse that was draped over the back of the couch. As I approached the front door, I felt a hand curl around my wrist before I could reach for the handle. I spun around, startled.

"I don't want you to think you can't come back."

My breath hitched as I stared up at Noah. His eyes were solemn, as if he needed confirmation that he hadn't scared me away for good—that they *both* hadn't scared me away for good.

"I'll be back." A forced grin settled in place as I finished, "You can't get rid of me that easily."

It was the truth. I had tried to stay away, but I'd missed Sam.

I'd missed them both.

"You have a place here... if you ever need it," Noah murmured softly. He took another step toward me.

If things don't work out with Devon.

"I know," I swallowed, pushing the thoughts out of my mind. I reached out to give Noah's hand a gentle squeeze before turning to open the door. "Tell Sam I said goodbye."

I hesitated briefly. It was the slightest pause, and one Noah may not have even noticed.

But I noticed.

Something ignited deep inside my bones. It was only a fraction of a second, but the feeling surged through me, leaving me rattled.

Remnants of it still lingered during my impromptu coffee date with Lisa later that morning. We had talked about new books we'd read, the good shows on Netflix, and our plans for the following week. Despite the easy conversation, every so often, I would drift away and ponder that moment.

As I walked into work that afternoon, my mind wandered, and I forgot my punch-in code. I was distracted, my thoughts cloudy.

"You're late," Jerry admonished. The pungent smell of his body odor assaulted me as he stormed by.

I fumbled with the keypad, finally regaining my senses. 5609 —the street number of my childhood home.

Yes, that was it. How could I forget? That place held my most precious and beloved memories. That house had my dreams and aspirations carved into its plaster walls. It was my first real home.

And that was why I was so shaken. That was why my mind kept recycling that moment over and over again.

Home.

For one alarming and consequential second...

Noah had felt like home.

It was a slow night at The Pit Stop. Tips were unkind, the music made my head throb, and Jerry was on a roll. I glanced up at the band playing on stage and recalled the night I'd met Freeze Frame for the first time—the night I had locked eyes with Devon Sawyer and my life was irrevocably changed.

A wistful sigh escaped me. I wanted to go back to that night. I wanted to turn back the clock and tell Devon the truth about my ugly past. I wanted to do things differently.

"Chelsie! Get these appetizers out."

Jolting where I stood, I trudged back into the kitchen with heavy feet. Sometimes I wondered why I kept my meager job as a waitress and allowed my boss to treat me like trash.

"You're on my last nerve. Get your shit together or go home," Jerry shouted. Beads of sweat rolled from his round face, soaking the front of his button-down shirt.

Home.

I picked up a tray of stuffed mushrooms labeled "Table 5" and looked out through the kitchen door at the bustling venue. I hated my job. I hated the noise. I hated Jerry. No matter how much my life had progressed, that man always managed to make me feel small.

Why am I here?

I froze when I realized I'd just spoken my thoughts out loud.

Jerry stopped in his tracks. His face was redder than a ripe tomato. "What did you just say?"

My heart raced. "I..."

"You're here because I pay your goddamn sorry ass to be here." His voice was loud enough to startle the kitchen help. They quickly averted their eyes.

Normally, I would cower like a scolded child, but today felt... *different*. I refused to be bullied by this brute any longer. I refused to work at a job I loathed. I didn't have a rent payment anymore, and while I hated falling into old, co-dependent patterns, I knew I'd be okay until I found a better job.

Right now... I just wanted to be free.

Setting the tray of appetizers back onto the counter, I unclipped my nametag. "I quit."

I didn't wait for Jerry's reaction, swiveling around and pushing through the double doors with a feeling of liberation.

As I weaved through the crowd of patrons, I pulled out my phone and sent a quick text to Lisa and Julia, accidentally bumping into someone along the way. "Oh! Sorry." I looked up and immediately recognized the man. "Miles?" My eyes drifted to his right, discovering a mysterious woman on his arm.

"Uh, hey, Chelsie. Forgot you worked here." Miles scratched the back of his neck and pulled away from the raven-haired beauty.

"Who's your friend?" I asked tightly.

I already knew.

"Oh, uh, nobody."

The woman scoffed, crossing her arms over her low-cut blouse.

"Well, good to see you," I said, biting at my lip.

Miles nodded and guided the woman away from me, toward the bar. My heart hurt for Lisa. There had been signs that Miles was being unfaithful, but nothing concrete until now. Lisa was going to be heartbroken.

Heaving in a deep sigh, I knew it was time for damage control.

The drive to Devon's condo had gone by in a flash. I'd been so lost in thought, I was driving on auto pilot. So many scenarios raced through my mind as I sat silently in the parking garage. None of them were good.

But I had to get this over with. I had to win him back.

Unlike the drive over, the elevator ride to his high-rise unit was painfully slow. Inch by inch. Second by second. I felt like I was choking on my own heartbeat.

When I arrived at his door, I knocked with trepidation. I didn't know why I knocked, as I had a key, after all. Yet I felt like a visitor—an outsider.

So, I knocked.

Devon opened the door, looking disheveled. His hair was a matted mess, and he was still wearing the prior morning's clothes. I supposed he was probably thinking the same thing about me—the difference was, I didn't have a choice.

I wondered if he'd been depressed over our separation when I got a whiff of alcohol on his breath. He was hungover or drunk. I wasn't sure yet.

"You have a key," Devon said.

"I know." He was standing in the doorway, leaning against the frame. "Can I come in?"

Devon moved to the side to allow entry, his movements sluggish. Was he hesitant to let me in, or were the effects of the booze slowing him down? Either way, I felt a potent lump growing in the back of my throat as I made my way into the living room.

I hadn't even set my purse down before he spoke.

"Are you fucking him?"

I froze. "What? No... God, Devon." I decided I was offended by the question. I probably had no right to be, but I was. I was angry and insulted.

"Do you think about fucking him?"

Outrage bubbled in my belly as my face grew hot. "Devon. Stop."

Devon began pacing the room, stopping only to grab a half-empty bottle of rum from his liquor cabinet. He took a swig straight from the bottle. "I'm not sure why you're surprised by those questions," he said, screwing the cap back on and dangling the bottle at his thigh.

My muscles locked. "I'm surprised you would think that of me." I stood firmly in place, only following him with my eyes.

He shot me an incredulous look. "Really? After all your lies? After all the late nights and cuddle-fests you two have had? The entire world thinks you're fucking each other, and you're shocked the thought has crossed my mind, too?"

"The world doesn't know me! *You* know me. I would never cheat on you. Noah is my friend. That's all."

Devon released a dry chuckle. "No. I *thought* I knew you."

His words stung, but he wasn't wrong. It was true—I had downplayed my life, omitting character-defining details about my past. I was prone to cowering and concealing, afraid of what Ian might think or do. I had progressed over the years, but old habits die hard when someone is programmed to constantly be afraid.

Devon was right... he didn't truly know me.

Not like Noah did.

My shoulders slumped, my body draining of the tension it had been holding onto. I let my anger dissipate. "Devon, I am so sorry. You're absolutely right. I made a bad call, and you have every reason to hate me for it."

Devon stopped pacing and tapped the bottle of Bacardi against his leg. "I don't hate you."

Tears rushed to my eyes, and I wanted to claw at them. I hated being so vulnerable in front of him. "I didn't mean to tell him," I confessed, flinching when my voice cracked. "It was the night we all went out for the first time. The night he got me drunk and had to take care of me."

"Okay." His gaze stayed fixed to the flooring beneath his feet.

Maybe if he just *looked* at me, he would see how much I cared; how much I was breaking inside.

"I don't even remember telling him, Devon," I continued. "I was drunk, and I guess it just came out. Noah stopped by my apartment the next day to tell me what I'd said. I would never *willingly* tell him something like that. Especially over you."

Devon finally glanced up at me. "Why didn't you just tell me that he knew? I asked you, and you lied. I'm just... I'm having a hard time getting over this," Devon bit out, taking another swig of the liquor. He set the bottle down on the coffee table before collapsing onto the loveseat across from where I was standing.

My bottom lip quivered, so I bit down hard. "I screwed up. I was so afraid of losing you," I pleaded. "I spent years of my life having to monitor every word that came out of my mouth because there might be consequences. This is my first relationship since Ian, and… and I'm still trying to figure everything out."

Devon's face was resting in his hands, elbows to knees. He sat upright, shaking his head, looking so… dejected. "That guy had it out for me, you know."

I looked up from the chipped nail polish on my forefinger. "Who?"

"Your ex. That asshole was out for blood."

"God, I'm sorry. I hate that he's here. I hate that he's trying to work his way back into my life. The things he's capable of…" My voice trailed off, old memories rushing back. The pain felt raw, the fear palpable. My trauma felt like it was yesterday, and I could almost smell him in the air.

His woodsy cologne. The gin on his breath. His peppermint shampoo.

"You need to go to the police," Devon muttered.

I shook my head, adamantly. "No, it's useless. Trust me."

"You can get a restraining order."

"Do you know how hard it is to get a restraining order?"

"He's a convicted felon."

"Even if…" I swallowed, pulling my lips between my teeth. "It's a piece of paper, Devon. If he wants me, he'll take me."

My own words sent a chill down my spine. I paced the room, my hands running through my stringy hair.

Devon finally stood, his balance unsteady. "I won't let anything happen to you," he said.

I stopped and lowered my arms. "I know."

He moved toward me, bumping into the coffee table along the way. Pulling me into a firm embrace, he rested his chin atop my head.

My worries washed away. I held him closer, nuzzling my cheek against his chest. "Are we okay?" I murmured into his t-shirt.

Devon was silent.

He never did answer the question.

He merely held me a little while longer, and then we made love as if nothing had ever happened.

I was restless that night. I felt cold, despite the warm blanket and Devon's body heat pressed into my back. Mysterious noises rattled my nerves, causing me to create elaborate stories in my mind of Ian breaking into the condo and shooting Devon in the face, then raping me until I went numb. The sounds were nothing but a whoosh of wind or a creak in the mattress, but my vivid tales played out for hours, until I fell into an uneasy sleep where Ian continued to haunt me.

And when I awoke, I was still so cold.

CHAPTER TWENTY

CHELSIE

I t had been a long time since we'd been out together, just the three of us.

Lisa and Julia sat on either side of me in a corner booth, sipping on martinis and shoveling sushi into their mouths. It was Friday night, and the boys were at band practice. It had been two days since my reconciliation with Devon, and while things were still marginally tense, we were steadily getting back into our old routine.

"I can't believe you quit The Pit," Julia mused, dipping a tuna roll into her soy sauce. "I wish I was there to see that asshole's face. You probably put him into cardiac arrest."

I shrugged, nursing a lemon drop martini. "I didn't stick around to find out. I took off my nametag and bolted."

The awkward run-in with Miles flashed through my mind, tickling my tongue as my gaze shifted to Lisa. I hadn't said anything about the suspicious meeting—not yet, anyway. I wasn't even sure *what* to say.

"I'm going to miss you," Lisa smiled.

I studied my friend's pretty features. Freckles stippled her nose and cheeks, as if someone had shaken a paint brush in front of her face. "I'm going to miss you, too. You guys are the only thing I'll miss about that place."

"How are things with Devon? I remember it had gotten a

little tense at our dinner date."

I realized then that my friends knew nothing about the altercation with Ian. I'd meant to tell Lisa during our coffee meeting, but I hadn't wanted to spoil the mood. We'd been having so much fun catching up on life.

Clearing my throat, I chugged down the rest of my martini. The vodka had settled at the bottom of the glass, and I shuddered when it slid across my tongue. "Guys... there's something you should know."

My two friends glanced up from their plates. Lisa wrinkled her brow in concern. "Everything okay?"

"Um... no, actually. Not really." My voice faltered, but I pushed through. "Lisa, you remember Ian, right?"

Her eyes popped. "Of course."

Confusion settled between Julia's dark eyebrows. "Kind of out of the loop here," she said, raising a hand in the air. "Was that your jerk of an ex?"

"Yes," I confirmed. "He was more than just a jerk. It was an abusive relationship, and he was in jail for a few years on a rape charge." I decided to leave out the rest of the gory details—there were a lot of them. "And... well, he's back."

Both girls fell silent as Lisa dropped her chopsticks with a *clank* against her plate.

I rushed to continue before they spoke. "I think he's still obsessed with me. I received a birthday card from him, and then he showed up at a bar that the guys were at last week. He was looking to fight Devon, but Noah beat him up and got arrested."

The silence from the rest of the table was deafening.

"Can I get you ladies anything? Another cocktail, perhaps?"

A lanky waiter stood beside our booth with a forced smile on his face.

"No, thank you. I think we're okay," I muttered.

Julia piped up. "We are not okay. Send over a round of tequila shots. Make mine a double."

"Certainly," the man nodded.

"Chelsie, why am I just now hearing about this?" Lisa asked. Tears were coating her copper eyes. "This is a big deal."

"And how come you didn't tell me about this, like... *at all?*"

Julia added.

Guilt threatened to swallow me whole. "Julia, I didn't even tell Devon. And now he hates me for it." I shifted my focus to Lisa and said with urgency, "Lis, I was going to tell you, but I didn't want to think about it. I just wanted to pretend this wasn't happening. Talking about it gives it life... it makes it all too real."

"How have we not seen it all over the media?" Julia wondered curiously. "Facebook is my news outlet and I've heard zip."

"Sean has been working overtime trying to keep this under the radar," I explained. "With the Grammy's so close, this could ruin them. But I'm sure there's no keeping quiet forever."

Lisa was silent as she swished her sushi roll around in a small bowl of soy sauce.

"Your drinks, ladies," the waiter said, popping over to the booth and passing out the shots.

Julia wasted no time in gulping it down as I took a small sip and placed it back down with a wince.

"Chels, you need to—"

I quickly cut Lisa off. "I'm not going to the police."

"I wasn't going to say that. I know how the police handled your situation in the past," Lisa told me. "I was going to say... you need to get a weapon to protect yourself. A gun."

Julia sucked a dollop of spicy mayo off her thumb. "That's a little dramatic, don't you think? Chelsie wouldn't even know how to use it."

I tilted my head back, staggered. "For your information, I have one. And I'll use it just fine if I need to." I knew my friends were angry with me. They were disappointed in my inability to let them in, as I was so apt at doing with the people I cared about. Truthfully, I had no one to blame but myself.

"Well, I hope to God you never have to use it," Lisa said as she popped the roll into her mouth.

Julia whistled loudly. "This conversation has gotten way too dark. Let's talk about sex. Specifically, sex between me and Noah."

We were accustomed to her lack of filter, but I gaped at her anyway.

"What? I know you've all been wondering."

I pushed my tongue against my teeth. The thought of Julia and Noah together like *that* made my stomach churn. Adding graphic details would be enough to send my sushi careening back up. I wasn't sure what it was about the two of them that gave me a queasy feeling in the pit of my stomach; it just did. Noah was a sexy, famous rock star and he had every right to indulge in cheap thrills as he pleased.

Then I winced. I'd manage to call Noah sexy and Julia cheap in the same thought. I didn't like where my brain was taking me.

"... and his size... Oh, boy... Let's just say he was touching parts of me only the Lord Jesus knows about..."

My head popped up, catching only bits of Julia's descriptive narrative. I found myself feeling both nauseated and oddly intrigued. Reaching for my shot glass, I let the rest of the tequila fall into my mouth, coating my throat with a smoky oak aftertaste.

Nauseated won out.

"And on that note," I muttered as I snatched my purse. "I'm going to head out."

Lisa took a sip of her dry martini, her fingers lingering on the stem of the glass. "I'm worried about you, Chelsie," she admitted. "Can the guys get a security detail on you?"

The thought had crossed my mind. Noah had even mentioned it.

But then I thought about how I'd feel with a muscle-man following me around, day in and day out. I would feel violated.

As violated as I would feel if Ian were to stick a knife in my gut?

"I'll think about it." I placed a wad of cash on the table, rising from the chair. "I had fun. Drive safe."

"Are *you* okay to drive?" Lisa wondered.

"I took an Uber."

I hadn't meant to leave in such a hurry. I hadn't meant to be rude or abrupt, either. But I didn't want to talk about Ian, or about how my life was in imminent danger, or about Julia's sexcapades with Noah. I didn't want to talk at all. I was sick of talking and apologizing and justifying everything I did—or *didn't* do.

I was just... tired.

So tired, in fact, that when I traipsed through the complex's parking garage and headed toward the elevator, I almost missed the figure looming behind a row of cars. He was far enough away that I couldn't make out his face, but I knew. He was wearing a dark hoodie, and his hands were stuffed into his pockets.

He was staring at me.

I could only describe the feeling as pure, undiluted fear. Not the kind of fear that made you run in the opposite direction, though—no, this was the kind that froze your feet to the earth. The kind that shut you down and made your mouth go dry. The kind that made you wonder if your heart was beating too fast, or not beating at all.

My eyes squeezed shut and I counted to three. I concentrated on my breathing. If I was breathing, I knew my heart must still be beating.

And when my eyes pinged back open, the figure had vanished.

Was I paranoid and delusional? Was this a prank? Had anyone been standing there at all?

My knees wobbled as I tried to regain the feeling in my legs and surveyed the parking garage with panic. I saw no one. I heard nothing.

When I was confident I wouldn't fall on my face, I took a hesitant step toward the elevator. As the doors closed me in, I envisioned Ian's hands wrenching the doors wide open and tackling me to the ground.

Stop it, brain. Please, stop.

I approached our unit and pulled out my keys with shaking hands. It took me four tries to fit the key into the keyhole. When I was successfully inside, I slammed the door and turned my back against the cold frame. I slid down the length of it, my bottom hitting the ground hard, then I pulled my knees to my chest and buried my face into my jeans. A wretched sob escaped my lips. The sound was so guttural, I wondered if it had even come from my own mouth.

This was my life now. I was doomed to live in a shroud of panic, always looking over my shoulder.

Ian had gotten one thing right—

He would always be with me.

CHAPTER TWENTY-ONE

NOAH

I f I wasn't already a household name, I sure as hell would be now.

The media had gotten ahold of some damning photos of my encounter with Chelsie's felon of an ex-boyfriend. Sean was livid, my bandmates were mopey, and Chelsie put the blame entirely on her own shoulders.

As for me? Well... I was indifferent. I didn't care what the world thought of me, and I didn't regret beating the crap out of that scumbag. The only thing I regretted was putting negative attention on the rest of the guys. While I didn't give a damn about my reputation, the music mattered. When our reputation suffered, the music suffered.

Sean was trying to put a positive spin on everything.

"Negative attention is attention. Your names are on people's lips. You're trending on Google. I'll take it," Sean had said at our most recent band meeting.

Sighing, I pulled my sunglasses off and set them on top of my head. I assessed my surroundings before letting Sam out of the car and chasing him toward the playground. It was a rare, quiet Sunday. Today I wasn't a Freeze Frame member. I wasn't the topic all over Facebook newsfeeds.

I was just Sam's dad.

"Look at me! I'm swinging so high."

I smiled with affection, watching as Sam used all of his strength to push his legs back and forth, gaining more momentum with each effort. "Great job, buddy."

I took a seat on a nearby bench, soaking up the sun and the crisp New York air. Woodchips crunched beneath my sneakers as I pulled a cigarette out of my pocket.

"I'm so sorry to bother you, but can I get an autograph?"

Inhaling sharply, I glanced to my left. I hadn't even noticed the soccer mom walking by with a baby stroller. "Of course," I said, hoping my tone sounded cheerier than I felt. I scribbled my chicken-scratch onto a notebook she'd pulled out of her diaper bag.

Just another day in the life of a music celebrity.

"It's for my cousin," the woman continued, boldly sitting beside me on the wooden bench. "I don't even like your music. No offense. But my cousin is a huge fan. She's even got tickets to see you guys on tour next spring."

I finally looked at the woman, truly noticing her. So many fans came in and out of my life, I couldn't recall a single face or name. It wasn't something I was proud of, considering these people paid my bills, but it was necessary for my sanity.

"Your honesty is refreshing," I replied.

She smiled up at me as I handed back the pen. "I'm Beth."

"Noah." It was a stupid response. She already knew that.

Her smile broadened. "Is that your little guy?"

Sam was climbing up the slide the wrong way, making funny sounds that mimicked a train or machinery. "That's him. That's my Sam."

Beth nodded to the stroller by her side. "This is Caden. I can't wait for him to be old enough to play here. I grew up at this park."

My gaze rolled over the small infant in the carriage. He couldn't have been more than two or three months old. "Enjoy it while you can," I told her. "They don't talk back at that age."

Beth chuckled, and I couldn't help but notice her resemblance to Chelsie. The long blonde hair, slender physique, and a dainty nose that curved slightly upward.

"I'm not used to people acting so normal around me

anymore," I said curiously, glancing back and forth between Beth and my son.

She shrugged. "My cousin says it's my super-power. I ran into Lady Gaga last year and we still text each other to this day."

I arched an eyebrow. "Impressive."

"Yep. Super-power," she laughed. A moment of silence passed between us before she stood from the bench. "Well, we were just passing through. Here's my number if you want to be added into my contact group of cool famous people I randomly meet."

She jotted down her number on another piece of notebook paper and placed it in my hand.

"Thanks," I nodded.

"Enjoy." Beth gestured toward Sam with a smile, then took off down the sidewalk.

I studied the wrinkled piece of paper in my hand. Every other phone number I'd been given by a fan over the years had gone straight into the trash. Yet, for some reason, this one I folded up and placed into my back pocket.

Twenty minutes went by, and I was texting back and forth with Sean when I heard a scream.

Sam's scream.

No.

I flew off the bench so fast, it felt like an otherworldly force had sprung me to my feet. When I raced around the corner of the playground, I discovered Sam lying crumpled next to the foot of the slide. Glancing up to the top of the play structure, I noticed an opening where a small child could easily fall through if they weren't careful. It had to have been at least a twelve-foot drop.

"Sam! Oh, fuck..." I rushed over to my son, pulling out my phone and frantically dialing 9-1-1. My hands were shaking so hard, I tried three times before finally getting the number combination correct. Crouching over Sam, I checked for a pulse.

Thrum, thrum, thrum.

He was alive. He was breathing. Sam was unconscious and his arm was twisted behind his back, but he was *breathing*.

"9-1-1, what's your emergency?"

"I'm at Holden Park off Center Street. My son just fell off the top of the playground and he's unconscious. Please... fucking hurry."

I knew enough to know that I shouldn't move Sam until the paramedics arrived, or I could potentially cause more damage. Instead, I sat beside him, running my hand over his forehead and gently moving his light brown hair out of his eyes. "You're going to be okay, Sammy. You're going to be okay."

The ambulance arrived within three minutes. They were the longest three minutes of my life.

The following moments went by in a daze. A neck brace. A gurney. Oxygen. Flashing lights. Bystanders gathering. Medical jargon. Sam's tiny body being lifted into the back of the ambulance. Someone was talking to me.

Someone was talking to me.

"Sir, are you going to follow?"

My vision blurred. The voice sounded like it was underwater. Or maybe the words were being said in slow motion. Possibly in a different language. I blinked. "What?"

The EMT continued to speak. "Sir, are you okay to follow? Are you his father?"

"My son... he's my son. Yes."

"Did you want to ride with us? We need to go now."

The words began to register, and I nodded slowly before following the paramedic into the back of the ambulance. There was IV equipment, cardiac monitors, and oxygen tanks. Sam's vitals were being taken as he laid there unconscious.

Why wouldn't he wake up? Was he in a coma?

The ride to the hospital was brief. When we arrived, I tried to follow the staff down the long corridor, but the EMT stopped me.

"A doctor will speak with you soon," the man said.

I didn't understand. "He's my son. I need to be with my son."

"Your son is in good hands."

All I could do was stand there, paralyzed.

Sam could die.

Sam could die.

The realization settled in, and I felt like I'd been sucker-punched in the gut. Sweat pooled at my hairline. I was dizzy, weak.

Chelsie. I had to tell Chelsie.

I fumbled with my cell phone, my fingers trembling as I paced the hallway back and forth. Back and forth. Chelsie picked up on the second ring.

"Hey, Noah."

"I'm at Presbyterian. Can you come?"

There was a pause of silence. "The hospital?"

"Yes. Can you come?"

More silence followed before fear threaded her voice. "Noah. What happened?"

I choked on my next words: "It's Sam."

CHELSIE

Racing madly through the emergency room doors, my eyes searched for Noah. When I spotted him sitting in a waiting room chair with his head in his hands, I rushed over, still wearing my frumpy sweater and house slippers, my heart in my throat. "Noah?"

His name was a question. A query. It was a yearning for answers, an apology, a solace, a hug, and a quiet consolation all in one breath. I found myself crouching down in front of him, situating my body between his legs. I splayed two unsteady hands on each knee, noting how they trembled ever so slightly beneath my palms. Noah raised his head, our eyes locking in a powerful hold.

"Noah."

This time it was permission. Permission to break, permission to cry. Permission to scream, curse, blame, and crumble.

He did break. He let his head fall between my breasts, his body overwrought with painful sobs. Pulling him closer, I rested my cheek against the top of his head and ran delicate fingers through his hair. Warm tears stained the front of my sweater.

I held him tight, lightly stroking the back of his neck until his tears subsided. Noah's face was pressed up against my heartbeat, and I hoped it was saying all the things I couldn't put into words.

"Mr. Hayes?"

We looked up to see a man in scrubs standing before us with a clipboard in his hand. Noah nodded.

"I'm Doctor Altschuler. I have an update on your son, Samuel."

Rising to my feet, I slid into the seat beside Noah. I still didn't know what had happened to Sam, except that he had fallen. That was all Noah had revealed before I dropped the dinner plate I'd been washing and watched as it disintegrated into a thousand tiny shards on the kitchen floor. I had left the condo so fast, I'd forgotten my purse and to change out of my slippers.

"Is he okay?" Noah was sitting up straight, his eyes troubled and bloodshot.

Please be okay.

The doctor smiled, and my chest fluttered with hope.

"Your son's prognosis is good. He suffered a severe concussion and cerebral adema, which is swelling of the brain. We had to perform a ventriculostomy to drain the fluid and relieve the swelling—but don't worry. He's doing great, even though it sounds scary. The fall also broke his proximal humerus, which is the upper arm bone. Luckily, the fracture looked clean, so we did not need to operate."

"Oh, thank God," I muttered, placing a gentle hand on Noah's shoulder. I glanced over at him, noting how the fear washed away. His features softened, his body relaxing.

"Can I see him?"

Dr. Altschuler shook his head. "Not just yet, I'm afraid. He will need about ninety minutes to recover before we allow visitors. I'll have the nurse come get you shortly. Sam will be transferred to the pediatric unit in roughly twenty-four hours for monitoring. If all continues to go well, he can go home in a couple of days. Are there any other questions?"

Noah swallowed. "Is he awake?"

The doctor nodded. "He's conscious. The effects of the anesthesia are still wearing off, but he should be fully alert in no time."

Noah rubbed his hands over his face and leaned back. "Thanks, Doctor."

The doctor offered a tight-lipped smile and disappeared down the hall.

I squeezed Noah's arm. His eyes were closed, and I wondered what was going through his mind. "He's going to be okay," I whispered.

Noah's eyelids fluttered. He placed his left hand on top of mine as I massaged his forearm with my thumb, then pivoted to face me. "Thank you for coming."

"Noah, you don't have to thank me. There's nowhere else I'd rather be right now."

Half of his mouth curved upward, as if he wanted to smile but didn't quite have the energy. "People talk about how hard it is being a single parent," he said, propping his ankle up on his opposite knee. "They talk about trying to work a full-time job, getting the cooking and cleaning in, helping the kids with school, trying to be present for all those special moments. But they don't talk about moments like this."

My heart stammered as I studied him, drinking in his words.

"I can juggle all those other things," he continued. "But not this. I couldn't do this alone. If I didn't have you, I..."

His voice trailed off, and I gave his arm another squeeze to let him know I understood. "I'm here," I assured him. "You don't have to do it alone."

We sat together in silence until the nurse fetched us an hour later.

Seeing Sam in his hospital bed with a bandaged head and arm cast was heartbreaking. He was so tiny, his legs only taking up half the bed space. Despite his condition, his eyes lit up like it was Christmas morning when we walked inside the room.

"Daddy! Miss Chelsie!"

New tears threatened to spill. He was so *happy*... even after all he had been through.

"Oh, Sam, you're so brave," I told him while Noah made a mad dash to his bedside.

"Sammy," Noah rasped out, climbing onto the bed and pulling his son into his arms. "My brave guy."

"I'm sorry, Dad. I didn't mean to fall. I hope you're not mad."

"I'm not mad, Sam." He peppered kisses along every inch of his face. "I'm just glad you're okay."

"They gave me a popsicle and said I was a good boy."

I beamed at him through misty eyes. "You're a very good boy. You deserve it."

"Miss Chelsie, come sit with us. It's like a slumber party."

Hesitation gripped me briefly. Would I be interrupting a significant father-and-son moment? I wasn't Sam's mother. I wasn't Noah's girlfriend.

Where did I fit in?

I eyed the narrow available bed space on the opposite side of Sam and carefully approached.

Right here, I thought as I laid down, my body barely fitting in beside him.

At the end of the day, I supposed titles didn't matter. I loved Sam. I cared greatly for his father. Maybe I would never be exactly what Sam needed in his life, but I would never stop caring about them both.

My arm wrapped around Sam's small frame, my hand reaching for Noah. He took it, squeezing with affection. Our eyes met over the white lump of hospital bedsheets, and for one powerful second, everything felt perfect. Absolute. It felt as if the universe had strategically placed me on this bed with these people at this exact moment.

What did that mean? I'd felt a similar feeling while leaving Noah's house the other day.

Home.

It was confusing, and I couldn't begin to understand it. The bed was squeaky and uncomfortable, the blanket scratched my skin, and yet... I had never felt more content.

"Miss Chelsie?"

"Hmm?" I answered.

"I love you."

I hadn't been expecting those words; I wasn't used to being loved. In my experience, love was control, abuse, and violence from Ian. Love was toxic.

This wasn't any of those things.

This was the purest thing on earth.

Overcome with emotion, I buried my face into the edge of the pillow to catch my falling tears. "I love you, too, Sam," I said quietly. Noah squeezed my hand again, dragging his thumb over my knuckles, but I couldn't look at him. I couldn't let him see how my heart was about to burst inside my chest. I couldn't show him the truth—that I had never truly been loved before. Only the dry, itchy pillowcase would be privy to my secrets.

"How about some cartoons?" Noah suggested.

"Yeah!" Sam squealed.

Noah let go of my hand, and I felt the bed shift as he reached for the television remote. I poked my head up, wiping away any remnants of my epiphany. Soon, *SpongeBob Square-Pants* filled the small recovery room and the afternoon progressed uneventfully. Sam appeared to be bouncing back like only a kid could. Nurses bustled in and out of the room, while Noah and I took turns stretching our legs and making coffee runs. Day turned into night, and it wasn't long before Sam was sound asleep.

"You should get going," Noah said as he sipped his watered-down hospital coffee. He rotated the Styrofoam cup between his hands as he spoke.

"I don't mind staying," I insisted. "I already told Devon it might be a late night. He's going to stop by to visit tomorrow."

"Yeah, he texted me," Noah replied. "I'm serious, though. You should go home and get a proper sleep. There's not really enough space for both of us here."

I was torn. I *was* exhausted, but what if something happened to Sam overnight and I was miles away?

It was as if Noah had read my mind. "I'll call you if anything changes," he assured me. "But I feel like we're out of the woods."

I relented with a sigh. "I suppose. It just doesn't feel right leaving you alone."

"Hey." Noah stood from the couch and stepped over to me. "You've done more than enough. You've been my rock this entire day. I swear... I would have lost it if you weren't here."

His gaze was so intense, I forced my eyes away, pinning them just over his shoulder. It felt like he was staring into the very naked parts of my soul. He was spying on all the broken bits that I kept locked away and hidden.

I froze when Noah took my chin into his calloused hand and tilted my head, forcing my eyes on his. "Hey," he repeated. "Thank you."

It was a simple "thank you," but it felt like so much more. *Everything* felt like so much more with Noah.

"You're welcome." It was a miracle I'd managed to speak under his heated gaze. What was he thinking? What was he trying to see? I swallowed. "Goodnight, Noah."

"Goodnight."

He took a step back, pressing his coffee cup to his lips as I turned away from him. I stopped briefly to glance at Sam, smiling warmly.

As I left the hospital, a chill washed over me. I knew it was for the best and that I needed to sleep—I knew there was nothing more I could do...

But I couldn't help but feel a magnetic pull back into that tiny, sterile hospital room.

There was love in that room.

There was home.

CHAPTER TWENTY-TWO

NOAH

"**S**urprise!"

Sam and I entered the house to a grand welcome of familiar faces. I had known about the celebration—it was all Chelsie's idea. She had texted me at two A.M. after leaving the hospital that first night, saying, *"Can't sleep. Planning an epic welcome home party for Sam in my head. Thoughts?"*

It was a great idea. Whether or not she could pull it off in thirty-six hours was the real question... but she had.

Chelsie Combs always came through.

I watched Sam's face light up as balloons floated to the vaulted ceiling and friends and family blew bubbles and blared noisemakers. The smell of homemade treats and confections assaulted my senses.

"Oh, boy," Sam shouted, jumping up and down. "Nana and Pappy are here, Dad!"

My parents, Lucinda and Robert Hayes, smiled as they approached us. They had flown in from Seattle after finding out about the accident. I didn't see my parents often with my busy schedule and the cross-country distance, so it was always special when they came into town, even when the circumstances were far from ideal.

"Sweet Noah," my mother said. She clutched my face between her hands, her assortment of rings and baubles pressing into the hollows of my cheeks. Mom was almost a foot shorter than me—a petite woman with striking silver hair and light green eyes. She stood on her tiptoes to plant an affectionate kiss along my jaw.

"Hey, Mom," I greeted.

Dad slapped a strong arm against my shoulder. "Son," his said. "We came as soon as we heard."

My father was a similar height to me, hovering around six-foot-two. He had always been on the leaner side, but a prominent potbelly was beginning to protrude from his belt buckle. His facial hair had been graying over the years, and the wrinkles on his face grew more visible every time I saw him.

"I know, Pops," I replied, watching as my son flew from person to person. Sam was being smothered in giant hugs and relieved kisses.

"I was really brave!" Sam declared. He held out the lollipop he had been clinging to on the drive home.

Chelsie appeared from the kitchen with Rosa close behind. "You're home," Chelsie grinned, bending down and holding her arms out to Sam. He ran full force into her embrace. "I missed the big entrance. I was helping Rosa with the lasagna."

"That's okay, Miss Chelsie. Daddy said to make sure I tell you thank you for my party."

I sauntered into the living room, my eyes catching with Chelsie's as she cradled Sam in her arms. The smile she sent me was brimming with affection.

"You're very welcome," she told Sam.

"Mi dulce niño," Rosa cried, tossing her potholders onto the back of the sofa and pulling Sam into a tight squeeze. "Your arm! Misericordia de mi." She did the sign of the cross while looking up to the Heavens.

"You can sign my cast, Miss Rosa." Sam lifted his elbow as high as he could with a proud grin.

Smiling, I stepped over to the group. "Do you think you can get every person here to sign your cast, buddy?"

Sam's eyes rounded at the challenge. "Good idea, Dad. Let me get my markers." He raced up the staircase at record speed, disappearing into the play room.

Chelsie's smiled bloomed brighter as she crossed her arms over her blush-colored blouse. "He's a fighter, that's for sure."

"Mmm." My answer was distracted while I studied her, her eyes still lingering on where Sam had vanished up the flight of stairs.

Chelsie had been a shining light during some of the darkest days of my life; a shoulder to cry on when I thought my world was falling apart. She had a way of peeling away my layers, one at a time, digging deep, and breaching every vulnerable, buried piece of me.

Chelsie Combs was so much more than she believed. She was a field of vibrant wildflowers. She was children playing on a sunny day. She was lightning bugs at dusk. She was lemonade. She was magic.

She was every little joy in life, all tangled together in her perfect smile.

"What?"

I blinked when she addressed me.

Apparently, I'd completely zoned out while gawking at her.

"Is it my hair?" Chelsie toyed with a brilliant blonde strand. "Is something in my hair?"

A grin pulled at my lips. "Your hair looks great."

"You were staring."

"You assume it was a bad thing." Taking a small step forward, I leaned in and whispered, "I was just thinking about how pretty you look today."

Color flooded her cheeks. She lowered her eyes, digging the tip of her pointed shoe into the area rug. "Oh... well, thanks."

I found a strange satisfaction in the crimson rouge that stained her skin. Compliments never came easy for her, and there was something inherently charming about that.

Chelsie cleared her throat, slapping a hand along her thigh. "Well, I need to get the lasagna in the oven."

She bolted back into the kitchen while my eyes trailed her.

Rosa approached me, whistling in way that sounded like pity. "Oh, Noah. You've got it bad, muchacho."

I scoffed at her, glancing around the room to make sure no

one had heard. "I don't pay you to analyze my personal life, Rosa."

"No, I do that for free." She jabbed a firm finger into my ribcage. "Tell her, señor. You must."

"This is not a conversation I want to have right now."

"Life is too short, mi amigo. There is only now." Rosa shot me a pointed look before following Chelsie into the kitchen.

Damn her and her sage wisdom.

A sigh left me as I pushed Rosa's words out of my mind and surveyed my friends and family. Miles and Lisa were munching on appetizers, a group of cousins were mingling by the dessert table, and my parents had joined Sam upstairs to fetch his arts and crafts bin.

Wait... where were Devon and Tad?

I migrated into the kitchen where the smell of fresh herbs enveloped me, watching as Chelsie and Rosa carried two large pans of homemade lasagna over to the oven. "Hey, where's Devon? You two didn't come together?"

She faltered, setting the dish on top of the stove. "He, uh... never came home last night." She swiped a lock of hair out of her eyes. "I haven't been able to get ahold of him all day. His phone is turned off."

Worry pinched at me. "Really? Do you know where he went yesterday?"

Chelsie looked flustered as she shook her head. "He said he was getting drinks with Tad last night around eight. That was the last time I'd heard from him."

Glancing at the clock, I noted it was a little after eleven A.M. It was possible they had drank too much and were still passed out. I nodded, biting my lip. "He'll turn up."

I'd be lying if I said I wasn't pissed. This was Sam's home-coming celebration after almost *dying*, and Sam was Devon's godson for fuck's sake.

Sometimes I really hated that bastard.

Chelsie smiled faintly. "I'm sure he will."

The doorbell rang, severing my next words. Excusing myself, I headed toward the front of the house, wondering why they didn't just let themselves in.

Running a hand through my hair, I pulled open the door and blinked when I noticed who was standing on the other side of the threshold.

I forgot I'd even invited her.

"Beth."

CHELSIE

I puttered around the kitchen island, mixing pasta salads together and slicing up French bread while Rosa pulled an apple strudel out of the oven.

"Deliciosa," Rosa exclaimed, lowering her nose to the strudel.

Standing on my tiptoes, I pulled a stack of party plates out of the cupboard. "That smells incredible."

"Muy," Rosa agreed. She turned to me, wiping her hands on a decorative dish towel. A question glinted in her dark eyes. "Señorita, forgive me if it's not my place, but I must ask. Señor Noah... you enjoy his company, yes?"

I stopped in my tracks, caught off guard by the query. "Um... yes, I do. He's a wonderful friend."

"Si. He's a good man. An honest man."

I tucked my lips between my teeth with an agreeable nod.

Rosa leaned over the kitchen island, taking my hands into her own. "My child. I see the way you look at each other. I see how happy you make him. You are an angel sent from Heaven." She squeezed my palms, shaking them vigorously. "Noah is a different man since you came into his life. You've put light back in his eyes. You must see it."

Air stalled in my throat as I stood there, frozen in place, processing Rosa's words.

No... *no.*

Rosa had it all wrong. It wasn't like that with Noah. "I appreciate your perspective... but Noah and I are just friends. Maybe you've misinterpreted something."

"I see what I see," she said with conviction. "And I will say this: I had a man like Noah once. His name was Paco. Back when I was a jovencita—a very young girl. But I did not follow my heart." Rosa held a hand firmly over her chest, her eyes misting. "I thought a better life was waiting for me in the states. Mi madre took me from my home in Mexico to start fresh here in New York. I married a man all wrong for me. He did not speak to my heart the way mi amor did back in Mexico."

Emotion sluiced me as I watched the tears well in Rosa's eyes.

"I wonder every day if he's waiting for me, but I cannot go back now. Too much time has passed. I failed my heart." Rosa reached for my hands again, squeezing my fingers. "You are a smart muchacha. Do not make the same mistakes I did. Listen to the song in your heart. It only plays for one."

Rosa let go of my hands as I blinked back my own tears. My feet were secured to the kitchen floor, my head spinning, mind racing. "I... I'm with Devon," I said with a crack in my voice.

She smiled knowingly. "I see what I see." Rosa turned back to the stove and began cutting into the strudel, serenading the kitchen with Spanish melodies.

I swallowed. Glancing down at my hands, I noticed they were holding onto the edge of the island so tight, my knuckles had gone white.

"Combs."

Noah appeared behind me. I whipped around, startled, knocking a serving dish to the floor. It cracked in half. "Crap."

"Here, let me help," said an unfamiliar female voice.

I looked up at the pretty blonde bending over to help me pick up the dish. "Thanks," I murmured.

When we stood back up, the woman extended her hand. "I'm Beth."

"How do you know Sam?" I asked guardedly, clearing my throat and returning the handshake.

Noah interjected. "I, uh, actually met Beth a few minutes before Sam's accident at the playground. I followed up with her when I was in the hospital to tell her about the fall, and we've been chatting ever since."

My lips drew together in a tight line. Noah met a random stranger at the park and invited her to his son's welcome home party a few days later?

Beth tucked a loose strand of hair behind her ear, revealing a golden hoop earring. "It's weird, I get it. I have this habit of making new friends everywhere I go," she laughed nervously. "Maybe we can grab coffee sometime?"

My eyebrows raised with skepticism.

I did not make new friends easily; I was a private person with years of pent-up trust issues. While I appreciated the sentiment, I didn't exactly foresee going on picnics and coffee dates with this woman—Beth was a stranger. "Sure. Sounds great."

I was also a people-pleaser, so I forced a compliant smile.

Beth smiled back, bobbing her head up and down. "I look forward to it."

My eyes roamed over the length of the young blonde, studying her—reading her. She was standing so close to Noah, their shoulders were touching.

Beth was beautiful, no doubt. Her skin looked like it had never seen a day of sun, and her features were feminine and delicate. She had chocolate brown eyes and perfect white teeth. Her smile was her finest attribute, and she was currently flashing it in Noah's direction.

Noah gazed back with a distinctive twinkle in his eye.

I ground my teeth together until my jaw ached, realizing that I was still holding onto the broken dish and the sharp edges were digging into my hand.

"Let me officially introduce you to Sam," Noah said, placing his hand on the small of Beth's back.

My gaze narrowed in on the gesture as I bit down on my bottom lip. I was surprised Noah felt inclined to introduce this woman to his son already. She could be a crazed, delusional fan.

Beth nodded. "I'd love that." She offered me a smile that reached her eyes. "It was so nice to meet you, Chelsie. I know how hard it is to find trustworthy babysitters these days."

Um... babysitter?

Outrage burned me. I couldn't help the queasy flutter in my stomach, or the rush of anger that made my skin flush.

Responding with a tight-lipped smile, I looked sharply at Noah. "Right. I feel honored to be his... babysitter."

Noah's face flashed with guilt as he turned and guided Beth out of the kitchen. My heart was racing, fists clenched at my sides.

"She is muy bonita." Rosa glanced over to where Noah and Beth had been standing. "Very pretty."

I shrugged, feigning indifference, before changing the subject. "Do you think these will be enough brownies?"

Rosa smiled. "Si. Now, go enjoy the party. You help too much."

"Chelsie?"

My head shot up at the familiar sound of my name.

Devon.

"Pardon me, Rosa." I darted out of the kitchen and into the living room, coming face-to-face with Tad and Devon. "Devon, you look..."

Awful. Terrible.

Drunk?

When I approached him, I didn't smell any remnants of alcohol. *Was he sick?*

"I made it," Devon grinned, his eyes glazed and bloodshot. He raised a victorious arm in the air, his balance teetering, and his hair looking like it hadn't been combed in a week.

"Devon, what happened? Where were you? We were worried..."

"Just having a little fun, eh, Tad?" he fidgeted.

Tad stuffed his hands into his pockets, rocking back and forth between both feet. He also looked disheveled.

I stepped closer to the two men, my stance guarded. "Are you... on drugs?"

Devon burst out laughing. "You're the only drug I need, baby," he said, bending down and scooping me up. He spun me in a clumsy circle as I pushed back at his chest.

"Devon, put me down. You're making a scene."

Noah and Beth appeared at the bottom of the stairs. "You're

alive." Noah's irritated tone morphed into anger as he moved forward, squinting at Devon. "Whoa, are you strung out?"

Devon set me down, almost dropping me to the floor. I smoothed out my blouse and crossed my arms over my chest, shocked by the display. I had never known Devon to abuse drugs. I'd been concerned about his increased drinking habits, but drugs had never crossed my mind.

Devon stepped over to one of the food tables and grabbed a large handful of potato chips. He shoved them into his mouth, dispersing crumbs all over the floor. Guests began to quiet their conversations to take in the scene.

"You've got to go," Noah ordered, grabbing his front man by the arm. "We'll talk tomorrow."

Devon yanked himself free with a dismissive huff. "I'm here for the party, bro. You invited me, remember?"

"Go home and fucking sleep it off. We'll talk tomorrow."

Tad nodded his head, signaling Devon to follow.

Devon sniffed. "Whatever, dude. Fuck this shit."

"Devon, what is going on?" I intervened, equally stunned and hurt.

"Let him go, Chelsie," Noah urged.

"Don't tell my girlfriend what to do." Devon pivoted, positioning himself in front of Noah. "Not your call."

Miles interrupted. "Knock it off. Go get some air—both of you."

"Fuck you," Devon snapped at the bassist. "This doesn't concern you."

"You want to do this, man?" Noah challenged. "In my goddamn living room with my entire family watching?"

I placed my hand on Devon's elbow to subdue him, but he swung it back without looking, forcing me to waver on my feet.

Noah shot him a death glare as he lurched forward, the veins in his neck distending. "Don't fucking lay a hand on her."

"You're just bitter because you never will."

Noah shoved at Devon's chest. "Get out of my house."

"Fine. But I'm taking my girlfriend with me." Devon glanced over Noah's shoulder at Beth, sneering as he added, "Enjoy your Chelsie clone."

"Get the fuck out."

Instinct had me backing away from Devon—I'd seen this look in a man's eyes before, and it scared me to death. He wasn't himself. "I'm going to stay here. Noah's right... sleep it off."

Devon stared at me in silence while a few harrowing beats ticked by. Then he sniffed with an icy laugh and wiped at his nose. "You know what? We're done. I'm going to Tad's to cool down." Devon issued me a disparaging wave. "Enjoy your last night in my million-dollar condo."

My heart sank.

He grabbed another fistful of chips and followed Tad out the front door, slamming it so hard, the pictures on the walls rattled. A stunned silence enveloped the crowd as nausea swept through me like a monsoon.

What in the world just happened?

Had Devon... *broken up with me?*

No, no, no. That wasn't Devon. That wasn't *my* Devon.

My Devon was kind and patient and loving. The person I just witnessed didn't hold a candle to the man I knew.

"I – I'm so sorry," I stuttered to no one in particular. "I don't know what that was all about."

Rosa was quietly praying in the corner. "The Devil got inside that boy," she murmured.

Noah's hands were balled into fists at his side, his eyes fixed to the floor before he pinned them on me. "Can I borrow you, Combs?"

Pushing back tears, I nodded.

I followed Noah downstairs into the finished basement, away from the crowd, away from the curious chatter. I was about to speak when he pulled me into a strong hug, his arms holding me close, firm and protective. I hadn't realized how tense I was until my body instinctively relaxed in his grip and I collapsed against his hard frame. He smelled like sandalwood and soap.

He smelled like home.

"Shit." Noah's chest vibrated as he spoke, his voice low and raspy. "Are you okay?"

My cheek grazed the front of his shirt as I nodded. "I think so." A tapered breath left me, sounding hopeless and uneven. "Did he really just break up with me?"

"He just needs to cool down. You can stay here tonight if you want."

Noah sighed, tickling the hairs on the top of my head, tempting me to say yes. I knew I shouldn't, though. "I'll be okay. Apparently, I need to start packing."

God, where would I go?

I had foolishly quit my job without a second thought, with no backup plan. I would be starting back from square one, no better off than I was when I'd walked out on Ian Masterson five years ago. How had I allowed myself to become dependent all over again?

Had I learned nothing?

The realization made me feel ill.

"I can't believe he's using."

Noah's words broke through my self-deprecation. He pulled back, but was still close enough that I could feel his breath against my face. "What do you think he was on?" I asked, looking up at him through watery eyes.

"Cocaine."

A chill raced down my spine. "I can't believe it..."

I never anticipated this—I never expected Devon Sawyer to fall down such a dark path.

He wasn't Ian.

I wasn't falling back into old patterns.

He. Wasn't. Ian.

Had my friendship with Noah triggered it? Was *I* responsible for his poor decisions? "This seems so out of character," I whispered raggedly.

Noah rubbed the back of his neck. "Tad used for over a year. It almost broke up the band. Drugs were never Devon's scene, but money and fame can be powerful things. He's never been satisfied... he's always needed more."

"What do we do?" I wondered. "We have to help him."

"Only he can help himself," Noah said gravely. "And I sure fucking hope he does. Fast."

I scrubbed both hands through my hair. Part of me couldn't

accept that. I needed to help him—I needed to *try*. It was in my bones. "He seems to really have it out for you," I said with a gulp. "Do you think he honestly believes... ?" My voice trailed off, my eyes hopefully finishing the question.

"That we're sleeping together?"

Blush tinged my cheeks as I nodded faintly.

"I think he thinks that I want to." His words didn't falter; his voice didn't waver. He was staring right at me, so unabashedly.

My breath caught.

Do you?

It was on the tip of my tongue, but God, I didn't have the guts to ask. "Rosa... she was talking to me earlier. She also thinks there's something going on between us." I studied him, monitoring his micro-expressions. "Or... that there should be, anyway. It was crazy talk."

Noah's eyes dipped. "We're an enigma. We're something people can't understand."

That made so much sense.

And... no sense at all.

"What are we exactly?"

That was the million-dollar question—as if my relationship with Noah could be explained away in a simple word or phrase. As if there was an appropriate title we could bestow upon ourselves.

There wasn't. There couldn't be.

We simply just... *were*.

Noah found my eyes again, his own flaring with something heated. A yearning of some kind. A carefully-veiled poignancy. "We're whatever you want us to be."

I sucked in a mouthful of air, almost choking on its density.

Was that an invitation? A starting point? It felt as if Noah had just handed me a box of crayons and a blank sheet of paper and told me to get to work.

I decided to gift him with the safest answer. "I like us the way we are."

It was the truth, after all, but the spark seemed to dim in Noah's eyes. His Adam's apple bobbed in his throat. "Right," he said in a low voice.

Forcing a smile, I wondered what Rosa saw. What Devon saw.

What Noah saw.

What kind of grand artistry unfolded on their pieces of paper?

I was too afraid to ask—a coward, terrified to give life to any of the illustrations.

"Beth seems nice."

The words fell out unplanned, and I wasn't sure why I said them—to change the subject? Redirect the conversation?

To hear from Noah what he really thought of the mysterious blonde upstairs?

"She is," he acknowledged.

Noah didn't indulge me. He didn't elaborate. He didn't give into my passive aggressive attempt at questioning his intentions.

"Let's get back to the party," he muttered, pivoting away, stuffing his hands into his pockets. "I just wanted to make sure you were okay."

I nodded mutely.

Something was tugging at me... a vague emptiness. A sense of regret.

It felt as if I had missed an opportunity, or passed up a critical moment.

Whatever it was, it was over, because Noah swept past me without another word and disappeared upstairs.

CHAPTER TWENTY-THREE

CHELSIE

The party eventually got back on track, despite Devon's dramatic entrance and exit. The food was delicious, and I had never seen Sam happier. That was all that really mattered—it was the whole point. So, even with the break-up hovering over me like a black cloud, I tried my best to enjoy myself.

I said my goodbyes a few hours later and headed back to the condo to pack, flipping on the lights as I entered through the front door in futile hope that Devon would be inside waiting for me.

He wasn't.

Sighing sadly, I moved through the condominium, tossing my purse onto the coffee table and kicking off my shoes. I pulled out my phone to see if Devon had contacted me, sucker-punched with disappointment when he hadn't. My bottom lip slid between my teeth as I debated reaching out to him, but I hesitated when I heard a noise coming from the master bedroom.

I froze.

A familiar fear rattled my bones. I had been so preoccupied with this new development with Devon that I'd forgotten to be more cautious. I'd forgotten to be afraid.

I had forgotten about Ian's shadow lurking around every corner.

As I approached the door to the bedroom, my bare feet

tiptoed across the hardwood floor with caution, a tentative hand reaching for the knob. My heartbeats thrummed in my ears, trouncing my senses like a bass drum.

When I pushed the door open, a gasp fell out.

I propelled myself backward, flush against the far wall, as I came face-to-face with Ian Masterson.

He was here. He was waiting for me.

And I was completely alone.

"Ian." My mouth was so dry, the word had barely squeaked out. Every extremity began to shake at the sight of him.

"Hey, Chelly Bean," he grinned. "It's been a while."

I pressed my fingernails into my palms, reminding myself that I was indeed awake. This was not a recurring nightmare. "What are you doing here?"

"I missed you."

Swallowing, my heart leaped.

Ian had changed over the years, his complexion haggard and gaunt. His cheeks were sunken-in, sharpening his already prominent features. Strands of silver hair peeked out through his mop of blonde curls. I idly wondered what I'd ever seen in him, aside from a broken man who needed fixing. "Ian... you need to leave. You need to stay away from me."

There was a wicked gleam in his eyes as he stepped toward me. "Oh, Chelsie. Innocent, naïve Chelsie," he sing-songed. "We have so much to catch up on."

Flustered, I pulled out my phone to dial 9-1-1, but Ian was on me before I could complete the call.

A scream pierced the air, echoing deftly through every room, every hallway, every nook and cranny. It was my scream. It was the same scream from all those years ago. The inflection, the pitch, the spectrum of fear. Nothing had changed. This scream belonged to Ian. He had dusted it off and brought it back to life like a special piece of china only unboxed for special occasions.

Ian knocked the cell phone from my hands, wrapping his fingers around my neck and pressing me further into the wall. "I wouldn't do that. Lover boy isn't gonna save you."

I lifted my chin with as much courage as I could muster. "I don't need saving anymore."

"No?" His fingers curled as he leaned in, alcohol-laced breath tickling my face and curdling my insides. Two slate eyes danced with amusement. "Little damsels always need saving."

"I'm strong now," I gulped, my quivering body betraying my words. "A fighter."

"I hope you *do* put up a fight," he leered, grazing his fingers down my throat, then my chest, until he was palming my breast in his dirty hand. "More fun that way."

I spit in his face.

Saliva dribbled down his cheekbone and along his jaw while rage blackened the humor in his eyes. Ian paused to study me, his tongue poking out to lick away the remnants of my spit. "You still taste sweet," he bit out, muscles twitching with anger. "Bet your pussy does, too."

Panic coursed through me as I began to struggle in his grip. "Get off me, Ian."

"How 'bout I get off *in* you?"

"Don't touch me. Let me go!" When I clawed at him, my fingernails raking down the side of his neck, he tackled me, tossing me to the floor like I was a bag of trash.

My head struck hard against the wood grains, and I saw stars.

They weren't stars, though. It was only my occipital lobe sending out electrical signals, forcing shocks of light to permeate my vision.

Stars were meant for wishes and fairytales.

This was no fairytale.

"Just like old times, huh?" Ian snarled as he mounted me, straddling my waist and pinning my wrists above my head with one hand. He used his free hand to unzip my jeans and tug them down my legs. "Time to take back what's always been mine."

Fear drenched me.

No, no, no.

I felt weak.

I had no fight in me when he overpowered me like this; I was accustomed to Ian taking what he wanted.

"No."

The word finally passed through my lips, but it only made him laugh. "You know that only gets me more excited."

"No," I repeated, louder, braver. I wasn't the same girl I was back then—I'd evolved. I was not the frail, lilting flower from years ago. I was a survivor, and survivors never gave up. "I said *no*," I hissed through my teeth.

My body began to resist him. A primal need to protect myself took over, and I lashed out at my attacker in every way I could. My legs thrashed about, trying to connect with some part of his body. And when my knee lifted and connected with his groin with more force than I'd expected, I yanked my wrists free from his punishing grip.

Ian growled in pain as I rolled onto my stomach and began to crawl away.

I was pulling myself to my feet when a hand wrapped around my ankle, sending me back to the ground. Another scream pierced the air, and I prayed someone would hear it.

Sluiced with horror, I eyed a decorative vase sitting on a shelf as Ian tried to mount me again. I only had a fleeting second, so I gathered every ounce of strength I had and careened my body toward the shelving display.

I just missed it.

Ian flipped me onto my back for a second time, wrapping his icy fingers around my throat. "You're going to pay for that, you stupid bitch."

I saw evil in his dark eyes as I gasped and choked, clawing at his arms while his hands tightened around my neck.

Was this it? Was I going to die here on Devon's living room floor? Was he going to rape and violate me before or after he squeezed the air from my lungs?

The thought was too much to bear.

I had built a new life for myself. I had too much to live for now.

Noah.

Noah's face flashed through my mind as my lungs burned, begging for reprieve. I pictured him barreling through the front door and saving my life.

Not Devon.

Noah was the hero in my story.

Ian kissed me hard, forcing my mouth open with his teeth and shoving his tongue in and out. His vile, disgusting tongue.

I gagged.

Then I bit down as hard as I could.

"Arrrgh!" Ian released his hands from around my neck as blood pooled down his chin.

I sucked in a giant gulp of air, sputtering on Ian's blood. I knew I only had moments before he struck again, so I lunged toward the vase, successfully wrapping my fingers around the glass neck. Without thought, I whirled around and smashed it against his face with a sickening *thunk*.

Ian cried out in pain, collapsing backward. "You're fucking *dead*."

Fear bubbled inside my gut at the realization that I hadn't knocked him unconscious—I hadn't even broken the glass.

The battle wasn't over.

Racing toward the guest bedroom, I looked over my shoulder to see Ian climbing to his feet. I threw open the door and ran to the bedside table, frantic, yanking out the drawer and snatching the pistol tucked inside. Terror consumed me when Ian's footsteps closed in.

"Boo."

I whipped around to face him, pointing the gun square at his chest.

Ian faltered.

Then he laughed with ice, as if to erase the fear that had flashed across his face. "You actually think I believe you know how to use that thing?" He wiped at his mouth with his shirt sleeve, leaving a bloody streak across his cheek.

"Feel free to call my bluff." My voice was calm, but my trembling hands betrayed me. I inched forward, my index finger on the trigger, my opposite hand trying to hold the weapon steady.

Ian held his palms up and slowly backed away. "I guess you are a fighter now, Chelly Belly. It's cute," he said with a smirk before spitting a dollop of blood to his right. The tone of his voice turned menacing as he finished, "Round two will be less cute."

"Get out of my house."

Moving forward, rage heightened inside of me. I wanted to

pull the trigger. I wanted to see him explode before my eyes, disintegrating into black ashes and dust.

But even more than that... I wanted him to live.

I wanted him to rot in a prison cell for the rest of his pathetic life, knowing I had won. He had failed to surmount me. His control over me had been permanently severed.

That would be a far worse punishment for a narcissistic pig like Ian Masterson... *knowing he had lost.*

"See you soon." Ian winked at me before turning on his heel and running out of the room like the coward he was.

Following, my chest heaved as I watched him disappear out the apartment door.

I lowered my shaking arms, shutting the door as hard as I could and double-bolting it. The pistol was dangling at my side. The weight of it was heavy, but not as heavy as the awareness that I had almost been raped and killed.

I almost died.

Setting the weapon down at my feet, I massaged my throat, running the tips of my fingers along where Ian had choked me.

I need to call the police. I stumbled into the hallway where Ian had knocked the phone from my grip before falling to my knees and punching in the familiar numbers.

"I'd like to report an assault," I said into the speaker.

I gave them the address. I told them his name. I detailed the attack to the best of my recollection, and when they advised me to stay on the line, I dropped the phone to the floor and fell back against the wall.

I crumbled.

I broke.

My face fell into my hands as years of pent-up torment and self-loathing spilled out of my eyes. I wailed and screamed and smashed my fists against the floor, releasing what felt like a lifetime of locked-up skeletons with every blow. I tipped over, lying sideways on the ground as warm tears pooled beneath my cheek. My knees curled up to my chest...

And I just sobbed.

CHAPTER TWENTY-FOUR

CHELSIE

I had given my statement and answered their questions, ultimately refusing medical treatment. Exhaustion had won out.

"Do you have a safe place you can go tonight?" an officer had inquired.

"Yes."

There was only one place I wanted to be.

I had tried contacting Devon multiple times to no avail. At one point, I'd even tried Tad, but his phone was also turned off.

So, there I was, standing on Noah's doorstep late into the evening hours with a blanket wrapped loosely around my shoulders. Officer Fenton stood beside me as I waited.

When Noah opened the door, the look on his face could only be described as shellshock. "Chelsie?"

He stared at me with a thousand questions in his eyes.

"Miss Combs was assaulted this evening and she asked me to bring her here. I wanted to make sure she had a safe place to spend the night before I left," the officer explained.

"Of course." Noah nodded quickly, his worried eyes never leaving me. Heaving in a rickety breath, he murmured, "Jesus... come in."

"Very well. Here's my card, Miss. Please don't hesitate to

contact me." The officer gave us a friendly nod and headed back to his patrol car.

I grazed the card between my thumb and finger before glancing up at Noah, who was still staring at me, his irises glimmering with concern beneath the porch light. Swallowing, he broke our gaze and opened the door wider to allow me inside.

I was about to speak when I noticed Beth sitting on the couch, gaping at me with wide eyes.

"Chelsie, what happened?"

Frowning, I swallowed back a sudden lump in my throat. I hadn't expected Noah to have company... let alone, *her*. "I'm really sorry... I can go. I'll call myself a ride."

"Nonsense." Beth stood, reaching for her cardigan and purse. "I'll go. I should relieve the babysitter, anyway."

I watched as Beth offered me a sympathetic smile, then inched up on her tiptoes to plant a kiss on Noah's cheek. "Call me tomorrow," she told him.

Then she was gone.

The door clicked shut as Noah turned to face me, our eyes meeting in a powerful hold.

While we stared at each other in silence, I recalled everything I'd felt when I thought I was going to die.

Through the horror and fear, I had seen... him.

Noah.

It was *his* face that had flickered through my mind in what I'd thought might have been my final moments alive. It was *he* who I pictured breaking down the door and coming to my rescue like my very own knight in shining armor. It wasn't my mother or father. It wasn't Devon.

It was Noah.

Why?

"Ian," I finally said in a croaked whisper, answering Noah's unspoken question. I hated saying his name; it tasted like kerosene and ash. Reaching for the scarf wrapped around my neck, I tugged it loose, letting it flutter to my feet.

Noah's eyes landed on the deep bruises already coloring my throat. I watched his jaw clench, the muscles in his face twitching. "He did that to you?"

I nodded. "He was waiting for me in the condo when I went over to pack. I managed to break free just long enough to grab your gun."

He stepped toward me, his features taut with something frightening as he reached out to cup my face. "Did he rape you?"

A gasp escaped when he lovingly cradled my jaw between his palms. His touch prompted a flurry of goosebumps to dance up and down my skin. I closed my eyes, finally feeling... *safe*. "No," I said softly. "He tried."

"Fuck." Noah tugged me to his chest and wrapped his arms around me in a fierce hug. His heartbeat vibrated into me, giving me comfort.

I was breaking again, the tears biting at my eyelids, begging to be set free. "I thought of you," I confessed. My words were barely audible with my lips pressed up against his t-shirt. His hand tangled in my hair, drawing me even closer. "I thought of you when he was choking me—when I thought I was going to die, and I... I don't know why, Noah."

I felt his heart rate speed up when my confession registered, so I inched back to look at him. I needed to see him.

I needed to know what he was thinking.

NOAH

She was peering up at me so intensely, it made my stomach flutter. Chelsie had thought of *me* when she thought her life was ending?

It was... profound.

Now she was begging me with her peridot eyes to tell her what that meant. But it wasn't the time for that because she was almost murdered.

Murdered.

My mind raced with madness, thinking about never holding her in my arms again, or watching her nose crinkle when I told a bad joke. I thought about never smelling the lavender in her hair or the citrus on her skin. It made my blood run ice cold.

I had to keep touching her. I had to keep feeling her warmth to remind myself she was okay. Yanking her back to my chest, I kissed the top of her head, exhaling my relief into her hair. Chelsie started to tremble in my arms as my shirt absorbed her tears.

She balled her fists next to her face as she cried. "I was so scared."

"You're okay now. You were so fucking brave." I rubbed the small of her back with one hand and massaged her scalp with the other, peppering more kisses into her knotted tresses. "You're okay."

She lifted her head, her cheeks damp. "What if he comes back? What if I don't survive next time?"

No... *fuck, no.*

"I won't let that happen."

Chelsie notably relaxed with a long sigh before pulling away and wiping at her eyes with the sleeve of her blouse. "I could use a drink," she told me.

I blinked, taking a moment to process her request. "I've got whiskey and wine."

Whiskey had been her choice. I brought her the bottle, along with two small glasses, as we situated ourselves on the couch. I sipped my drink over ice, while Chelsie swallowed the liquor in one shot. Her head collapsed against my shoulder as she clutched a pillow between her arms, picking absently at the embellishments along its edges.

"Thank you," she said, using her other hand to twirl the glass between her fingers. "I just needed something to help me wind down. I still feel... frazzled."

"That's understandable. You experienced a trauma." I felt her body rise and fall against me, warm and alive. She reached for the whiskey and poured a few more ounces into her glass.

"I just want to pass out," she admitted. "I know I won't be able to sleep tonight."

She downed the second shot, gagging slightly, then poured another. "Don't overdo it, Combs," I warned, handing her a bottle of water.

Chelsie set the whiskey on the coffee table before gulping down the water. "I just want my brain to stop replaying everything. I'll never forget the look on his face when he was strangling me, Noah. I can't get it out of my head."

My heart ached. I could only imagine how scared she was fighting for her life. "You should try to get some sleep."

She nodded against my shoulder and stood up, wobbling on both feet, before collapsing back down to the couch with a sheepish expression. "Oops. I think the alcohol is starting to hit me."

I pulled her to her feet. "I think you're going to pass out just fine. I'll help you to my room. I can take the couch again."

Chelsie clutched my arm with both hands as we made our way up the stairs. When we entered the bedroom, she staggered over to the bed with clumsy feet, then disappeared under the comforter. After I pulled the curtains closed and flipped off the light, I stopped briefly by the side of the bed to say goodnight. "I'm just downstairs if you need anything. You're safe, okay?"

The pillow shifted as she nodded.

I faltered for a moment, hesitant to leave her.

"Noah?"

It was dark in the room, but I could see her face peeking out from under the covers. Swallowing, I took a small step toward her. "Yeah?"

"Can you stay with me? I don't want to be alone tonight."

Inhaling sharply, I studied her outline masked in shadow while I registered what she was asking. I bit down on my cheek and moved in closer. "Combs..."

She was broken, vulnerable, and intoxicated. What would Devon think if he ever found out about this? Separated or not, she was still Devon's girl. Sharing a bed with her directly after a trauma—not to mention, a woman I had feelings for—did not seem like a rational proposal. Chelsie wasn't thinking clearly.

I needed to be the logical one.

Her voice was muted against the bedsheets as she added, "You make me feel safe."

Fuck.

She needed me; she shouldn't have to sleep alone tonight, and Devon wasn't here.

Screw logic.

I approached the other side of the bed, climbing in and situating myself underneath the covers. The bed squeaked beneath my weight as I moved toward the center of it, just close enough that I could feel her body heat emanating into me. A few rogue strands of her hair tickled my forehead as they fanned out across her pillow.

Chelsie rolled over to face me.

Don't do that. Just go to sleep. Don't do that.

We were close, with only a few inches between us. I felt her knees graze my own as she stared at me through the dark. "You should get some sleep," I prompted, mentally erasing the catch in my voice. It was stark against the shroud of silence.

"Will you hold me?"

Damnit.

Another terrible idea I was absolutely going to do. "Of course."

Chelsie scooted her body over to me, closing the gap between us as she nuzzled her face beneath my chin. I wrapped my arms around her, inhaling the whiskey on her breath and the lavender in her hair. She was warm, soft, intoxicating, and...

Mine.

It was a foolish thing to think. Only a goddamn fool would have fallen for the one woman who was off-limits.

But right now, in this room... I did have her.

She was in *my* bed; in *my* arms.

She was mine.

My fingers weaved through her hair, stroking gently, and I could have sworn she let out the tiniest moan. The sound sent shockwaves through my body, and my cock twitched in reply. Our legs were beginning to intertwine on their own accord as Chelsie inched her way closer, as if there was anywhere else to go. She was already pressed fully against me, impossibly and dangerously close.

She peered up at me, tipping her head until our eyes locked, our noses nearly touching.

"Thank you," she whispered.

Her breath caressed my lips like a forbidden kiss. "For what?"

"For everything. For making me feel."

I swallowed, my body humming. "For making you feel what?"

"Everything," she echoed.

Everything.

I didn't know what to make of that answer. The collection of meanings I could come up with were endless and could easily drive me mad, so I chose not to read into it. She was tipsy, rattled. Traumatized.

She was also cocooned against my torso, warming me up from the inside out. Chelsie was shameless in her proximity—almost every inch of her body blanketed me in some way, from her forehead, to her toes, to her wildly beating heart. I felt it rumble through my veins like a ticking time bomb, reminding me that this moment was fleeting. She was *not* mine.

She never would be.

"You're drunk," I murmured. It needed to be said, and maybe I needed the reminder more than she did.

Chelsie chewed her bottom lip, her eyes dancing across my face. "Is that all this is? A drunk moment?"

Don't go there, Combs. Not now. Not when you're pressed against me like the perfect lover.

My tongue disobeyed, begging for her to indulge me. "You tell me."

I'd given her the opportunity earlier in the day, but she had shot me down, insisting that she liked us the way we were.

Platonic.

Despite the dagger to my heart, that had settled it. I had made a conscious effort in that moment to move on. To get over her.

To pretend we were just friends.

And yet... here she was, our bodies twisted together, and her lips a hair's breadth away from mine.

Chelsie lowered her eyes. "What if I don't know what we are?"

"You know."

Her heartbeat danced with my own.

Th-thump, th-thump, th-thump.

The air was charged between us. If a match were lit, we would both go up in flames.

Or maybe we already had.

Chelsie glanced back up, her lips parting with my name. "Noah..."

"You don't have to say anything. We can talk more tom—"

But my words were cut short, stolen by her perfect mouth.

She was kissing me.

She was *kissing* me.

I froze with disbelief.

Fuck, Chelsie was kissing me.

When she made a little mewl, something in me ignited; my brain kicked back on, and I grabbed her face between my hands and shoved my tongue into her mouth. She went limp in my arms, making that sound again, as she succumbed to something bigger than us both.

Her hands clung to my t-shirt, tiny groans escaping her as my tongue plunged in and out, knotting with hers. Chelsie's legs continued to entwine with mine, a mess of tangled limbs, while she raised her left leg to wrap around my waist, her pelvis grinding into me.

I was hard. I was really fucking hard.

Eager fingers moved to grip my hair while our tongues danced, hers sweeping over the roof of my mouth, sliding in and out.

Goddamn... she tasted fucking magical. Like taffy apples at the fair. My entire body was on fire as I moaned into her mouth, and she replied by pressing herself harder against the rock-hard bulge in my jeans. My hips involuntarily bucked against her, craving her heat. "Fuck, Combs... you're killing me."

She reached for my belt buckle, and my dick beckoned for release. I wanted to be inside her. I wanted to pound her into the mattress while my name fell from her lips over and fucking over again, until she had no other choice but to be mine.

God, but we can't. We shouldn't.

My erection strained against denim as Chelsie's fingers fumbled with my zipper. Our mouths were still fused, bodies writhing, hands everywhere. Teeth crashed together as a deep growl rumbled in my chest, and I sucked her tongue into my mouth.

Maybe just the tip.

Fuck, it's never just the tip.

Chelsie released my pants to grip the hem of her shirt and pull it up over her head until her breasts were exposed, bathed in a sliver of moonlight from the crack in my drapes.

My eyes dipped, heart stuttering.

She arched her back, palming the nape of my neck and tugging my face to her chest. I groaned, nearly fucking losing it when my mouth closed around a dusky nipple, and she cried out. Chelsie's nails dug into my neck as I nicked her with my teeth, then laved my tongue over the pebbled bud before tasting the other.

I rolled her onto her back, moving over her and interlacing our fingers together while my lips trailed south. Her stomach fluttered beneath my wet kisses as I inched lower, grazing her belly button and landing at the edge of her jeans.

Glancing up, I wavered.

We shouldn't do this, my mind chanted.

She bowed her body, lifting her hips, seeking more attention. "Noah, please."

My eyes closed, overcome with lust and need and...

Everything.

Chelsie's hands trembled as she unhooked the button on her pants, jerked the zipper down, and shoved them off her waist until they bunched around her knees.

The animal in me took over when a hint of lavender silk caught my eye, stained with a pool of her wetness. I grabbed her jeans and tugged them all the way off her legs before moving the slip of underwear aside and diving between her thighs.

She practically screamed.

A moan of unparalleled satisfaction poured out of me when my tongue plunged inside her. I couldn't even spare the few seconds it would take to fully remove her panties, and instead, just pulled the small slip of silk to the side while my mouth feasted.

"Noah, Noah... oh my God..." She panted and squirmed, her hands landing in my hair and fisting. "Don't stop, please..."

Gripping her outer thigh with my palm, I drew her legs farther apart, sliding my tongue up her slit. "I want to make you feel good," I murmured against her, teasing her clit. She bucked upward with a sharp cry. "God, you're soaked."

My head lowered and I sucked her clit, finding the perfect rhythm as I inserted two fingers inside of her. Her thighs clamped my face, her body raising off the mattress, her whimpers desperate and erratic. Before bringing her over the edge, I lifted my face and removed my fingers, watching her writhe beneath me with tortured urgency.

"Please, don't stop," she begged.

I crawled my way up her body until we were face-to-face. Her eyes fluttered open, glazed over and laden with lust. Deep flush stained her cheeks while her hair splayed across the pillowcase in golden, chaotic waves. When our eyes locked, I reached down between her legs and pushed my fingers inside her again.

Chelsie's breath caught, her lips parting with a small squeak of surprise. We didn't break eye contact as I inserted a third finger and pumped roughly into her, my thumb working her clit. Our noses touched, our lips grazing, and I whispered raggedly, "I want to watch you break apart."

Her eyes flared, mouth still parted, as if words were caught in her throat with no way out. But I didn't want her words. I just wanted her to come.

I thrust my fingers in and out as her knees spread wider, her body tensing with a prelude to release. Wet, slippery sounds echoed throughout the quiet room as she soaked my fingers, and I bit down on my inner cheek to distract myself from the painful erection still straining my pants.

But this wasn't about me. This was about her—making her

feel safe, adored, cherished, especially in the aftermath of something so evil and violent.

This was about telling her exactly what I wanted us to be.

A sharp breath hitched in her throat as her body arched up, hands gripping my shoulders, fingers bruising.

"Come for me," I said against her lips, my thumb massaging harder.

She broke. Keeping her gaze fixed on me, Chelsie came with a throaty moan, squeezing me tight as I slowed my pace and leaned down to kiss her.

I stole the rest of her cry with my mouth, pulling my fingers out of her as I cradled her face, gently caressing her tongue with mine until she collapsed into a satiated heap below me.

But when I lowered my hands to her neck, she flinched, hissing through our kiss.

Shit.

Her bruises.

I pulled back, breathless and still in a daze. "I'm sorry."

"It's okay." Chelsie nicked my bottom lip with her teeth. "Keep kissing me."

A groan escaped me, my inner caveman demanding to be unleashed.

Want. Take. Have.

Her honey still slicked my fingers, and my lips tingled from our fevered kisses.

But hell... seeing her wince in pain when I touched her neck was a sharp slap back to reality. She'd just been assaulted by a madman; nearly raped.

As much as I wanted her, I cared about her too much to continue while she was intoxicated and traumatized.

I'd already taken it too far.

Somehow, I resisted, finding an ounce of strength and common sense. I ducked my head, moving off of her, just before her mouth claimed another kiss. "Chelsie, we should stop."

She touched her forehead to mine as she rolled over to face me, her hand curling behind my neck. Tilting her chin up, she placed a kiss to my lips. A sweet, perfect kiss. A promise of so much more. "Please... make love to me."

My eyes fluttered closed, willpower waning. "God... we can't. I don't want our first time to be like this."

"But we already—"

"That was for you. I wanted to make you feel good."

When she finally pulled away, she blinked with confusion.

Her eyes turned wounded.

"You know we can't," I said gently. "I refuse to be selfish when you're still in shock. You'll hate me in the morning."

"I could never hate you."

I massaged my thumb along her cheekbone. "I would hate me."

Reality seemed to claim her as she inched herself backward. "God, I'm sorry..." Chelsie reached for her discarded shirt and pulled it back over her head, then tugged the bedcovers up over her half-naked body. "I'm a mess. I didn't mean to pressure you. I—"

"Whoa, that's not what happened, okay?" I didn't want her regret, or her shame. I didn't want her apologies. I just wanted her to understand. "We can discuss in the morning when you're feeling more yourself. I'm not saying I don't want to take this further because I do. I really do." My cock twitched in agreement. "When the circumstances are right."

She nodded slowly, processing my words. "Okay."

"Get some rest. We'll talk tomorrow."

Worrying her lip between her teeth, she nodded again before rolling over and facing away from me.

Emptiness settled in the moment she was out of reach. I tried to get comfortable on my own side of the bed, my tongue still buzzing with remnants of tasting her, but Chelsie surprised me by turning onto her back to glance at me.

"Can you still hold me?"

My heartstrings tugged inside my chest—strings I thought had been tied into unbreakable knots a long time ago. "Of course," I said, echoing my answer from earlier. I would never say no to holding her; she was one of the few good things in my life, and I couldn't let go of something like that.

I moved across the bed and wrapped my arms around her, pulling her close to me. Her skin was warm, like a languid day at the beach. I could almost smell the saltwater and seashells in her hair.

It was winter in New York, but she would always be summer.

"Goodnight," she whispered into the crook of my arm, falling asleep in an instant. I could tell by the way her breathing slowed to placid, heavy breaths. I counted them for a while as if they were sheep. Perfect, brilliant sheep.

One. Two. Three.

In and out.

In and out.

I started timing them. Eight seconds per breath. If we slept for six hours, that would be 2,700 breaths she would take in my arms.

I tried to quiet my brain. At this rate, I would never sleep.

How could I, though?

Chelsie Combs was passed out in my bed, curled up against me like a fervent lover. We had kissed. I had sampled her sweetness. I knew the curve of her tongue and the way she arched her back when I gently tugged at her hair. I recalled the sounds she made when her bottom lip caught between my teeth.

I'd memorized the look in her eyes when she came.

Above all, I wanted to know more.

I wanted to know *everything*.

Sighing deeply, I nuzzled my face against her hair, giving her a tender squeeze. Despite my efforts to savor as many seconds as possible, sleep overcame me, and my breaths settled in time with hers.

CHAPTER TWENTY-FIVE

CHELSIE

I could have sworn I'd been awoken by the sound of giggles—giggles from a person of small and childlike stature. I felt tiny fingers playing with my hair, singing the theme to *Daniel Tiger's Neighborhood*. I tried to open my eyes, but the light was blinding, as if a thousand suns had been strategically placed into the room and their sole purpose was to burn out my retinas. Pressing a hand against my forehead, I tried in vain to cease the incessant pounding.

Then I realized there was, indeed, a child beside me.

"Sam?"

Was that my voice? I sounded haggard and feeble.

It didn't seem to faze the young boy bouncing to my right. "Good morning, Miss Chelsie! You had a sleepover again."

I blinked half a dozen times before Sam came into focus. He was kneeling between me and... Noah.

... Noah?

... *NOAH!*

Shit, shit, shit.

"Daddy was cuddling with you like he cuddles with me."

Shit.

Noah finally shifted on the bed, and my eyes panned over to him as I swallowed.

It hurt like hell to swallow.

I touched the bruised flesh along my throat, which spurred all the prior day's events to come rushing back like a violent windstorm.

"Can we make pancakes?" Sam inquired.

Noah was staring at the ceiling with his hands behind his head. I used what little energy I had to push myself up into a sitting position.

"Pancakes sound great," I said. My voice sounded like I'd smoked a pack a day for the last twenty years. "You know how to make them, right?"

Sam gaped at me with wide eyes and messy hair. "No, silly! I'm just a kid."

Noah cracked a smile, also not immune to his son's charms. "Why don't you go brush your teeth, buddy. We'll be down in a few minutes."

"Okay." He crawled off the bed on all fours and flew out the door, leaving us alone with our inevitable morning-after chat.

Oh my God. I'm having a morning-after with Noah.

When Noah turned to face me, I pulled the covers up to my chin, trying to hide from him—trying to hide from my indiscretions. "Before you say anything," I began, "I owe you a huge apology." I refused to look at him, even though I could almost see his brow contorting into a furrowed state. I envisioned his lips drawing into a thin line.

"For what?" he asked. "You didn't do anything wrong."

I forced my eyes in his direction, and it *hurt* to look at him. It pained me to gaze upon the man I crossed a massive line with.

I almost had sex with him. I'd wanted to.

My best friend.

My belly ached, insides twisting. "I did everything wrong," I said softly.

How did he not see that? How was he looking at me with anything other than disgust?

Sure, Devon had dumped me, but he was coked-up and not thinking clearly. We hadn't even discussed things yet.

I messed up.

Noah wasn't looking at me with disgust, though. He was

looking at me, yes—he was staring at me with such an impassioned gaze, I had to pull the covers up farther until they were tickling my nose. But there was no disgust. No regret or animosity.

There was something else.

"You remember what happened?" There was mild trepidation in his voice, and I wasn't sure what he wanted the answer to be.

"Yes," I squeaked out.

Oh, I remembered. Memories flashed through my mind of forbidden kisses, entangled limbs, and his face buried between my thighs.

I remembered wanting more. I had wanted *all* of Noah Hayes.

My cheeks burned, while other parts of me cheered.

"I'm so sorry, Noah," I rushed out. "I practically threw myself at you. I was just... drunk and upset."

Noah's expression changed. He looked... wounded. Like I'd just stolen something of great value from him.

"I'm glad I could be of service," he snapped. His features hardened, jaw tensing. The familiar sparkle had left his emerald eyes.

"God... I'm sorry I dragged you into my drama."

"Stop apologizing. You didn't drag me into anything. You really think you could force me to do something I didn't want to do?" Cynicism laced his tone. Every syllable was dripping with bitterness.

I swallowed again, my throat sore and scratchy. "You probably felt obligated to comfort me."

Noah laughed, but it wasn't a happy laugh. It was a contemptuous laugh that sent a shiver down my back. He sat up and leaned against the bed frame. "Obligated," he repeated, as if it was the most abhorrent word I could have uttered. It sliced through the air like a crude cut.

"I wasn't thinking clearly. I didn't mean to—"

"Just stop," he said.

Anxiety bubbled in the pit of my stomach. "What?"

"Stop talking." Noah pulled the covers off and threw his legs over the opposite side of the bed. His head was down, shoulders taut. "I don't want your excuses or justifications."

My fists clenched around the blanket. It was the only thing sheltering me from his hostility. He was facing away from me, so I watched as the muscles in his back flexed with indignation beneath the constraints of his white t-shirt. "They aren't excuses, Noah. It's the truth. Why are you punishing me for apologizing?"

He was silent as his hands gripped the side of the bed.

"Noah..."

"Go home, Chelsie."

Hot tears clouded my vision, my face flushing with chagrin at his dismissal. "Why are you being like this?"

He finally stood and faced me with a look that could only be described as audacity, his arms extending at his sides. "What the hell do you want from me, Combs?"

My knees were pulled up to my chest as tears began to fall. His tone was full of exasperation, as if he'd reached the end of some invisible rope. But I didn't know there was a rope. I wanted to give him more slack, but I didn't know how, and I couldn't conjure up the words he needed. "I don't know."

I knew I'd failed.

I'd pulled the rope right out of his hands.

"Go home."

Home.

Why did it feel like I was already home?

Inching toward the edge of the bed, I hesitated when my bare feet touched the cool surface of the floor. "What do you want from *me*?" I countered. My back was facing Noah, but I could picture his slow blink of frustration.

"Chelsie..."

Resignation. Weariness.

I rose from the mattress, turning to look at him, needing to see his face.

"I can't give you that answer," he said. "Not because I don't know... but because there's no point."

Chewing on my lower lip, I wrapped my arms around myself like a security blanket.

"I can't be what you need," he finished.

Panic erupted inside my chest at the finality in his tone. "What are you saying? We can't be friends?"

"I'm saying there is no *we*."

His words stung. The slow burn of dissolution and guilt rattled me as I rubbed my hands up and down my upper arms, my chin quivering. Only a king-sized bed stood between us, but it felt like a million miles.

I knew there was nothing more I could say. How could I possibly convey what he meant to me?

God... what *did* he mean to me?

Last night I had begged him to make love to me.

Today I was desperate to have my friend back.

"I'll call myself an Uber," I said, turning to exit the room.

When I glanced back over my shoulder at Noah, he was looking away from me, rubbing a hand down his face and shaking his head.

Disappointment.

I was good at disappointing people.

Maybe it was better this way.

I passed by Sam's bedroom before I reached the staircase. He was sitting on the floor, playing with cars and trucks, talking to himself as he pushed the tiny vehicles around the carpet. There were clothes popping out of his chest of drawers; an assortment of blues and oranges and yellows peeking out the tops. I closed my eyes for a moment, etching the image into my memory, envisioning the navy walls and plush white carpet. A dinosaur border displayed along the edges of the room, accenting all four walls. The ceiling fan circling around and around, sending the green and white striped drapes fluttering back and forth.

Sighing, I continued down the stairs, running a hand purposefully along the rail. It was cool beneath my fingertips. Eyeing the framed photos as I stepped down, I noticed the family photo with Ruby had been removed, replaced by a small cell phone picture of Sam and me eating ice cream together with goofy smiles on our faces.

Tears spilled down my cheeks as I inhaled a frayed breath and continued my descent.

When I scooped up my purse, I pulled out my phone and

checked the notifications. There were a ton of texts from Lisa, Julia, and Devon.

Lisa: *Are you okay?*

Julia: *I just saw you on the news!*

Devon: *Where are you?*

Lisa: *Did they catch him?*

Devon: *Call me.*

I shut off my phone and stuck it back into my purse.

Surely, Noah was going to follow me down the stairs and tell me not to leave. Then he was going to make his way into the kitchen to cook cinnamon pancakes, sausage, and scrambled eggs, while Sam helped crack the yolks and set the table. I'd help him wash the dishes as we exchanged familiar banter and discussed plans for the week.

But… none of that happened. The shower turned on upstairs, and I resigned myself to the fact that Noah was not going to pursue me. This time, I was on my own.

As I slung the purse strap over my shoulder, there was a persistent knock at the front door. My chin popped up, knowing exactly who it was.

I opened the door, revealing a sickly-looking Devon.

His eyes were bloodshot. His face looked gaunt, his skin lack-luster—almost gray in color. "Devon," I croaked out.

"Shit, Chelsie."

He charged through the entryway and wrapped his arms around me in a tight hug. My arms didn't instinctively rise to return the embrace like they used to, and instead, remained at my sides, limp and apathetic. I let out a long breath, muttering, "I needed you."

I was angry because he wasn't there for me when I was being strangled. He wasn't there to fight off my attacker when Ian had tried to murder me in cold blood on his living room floor.

Devon wasn't there.

And not because he'd run to the grocery store, or left to pick up Chinese take-out at our favorite place on Cedar Street—no, he was coked-out somewhere, oblivious to the world around me. He had deliberately turned off his phone to cut off communication with me. He chose to remain camouflaged in his seedy world of drugs and darkness.

I was also angry with myself.

I'd kissed Noah. I'd allowed him to do things to me—things I'd enjoyed, things that currently had my heart rate increasing and my thighs clenching as hazy memories swept through me.

Things I wanted to do again?

Confliction poked at me, making me feel itchy inside.

"Fuck," Devon whispered into the crook of my neck. "I've been blowing up your phone, worried sick. Did they catch that motherfucker yet?"

I pushed my palms against his chest and inched the sleeves of my sweater over my hands as I brushed a defiant strand of hair from my face. Devon skimmed my face with a blank look in his eyes, awaiting my answer.

A few beats of heavy silence ticked by.

"I kissed Noah last night." The words escaped my lips with rebellion. I hadn't planned on confessing my sins to Devon—not yet. Not in Noah's house with Sam playing with his *Hot Wheels* directly above us.

A wave of nausea unraveled in my stomach as I studied Devon's face for some sort of reaction.

Devon flinched at the confession, albeit brief and subtle. If I had blinked, I could have missed it. "I figured," he replied, his tone exuding nothing at all. Even indifference sounded like too bold of a reaction. "I figured it enough to come here and look for you."

"He was there for me, and you weren't."

Devon shuffled his feet and looked down at his shoelaces.

Still silent. Still unreadable.

Why wasn't he mad? Why didn't he hate me? The moment we separated, I'd run into the arms of his friend... just as Devon had suspected I would.

He swallowed, glancing up at me with only his eyes. "You fuck him?"

Heat flamed my cheeks as I bit my lip, shaking my head a little. "No, but..."

I wanted to.

I'd been shameless, begging for Noah to take me.

"But what?" he pressed.

Mortified, I looked away, unable to face him as I admitted, "We... fooled around." I tried to hide my shame by ducking my head. "Y-You broke up with me, Devon, and then I was attacked. I couldn't reach you. You came to the party completely high and embarrassed me, told me we were over, and then—"

"I know what I said yesterday, but I don't want to lose you."

I hesitated, drawing in a quick breath.

Devon rushed forward, clasping my face between his hands, his eyes finally shimmering with something more than disregard. "You want to know why I got so fuckin' high?" he rasped out, squeezing my cheeks. "Because of you."

My chest tightened. "What?"

"I've been so fucked-up over you, babe. All this shit with Noah. I'm pissed and jealous, okay? I've seen the way you two look at each other. You look at him the same goddamn way you used to look at me, before everything started going to shit," he bit out. "You want him. I see it all over your pretty fuckin' face whenever he's around."

"That's... that's not..." My breathing unsteadied as my hands balled into fists. Tears burned my eyes, his words registering and settling deep.

"It is. And that's why I've needed this distraction—to keep myself from losing it. I've got the Grammy's to think about; my career. You make me crazy, Chels." Devon stroked my hair, tugging me to his chest. "Pick me for once, will you? Help me. Fix me. I don't fucking know, just... *stay*."

A frown furled as my voice caught in my throat, words stuck like taffy. Warm tears soaked through the front of his t-shirt as I strove to process everything. "I-I'm sorry," I stuttered, trying to catch my breath. "I didn't mean to upset you so much. I didn't know I was the reason you—"

"Hey, it's okay. We can start over, yeah?" He sighed into my hair. "Two broken people, piecing each other back together."

Was that it?

Had we both screwed up so bad, we canceled each other out?

Did that make everything... okay?

Is that what I wanted? For us to be okay?

The stream of the shower jets from the second floor sounded louder, and I pictured Noah standing beneath the hot water washing me away, while Devon held me in his arms and begged for a second chance.

"Okay," I finally whispered.

Guilt and a debilitating sense of responsibility carried my feet forward and out Noah's front door.

Devon needed me right now.

He needed me.

And I couldn't turn my back on him.

CHAPTER TWENTY-SIX

CHELSIE

The following week had flown by—a whirlwind of reporters, lawyers, detectives, photographers, media, and security. I had become an instant celebrity; a victim to some, a role model to others, and a liability to the higher-ups in the industry. I hadn't left the condo without sunglasses and over-sized sweaters for as much anonymity as possible. It was exhausting.

Devon and I had fallen into a new routine. Things were different between us now. There were no late nights on the couch with popcorn and Netflix binges. There hadn't been any stolen glances, or romantic gestures, or passionate lovemaking.

We weren't quarreling, either. No arguing or heated words. Our arrangement was... stale. Boring. Exactly *that*—an arrangement. I hadn't seen Devon much that week due to his band schedule, having had two shows and three separate practices to prepare for the Grammy's.

To say I'd been on edge was an understatement.

Ian was still out there unaccounted for, so I kept my phone attached to me at all times just in case I received that call... the call that assured me Ian was off the streets and could no longer hurt me.

Devon had installed a high-tech security system and added more locks and deadbolts to the door. A security guard was on site of the complex 24/7, and it was a relief to have the added protection. Yet, nothing seemed to erase the constant paranoia. To me, Ian was always there, peeking in my windows and whispering in my ear. He lived in the tiny hairs on my arms that stood to attention when I heard an unfamiliar sound, or saw a strange shadow dance across my wall.

Perhaps he'd always live there.

As for Noah, things hadn't been the same between us since that night.

How could they?

I'd only seen him once that week, at one of the shows they had played in New Jersey. The whole band seemed disjointed and distant from one another. Devon had barely spoken, which set the tone for the rest of the members. Their performance had been muddy and amateur with little communication.

I'd fidgeted restlessly backstage with Lisa, unable to dismiss the overwhelming feeling that it was all my fault.

"Don't you dare blame yourself, Chelsie," Lisa had told me, linking her fingers in with mine and giving my hand a tender squeeze. "You're not responsible for having a psycho ex. You didn't make Devon do drugs. Don't do that to yourself."

"I just can't shake this feeling that if I wasn't in the picture, everything would be okay."

Lisa had shaken her head, her red curls bouncing with earnestness. "Nothing would be okay because that's life. Nothing is ever 'okay.' There's always some kind of battle."

I had tried to take Lisa's words to heart, but they didn't quite resonate.

"Chelsie..." Lisa had said later that night. "Why are you still with Devon?"

The question had thrown me.

My mind had fumbled for an answer, and the fact that I had to search for one made me question my decision to stay with him in the first place.

"Because I have to keep hoping things will get better," I'd eventually replied. "I need to believe the Devon Sawyer I met at The Pit Stop is still in there somewhere."

Lisa had sighed in a way that had made my skin bristle.

"Chels... hope and denial are two different beasts. Devon isn't the same guy he was when you started dating. You're reverting into old patterns. You couldn't fix Ian, and you can't fix Devon."

"Devon isn't Ian. He's just not."

"Not every toxic situation is the same—doesn't mean it isn't toxic."

I had stiffened against the wall, my eyes inspecting the tips of my fingernails. Lisa had rubbed my back, as if to offer a silent apology for her truth. I supposed I hadn't thought about it in that way before. I was a nurturer; a hopeful optimist. A lifelong *helper*. I'd always chosen to see the good in people and felt determined to fix their fractured bits whenever they fell apart.

Ian had been a lost cause, but there was still hope for Devon.

Noah had exited the stage after the show, his features etched with disappointment.

"You did good out there," I had told him, forcing a small smile.

It had been the first contact between us since I'd left his house that fateful morning. There had been no texting, no phone calls, and no offers to babysit Sam.

Nothing.

Still, I had wanted him to know that he *had* done good out there. He always did. It never mattered what demons he was grappling with, or what the band was or wasn't doing—Noah was steadfast in his craft. He plucked away at his guitar strings with accomplished finesse. He rarely faltered, but even when he did, his mistakes still felt like art. And that night, while the men on stage had stumbled and faked their way through the set for their fans, Noah had shined.

I'd really wanted him to know that.

"It was a mess," Noah had said, pulling his guitar strap over his head. Beads of sweat had rolled down his face, his hair stuck to his forehead as he kept his distance from me.

He never once looked at me that night.

I'd wanted to shake him for it. I'd wanted to pummel my fists against his chest until he *saw* me. I'd wanted to scream that what we had was still there... it was just buried beneath the layers of baggage and dirt and piss-poor decisions.

It had felt like I was six feet under, and if I'd just kept digging and clawing, a ray of light would penetrate through the heavy soil. Noah would be waiting for me. Things would go back to the way they used to be, and I would have my friend back.

I would be home.

But I hadn't done any of those things. "It wasn't that bad," I'd replied.

It had been a weak response, not alluding to any of the things I'd been feeling, or to the novel of words on the tip of my tongue. I had bitten down hard on that tongue, as if to punish it for its failure.

Noah had continued to fiddle with his guitar as the rest of the guys muddled around the small back room. "Well, thanks."

That was it. That had been our only correspondence. Devon couldn't wait to get out of there, so he'd guided me out the back door and to his car.

I chewed on my fingernail, making a mental note to get a manicure before the Grammy's. Brisk January air bit at my nose as I walked through the local downtown, tightening the scarf around my neck while looking in through storefront windows. I was desperate to clear my head. I'd kept myself locked up for the past week because of Ian's unknown whereabouts, making myself stir-crazy.

Even though it was a frigid twenty-two degrees outside, it was exactly what I needed—the refreshing outdoors. Inhaling big gulps of air, I traipsed along the sidewalk, dodging small patches of ice along the way.

I stopped in my tracks when I came upon a charming-looking hair salon, peering in through the foggy glass and debating whether or not I should go inside. I'd been considering a new look for myself... a change. Change was always good.

Change had saved my life once.

"It's rude to stare. C'mon inside!"

I stumbled back when the door opened, and a middle-aged lady poked her head out. She gestured enthusiastically with her arm.

"Oh, I don't know. I'm still thinking," I explained, stuffing my glove-covered hands inside my coat pockets.

"Well, you're not getting any warmer thinking on that side of the glass," the woman said. "Take a break from the cold and have a cup of coffee."

Smiling, I nodded. "Okay. Thanks."

The salon smelled of warm blow-dried hair and orange honeysuckles. I breathed in the aroma as I began to remove my coat.

"Here, let me. I'm Lilah." The dark-haired woman in stylish black suspenders pulled the jacket from my hands and hung it on a nearby hook. "I'll get you some coffee. Cream and sugar?"

"Just black, please. Thank you," I replied, looking around the small salon. Two washing stations, two dryers, and four salon chairs adorned the quaint space, perched on both sides of the room. Another stylist was already tending to a client, chit-chatting about her holiday break. The large sign above the check-in desk read "Bliss Bar."

Lilah returned a few moments later with a hot mug of coffee in her hands. It wasn't one of those disposable cups I'd been expecting. "Careful, it's pipin' hot," she warned. "It's a dark roast. Hope that's all right."

"It's perfect," I said with an appreciate gaze. "You have a cute place here. I've never noticed it."

"We just opened last month," Lilah answered, leaning over the waiting area's coffee table and shuffling through the assortment of magazines. She picked one up and flipped through it, licking her thumb as she plucked over the pages. "This." Lilah folded the magazine in half and handed it to me.

I glanced over the model with a medium-length, angled bob and bangs. It was a bold cut for someone who'd rarely done anything with her hair. My hair was strikingly long, ending just above my hip bone, all one length with no dimension. The extent of my hair routine was letting it air-dry, or pulling it up into a messy bun.

This haircut looked fierce and sexy. It looked like I wanted to stand out instead of hide.

"I kind of like it," I confessed, the corners of my mouth tipping upward. "It's... different. I think I need different."

Lilah gave me a knowing smile. "You're that girl on the news, huh?"

I blinked a few times as I registered the question. "Um, yes. I mean... probably."

"You're dating that musician, right? Imagine Dragons or somethin'?"

"Freeze Frame," I corrected with a chuckle. "And yes, that's right."

Lilah clicked her tongue as she removed the magazine from my hands and plopped it down on the table. "I heard about your attack. How are you holdin' up?"

Swallowing, I touched a hand to my throat, where a burgundy scarf hid my fading bruises. "It's been a tough week."

"I'll tell ya what," Lilah said, placing her hands on her hips. She tilted her head to the side, eyeing me up and down. "This one is on the house. Tell your friends to come see me, and we'll call it even. You deserve a little pampering."

My eyes widened at the offer. "I can't accept that..."

"Nonsense. Now, go sit your pretty butt down."

I wasn't well-versed in accepting favors or handouts, but it was as if this woman somehow knew that as she took me by the crook of the arm, guiding me to the first chair on the left.

"You have such a pretty face to be hidin' behind all this hair."

I watched in the mirror as Lilah ran her chocolate brown fingernails through my long, drab locks. She removed my scarf and set it on the small tabletop in front of her. The bruises beneath it stared back at us, boasting their purple and green composition.

Lilah only glanced at them for a moment before resting her hands on my shoulders. "Are you ready for a new you?"

I couldn't help but smile. "I'm ready."

NOAH

It was the night before the Grammy's.

I was tuning my Gibson guitar while the guys chain-smoked in between songs. Sean was pacing the room, finalizing details for our very public performance tomorrow evening.

"You keep fucking up that note," Devon scolded Miles, a cigarette dangling between his lips. He took a swig from his flask and wiped his mouth with the back of his hand. "When I sing 'believe in you,' you're supposed to play an *E*."

Miles scoffed at him. "I got it."

I ignored the bickering. I couldn't wait for the Grammy's to be over so I could announce my break from the band.

It had been a daunting decision, but I needed to take a step back. I needed a goddamn soul cleanse.

Music had always been my life, but it wasn't speaking to me the way it used to. My muse had been bogged down with politics and bitter grudges. Tad and Devon were getting loaded almost every night, and the entire band's integrity was slipping. It was eating at me.

Besides, I wanted to spend more quality time with my son. I had enough money saved up to take a few months off. Sam and I could travel the world together. And hell, maybe a few months was all I needed to find my muse again.

Maybe I could finally forget about her...

I'd been avoiding Chelsie since she left my house that morning. I needed to. She'd broken my damn heart, and she didn't even know it.

I had been nothing more than a shoulder to cry on, a warm body to escape to, and I was stupid to think we would wake up the next morning and our new life would begin. We'd be a happy little family.

Ridiculous.

Chelsie Combs had softened my once-cold heart to the point of believing in fairytales and it made me sick.

My phone buzzed in my pocket, and I reached in to grab it.

Chelsie: *Tell Sam I said hi.*

I blinked at the message, holding the phone in my hand for a long time, wondering if I should call her.

I wanted to. I wanted to hear her voice. I wanted to tell her how much Sam missed her... how much *I* missed her.

But we were different now.

Instead, I shot off a brief, noncommittal text: *"Ok."*

My response was stony, but it had to be. I couldn't let myself go back to that place of *feeling*, or I would break all over again. I'd be carried away to the night she was mine—when I fell asleep counting her breaths with the taste of her honey still on my lips.

I couldn't do that.

"I gotta go."

My head shot up when Devon's voice traveled over to me. He was staring at his phone, furiously texting something as he put out his cigarette.

"What the hell, man, this is our last practice," Miles argued.

Devon threw on his coat. "I have to take care of something."

"Shit," Tad muttered under his breath.

"I guess that's a wrap for tonight," Sean lamented. "Let's try to squeeze in an early-morning practice. I'm still not feeling confident."

I packed up my guitar with indifference. "Sounds good. See you assholes tomorrow."

I wasn't much for conversation these days. All I wanted was to do my job and get out, all while hating that music had become a *job*.

That's how I knew it was time to step away.

CHAPTER TWENTY-SEVEN

CHELSIE

I'd awoken that morning with a bounce in my step.

I was going to the Grammy's.

The only thing that would make the day better was if I received a phone call telling me that Ian was in custody. Until then, his shadow loomed over me like an ominous rain cloud.

Devon had been up first that morning, and I wondered if he had slept at all that night. I recalled his pacing feet around our bed and the glow of his cell phone brightening the room for hours. He was fidgety and restless.

I hadn't tried to initiate intimacy at all since our tentative reunion, and neither had he.

All I felt was... *relief.*

Maybe after the stress of the Grammy's passed, we would be able to talk and repair the damage in our relationship.

Devon left early, as soon as the sun came up, and I'd given him a quick peck on the lips before he disappeared out the door. He had a lot to take care of before the big show, and I had a date with Lisa.

My friend and I sat in our respective salon chairs, while Lilah and another employee primped our hair and applied makeup.

"This is such a cute place," Lisa exclaimed as the curling iron wrapped around her thick curls.

"The people are even better," Lilah said with a wink.

I was deeply grateful for Lilah's hospitality at my last visit. The haircut had turned out perfect; so perfect that I didn't want it styled too much for the awards. I just wanted it blow-dried straight with a little teasing on top. The bangs framed my face nicely and brought attention to my jade-colored eyes.

I was excited to bring Lisa to the salon for our award makeovers. After the appointment, we were picking up our dresses and heading over to meet the guys for the pre-party. The Grammy Awards were taking place at Madison Square Garden this year, which made the travel arrangements convenient.

"I can't wait to watch you guys tonight," Lilah gushed as she applied a rosy rouge to my cheekbones. "I've never had a famous person in my chair before."

I chuckled at the assessment. "I'm only famous by association," I teased.

"You're one-hundred percent famous," Lisa argued. "You're sitting next to Taylor Swift tonight."

The nerves began to bubble in my belly. I'd always chosen to stay out of the spotlight—I didn't mingle with the A-listers or attend socialite parties. I would much rather partake in a date night on the couch watching movies in my pajamas.

I took a deep breath to ease my jitters.

A few hours later, we stopped by the dress shop to collect our gowns for the evening.

"I feel like a princess," Lisa exclaimed when she spotted her dress. "Pinch me, please. This cannot be real."

I studied my own reflection in the mirror, my jaw dropping. I'd chosen a deep turquoise, strapless dress. The top portion had a sweetheart neckline bodice, and it hugged my curves in all the right places. A ruffled, floor-length organza skirt adorned the bottom half of the gown. I twirled my hips back and forth, watching as the layers of chiffon splayed around my feet and rhinestones twinkled under the glow of the boutique lights above my head.

Lisa exited the dressing stall, clapping her hands with enthusiasm. "I think I'm going to pass out."

My friend was wearing a formfitting red gown with long sleeves and a plunging neckline. "You look sensational," I said in an excited breath. "A classic beauty."

When we finally met up with Devon and Miles at the studio to catch our limo, Devon smiled for the first time in over a week.

"Goddamn," he muttered, eyeing me up and down before wrapping his arms around me and kissing my temple.

I allowed myself to pretend for a moment that everything was okay between us—we were blissfully in love in a utopian world. I imagined it was just like it used to be when we had first started dating: tender, exciting, and full of possibility.

When he let me go, the moment ended. I regarded the dark circles under his eyes and his lifeless expression. Nothing was okay.

But tonight, we would lie.

The drive to the award ceremony was long and painfully quiet, with Devon on his phone the entire time. I let my gaze fall upon the man I had given myself to over the past year, knowing he wasn't that man anymore. It ate me up inside.

My rock star boyfriend was still a star, but he was no longer my rock.

What if I just needed to try harder to bring him back to life? What if there was still hope for him to change?

"You excited?"

The sound of his voice startled me, breaking through my thoughts like a jagged thorn. He didn't look up from his phone when he addressed me. "Very excited," I answered. "Nervous?"

Devon was typing away on his digital keypad, and I wondered if he'd even heard me until he finally shrugged. "Nah."

Miles shifted in his seat across from us. "Don't know about you, bro, but I'm about ready to shit myself."

Lisa laughed. "I'm excited *and* nervous. I've had this recurring dream that I'm going to trip on my chunky heels and face-plant on the red carpet in front of Brendon Urie."

"Stop... I've been having that *exact* same dream," I joked.

"I won't let you fall, babe," Miles said to Lisa as he reached his arm over her shoulders.

Do you say that to all your women, Miles?

I never did tell Lisa about my suspicious encounter with the bass player. The Grammy's had been so close that I hadn't wanted to take such a lifechanging experience away from my friend. I didn't want to be the messenger that broke Lisa's heart.

She would always have your back, though.

The nagging thought flooded me with guilt as I watched how unaware Lisa looked in the arms of her lover. Lisa would never let me get played like that.

I sighed, slinking back against the seat—I would tell Lisa after the Grammy's.

"Check it out!" Lisa pointed out the window as we ventured through Midtown Manhattan. The iconic building came into view, bustling with reporters and important people.

Our limo pulled up behind a sea of black luxury vehicles and SUVs, all with tinted windows. It was a mystery who may be inside: Katy Perry, Bono, Jennifer Lopez. I felt small among the quintessential stars.

As our transport came to a stop, Devon finally put his phone away and slipped his Tom Ford sunglasses over his eyes, hiding how jaded they looked. He held his hand out to me. "Ready?"

I nodded through a gulp. The driver came around to open the side door, and we were instantly greeted with security guards and flashing camera lights. I stepped onto the concrete, holding up the heavy fabric of my designer gown with Devon's hand firmly linked with mine.

A newscaster stood behind the rope, his back to us as he introduced our arrival.

"Devon Sawyer of Freeze Frame and infamous girlfriend, Chelsie Combs, make their way out of the next vehicle. Freeze Frame is performing tonight, up for two separate awards..."

Infamous.

I plastered a dazzling smile across my face as I followed Devon onto the red carpet. My heart was racing. Glancing behind my shoulder, I spotted Lisa waving madly to the masses and my smile broadened.

When we entered the venue, swarms of media with microphones in hand were waiting to get an interview. Devon and I posed for photos, shaking hands with superstars.

One of the reporters pulled me away from Devon while a camera followed. "Miss Combs, a word?"

Smiling, I hoped my nerves wouldn't get the best of me.

"Miss Combs, your name has been in a lot of people's mouths lately. How does it feel to go from a struggling waitress to a house-hold name?" the woman asked.

"I count my blessings every day," I answered simply.

"You don't do many interviews, so you're kind of a mystery to Freeze Frame fans. Is there anything we should know about you?"

I froze as my mind scuttled with hundreds of fun facts about myself. I was an only child. I hated flying. I could curl my tongue. I was a hula-hoop champion when I was twelve. I liked mush-rooms. I wanted to visit Ireland someday. But I hated flying...

"I'm honestly not that interesting," I concluded. "I'm prob-ably no different than you. I'm obsessed with my cat, and I spend most of my time reading or watching *Buffy the Vampire Slayer* reruns. And I can rock a messy bun like nobody's business."

The reporter laughed, so I relaxed, suspecting I hadn't completely flopped.

"Well, we're rooting for Devon tonight. Thanks for stopping by to chat."

I gave an appreciative nod and continued walking.

"Love your new hair, Chelsie!" someone shouted from behind the ropes.

Waving, I shot off another smile.

Where did Devon go? I wasn't good at this celebrity thing. I needed someone to, quite literally, hold my hand.

As I surveyed my surroundings looking for a familiar face, I stalled in my tracks.

There he was, only a few feet away.

Noah.

He was chatting with one of the reporters with Beth by his side.

He brought Beth to the Grammy's?

My stiletto heels felt stuck to the carpet as my eyes examined him. He was wearing a slate-gray suit with a baby blue bowtie.

His hair was still grown out, styled and tamed with gel. A week or two worth of stubble adorned his handsome face.

Beth stood next to him, smiling softly, with a hand clamped around his upper arm. A striking purple dress kissed her ankles as she absorbed the scene, her sunny blonde hair pulled back into a sharp, elegant bun.

Noah was mid-sentence when his eyes broke away and fell in my direction.

My heartbeats thundered beneath my ribcage when our gazes locked. It felt like a forest fire had been lit underneath my skin.

He's never looked at me like this before.

NOAH

I was good at faking things.

Smiles for the press. My love for Rosa's pineapple upside-down cake. The eye exam for my driver's license test. My enthusiastic interest in Candyland.

But *fuck...* I couldn't hide the feeling that came over me when I saw her standing there.

I was dumbstruck.

Chelsie stared back at me, her eyes burning hot like embers. I didn't hear the reporters speaking to me. I didn't hear Beth repeating my name. The voices were a quarry of gibberish in the back of my mind.

All I could see was her. All I could hear was the rush of heat surging through my veins.

All I could envision was her writhing beneath me while I brought her to ecstasy.

She picked up the skirt of her dress and began to approach me. Our eyes were still connected by an invisible wire as Chelsie stopped a foot away and licked her lips. She dropped the dress, pressing her palms against the bustle of fabric. "Hey."

Hey.

It was easy enough to say back. One syllable. A commonly used word in my vocabulary. An appropriate response. Instead, I blurted, "You have bangs."

I watched as she raised a hand to fiddle with her hair, ducking her head with a semblance of modesty. "Yeah... I'm still getting used to it," she murmured.

Beth coughed beside me. "I think it looks great."

Blinking, I felt Beth's hand give my arm an effective squeeze, snapping me back to reality—the reality where Beth was my date and Chelsie was the woman who told me she'd only let me go down on her because she was drunk and upset. I cleared my throat. "Chelsie... you remember Beth," I said, redirecting the conversation.

Chelsie gave a thin-lipped smile, her eyes only briefly leaving mine. "You look beautiful, Beth. I'm sure you'll have a great time tonight."

"Thank you," Beth replied.

Chelsie returned her attention me. "Is Sam with Rosa?"

"Yeah," I nodded, scratching at the nape of my neck. "He misses you."

I miss you.

Flecks of teal and aqua sparkled in her eyes, reflecting the brilliant colors of her dress. "I miss him, too."

I was doing a terrible job of redirecting the conversation.

A photographer appeared in front of us, breaking the tension that had developed like a third party. "Noah Hayes—can I get a picture of you and Chelsie?"

I'd forgotten where we even were. There were cameras and reporters and A-list musicians surrounding us, and there I was, making puppy dog eyes at a woman who very publicly belonged to someone else.

"Uh... sure," I replied, flustered.

Beth pursed her lips together and took a step out of frame as I gave her hand a light kiss before letting it go. Chelsie moved closer to me.

"Closer, please," the photographer ordered.

Clenching my jaw, I wrapped an arm around Chelsie's lower waist and pulled her in until our bodies were touching.

Electric.

We were fucking electric.

Energy crackled, sparks flew, heat mounted. I could feel her heart beating swiftly through our layers of clothing. I could smell lavender and lilacs in her hair.

I could practically taste her.

"Thank you!"

The photographer snapped the photo and moved along to his next subjects, forcing me to drop my arm and step back.

A chill whispered down my back at the loss of her.

"I should go find Devon," Chelsie rushed out, fisting a white clutch between her hands. The tips of her fingers were painted a deep berry. "You're going to do great tonight."

My mouth quirked with a semblance of a smile. "Thanks."

She hesitated, and I wondered what she wanted to say. I could see the words climbing up her throat, stopping just before they touched her glossy lips.

I wondered if those words echoed my own.

But Chelsie said nothing. She gave me one fleeting glance before pivoting away, disappearing into the myriad of flashing lights.

Beth leaned back against the wall, taking in the scene. "You like her," she said.

Frowning, I removed my gaze from Chelsie's retreating back. Beth had her arms crossed over her chest, but she didn't look angry. She looked objective. "I like *you*," I countered.

"Not the same way you like her." There were no jealous undertones or bitter inflections. Just facts. "It's okay, Noah."

I ran a hand over my face and let out a sigh of resignation. I was going to protest, but I couldn't seem to find the words. The truth was, I *did* like Beth—she was refreshing, funny, and exactly what I needed in my life.

Her only flaw was that she wasn't Chelsie Combs.

"Walk me to my seat?" Beth held out her arm with a faint smile.

I nodded, deciding not to address her statements. There was nothing I could say that she didn't already piece together.

A few minutes later, we parted ways with our women, making our way backstage and getting ready to play.

"Break a leg, boys."

I glanced up to see Steven Tyler giving us a friendly wave, and I nodded my thanks.

"Hey, where's Devon?" Tad asked as we tweaked our gear.

I noticed the lead singer was no longer trailing behind us. "Bathroom break?"

"Cuttin' it close," Miles scoffed.

"Just had to take a piss. Shit." Devon hobbled over from the bathroom looking jittery and strung out. "Let's fucking rock this."

"Did you seriously just get high?" I frowned, stepping closer to my front man. "Right before the show?"

Devon was sweating, wiping at his nose. "I'm good, man. Let's do this."

"Fuck you." Getting right in Devon's face, my anger spiraled to the surface. "What the hell is wrong with you?"

He pushed defensively at my shoulders. "Back the fuck up, Hayes."

I shoved back.

"Jesus Christ," Miles shouted, jumping between us. "You seriously think this is the time for this shit?"

"A little professionalism would be excellent," Sean said, appearing from behind the stage with a headset on. "You're almost up."

Regaining control, I adjusted my bowtie, grinding my teeth together. Any doubts I may have had about leaving the band were officially put to rest. I couldn't do it anymore. Devon had chosen his path, and now it was time for me to choose mine. The music had brought us together, but it wasn't enough to keep us together —Devon had allowed himself to be sucked into the blinding lights of stardom; he'd gotten swept away in the cheap thrills.

As much as it killed me to watch my old friend make a swift descent toward rock bottom, I couldn't stick around to watch him crash and burn. Devon needed to pull himself out on his own.

"Five minutes," one of the producers shouted.

I picked up my guitar, needing to re-focus and remove the mindless clutter from my thoughts. There was no Devon, no band drama, no Chelsie. None of that existed. It was just me and my guitar—like old times. I grazed my thumb against the strings, basking in the reassuring chords that reverberated through me. I played the first few notes of *Hometown Girl*.

"You're up!"

The announcer introduced us as we got into position.

This was it.

This was the moment every musician dreamed about: The Grammy's. Performing in front of hundreds of acclaimed performers and celebrities. We were among so much talent. Hell, we *were* the talent. I had envisioned this moment since I was a small child sneaking into my father's closet and play songs by The Beatles on his rust-colored acoustic guitar. I'd fantasized about being on a stage like this with smoke and strobes and colorful lights.

My heart rumbled in my chest as the curtains were pulled, revealing the most high-profile audience I had ever performed for.

No pressure.

I strummed over the first note, the chords vibrating through the expectant auditorium. I closed my eyes.

Here we go...

Tad jumped in with a "one, two, three" on his drums and the song took off. I had played this song so many times, I could do it in my sleep. I glanced over at Devon who was already dancing around, head-banging on stage, and I couldn't help but smile. The energy was contagious. If I was going out, I wanted it to be like this. It was almost like old times again as I watched my friends bounce around with a vitality I hadn't witnessed in months. My eyes narrowed through the smoke as I looked out at the sea of artists I'd admired since I knew what music was.

Devon's raspy voice echoed through the music hall and recoiled through me like an old friend. There were no fumbles. We didn't miss a note or a beat. We were young, bright-eyed musicians again, running on pure adrenaline and a genuine love for performing. We weren't jaded. There were no vices.

There was only music.

We ended the song with passion and efficiency, and the crowd went wild with whistles and applause. I let the emotions wash over me, throwing my arms up and lifting my guitar in the air like a well-deserved trophy.

I shared a triumphant look with Devon.

And for just a moment, everything was perfect.

CHAPTER TWENTY-EIGHT

NOAH

As soon as the awards ceremony concluded, it was all about the after parties. It felt like my high school prom, only with million-dollar estates and the finest recreational entertainment.

The band and I mingled outside the venue, signing autographs and posing for more photo ops, while Beth, Chelsie, and Lisa waited in the SUV as we wrapped up. We'd decided to continue the party at Marley's—it seemed like an inevitable end to the evening, since we were discovered on that small, dark stage in front of thirty people two years ago.

Devon waved to the crowd as he jogged over to our stretch limo, the coattails of his tuxedo billowing behind him. Following, I slid in next to Beth and across from Devon, Chelsie, and Lisa. Miles slipped in beside his girlfriend while Tad piled in last, falling back onto the cushioned seats with an exhilarating "whoop."

Tad was the only band member who chose not to bring a date. Not because he couldn't find anybody to go with him, but because Tad never really "dated" anybody in the time that I'd known him. We insisted he take Julia, but he'd refused. I never understood why fame and fortune hadn't given him a newfound confidence with the ladies, but he didn't seem to care.

"That may have been the best night of my life," Lisa said, digging her fingers into Miles' upper thigh.

I watched as Chelsie rested her head on Lisa's shoulder as the vehicle began to move.

Fuck, she was pretty.

From her heart-shaped lips, to her milky white skin, to her meticulously manicured toenails peeking out through strappy heels. She was the type of woman other women wanted to hate because she was just *so damn pretty*, but they couldn't because she was also sweet and kindhearted. Chelsie Combs was one of those rare females who didn't fit into any category.

Beth sat beside me in silence with a passive disposition. Her hands were folded neatly in her lap as she gazed out the window over Lisa's shoulder. She probably felt out of place among strangers, so I placed my hand atop her interlocked fingers and offered a smile when she looked up at me.

I'd intended the smile to come off as comforting, but I feared all it said was... *I'm sorry.*

Beth didn't smile back, but she did lace her fuchsia-tipped fingers with mine, as if to reiterate her earlier statement of... *it's okay.*

"Marley's... gosh, that brings back some memories," Chelsie mused, her head still leaning against Lisa's shoulder. "I think my whole life changed there."

I tried to pinpoint when *my* life had changed and was brought back to a hotel room in Manhattan with a girl who had unknowingly spilled her guts to me.

"Those were some good times," Devon agreed. "I had a lot of big moments there."

Nostalgia swept through me, recalling how Chelsie had stormed out on us that first night after I'd pushed her buttons. *Ballsy.* She hadn't cared how famous we were—she'd simply demanded respect.

Maybe I'd started falling for her right there in that V.I.P. lounge.

The limo rolled up to the side entrance where dozens of fans were already waiting. Word traveled fast. Two bouncers exited the building and assisted our group inside while we quickly dodged screaming women and frantic requests for autographs.

"I love you, Devon!"

"Noah Hayes is my soulmate!"

"Please have my children!"

"I hope you die, Chelsie!"

I froze as I ducked inside, canting my head to see who had threatened Chelsie. There were too many fans to pinpoint the culprit.

Glancing at her, I pressed my palm to the small of her back as a gesture of solace. "They're just crazy fans," I muttered softly into her ear.

She rubbed her hands up and down her arms, gifting me a weak smile as my fingers trailed down her spine, then fell away. "I know, but it's not something I'll ever get used to."

"Fuck 'em," Devon piped up, staring into his cell phone. "Jealous ass bitches."

Chelsie's eyes were on me as she murmured back, "Yeah."

We retreated up to our private V.I.P. quarters above the bar as two cocktail waitresses flittered around, pouring glasses of water and stocking the fridge with beer and champagne.

"I'm Tiffany," one of the waitresses greeted, her eyes undressing me as she gave me a onceover. "Let me know if you need... anything at all."

The only thing lower than her neckline was probably her IQ.

I raised an eyebrow, recalling a time when I would have eaten that shit up. It wasn't even that long ago. "Sure," I said flatly.

"Check this place out."

My gaze traveled to Beth as she perused the lush suite. "Pretty cool, huh?"

She shrugged. "I guess if you're into this sort of thing."

I studied her with bewilderment.

Beth was a mystery. She never acted like she was hanging out with a celebrity, and I supposed that was part of why I found her intriguing. Her nonchalance to my notoriety was genuine, unlike most of the females I'd pursued. "Are you implying you're not into this sort of thing?"

I was half-joking, but Beth hesitated and turned to face me, a rueful smile on her lips. "Noah... this isn't for me."

My amusement waned.

The truth was, I liked Beth. I'd been enjoying her company over the last couple of weeks, and I'd be lying if I said her admission didn't tickle me with disappointment. "Do you want to talk?" I asked, feeling the eyes of my bandmates lingering in my direction.

"Sure."

Taking her by the arm, I led her outside the private lounge. Beth peered down at her hands folded in front of her, looking wistful yet resolute.

"Noah, I'm not trying to put a damper on your night," Beth began, pressing her thumbs together. "I'm honored you invited me to such an iconic event, but... I don't feel like I fit in here. I'm just a single mom who fell for a superstar. I'm in over my head."

"I'd like you to stay," I replied gently. "Screw fitting in. I don't even fit in here."

She smiled again, her eyes softening. "That's why I like you," she admitted. Then her smile faded, and she let out a deep sigh. "But your heart is with someone else."

My jaw tightened as I looked up at the ceiling, images of Chelsie flickering to mind. "Beth, the thing with Chelsie... it's not going anywhere."

"Whether it is or it isn't, you can't change how you feel, Noah. The heart wants what the heart wants. It wasn't in the cards for us, and that's okay. I just need to move on." She reached up and touched her fingertips to my cheek. "I'm glad I met you, Noah Hayes. No regrets."

I parted my lips with protest, but couldn't seem to find the words.

I hated that Beth was right, and I was angry at Chelsie for creeping her way into my world and clinging for dear life. I couldn't shake her; I felt ambushed. "I'll have my driver bring you home," I said tersely, nodding my head and stuffing my hands into my pockets.

There were no long goodbyes or mournful embraces. I just

walked back into the suite, called the driver, and grabbed a beer out of the fridge.

Beth was gone because my heart was with a taken woman.

Fuck.

Five beers and a shot of whiskey later, a buzz crawled through me as I sat alone on the red couch, watching as my friends mingled and laughed. Waitresses filtered in and out of the room, their hips swaying dramatically as they entered and exited. Most men would do anything to have buxom blondes throwing themselves at them, but not me. Not anymore.

The only blonde I wanted was curled up in a loveseat with my strung out lead singer.

"I want to make an announcement," I blurted, taking my own self by surprise. I hadn't intended on making any announcements tonight.

Everyone stopped what they were doing and gave me their full attention. Chelsie sat up straight, looking at me with cautious anticipation.

Rising to my feet, I cleared my throat. "After much deliberation, I've decided to take a break from the band."

The silence was deafening.

I took a swig of beer while awaiting a response.

"Are you fucking joking?" Devon demanded.

"No, I'm not." I shuffled my feet, glancing around the room. Chelsie's mouth was agape, her eyes wide and incredulous. "I'm burned out. I need to find my muse again."

Devon let out a scathing laugh as he stood. "Don't give me that hippie-dippie bullshit. We're all burned out. Every motherfucker with a nine-to-five is burned out. You keep going."

"Is this... temporary?" Chelsie squeaked out.

I gritted my teeth, shrugging. I wasn't even sure. "Maybe. Probably."

"How can you leave after the show we did tonight?" Miles inquired, looking rattled as he stepped toward me. "It was like old times again. We killed it."

"They're right, man," Tad added. "We're in our prime right now. We can't stop."

"I never said you needed to stop." I tossed the empty beer can into the trash, flinching when it clanked against another glass bottle. "I'm sure you can find a fill-in."

Chelsie approached me, concern glimmering in her emerald stare. "Noah... are you sure you've thought this through? The music means everything to you."

I could see the distress on her face. The worry, the empathy. I softened my stance and let out a weary breath. "I need a goddamn break," I told her, my words clipped with honesty. "Everything's a mess. Devon and Tad are always high as a kite. You almost got raped and killed, and then we—" I caught myself before the alcohol had me saying too much. "I rarely see my son. We've lost our way."

Devon stormed over to me, glaring daggers. "Go fuck yourself."

"Devon," Chelsie scolded, swiveling toward him with a stunned frown.

"What?" He threw his hands up in the air. "What do you want me to say? Noah knows everything. Noah thinks he's better than all of us. I say let him go. He's replaceable."

"Come on, dude," Miles spoke up.

I bit down on the inside of my cheek as the anger prickled the back of my neck. "I'm the reason this band even exists. You'd still be fixing brake pads if it weren't for me."

"And now, I'll be just fine without you," Devon sniffed. "Replaceable."

The whiskey coursed through me, and my fists clenched to stones. "Out with it, Devon. What else do you want to say to me? Don't hold back now."

"Stop. Both of you," Chelsie chided, stepping between us. "This is so unnecessary. You two are friends."

"We stopped being friends a long time ago," I muttered, reaching for the open bottle of Jameson and drinking straight from the spout. I wiped my mouth with my shirt sleeve and eyed Devon with resentment. "Right around the time he screwed Ruby in the front seat of my car."

Chelsie blinked, then faltered. She looked like she'd been slapped. "What?"

Devon curled his lips into a sneer, his eyes narrowing. "It eats you up, doesn't it?" he said. "I've always had everything you wanted. The center spotlight. The recognition. The women. Hell, even Ruby." Years-worth of harbored grudges encompassed the room. Devon took another step toward me and cocked his head to the side. "And now... Chelsie."

Something inside of me snapped. I lunged at Devon, getting in one solid punch to his face before Miles and Tad grabbed me.

"Jesus Christ," Tad cursed. He held my arms behind my back, while Miles stood in front of me, blocking Devon from any further attack.

Chelsie stood frozen in place, one hand clutching her elbow, the other resting against her chest.

Freeing myself from Tad's grip, I spun around, running both hands through my hair. Tad started to reach for me again, but I threw my arms up. "I'm good... I'm good," I spit out through gritted teeth.

Miles helped Devon to his feet while Devon wiped a smear of blood from his lip as a result of the single blow I'd managed to get in.

"We're done here." Devon grabbed his leather jacket from the back of the loveseat, nodding at Chelsie as he put his arms through the sleeves. "Are you coming?"

She stood there quietly, her eyes darting between me, Devon, and Lisa. Indecision pinched her brows. "I—um..."

"Suit yourself," Devon cut her off. He glanced at Tad, and the two men left the lounge.

Chelsie's eyes widened with disbelief as she stared at Devon's retreating form. He hadn't even given her a chance.

I fished through my pockets for a pack of cigarettes. "I need some air."

Pulling one from the box, I headed out of the private suite and snuck outside through a side door, away from the crowds. My hand was shaking as I lit the butt.

As soon as I inhaled, the door creaked open beside me, and I silently cursed whoever had witnessed my getaway.

To my surprise, Chelsie poked her head out, closing the door behind her as she joined me. "Sorry. Did you want privacy?"

She was still in her designer gown. The gems sewn into the

bodice were reflecting shades of indigo from the overhead street-lamp. "Nah," I muttered softly. "You can stay."

Chelsie wrapped her arms around herself, shivering against the frosty January air.

"You're going to freeze," I noted, my eyes skating over her. I watched as the skin on her arms began to pimple with goose-bumps. "Where's your coat?"

She shrugged. "I didn't bring one. It didn't go with my dress."

I arched an eyebrow as I flicked the embers from my cigarette. "Typical woman. How about we get a drink at the bar down the street?"

It was a daring proposal, but the whiskey running through my veins didn't seem to care.

We hadn't been alone together since our intimate sleepover—we hadn't even talked about it. I was anticipating a firm rejection, but was surprised when she conceded with a quick nod. Maybe it was the bitter cold shocking her into submission, or maybe it was the fact that Devon had left, and she was lonely and upset.

That was always what it was, right? That was her way—running into my arms anytime she needed comforting. And I ate it right up.

I always would.

Chump.

But I knew that if the opportunity arose and I found myself entangled with her warm body again, our lips fused together, tongues hungry, my fingers inside of her while she begged me to make love to her... well, I wouldn't say no.

Snuffing out my cigarette, I reached for her hand. "Let's go."

CHAPTER TWENTY-NINE

CHELSIE

I could see my breath as we walked briskly down the city sidewalk. Noah's hand was my only source of warmth, so I clung to him, using my other hand to hold up the bustle of my dress. I felt out of place as we entered a grungier side of town.

People stopped to offer curious glances, some even shouting at us.

"You folks lost?"

"Drinks on those two tonight!"

I ignored them and kept my eyes forward, wondering if anybody recognized who we were—or why Devon Sawyer's proclaimed girlfriend was holding hands with another man, clinging to him for more than just warmth.

He felt safe. He felt good. He felt like...

"We're here," Noah said, pulling me into a little hole-in-the-wall pub called Ernie's.

As soon as we entered, we garnered the attention of everyone in the room. I tried to slink behind Noah, still holding his hand. "Think we stand out a little?"

"Don't worry about them." He spared me a quick glance over his shoulder, his eyes dipping to our still-interlocked hands. "Let's grab a table."

I followed him to a high-top table in the corner of the small bar, tripping on my dress three times along the way. Color crept into my cheeks as patrons chuckled at my clumsiness. "I swear I'm not cut out for this glamorous stuff," I mumbled, finally letting go of Noah and instantly feeling a chill race down my neck at the loss of contact. Nibbling my lip, I hopped onto a bar stool and cringed as the heel of my stiletto caught on the inner layer of my dress, tearing the fabric. "I would give anything to be in jeans and a t-shirt right now."

Noah smiled at me from across the table, and I swore it was the first genuine smile I'd seen from him in weeks.

"I've missed seeing that," I whispered. Clearing my throat, I dipped my chin. "Your smile."

The smile faded as he waved over a waitress. "Haven't had much to smile about, I guess."

Guilt flooded me because I knew I'd contributed. "Noah... I can't help but feel like all of this is my fault."

His eyes narrowed, studying me for a moment before shifting to just over my shoulder. "All of what?"

"Everything," I swallowed. "You and Devon fighting. The band falling apart. Beth leaving."

Noah's mouth twitched. "You give yourself too much credit, Combs. Sometimes life just sucks."

A waitress appeared at our table and jotted down our drink orders.

"Don't pretend the thought hasn't crossed your mind. I'm bad luck," I told him. When my rum and Coke arrived, I sipped on the small straw and lowered my eyes. "I feel responsible."

Noah downed his shot in one swallow, clinking the glass onto the table when he finished. "Don't do that," he murmured after a beat. "You and Sam have been the only ray of fucking sunshine I've had in a long time."

My hands folded around the cold glass as I gazed down at the disappearing ice cubes. As much as his statement drenched me in warmth, I knew it couldn't be true. All I'd brought was hellfire into his life.

It burned, yes, but it wasn't sunshine.

Part of me wished I could turn back time and call in sick that fateful night at The Pit.

Then I remembered Noah's earlier confession about Ruby.

"Is it true?" I suddenly wondered aloud. Our eyes met. "Is it true what you said about Devon and Ruby?"

Noah leaned back in his chair, the muscles in his cheeks ticking. Saying Ruby's name always seemed to pull a physical reaction out of him. Sometimes it was a wince or a flinch; sometimes he clenched his jaw. This time he creased his lips together in a thin line and tapped his foot against the rung of his chair.

"Yeah," he finally answered. "I hated them both for a long time."

I felt Noah's pain radiating into me. I could only imagine what it would feel like to find the person you loved with your best friend like that. Ruby was clearly a narcissistic wench, but Devon? How could he do that?

"I'm so sorry, Noah. That's awful." My words sounded trivial. All I really wanted to do was take him in my arms and hold him tight, just like he had done for me so many times before. I wanted to press my cheek against his chest and breathe in his sandalwood scent. I wanted him to confide in me like he used to.

But things were different now.

We were different—ever since I had crossed that line and stuck my tongue in his mouth.

The memories plagued me. There hadn't been a single day I hadn't thought about the way his lips felt pressed to mine, or how natural it felt to be entwined with him in his bed. His erection had ground into me, yearning to take what I was so freely offering. His lustful groans still infiltrated my mind, haunting me.

I often fantasized about unraveling into his hand while his fingers pumped into me, and he kissed away my cries of pleasure.

The thoughts warmed me up from the inside out, and I wondered if Noah noticed me squirming in my seat with clenched thighs.

"Yeah, it was pretty shitty. But I got over it," Noah replied, tapping his finger against his empty shot glass. "Just like I get over everything."

His stare bit into me like the edge of a dagger. I swallowed back a thousand responses and raised my cocktail to my lips, sucking down the rest of the liquid with frenzied gulps.

"Want another?" he asked, watching as I inhaled the drink.

"Yes, please."

My insides felt tingly as I studied him. His striking good looks hadn't resonated with me at first, overshadowed by his crude attitude.

He was just Noah the Asshole.

Then, he was Noah the Friend.

Now... well, I wasn't entirely sure what he was. "Noah, can we talk about what happened?" I asked, pulling my lip between my teeth. Nerves raced through me.

He straightened in his chair, reaching for his beer with a shrug. "About when I was *obligated* to go down on you because you were drunk and upset?"

Taking a few swigs of beer, he eyed me with a mix of pain and frustration. I fidgeted in my seat, my cheeks heating. "Noah..."

"I mean, I don't know what there is to talk about. You made yourself pretty clear."

"I panicked, okay? I was freaked out and scared because I felt something," I confessed, the words spilling out of me, leaving me winded.

His eyes flared. Noah went still, faltering mid-sip of beer as he awaited more.

Licking my lips, I blew out a breath and finished, "I never meant to imply that it didn't mean anything. In fact... it meant more than I ever thought it would," I said. "*You* mean more to me than I ever thought possible. So does Sam. And I feel guilty for that because you're my friend, and I was with Devon for so long, and I just..." I trailed off, my tongue tying into knots.

Noah stared at me with hopeful anticipation, a spark of life returning to his eyes. "Was?"

I blinked. "Was what?"

"With Devon. Past tense."

Oh.

He wanted to know if I was single.

Am I?

"He, um... asked me for a second chance. I was terrified Devon would go on a bender before the Grammy's, or overdose or something. I feel responsible for his downward spiral. So, I'm not really sure where we stand right now, but I'm confused and conflicted, and I don't know how to fix any of this..." Heaving in a giant breath, I was about to continue when I noticed Noah shaking his head with that look of disappointment again.

But before I could try to further explain my rambling, his gaze shifted over my shoulder, twisting into something akin to apprehension.

"What?" I frowned. "What is it?"

"I know those guys," Noah said, nodding toward a group of men on the opposite side of the room. "They were with Ian the night I beat the shit out of him at this bar."

I swiveled in my seat, looking back at the three men laughing with each other. My blood ran cold. "I know one of them. That's Brad, Ian's brother. He's bad news."

"Well, it looks like Brad just spotted you."

Brad locked eyes with me and stood from his chair, almost knocking it backward.

"Shit," I whispered, dread simmering beneath the surface of my skin. If Brad and his cronies were here, Ian couldn't be far.

He sauntered over to our table with his hands in his pockets. "Well, well, well. What are you fine people doing in a place like this?"

"Same as you, man," Noah shrugged, propping his ankle up on one knee, giving off the impression of casual indifference.

I tensed in my chair, unable to keep the anxiety from creeping into my bones. Just the sight of Brad brought back all sorts of haunting memories. Ian and Brad had always been incredibly close—a deadly duo. Brad had been in and out of jail most of his life for assaults and petty crimes, and on one occasion, he had beaten a man unconscious for lightly rear-ending Ian's car.

And the things he had done to Riley...

He was evil, just like his brother.

Brad turned to me, an eerie smile forming on his lips. "Look at you, princess. A true "rags to riches" story. Can I get your autograph?"

"Look, we don't want any trouble," Noah said, clearing his throat. He stood from his chair and tossed some cash down onto the table. "Let's go, Chelsie."

Brad threw his hands up. "Hey, I have no trouble to give. If I remember correctly, you're the one with the anger issues." His smirk contorted into a malevolent scowl as he leaned in close to Noah's face. "But if you lay another hand on my brother, you'll be in for a whole *world* of trouble."

He ignored the threat.

I shuddered as Noah helped me hop down from the chair and led me to the door, while Ian's gang of losers whistled and cheered as we exited the bar.

Stalling for a moment on the sidewalk, Noah snatched his smokes out of his back pocket. "Fucking assholes," he mumbled around the cigarette, fumbling for a lighter. "Let's get out of here."

He started walking.

Then he stopped.

Releasing a heavy sigh, he took me by the elbow and guided me into an alley adjacent to the bar.

"Noah?" I glanced around, confused, watching as he began pacing back and forth.

"You know what?" he blurted, hands linked behind his head. "I can't do this anymore. This ends now."

"What?"

"This." Noah spun toward me, flicking his finger between us. "You and me."

"Noah, please..." My heart raced with fear, my skin growing hot; a welcome contrast to the elements. Noah's eyes were searching for answers, his cigarette dangling between his fingers, and I couldn't tell the difference between its puffs of smoke and his breath hitting the icy air. "I just want things to go back to the way they were," I told him. "I miss you. I screwed it all up."

He shook his head, running a hand through unruly hair. "You miss me? Well, I'm right fucking here." He threw his arms out with frustration. "You're hot and cold. You're running into my arms, and then you're running back to Devon. You want to be friends, but then you kiss me and let me between your legs. You say it meant something, but what? What did it mean?" he demanded, his tone escalating. "What do you *really* want, Chelsie?"

A vision popped into my head.

Noah, Sam, and I snuggled up on the living room couch watching *Toy Story* on repeat. There was popcorn and tickle fights and unrestrained laughter. There was dinner in the oven and cookie dough ice cream for dessert. There were drawings painted on bright colored construction paper, hanging up on the refrigerator.

There was warmth, music, and hope.

Home.

Tears welled in my eyes as I bit down on my bottom lip to keep it from quivering. The words were on the tip of my tongue—words I'd kept buried for a long time. Months, maybe.

Words that would change everything.

"Noah, I have feelings for you. Strong feelings." I wondered if the breath left Noah the same way it just left me. His angsty eyes shifted into something else. Something softer, yet infinitely more powerful. I squeezed my own eyes shut to avoid his gaze. I couldn't concentrate with him looking at me with such intensity. And I had to concentrate... the words needed to be right.

They needed to be *perfect.*

But when I opened my eyes to continue my overdue confession, I was silenced by a familiar figure standing behind Noah at the opening of the alley. I jumped back with a gasp of horror. "Noah... oh my God..."

Ian.

No.

Noah whipped around, quickly shoving me behind him, using his body as a shield. I clutched his arm as Ian stepped toward us.

"You look like you've seen a ghost, Chelly Bean. I hope you didn't think I skipped town," Ian mocked, letting out a malicious laugh. "I'd never leave you."

I paled, my stomach twisting into knots. "Leave us alone."

"You don't want to make any more trouble for yourself," Noah reasoned.

Ian cackled in reply. "You think I've got anything left to lose?"

He pulled a pistol out of his coat pocket and brandished it in front of us.

"Jesus, Ian," I startled, pulling away from Noah and taking a step toward my armed ex. I wasn't sure why my reaction was to approach the unhinged assailant instead of flee, but my blood coursed with fire, and my limbs twitched with purpose. "You're fucking crazy. You always have been. Are you going to shoot me?" My fear escalated into blind rage. "Get it over with!"

"Christ, Chelsie..." Noah grabbed me by the arm and yanked me back. "What the hell are you doing?"

"I'm sick of this, Noah. I'm sick of living in constant fear." I glanced back at Ian, my heart nearly beating out of my chest. "Just shoot me, goddammit!"

Ian laughed again, twirling the weapon between his fingers. "You've got a little spunk left in you, after all," he said with a wink. "We had some good times."

"Either shoot me, or leave me the hell alone. I'm done playing your games," I pleaded. I only realized I'd been crying when the hot tears spilled onto my lips, my chest heaving with anger. I had meant it—I'd rather be dead than living in Ian's perpetual shadow.

That was no life at all.

"Listen, just put the gun down," Noah urged, moving in front of me, holding his arm out for protection.

Ian shrugged as he eyed the shiny pistol, running his finger along the barrel. "I rather like it. Chelsie got herself a pretty little gun here."

Frowning, I squinted my eyes at the weapon. "That's... your gun," I whispered to Noah. "He stole your gun." I gritted my teeth and looked back at Ian. "You broke into my house?"

"*Your* house?" Ian sneered. He clicked his tongue against the roof of his mouth. "You mean the residence you occupy with your millionaire boy-toy? We both know that will never be your house. That will never be your life. You're a bottom-feeder. You're just like me, Chelly Belly."

I couldn't help the wave of insecurity that washed over me as old demons resurfaced. "Fuck you."

"Ooh," he taunted. Ian scratched his head with the butt of the gun. "You play the part well enough. I'm sure you've fooled a lot of people with your Cinderella act."

"It's not an act."

"Oh, darling, it's a complete façade. If only lover boy knew the real you."

My fists clenched at my sides, my fingernails leaving tiny half-moon prints on my palms. "That's not me, Ian. I'm not broken anymore."

"You'll always be broken. You'll always be weak."

"No!" I rushed forward, pushing Noah's extended arm out of my way.

"Damnit, Combs!"

I ignored Noah's plea and faced my attacker with newfound courage. "You have no power over me, Ian. I won. I *survived.* You can shoot me dead right now and that won't change." Advancing on him, I basked in the startled look on his face. "You're the weak one. You feed off damaged women. You rape because no self-respecting woman would even look in your direction. You spent years in jail *obsessing* over me." I looked him up and down with pity, then spat at his shoes. "You're pathetic."

Only a swift beat passed before I found myself staring down the barrel of a gun.

I inhaled sharply.

Ian's hand was shaking as he pointed the pistol between my eyes. "You're a dumb bitch," he growled.

"Jesus, just stop," Noah blared from behind me. "We can work this out. You don't need to do this."

I glanced back at Noah. He was stepping forward with his hand out, as if to offer a truce. The fear was evident on his face. Beads of sweat pooled along his dark hairline despite the frigid temperature. "Noah, get out of here," I ordered. "I'm the one he wants."

"Neither of you are going anywhere," Ian snapped, waving the gun back and forth between us. "You think I won't do it?"

"Please," Noah begged. "Please... don't hurt her."

Ian let out a scathing laugh and pointed the gun back at my forehead. "Give me one good reason I shouldn't blow her brains out all over your snappy dress shirt."

My eyes squeezed shut. All I could hear was the sound of my pounding heartbeats thudding against my ribcage.

Th-thump. Th-thump. Th-thump.

Then Noah's words fell out, stealing my breath:

"Because I'm in love with her."

The world went quiet.

My eyelids shot open as I turned to face Noah, who was standing a few feet beside me. Everything around me faded away except for him. There was no gun. There was no Ian.

There was only Noah.

He wasn't looking at me. His hands were raised in surrender, the words coming so naturally—as if it was the obvious response.

The *only* response.

I wanted to race over to him. I wanted to wrap my arms around him and bury my face against his neck. I wanted to kiss him. I wanted to feel his tongue twining with mine, saying those words over and over again, in a thousand different ways.

Did he mean it? Did he really... *love* me?

There was a loaded handgun pointed at my head, and I didn't even care.

Noah Hayes loved me.

But the world came rushing back when a loud crack pierced my eardrums.

Then another.

My ears rang, everything moving in slow motion. My brain felt cloudy, so I blinked rapidly, trying to clear the smoke as I glanced down at my dress.

There was no blood, no pain. I hadn't been shot.

Noah.

I lifted my chin.

That was when I felt pain.

I felt more pain than I ever thought possible.

Our eyes locked for a brief, poignant moment before we both glanced down at the red stains blooming on the front of Noah's dress shirt. One just between his neck and his shoulder, and a second on the left side of his abdomen.

Ian shot him.

Ian shot Noah.

Lowering his weapon, Ian took a step backward. "Fuck you, and fuck love."

Commotion rumbled at the opening of the alley as people

began to flock to the sound of gunshots. As Ian spun around to look, Noah took the opportunity to lunge at him with a menacing growl, knocking the gun out of our attacker's hand.

"Chelsie... run," Noah ordered, stumbling, while Ian broke free from his grasp.

I kicked the gun away before Ian could snatch it back up.

Ian glanced down at the weapon, then at me, hesitating with indecision, before taking off running out of the alley.

And to my surprise, Noah chased after him.

"Noah!" I shouted, hiking up my gown and following.

Noah was shot. Twice.

Oh my God.

Adrenaline coursed through me as I raced through the alley in my six-inch heels. My ankle twisted as one of the stilettos broke off, and I winced in pain, pulling off both shoes and continuing my pursuit on bare feet. Gravel and shards of glass pierced through my skin, but I ignored the pain, half-limping as I tried to catch up.

"Noah!" I called again. Noah was about to chase Ian into the street, but a taxi cab was careening around the corner. He reached out, snatching the back of Ian's shirt while I froze in place, a desperate shriek shredding my throat: "Noah, *stop!*"

Noah let go, halting at the curb. We both watched as the vehicle smashed into Ian with a sickening thud, just as he was crossing the busy intersection.

I brought a startled hand to my mouth as I witnessed his body bounce off the windshield and collapse onto the street, lifeless and still.

Bystanders screamed with horror.

Brad ran toward the scene from the front of the bar, shouting and cursing. "You pushed him! You pushed my fuckin' brother, you son-of-a-bitch!" As Brad raced to Ian's crumpled body, my own legs regained movement.

"Call 9-1-1!" I called to the crowd, catching up to Noah as he fell to his knees on the sidewalk. I dropped beside him. "Noah, Noah... oh my God..."

"Fucking bastard shot me," Noah bit out, the adrenaline wearing off, replaced with shock. He raised a hand to his neck and pulled it back, inspecting the crimson fluid left behind on his fingers.

"No." I grabbed him by the shoulders just before he fell backward. "No, please." Sobs poured out of me as I pulled him to me, feeling the sticky blood smear against my chest. A crowd gathered around us.

Noah wobbled, his weight becoming unsteady. "Hurts like a bitch."

"God, Noah…" I lowered him back, carefully resting his head along the concrete. Leaning over him, tears dripped down my cheeks, mixing with the blood on his shirt. Sirens blared in the distance as I pressed down against both wounds with the front of my palms. "You're going to be okay," I sniffed, placing a soft kiss against his forehead. Hysteria tried to claim me. My cries turned into hiccups. "Y-You're going to be fine."

Noah's eyes fluttered. He reached his hand out, wrapping it around my wrist. The pools of blood grew larger, like fragile azaleas bursting to life. I pressed harder against the bullet holes, gasping and sniffling. "Th-there's so much blood. I can't stop it, Noah. I-I can't—"

"Hey, look at me."

His grip on my wrist grew weaker, and I choked back another strangled cry. "Noah… I can't stop the blood." I addressed the crowd that had circled us, drinking in the looks of panic and concern. "Is anyone here a doctor?"

"Look at me, Combs," Noah pleaded.

I glanced back down into his green eyes, trying to convey everything I wanted to say to him in a single look. Everything I was *going* to say—right before our worlds were rocked by a madman with a vendetta. "I won't lose you," I rasped. I said it with more conviction than I'd ever felt for anything in my life. "I won't."

His hand rose and touched my cheek, so delicately. So lovingly. I pulled his hand closer until he was cupping my jaw, and then he whispered raggedly, "Promise me… you'll take care of Sam if…"

Noah trailed off as I whipped my head back and forth. "Don't you dare say that."

"Please."

I shut my eyes, squeezing out fresh tears, using Noah's fingers to brush them away. "I promise."

Curious whispers echoed around us.

"Is that the band guy?"

"What happened?"

"Aren't they famous?"

The sirens grew louder. I lifted my head as an ambulance sped toward us.

Brad was cradling Ian in his arms, rocking back and forth on the roadway as traffic came to a stop.

My blood burned with rage, but I needed to focus.

I needed to focus on Noah.

"Noah, they're almost here. Help is coming." I applied more pressure to the two wounds as his hand dropped from my face, his eyelids fluttering closed. His skin was ice cold, so I draped my body across him, trying to give him as much heat as possible. His heartbeats sounded slow and far away as the coppery scent of blood invaded my senses, mingling with his musky aftershave. "Stay with me," I begged, my face pressed against his chest, savoring every precious heartbeat. "Stay with me, Noah..."

CHAPTER THIRTY

CHELSIE

There weren't many things in life I hated more than hospital waiting rooms.

Unfortunately, I had seen my fair share.

Riley's overdose. My grandfather's heart attack. Two separate car accidents for old friends. Sam.

Now... *Noah*.

Numbness settled in as I sat in the stiff burgundy chair. Home and Garden magazines were strewn atop a small table to my left, and *Friends* reruns echoed throughout the small room. There were others waiting, all with different stories—strokes, pneumonia, broken bones.

I was certain I was the only one waiting for a famous rock star who had been gunned down by a psychotic ex-boyfriend.

I'd been dodging curious stares all evening, and I couldn't blame them. I was a sight to see in my designer ball gown, covered in blood, and my brutalized bare feet. Glancing down at my ankle, I noticed minor swelling along with an abundance of cuts and colorful bruises. I had denied medical treatment for my ankle because it was an *ankle*. It was nothing compared to what Noah had suffered.

The nerves and anxiety were all-encompassing as my mind kept reliving those moments of terror and disbelief. The look on Noah's face when he realized he'd been shot. His confession. The blood. *So much blood.* I could still hear the ringing in my ears from the gunshot. It was a sound I would never forget.

I looked down again, my stomach souring at the sight. Dried bloodstains saturated the front of my gown where stitches had come loose on the bodice. I was one wardrobe malfunction away from flashing everyone in the waiting room. The bottom portion of the dress was shredded and torn, and my chest was still painted in Noah's blood from where he'd laid his head against me. Emotion caught in my throat as I recalled his life slipping away in my arms.

Ian had also survived the accident and was brought in by a second ambulance. They were both in surgery fighting for their lives.

I had never wished death upon another person before, but I hoped to *God* Ian Masterson choked on his own blood.

I looked up when familiar faces rushed through the revolving doors—Devon, Tad, Miles, and Lisa. Devon and Tad looked strung out as the group approached me.

"Holy shit," Devon said, eyeing me up and down.

Four incredulous expressions stared at me. "Yeah," I mustered. My eyes drifted to Lisa's stricken face, and I couldn't help the tears from resurfacing.

"Oh, Chels... come here."

I broke down, collapsing into Lisa's arms. She didn't say anything because words could never express how any of us were feeling. There was nothing to do but cry.

When Lisa pulled back, she wiped her own wetness from her cheeks. "Are you hurt?"

I shook my head. "The blood isn't mine. It's all Noah's."

"Fuck," Tad said, running his hands over his face.

The group followed me to a far corner. Devon took a seat beside me, wrapping his arm around my shoulders. "It's crazy out there with security and police. They're swarming the place."

I shuddered, wishing it was all a bad dream. "I'm glad you made it," I said to Devon, inching away from him slightly. "I wasn't sure if I'd be able to get a hold of you."

Devon leaned back in his seat and tapped his feet in anxious unison against the waiting room floor. "I'm glad you did."

"Holy fucking shit, Chelsie!"

I jerked my head up to see Julia running through the main entrance. Standing, I gave my friend a tight hug. "Hey," I whispered, my voice ragged and dry.

"It's a madhouse outside the hospital," Julia said. She sighed with worry. "God, I don't even know what to say. Any word on Noah yet? Any updates?"

Disappointment rippled through me. "Nothing yet."

"This is so messed up," she murmured, taking a seat next to Lisa.

When I sat back down, I couldn't help but notice Devon playing a game on his cell phone. He cracked a smile as his points accumulated. "Really?"

Devon glanced in my direction, then back to the game. "Something wrong?"

I stared at him, my mouth open with amazement. "Yes, something's wrong. Noah is fighting for his life a few feet away and you're playing video games?"

"I need the distraction," he said. "Why does it matter?"

I was about to speak, but the words stopped at my lips. *Was I overreacting?* Shifting in my chair, I cleared my throat. "Sorry."

A few moments of silence passed, and Devon slipped his phone into his pocket. "Chelsie, I care about Noah. I'm worried, just like you."

Nodding, I looked down at the scarlet stain in my lap as I folded in my lips and ran a hand through knotted hair. When my fingers caught on a patch of dried blood, I winced.

The thought of Devon and Ruby crossed my mind, and suddenly, I wanted answers. Maybe I was looking for a fight—maybe I was trying to see the worst in Devon to make my feelings for Noah more justified. Whatever the reason, I needed to know. "Devon... what happened with Ruby?"

He didn't flinch at the question. Perhaps he'd seen it coming. "Is this really the right time to bring up past indiscretions?" he asked, his eyes fixed straight ahead.

"Probably not," I admitted. "But I'm curious."

He sighed and continued to fidget in his seat. "It was a dick move. Not much more to it."

"So, you slept with your best friend's girl? The woman he was crazy about?"

"You don't know anything... *she* was the crazy one. We both got drunk one night, and it just happened. I barely drank alcohol after that point. I felt terrible—I didn't give a shit about anyone but myself back then."

Swallowing, I pursed my lips together. "Doesn't seem like much has changed."

"What?"

"I'm just saying, you've been acting like an asshole lately. You haven't been there for me. You've been treating the band like crap. The things you said to Noah earlier were shitty," I told him, worrying my lip between my teeth. "I'm wondering if something changed in you, or if this is who you've always been... and I was too blind to see it."

An eerie silence enveloped the room; maybe I'd said too much. Devon's expression shifted from indifference to agitation. He sniffed and folded his hands together before leaning his head back against the seat. "That's something only you can decide," he said with closed eyes, shutting himself off from me.

I blinked slowly as the guilt hit me.

I was angry.

I was angry at Devon for letting me down in so many ways. I was angry at myself for putting up with it and ignoring all the red flags along the way. I was angry at Ian for worming his way back into my life and destroying all the progress I'd made. I was angry for pushing my parents out of my life and being too much of a coward to reconnect.

I was angry that Noah was lying in a hospital bed unconscious when we should be out having celebratory drinks until the bar kicked us out.

I was just *angry*.

And I knew it was all my fault.

I had found solace in another man, prompting Devon to push me away. I had brought Ian into my life in the first place, setting off the domino effect of trauma and bloodshed. I had chosen a chauvinistic rapist over my parents when they'd only tried to help me.

And Noah... I had dragged him into all of it, putting him in the line of fire.

"I need some coffee." Rising from the chair, I headed down the long corridor, trying not to put pressure on my right ankle. I did my best to ignore the horrified looks I received as I approached the coffee machine, looking like a scene out of a Stephen King movie.

The coffee dispensed into a paper cup, the hot steam wafting from the top. The cup warmed my hands, and I wasted no time in bringing it to my lips. I didn't even wince as the piping hot liquid scalded my tongue.

I didn't want to head back to the waiting room, so I leaned my back against the wall and slid down until my bottom hit the cold floor.

"Because I'm in love with her."

Noah's words had been plaguing me all night. Did he mean it? Did he just say it to throw off Ian? Did he say it because he thought we were both going to die?

Devon had never uttered those elusive words to me. Not once. Truthfully, I wasn't accustomed to being loved. I had taken the broken pieces of my life and put my world back together, all by myself. I didn't have anyone cheering in my corner. I never had a partner in crime. There was no one I could ever run to when life got hard.

Until there was Noah.

He had become my rock. He was the one wiping away my tears and calming the demons in my soul. He was the one cooking me pancakes and giving me relationship advice. Noah was there when I wanted to see a new movie and everyone else was too busy. Noah knew my birthstone, and my favorite toothpaste, and the name of my childhood goldfish. He was the first to show up when I needed a friend, and he was the last to leave.

I recalled a wintery night not long ago, days before I had quit my job at The Pit Stop. It had snowed all night and into the morning hours, and I was on the closing shift that evening. I'd been dreading cleaning the snow off my car at three A.M.

When I'd finally trudged through the eight inches of heavy snow with soggy socks and a frosty face, I'd noticed my car was the only one to be brushed clean. I had been dumbfounded. It was only when I'd gotten closer to the vehicle, I saw the words drawn into the snowy side: *"Noah was here."*

He had shrugged it off when I'd called him the next morning to thank him.

"It was nothing," he had said.

But it wasn't nothing. It was the nicest thing anyone had ever done for me.

Maybe that was love. Maybe love was clearing snow off someone's car in the middle of the night, just to make their life easier.

The revelation brought me to tears. I set down my coffee cup and clutched my legs to my chest, sobbing into my knees.

"Miss?"

I lifted my head and sniffed. A nurse stood over me with a look of concern.

"Miss, there's an officer here to speak with you. I'm very sorry to interrupt."

Wiping my nose with the back of my arm, I nodded. "Thanks," I said, rising to my feet.

A police officer approached me with two more men in uniform trailing behind. "Chelsie Combs?" he asked.

"That's me."

"My name is Detective Brennan. I know this is a difficult time, but I'd like to ask you a few questions about what happened tonight. Is that all right?"

I nodded.

"Good." He flipped back a piece of a paper on his college-ruled notepad. "I know you gave a statement to the officer on the scene, but I understand those were difficult moments. You stated your ex-boyfriend shot Mr. Hayes two times. Is this true?"

"Yes," I said. "Noah and I had stepped into the alley behind Ernie's to talk in private. Ian approached us with a gun and began to threaten us."

"Do you know of any reason he would want to harm Mr. Hayes or yourself?"

"He's insane," I answered flatly.

Detective Brennan jotted down notes and glanced at me. "I see. Are you able to elaborate?"

"I dated him a long time ago. He was abusive. I found the courage to leave him, and he ended up raping some poor girl. He was sent to prison, but he was released on good behavior a couple of months ago."

"Mmm-hmm."

My eyes narrowed. I hated the sound of his pen scratching against the yellow paper. "He's crazy. He was stalking me, and then he broke into my home and attacked me."

"Okay," the detective said, scribbling his notes. "Do you know how he could have found you this evening?"

I paused for a moment, remembering Ian's brother at the bar. "I think his brother called him. Brad. We ran into their group at Ernie's."

"I see," he replied. "So, he sees you and Noah in the alley. What happened next?"

I sucked my bottom lip between my teeth and fingered the coffee cup, my eyes closing as the memories consumed me. "He said he had nothing else to lose. I started yelling at him, telling him to just shoot me and get it over with."

"Why would you instigate him? You seemed to have known what he was capable of, yes?"

My brows furrowed into a scowl. "Are you saying it's my fault?"

"No, no. Of course not." Detective Brennan crossed his arms across his chest and softened his gaze. "It's my job to try and understand why things happen the way they do. Some questions may sound offensive at times, but I assure you, I only have your best interest in mind."

I swallowed as I continued to chew on my lip. "I was tired of it. I was done running from him. I was sick of being scared all the time. I never thought..." Tears stung my eyes, and I forced them back. "I never thought he would hurt Noah. I thought all he wanted was me."

The detective nodded with a sympathetic expression. "What happened next?"

"Um... he told me he stole the gun out of my house."

"He used your own weapon against you?"

"Well, it was Noah's gun. He gave it to me for protection." I shook my head with a sigh. "That backfired."

More furious note scribbling. "How did the altercation transpire? Was there a physical quarrel?"

"No. He just... shot him."

"Unprovoked?"

My eyes shot up. "No, not unprovoked. He's been 'provoked' his entire life. He never should have been let out of prison."

"My apologies, Miss. I didn't mean it like that."

"Noah didn't do anything wrong. All he tried to do was protect me. Those bullets should have been mine." The realization hit me hard, and my chin quivered, tears breaking through. "Those bullets should have been mine."

Detective Brennan stopped writing and took a careful step toward me. "I understand if you need more time. Would you rather come by the station tomorrow?"

I placed an unsteady hand over my mouth, my eyes squeezed shut. "Is he going to be okay?"

"I can't answer that, unfortunately. Mr. Hayes is still in surgery. Both of the victims are."

"Ian is not a victim." I opened my eyes and pushed my bangs out of my face. "Write that down. Ian Masterson is no victim... he's a monster."

"I appreciate your cooperation, Miss Combs. Let me give you my card." He reached into his front pocket and handed me a business card. "I hope we can talk more tomorrow."

I watched the three men walk away, disappearing down the white corridor. Blinking back tears, I placed the card in the front of my dress.

As I took another sip of stale coffee, I heard commotion coming from the waiting room. My heart rate picked up when I recognized a familiar voice.

Brad.

"That celebrity prick is a dead man!" I heard Brad shout as I hurried through the double doors. A security guard was attempting to subdue him. "He pushed my goddamn brother—I saw him do it. He fucking *killed* him!"

I stopped short of the scene, my chest heaving.

Ian was... dead?

My friends had moved away from the altercation, along with the rest of the waiting room occupants. I brought a hand to my heart as I witnessed Brad thrash around in the guard's grasp. More guards bounded into the room to assist.

"Get the fuck off me!" Brad blared, kicking his legs and trying to throw punches. "I need to see my brother."

"He didn't make it, son. You need to leave and calm down." The guards gained the upper hand and dragged Brad out of the hospital. Brad continued his threats and obscenities until the glass doors sealed shut and silenced him. I let out a relieved sigh as the tension in the room began to settle, and I returned to my previously occupied seat and closed my eyes.

Ian was gone. Thank God Ian was gone.

That's where I spent the next five hours—curled up in the burgundy waiting room chair. Every time a door opened, my head shot up. Every time a nurse or doctor stepped out, my heart skipped a beat. My friends had all stayed except for Julia, who had to get back to her shift at The Pit Stop. Tad, Miles and Lisa were asleep, while Devon kept himself occupied with his video games. I hadn't said a word to him for the remainder of the night.

As the sun began to peek through the hospital windows, a doctor emerged from the emergency room doors. The look on his face was unreadable. I straightened in my seat as a lump formed in the back of my throat, squeezing Devon's arm.

"Are you here for Noah Hayes?" the doctor asked, approaching our group.

I stood on shaky legs as my friends stirred awake. Devon moved in beside me.

"Is he okay?" I barely recognized my own voice as it trembled. "Is Noah okay?"

The doctor smiled and held out his hand. "I'm Doctor Alverez. You must be his significant other?"

Swallowing, I glanced at Devon before accepting the doctor's hand. My grip was weak as my body struggled to stay standing upright. "Do you have any updates for us?"

"I'm pleased to report that Mr. Hayes made it through surgery and is resting comfortably," Dr. Alverez explained.

A sigh of relief resonated among the group. An enormous weight fell away, and I closed my eyes, thanking whatever higher powers existed.

The doctor continued. "He's not out of the woods just yet, and he has a long road ahead. But he's a fighter; I'm optimistic he'll get through this. I want to mention that Mr. Hayes did suffer some extensive nerve damage. It's too soon to tell how this will affect him, but there's a chance he may lose function in his left arm. The bullet near his neck damaged his brachial plexus, which conducts signals to the shoulder. Some patients do lose complete function."

My eyes widened at the thought of Noah unable to play guitar again.

It's all my fault.

"... but I have high hopes that Mr. Hayes will make a full recovery. He lost a great deal of blood and went into hypovolemic shock, so we'll need to monitor him for long-term side effects."

"Can I see him?"

Dr. Alverez shook his head apologetically. "I'm sorry, not just yet. He's under heavy pain medication and should not have visitors for a couple of hours. I'd suggest going home and resting, then returning later."

"Thanks, Doctor," Devon said, shaking his hand. "We appreciate it."

"I'm just happy to have good news for you," he replied.

I offered a grateful smile and took a deep breath.

"Chelsie, you should take a shower and get some sleep," Lisa told me, placing a comforting hand on my shoulder. "Why don't you come by my apartment, and I'll drive you back here in a few hours?"

I didn't want to. I didn't want to go anywhere until I saw Noah—but I was smeared in crusty blood with my dress torn to shreds. A shower would probably do me good. Taking a nap was the last thing on my mind, but my body was crumbling from exhaustion.

"Thanks, Lisa."

"Do you need to pick up some clothes from my place?" Devon asked, tucking his hands into his pockets.

I flinched.

My place—not *our* place.

I supposed it was better that way.

"She can wear something of mine," Lisa offered. "It's not a problem."

"All right," he shrugged. "I'm sure I'll see you back here later. Keep me posted if you hear anything."

I watched as Devon and his bandmates exited out the hospital doors before I felt Lisa's reassuring touch on the small of my back.

"Let's get you cleaned up," Lisa said, pulling me into a hug with a gentle squeeze.

I returned to my chair to fetch my purse, pulling out my phone to call Rosa.

Rosa was frantic when she answered. "Mi muchacho, Noah! I need good news, señorita. Por favor..."

"He's okay, Rosa. He's stable and resting now. They think he's going to be okay."

"Gracias a Dios!"

I could almost see Rosa making the sign of the cross. "I'm going to my friend's place to freshen up and I'll head back to the hospital later. Can you bring Sam over when Noah is allowed visitors?"

"Si. Of course, mi querido."

"Thanks, Rosa. For everything." I pulled my purse strap over my shoulder and smiled my first real smile since sitting in the pub with Noah. "I'll see you later."

"Gracias, muchacha."

I popped my phone into the center of my purse and followed Lisa out of the hospital. I couldn't wait to breathe in the crisp morning air.

Noah had lived to see another morning.

I awoke to Lisa nudging me as I laid curled up on my friend's sofa.

"Chels, wake up."

I rubbed my eyes to correct my blurred vision. My mind was groggy, my limbs like jelly. "How long was I out?"

"Almost three hours," Lisa replied. "The hospital called your phone, so I answered it. They said Noah's awake and asking for you."

Jolting into a sitting position, a gasp left me. "Oh my God. I need to go. Can we head over now?"

"Of course. I'll grab a coat for you."

Rising from the couch, I winced as my right foot connected with the floor. My ankle was still swollen and tender. I slipped into a fleece jacket, already dressed in slightly oversized sweat-pants and a white tank top. I combed my fingers through my hair and coated my lips in a kiwi Chapstick. "Let's go."

It was a quiet drive to the hospital. I had called Rosa to tell her the news, causing her to shriek with joyous gratitude. Little Sam would be reunited with his father soon.

I was trying to prepare for my own reunion with Noah Hayes. What could I possibly say to him?

Oh, hey. Sorry about that whole multiple gunshot wound thing. My ex gets a little crazy sometimes. But don't worry—he's dead now.

Hey, Noah. I heard you might never be able to play guitar again or gain feeling in your arm. Kinda my fault. So sorry.

Hi, there. You sort of confessed your love to me and then almost died. I feel like this complicates our friendship a little.

I wrung my sweaty palms together and tapped my foot against the floor of the passenger's seat. The radio played at a low volume, serenading us with the vocal talents of Stevie Nicks. When we arrived at the hospital, I felt my heart beating in my throat. I was anxious, nervous, and eternally grateful. I was also teetering on the edge of an imminent breakdown...

It was a complex mix of emotions.

"Are you ready?" Lisa turned the engine off as we sat in the parking garage, an eerie silence sweeping over us. "I can stay in the waiting room if you want some private time with Noah."

I found myself nodding. "I think I would... if that's okay."

"Whatever you need, Chels. I'm here for you."

The walk down the white corridor felt long and foggy. My

feet were heavy, as if I were trudging through wet sand. Noah's room appeared before me, and I glanced down at the sticker on the front of my shirt that read 'Visitor.' I gulped.

Then, I knocked.

"Come in."

That voice. Oh God, that voice.

I turned the handle, cracking open the door. My steps inside the room were hesitant and guilty as I swallowed back my reservations and walked inside.

My eyes landed on Noah. He was connected to IVs and monitors that beeped and buzzed, lying partially upright on the narrow hospital bed.

His eyes flickered with recognition when he saw me, flashing with relief. "Chelsie."

I was torn between keeping my feet frozen to the ground and dashing over to him like a star-crossed lover.

"I didn't know if I'd ever see you again," I whispered from across the room. My admission gutted me. I tried to keep the tears at bay, but my lip quivered with betrayal.

Noah's trademark smirk danced to life. "You can't get rid of me that easily."

My feet carried me across the room, and I dropped to my knees at his bedside, cradling his hand between my palms and pressing my forehead to our interlaced fingers. I squeezed my eyes shut, ugly-crying until I felt his hand break free to tangle in my hair.

"Don't cry, Combs," Noah said, running his fingers along my scalp. "I'm right here."

His voice was low and scratchy, tickling my insides. Sniffling, I wiped at my eyes. "You're not dead," I croaked out.

"Pfft. From multiple gunshot wounds? I assure you my death will be much cooler," he teased.

I let a smile slip, but it didn't stick. "I'm sorry, Noah. I'm so sorry. You didn't deserve any of this."

Noah forced me to look up at him, dipping his index finger beneath my chin. "Neither did you," he said gently.

I took a moment to drink him in, from his messy hair to his bloodshot eyes. He looked tired and worn, but he was still Noah.

And he was alive.

"He's dead, you know," I told him. "Ian... he didn't make it."

"Are you okay?"

The question threw me. "I'm ecstatic. Relieved."

"I guess it's over then," Noah replied with a nod. "You're finally free."

I nibbled on the inner lining of my cheek.

Was I, though? Was I... *free*? My experiences with Ian forever changed me as a person. My life would never be the same because of him. Maybe, even in death, he would still hold onto me with a merciless, unforgiving grip. When I closed my eyes, he would be there laughing at me. Mocking me. Squeezing his cold, dead fingers around my neck.

No, I would never be free.

I didn't relay my thoughts to Noah, and instead, forced out the faintest of smiles.

"I'm really glad you're okay." Noah grazed his finger along my jawline, shooting goosebumps across my skin.

My breath caught.

Our gazes locked again, and I flashed back to the alleyway, recalling the look in Noah's eyes after he had just been shot.

Confusion. Incredulous disbelief.

"Because I'm in love with her."

His confession rocketed through me, forcing my heart to thunder inside my chest. I replayed those words a thousand times since they'd reached my ears, but not with him so close. "Did... did you mean it?" The question escaped my mouth before I could stop it.

I watched his micro expressions carefully. The slight twitch of his jaw. A single blink. The way his tongue poked out to moisten his dry lips.

"Mean what?"

He *knew* what I meant; he had to. Did he want me to say it? Bring it back to life?

"Noah..." I breathed out.

He shifted on the bed and looked away. "I'm sorry. I'm not sure what you're referring to."

I frowned, my chest squeezing tight. "In the alley," I

explained. "Right before... you know..." I couldn't bring myself to say the words.

Noah hesitated, parting his lips and then closing them. He glanced back at me, his eyes shimmering with something unreadable. "I can't remember. Everything is such a blur."

Don't you lie to me, Noah Hayes.

My jaw clenched as I nodded with acceptance.

It was too much.

Too soon.

"Don't worry about it," I told him, forcing another smile through the tears. I brushed the tips of my fingers through his hair, grateful he was still here, and pressed a light kiss to his forehead. His eyes fluttered closed, his breath hitching. "It's not important," I whispered.

Now, I'm the liar.

The truth was... it *was* important.

It was, in fact, everything.

CHAPTER THIRTY-ONE

CHELSIE

A tub of peanut butter fudge ice cream was clutched in my hands as I sat propped in front of the television on Lisa's couch. My friend was beside me, flipping through the new Netflix releases and texting Miles.

"I don't understand men," Lisa said with exasperation. "They're so hot and cold—one minute their entire universe revolves around you, and then the next day they can't even text you back."

I wiped at the ice cream dribbling down my chin. "You know how Miles is," I shrugged.

"Disinterested?" She tossed her phone onto the couch cushion between us.

"No, Lis. He's distracted... busy. You know, doing famous people stuff."

Lisa clicked her tongue. "Noah's never too busy for you. And you're not even his girlfriend."

My heart fluttered at the sound of his name. "Noah's... different." I handed the pint of frozen dessert to my friend. "You need this more than I do," I said with a sympathetic smile.

Lisa snatched it up without hesitation. "Do you think now that it's over between you and Devon, something might happen with Noah? The chemistry you two have is undeniable."

A warmth crept into my belly as I squirmed in my seat. The

thought had certainly been weighing on my mind. There were moments when I fantasized about barreling through Noah's front door and leaping into his arms, wondering how it would feel to give in. But then the logical part of my brain reminded me that Noah was still recovering from near-fatal gunshot wounds he received because of me.

It was *my* past; *my* baggage.

I was the reason he was temporarily wheelchair-bound with little feeling in his left arm.

I was a tornado of darkness and bad luck. My own unsavory choices had led to Noah's life being forever changed, and the guilt and self-loathing had been keeping me away. "Oh, I don't know about that. I think it's better if I just stay single for a while."

Lisa popped the lid on the ice cream tub and rose from her seat. "I hear you. Can I get you anything?"

Slinking back against the couch, I moped, "A job. A shiny new savings account full of unspent money. Assurance that I'm not actually back at square one after all my hard work."

"Oh, Chels. You'll get back on your feet soon."

I sighed. This was my home for the time being. I'd finally broken things off with Devon shortly after visiting Noah at the hospital and stopping by the police station to discuss the case with Detective Brennan. Luckily, I was able to compose myself with grace and a clear head, and the detective had considered the case closed.

That dark chapter of my life was over.

But... I'd known in my heart that there was another chapter that had needed closing.

"I had a feeling you'd be stopping by," Devon had said after discovering me standing in his doorway that afternoon.

I'd entered the condo, fidgeting with the sleeves of my fleece jacket. "Sorry to show up unannounced."

"You do live here."

I'd looked around, basking in the unfamiliarity of it all. Devon's condo had never felt like home. There was no warmth or laughter or nostalgic memories. There were no feminine touches, or any trace of my occupancy, save for a closet filled with my clothes and my toothbrush on the sink. There were no photos adorning the walls, or canvas art pieces we had lovingly picked out together. Perhaps that was my own fault.

Perhaps Noah Hayes had stolen my heart long before I realized I'd given it to him.

On the flip side, it had made everything so much easier.

"I don't live here anymore," I'd told him, dropping my arms at my sides with a heavy sigh. "It's over, Devon. I think it was over a long time ago."

Months of stress, anxiety, and indecisiveness had escaped me in that moment. It was the right thing to do.

It was a long time coming.

There had been no noticeable reaction from Devon during the few seconds of silence that had passed between us. I had watched for a flicker of sadness or regret in his eyes, but there was nothing. He hadn't begged me to stay, or pleaded his case. He hadn't asked for another chance.

I think he knew—I'd made my choice.

And he'd made his.

"Yeah," he had said, leaning against the back of the couch. "I guess it is."

"I'll find a way to pay you back for the car."

"No, it doesn't matter," he'd told me, scratching at his hair. "None of it matters."

That had been it.

My whirlwind romance with Devon Sawyer had come to an end.

Even though I knew it was for the best, I couldn't help but reflect on our fonder memories together. It had all felt so right in the beginning; there had been so much infatuation and high hopes. I'd known our relationship wouldn't be easy due to Devon's notoriety, but...

I'd never expected Noah Hayes.

And I'd never expected that fame and fortune would lead Devon down such a destructive path, turning him into a completely different person.

My thoughts were interrupted when Lisa strolled back into the room.

"Do you think Miles is cheating on me?" Lisa wondered.

I blinked. "What? Cheating on you?"

Lisa crossed her arms over her chest, pursing her lips together. "There have been signs. He's always flirting with other women and checking them out in front of me. Then he'll go days without texting me back. Sometimes he's vague about where he's been or what he's been doing."

My face flushed with shame. I had suspected Miles was cheating on Lisa for months and I hadn't said a word to my friend. "Lisa, I should probably tell you something..."

Her eyes widened, her fiery red curls bouncing as she stormed over to the couch. "Tell me what?" she asked in a panic.

"I mean, I don't have any concrete evidence, but there was something... suspicious," I said. "It was my last day at The Pit. I had just told Jerry I quit, and when I went to leave, I ran into Miles. He was there with another woman."

Lisa looked as if she'd been slapped.

I rambled on, flustered and guilty. "You were so happy, Lis. I didn't see anything sexual going on between them. A-And then the Grammy's happened, and I didn't want you to miss out on such an iconic event. You deserved to be there... you know?"

Swallowing, she looked down at the llama slippers on her feet. "I'm such a fool," Lisa whispered, shaking her head. When she returned her gaze to me, her eyes narrowed with indignation. "I trusted you to have my back."

My cheeks grew hot as I stood to face her. I reached for her hand, but she pulled away. "Lisa, please. I never meant to hurt you. It was the opposite... I was trying to protect you."

"I don't need your protection. I need your friendship and loyalty." Her expression morphed into hurt.

No.

Could I ever do anything right? How could one person make such a mess of everything?

"I'm so sorry. I screwed up."

"Yeah," she agreed, stepping away from me and muttering under her breath, "You're good at that."

I flinched as the bedroom door slammed shut before collapsing back onto the couch, burying my face into my hands.

It was true. I was a bona fide genius when it came to dissolution and disappointment. I had a magical way of sabotaging relationships and bringing chaos down upon everyone I loved.

Noah's face popped into my mind. He had received the shittiest end of my destruction stick. I'd managed to exacerbate his friendship with Devon, triggering Noah's departure from the band and thriving musical career. I had ruined any possible romance between him and Beth.

Above all, he'd been shot—*twice*—by my psychotic ex-boyfriend.

Someone from *my* past.

I was poison.

No wonder Noah couldn't admit to his love confession.

How could anyone possibly *love* me?

"No one will ever love you, Chelly Bean. You're a disaster—people run from disasters."

I jolted in place when my phone vibrated in my pocket, Noah's name lighting up the screen. "Hello?"

"Hey, Combs. It's great to hear your voice."

I couldn't help the smile that pulled at my lips. Clearing my throat, I asked, "How are you?"

"Oh, you know," he sighed. "Hanging in there. Glad to be home."

"I'm so glad you're home..." A pang of guilt swelled in the pit of my stomach. I had only visited Noah once in the last two weeks, right after he'd been released from the hospital.

Rosa had a background in nursing and seemed to be holding down the fort just fine. I had helped Noah settle in and enjoyed a *Paw Patrol* marathon with Sam, but when they'd insisted I stay for dinner that night, I'd declined. I had wanted to stay, more than anything... but seeing Noah sitting in his wheelchair, unable to play on the floor with his son or cook his own meal—well, it was heartbreaking.

And I'd felt wholeheartedly responsible.

While we'd stayed connected with texts and phone calls, I felt that keeping my distance was for the best.

"I'm not gonna lie," Noah whispered after a few beats. "I miss you."

The guilt in my belly turned into a kaleidoscope of butterflies. "I miss you, too. I'm sorry I haven't been over to see you lately."

"Yeah. Me, too."

I swallowed, closing my eyes. "It's not that I don't want to... I hope you know that."

"You feel responsible," Noah said. "You think you're the reason I was shot."

How did he do that? How was he always able to strip down my walls and access my tormented center?

"Noah... God, I'm so sorry."

"Stop being sorry." His tone was adamant and firm. "You're not responsible for what happened to me. You're not responsible for what happened to *you.* You need to get the hell away from that toxic mindset and realize that sometimes bad shit just happens. Bad people happen. It's not your fault."

My breath caught as I absorbed his words. My mother had always told me that my self-deprecating thoughts would be the end of me someday. "You're right," I conceded, running my fingers through my hair. "I'm just making everything worse. When can I see you?"

"Really?" Noah hesitated, thrown by my question. "Oh... well, I'm free right now."

It was my turn to be thrown as my insides hummed with anticipation. I glanced at the time on my phone, noting it was a few minutes after eight P.M. If I hurried, I could tuck Sam into bed. "Okay, I'll head over."

"Yeah?" Noah sounded surprised.

Hopeful.

"Is that okay?"

"Of course," he said. "It's definitely okay."

Tension swirled between us, loud and heavy. It was full of unspoken words, months of pent-up feelings, and something so powerful, it made my hand start to tremble as I held the phone to my ear. "I'll see you soon."

"See you."

When the call disconnected, I lifted a hand to my heart, feeling it thump wildly beneath my pink hoodie. I squeezed the fabric between my fingers and sucked in a nervous breath.

I felt like a frumpy mess in my hoodie and leggings. My shorter hair was tossed up into a small ponytail, while yesterday's mascara still adorned my eyelashes.

Jumping off the couch, I stepped into the room adjacent to Lisa's, careful not to disturb her, and changed into a pair of skinny jeans with a tank top and cardigan. I spritzed my favorite perfume onto my pulse points, pulling my hair down and untangling the strands with my fingertips. I touched up my mascara and reached for my blush, only to realize my cheeks were naturally flushed pink. My palms trailed to the rosy stains on my face, cursing myself for feeling like a giddy junior-high girl with a first crush.

"It's just Noah," I said to myself, studying my reflection in the mirror. I gulped back a lump in my throat and flattened out the wrinkles in my cardigan, wondering why I even cared about my appearance. Noah was used to seeing me in sweatpants and no makeup.

Why did this visit feel so... *different?*

Because it was different. Everything changed in that alleyway.

I stepped out of Lisa's apartment complex, biting my lip at the sight of the freezing rain. The temperature had warmed over the past couple of weeks, the snow turning into icy droplets. Pulling my hood up over my head, I made a mad dash to the BMW Devon had bought for me.

When I parked the car in Noah's driveway, I sat in silence.

I watched as the windshield wipers darted back and forth, unable to keep up with the falling rain.

Swish, swish.

Glancing up at the living room window, I squinted through the half-parted curtains. A welcoming yellow light beckoned me inside as shadows scattered across the room. I didn't even know why I was stalling.

It was just Noah.

The front door opened, and Rosa stepped outside with a giant red umbrella. I finally removed my keys from the ignition and hopped out of the car to greet the caretaker before she disappeared into the night.

"Rosa," I called out, trying to overpower the sound of the howling wind and rainfall.

"Señorita." Rosa quickened her pace. "You're going to freeze out here in this storm. Hurry on inside and get warm."

I huddled into Rosa, sharing her umbrella. "I just wanted to say thank you for everything."

"Que?"

I didn't know why I needed to say it—I just did. "Thank you, Rosa. I hope one day you'll see your Paco again."

Her eyes widened, then glazed over with a thousand memories. "Muchacha..."

"It's never too late. You can screw it up a million times, but love is love. It will always be there, waiting."

The rain and wind seemed to go silent as we faced each other. I wasn't sure where the words were coming from—I had no intention of offering sage wisdom to this woman in Noah's driveway, freezing cold and soaking wet.

Rosa extended her free hand, cupping the side of my face. "The song in your heart... it only plays for one."

I smiled as my eyes closed.

"Chelsie?"

My head turned, finding Noah standing in the doorway with his arm in a sling.

"Adios, mi querido."

Rosa gave my cheek a strong pinch before hurrying to her car. Returning my attention to Noah, I made my way up the pebbled path to his doorstep. "Hi."

Noah moved aside so I could enter. "Jesus, Combs. You're drenched."

I pulled back my hood, shaking out my arms and watching as the raindrops dispersed across the room. Glancing up at the mirror across the way, I chuckled at my appearance—I'd actually put effort into not looking homeless, and I still ended up resembling a drowned rat. I scrubbed the mascara streaks from under my eyes and slipped out of my soggy coat.

Noah was leaning against the wall with his good arm, holding himself steady. His wheelchair was abandoned next to the sofa.

"Are you walking okay?" I inquired, hanging my jacket up on an adjacent hook. I pivoted toward him, my eyes casing his appearance. Worry fused with affection as I awaited his response.

Noah gave a dismissive shrug. "Working on it," he said. "I'm improving with my physical therapy and moving on my own pretty well now."

He removed his hand from the wall and straightened, approaching me on unsteady feet.

I couldn't take it anymore. I closed the gap between us, wrapping my arms around his neck and releasing a sigh of relief into the collar of his shirt. His right arm encircled my waist, pulling me into a tight hug. "I've been wanting to do this for weeks," I whispered against his shoulder.

Noah gave me a squeeze, his breath tickling the hairs on my head. "I can't say I haven't missed having you around," he murmured. Then his voice lowered as he said, "And I can't say I haven't thought about—"

"Miss Chelsie!"

Sam's voice interrupted us as he darted down the staircase, his feet eliciting a loud thunk from each step.

I pulled away from Noah carefully, so he remained balanced, just as Sam came barreling into me. "Oh, Sam," I greeted, lowering myself to his level. "Did you get taller?"

He beamed, swaying back and forth, his arms swinging in time with his body. "Uh-huh. I'm growed-up now."

"I see that," I smiled. "Are you taking care of your dad?"

"Yep. I'm helping him get better with my doctor tools and my thermometer. Daddy had a *bad* fever today."

Noah chuckled behind me. "Sammy has been very attentive. I feel better already."

"It sounds like you're in excellent hands." Nibbling my lip, I addressed the littlest Hayes. "Sam, do you want me to help you pick out your pajamas and tuck you into bed?"

He bounced up and down. "Yes, please! I want my dinosaur jammies."

"I think that can be arranged." I glanced at Noah who was leaning against the door frame. Our eyes fused as I swallowed. "I'll be right back."

Noah nodded, a ghost of a smile lingering on his face. Sam snatched my hand before I became too lost in Noah's stare and pulled me toward the staircase.

"You were gone a long time, Miss Chelsie," Sam said as we made our trek up the stairs. "Were you sick like my dad?"

I guided him to his room before spinning toward his chest of dresser drawers to sort through the assortment of bright colors and patterns. A green set of pajamas decorated in cartoon dinosaurs came into view, so I reached for it with a triumphant smile. "I was waiting for your dad to get better, Sam. I didn't want to bother him while he was healing. Does that make sense?"

Sam jumped onto his bed, sitting cross-legged and tracing the stitches in his comforter with a clumsy finger. "I think so. Like how I stay in my bed under my blankets when I'm sick, so I don't get my friends sick, too?"

I sat down beside him and handed him the pajamas. "Just like that," I grinned through a nod.

"Miss Chelsie?"

"Yes?"

"My dad won't die... will he?"

My heart raced at his question. The last two weeks flashed through my memory like an old movie reel. "Oh... no, Sam. Your dad is very lucky. He's going to be okay."

Sam chewed his lip with consideration, then changed into his special pajamas. I helped tug his feet through the small foot holes.

"Will you read to me?"

I ran a hand through his brown mop of hair. "I would love to. *Curious George*?"

"Yes!"

I spent the next thirty minutes snuggling next to Sam, reading him outlandish adventures of a curious monkey. He would giggle every so often, pulling the blankets up to his chin and nuzzling his head against my shoulder, and I savored every moment. I was almost finished with the story when I looked down, noticing that his eyes had closed. His breathing became rhythmic, his arms falling still at his sides.

"Sweet dreams, Sammy," I whispered, placing a delicate kiss on his head before carefully removing myself out from under him. I switched off his lamp and turned on his Buzz Lightyear night-light, closing the closet door so there would be no conjuring of monsters or boogeymen.

As I turned to leave, I halted in the doorway, overcome with emotion I couldn't quite pinpoint. A solemn disquiet washed over me.

"Chelsie?"

I poked my head out into the hallway and spotted Noah at the bottom of the staircase. "I... I'm coming." Sparing Sam a final glance, I closed his door. "Sorry... we got caught up in *Curious George*," I explained as I made my way down the stairs.

Noah was leaning against the railing, his right hand holding up a glass of sparkling wine. "It's all good. It took me that long just to get the damn wine bottle open."

A smile tipped my lips as I accepted his offer, eyeing the glass curiously. "Are you trying to get me tipsy, Mr. Hayes?"

"You know I would have brought out the whiskey for that."

His eyes sparkled with flirtation while my mind wandered back to the last time I'd had whiskey with Noah. Illicit memories swept through me, causing my cheeks to flush hot.

"Where's your drink?" I inquired, biting my lip.

His eyes darted toward the kitchen. "On the table."

Faltering briefly, I walked over to find two plates of spaghetti and a bottle of champagne set up at the quaint table. It was adorned with silverware, napkins, and a sea breeze candle burning in the center. Soft music played as romantic ambiance kissed the air.

My lips parted to speak, but no words escaped.

Was this... a date?

CHAPTER THIRTY-TWO

NOAH

Monitoring Chelsie's reaction, I waited for her to speak.

Or smile.

Or breathe.

She didn't seem to be doing any of those things.

Did I misinterpret everything?

"I just figured we could relax and talk things out over wine and food," I tried to explain. "I hope it's not weird."

Chelsie looked up at me, her eyes as wide as emerald saucers. "I don't know what to say."

Well, fuck. That was not the reaction I'd been hoping for.

"It's honestly nothing." I scratched at my overgrown hair, my balance steadied by the railing. "Rosa made some spaghetti before she left, so I thought maybe you'd want to have a late dinner with me."

"I do. Of course, I do..." she said, nodding swiftly. "Sorry, I was just... caught off guard. This is a sweet surprise."

I tried to read her. Her knuckles had gone white from her deathlike hold on the champagne flute. There were mascara smudges under her eyes and her hair was still damp from the rain, spilling golden waves over her shoulders. She looked nervous, frazzled. "Are you sure you're okay?"

Maybe it was too soon, and I'd dropped the ball.

Chelsie flashed me a smile. "It's really great, Noah."

I began to relax until I noticed her face crumble into a mask of tears.

Double fuck.

"Shit, Chelsie." The bubbly liquid swished back and forth in her glass as her body shook with sobs and she buried her face into her opposite hand. I stood there, frozen to the floor, unprepared with how to handle the situation.

Should I hold her? Run away? Jump off the roof?

"Damnit, Combs, I didn't mean to upset you. It's just spaghetti."

"It's not the spaghetti. I love spaghetti," she cried, sniffling into the palm of her hand. "It's everything else."

The roof was sounding appealing.

"What did I do?" My voice cracked with vulnerability. This was not how I'd pictured the night unfolding.

Chelsie shook her head and looked up at me with swollen eyes. "I almost killed you... and you made me spaghetti."

She spoke as if there could be no other answer.

That's what this was all about? Guilt for a crime she didn't commit?

"First off, Rosa made the spaghetti. You give me too much credit," I said. "Secondly, you need to stop. We've been over this, Chelsie."

She set her glass down beside her. "It doesn't make it not true."

My shoulders sagged with defeat, but I knew I needed to get through to her—it was imperative.

Otherwise, there would be no hope for us.

"Chelsie... listen to me." I used my good arm to reach out and take her hand. She startled before relaxing beneath my touch, her breaths choppy as she inhaled. "I'm okay. I survived. I'm here, right now, with you. You need to stop dwelling on what might have been and start celebrating the fact that we got through it."

"What about your arm?" she sniffled. "What about your music?"

"Whatever happens, happens. I'm just happy to be alive."

I watched her features soften. She squeezed my fingers, as if to make sure I was real, running her hand up my other arm and pausing when it reached the juncture between my neck and shoulder. Thick bandages were hidden beneath the confines of my t-shirt, but we both knew they were there. Chelsie's eyes flared, fixed on my wound, her fingertips dancing along the surface of my cotton shirt.

She took a step closer. I tensed with anticipation at her nearness, blinking lazily. My breathing unsteadied.

"I keep replaying that night," she started, her tongue poking out to wet her lips. She fingered my collar, her touch featherlight and curious. "The sounds. The smells. I feel like I can taste the gunpowder in my mouth."

My jaw tensed while I tried not to put myself back in that alley. "It's over."

"I still see that look in Ian's eyes. That lifeless, horrible look," Chelsie continued. "I can feel myself running across the pavement, rocks cutting into my heels. I can hear my heart thumping in my ears. And I always see... you."

I reached up and grasped her hand, moving it downward and placing it over my heart. "I'm here." The steady beats were a solace to us both as I grazed my thumb over her knuckles. "I didn't die in that alley, Combs. If you keep living in a reality where I did, I'm going to lose you."

I couldn't lose her.

We finally had a real chance, and I fucking *knew* Chelsie wanted this as much as I did. Not to mention, she was single now.

Miles had stopped by with coffee and donuts one morning, filling me in on everything going on with the band. They were still practicing. They were trying out a guitar player that Devon knew through one of his social circles. According to Miles, the potential guitarist came from the social circle that involved all-night benders and cocaine. Miles hadn't seemed hopeful for the future of Freeze Frame, and I couldn't help but feel somewhat responsible for the band's downward spiral. The media was under the impression I had taken a break to heal from my gunshot wounds—they were unaware I'd made my departure before the attack had even occurred.

Miles had said Devon showed no remorse over his breakup with Chelsie. He'd barely said a word about it, acting numb and indifferent—a zombie. Drugs had turned him into a whole new person, and while we'd always had our ups-and-downs, I never could have anticipated this. I never wanted our friendship to end this way.

And while part of me was grateful for Devon's nonchalant reaction to losing Chelsie, I couldn't help but feel enraged by it as well.

How could anyone be so apathetic about losing a woman like Chelsie Combs? The thought alone burned me. She was the kind of woman a man fought hard for. There was no white flag or cordial surrender—there was bloodshed. There was impenetrable armor and steel swords.

There was the knowing that you might not make it out alive, but nothing would ever be more worth it.

I made a valiant effort not to think about the attack, but when I'd wake up at night in a cold sweat, I always saw her. I saw the look in her eyes when she realized I'd been shot.

She'd looked like she'd lost everything.

That's how I knew she felt it, too.

Chelsie was biting her lip, her face a canvas of emotion. "I wish I could be what you need," she whispered.

Her words cut me down like a gallant soldier as her fingertips pressed into my chest, her eyes lifting to mine. They shimmered with apology.

I wanted to shake her.

But even more than that, I wanted to kiss her.

Chelsie released a startled gasp when I wrapped my arm around her waist, tugging her to me. I ignored the pain in my side and walked her back toward the wall, leaning us both against it to steady my balance.

Her chest heaved as she stared up at me, our faces only inches apart. She looked unsure. Drenched with uncertainty. But then she raised both hands to my face, falling limp against the wall, and pulled my lips to hers.

I groaned with desire and relief when our mouths locked. Fuck... *yes*. Tasting her again was pure ecstasy. With one hand planted against the wall beside her head, I used my other to fist her hair and deepen the kiss. She tasted like spearmint gum and fucking sunbeams.

She tasted like my life was never going to be the same again.

Chelsie pulled me as close as possible, one of her hands reaching around and clutching the nape of my neck, while the other found my hair. She plunged her tongue in and out of my mouth, eager and impatient, her whimpers shooting shockwaves straight to my dick. Angling my face, I kissed her deep, desperate, unrestrained. I kissed her like a madman devouring his last meal. Her leg raised, wrapping around my upper thigh as she ground herself against me, turning me on even more.

I was painfully hard. I needed to be inside her.

But I also needed to breathe, so I pulled back for air, pressing my forehead to hers. "God, Chelsie..." I rushed out, ignoring my aching wounds warning me to slow down. "You're exactly what I need."

She lifted her chin to close the gap between us once more, her lips swollen and bee-stung as they found mine. But before I could deepen the kiss, Chelsie made a little gasping sound, almost like a cry, and withdrew from me. She shook her head, breathless and distraught. "I can't, Noah." Slipping out from under my arm, she dragged frustrated fingers through her hair and turned her back to me. "I thought I could, but I can't."

What the hell?

I straightened, staring at her with addled confused. "Why can't you just admit this is what you want?" I demanded, my heart straining my chest and my cock straining my jeans. "What are you so afraid of?"

Chelsie headed toward the front door and reached for her coat.

"Abandonment?" I called out. "I would never leave you."

She paused, jacket in hand. Chelsie swiveled around to gaze at me with a poignant clarity in her eyes. "I'm not afraid for me," she confessed. "I'm afraid for you."

My teeth scraped together. "That's ridiculous, and you know it."

Did she know it?

She looked pretty damn convinced.

"You'll regret this, Noah. It's for the best."

"I'm a grown ass man, Combs. I'm willing to take that risk." Except she wasn't a risk at all. I had never been more certain of anything in my life. "Is it Devon?" I wondered, flustered. My fists curled at my sides. "Do you still have feelings for him?"

Chelsie was pulling her arms through her coat sleeves, flipping her hair out over her shoulders. "No. It's over with Devon."

"Do you have feelings for me?"

She paused, locking her eyes with mine. There was no hesitation as she whispered, "Yes. So much."

I walked toward her with caution, as if any sudden movement might scare her away. "Then stop punishing yourself."

Chelsie's eyes watered as she shook her head, just a little. "I care about you too much to let you get hurt. I'm poison... a disease."

"Those are the words of a psychotic, murderous abuser—not yours. And sure as fuck not mine. You have to believe that."

Chelsie looked reflective for a moment, her eyes glimmering with possibility. For a split second, there was hope—there was a future.

There was spaghetti to be eaten.

"Give us a chance," I begged on a quiet breath.

But the hope dissipated when Chelsie zipped up her coat and spared me an apologetic glance. "I'm so sorry, Noah. It's for your own good."

Don't walk out that door.

The sound of the door rattling shut echoed through the house, a metaphorical closed door on everything I thought might be.

Anger bubbled. Disbelief seized me.

"*Fuck,*" I bit out, storming through the living room toward the kitchen, kicking my wheelchair as I passed. I grabbed the dinner plates off the kitchen table and tossed them both into the garbage can, dishware and all. Pouring the rest of the champagne into the sink, I threw it into the trash, wincing as the glass bottle clashed against the plates.

I still felt her presence. I still tasted her fruity lip balm.

Drinking in a calming breath, I walked back out into the living room, feeling hopeless and defeated.

I was about to make my way up the stairs when the front door burst open.

Chelsie stepped inside soaking wet, her hair matted against her cheeks and forehead. I froze, my attention pinned on her as she advanced on me. With our gazes locked tight, her eyes reckless and wild, she pulled off her coat and let it fall to the floor.

"What are you—" My question was silenced by her mouth when she closed the gap between us. She was radiating furious passion, her movements desperate as I parted my lips to let her in. We both groaned, our tongues colliding, her hands everywhere—tugging at my hair, cupping my face, sneaking their way up my t-shirt. My body buzzed and hummed as her fingertips grazed over the planks of my stomach.

I walked backward, our feet awkwardly stepping on each other's as she followed my lead, our lips still fused. When the back of my legs found the edge of the couch, I collapsed onto the cushions while Chelsie climbed into my lap, straddling me and reaching for the edging of my shirt.

I grabbed one of her hands and we locked eyes, both of us panting and wanting. As I held her heated gaze, I was transported back in time to that night in Manhattan—a night in which I'd fully intended on sabotaging Chelsie and Devon's budding relationship. My goal had been to cast her out of our lives forever.

Instead, she had wormed her way into my heart after baring her soul to me in a hotel room. She'd burrowed deep and never left.

I would never forget the tortured look in her eyes as she'd confessed her darkest secrets. I would never forget the way her body felt when she'd crawled into my lap and forced me to look at her; to truly *see* her.

And I had.

I'd seen all of her broken bits and unparalleled beauty.

In that moment, she had made her mark me on, destined to leave a permanent scar.

We were in that same position again, right now, with Chelsie in my lap and an identical look in her sea-spun eyes. There was no metaphor more perfect than that: Chelsie's eyes were the ocean. Tranquil, yet turbulent. Vast and full of life. Mysterious.

Dangerous in the most beautiful way.

Chelsie leaned into me until our noses were touching. Her fingers disappeared underneath my shirt as she closed her eyes, her hot breath tickling my face. I ran my hand up the length of her arm, pulling her cardigan down over her shoulders. Raindrops dripped down her collarbone and onto her chest, then disappeared between her breasts as icy, wet hair tried to cool the heat between us.

"Noah..."

My name fell out of her like a small whisper. I wrapped my arm around her waist and pulled her closer, until my erection was grinding right between her thighs. She let out a breathy moan as I inhaled sharply, her body moving, seeking more friction.

"Noah," she repeated. "Did... did you mean it?"

I knew what she was referring to.

Of course, I knew.

Leaning forward, I moved her hair over her shoulder, kissing along her collarbone, up the expanse of her neck, and nibbling the lobe of her ear. She squirmed in my lap as her back arched, her hands squeezing the fabric of my shirt for dear life. Grazing my palm up her spine and holding her to me, I whispered huskily against the shell of her ear, "Yes."

Chelsie froze, her body going still and limp, her breaths quick and frayed. A few silent beats passed before she pulled back to look at me with a dazed expression. I cupped her face with my good hand, my thumb grazing over her cheek. She relaxed with a sigh, then leaned in to breathe her reply against my mouth. "I love you, too."

It was my turn to go still.

My eyes flared, my grip on her cheek tightening as my insides swirled with disbelief. "Chelsie..." I said, my hand moving to palm the back of her head, my fingers fisting in her hair. Words were elusive, so my only response was to kiss her senseless.

She whimpered, our bodies becoming a mess of tangled limbs and tongues. When she pulled her arms out of her cardigan, I yanked her tank top up over her head, one-handed. Her hair sent a shower of raindrops over me as it fell back down, and she bent to yank at my belt buckle. Her hands trembled as she unlatched it.

When the belt came loose, Chelsie unbuttoned her own jeans, sliding the denim and lace panties down her legs and wriggling free. She lifted my t-shirt, pressing a delicate hand against my bandaged wounds. "I don't want to hurt you, Noah," she said, trailing her fingertips over the gauze.

I sensed her double meaning.

Chelsie was perched in my lap, only wearing a bra, and I'd be lying if I said I'd never imagined this moment before. But in my own fantasies, I didn't have multiple gunshot wounds and a defective arm. "You won't," I assured her, my palm splaying against her chest and trailing downward, memorizing the silk of her skin. "But I have to say, I had every intention of going crazy on you if we ever made it to this point. I'll make it up to you when I'm healed."

She moaned a little, arcing into me, before shoving at my jeans. I tried not to wince as I lifted up, allowing her to drag my pants and boxers down my hips until my cock was freed. Chelsie's breathing picked up when she gazed down between us, our naked bodies almost touching. She swallowed. "You've... thought about this?"

Tugging her hair back, my mouth found the swell of her breast, and I murmured, "Every damn day."

Chelsie released a breathy moan as our mouths collided and reached down to wrap her hand around my cock.

Fuck.

My head fell back against the couch when she fisted me, stroking up and down and raising her hips. She situated herself over me, pressing her forehead to mine. And when she slid down slowly, taking me inside of her for the first time, I nearly fucking died.

Chelsie cried out when I was fully sheathed inside her, digging her fingernails into my shoulders. A moan fell out of me as my grip on her tightened.

Goddamn.

She went motionless for a beat. A heady potency wrapped itself around us as we clung to each other, each of us lost to the power of the moment—each of us utterly bewitched. It was a culmination of nearly a year's worth of almosts, maybes, and if onlys. It was the pinnacle of the ultimate slow burn.

It was a divine inevitability.

She began to move, her forehead still glued to mine, as if she needed to feel every inch of me. I groaned, reveling in the way our bodies melded together, savoring the sheer magic of it all. My fingers tangled in her hair as she moved in my lap, and I gently pulled her head back. "Look at me, Combs."

I needed to see her eyes.

Chelsie blinked slowly, tugging her bottom lip between her teeth. The chemicals danced between us, flickering, sparking, exploding. Her cheeks were flushed pink, her skin warm and intoxicating. "Noah..."

The sound of my name passing through her lips as she rode me, clinging tight, lifting up, then slamming back down—*Jesus Christ*.

I kissed her hard. Recklessly. My tongue twisted with hers, growing clumsier as she bounced up and down and the pleasure swelled. Fevered moans escaped her, the sounds vibrating right through me. She picked up her pace, wrapping her fingers around the nape of my neck and squeezing.

I pulled back to speak. Not to breathe, or to regroup, or to collect my thoughts. I only pulled back to speak the words that had been sweltering inside me for months. "I fucking love you."

Chelsie tensed in my arms, burying her face against my neck and letting out a primal gasp as she ground against me. I felt her shudder and peak. I felt her rise and fall like a tempestuous tide. I felt her break and burn, and above all, *surrender*. Her orgasm gripped her, spontaneous and furious, a consummation of everything we were always meant to be.

Ignoring the shooting pains from my healing body, I held her tight, bucking my hips and slamming into her, grunting with every thrust. Unraveling with every squeaky moan that spilled from her lips.

I growled as I came, following behind her as we rode out the waves together. Chelsie still clutched me, her face concealed in the crook of my neck, her breathing low and heavy. Warm and comforting. I ran my hand up and down the curve of her back, which was slick from sweat and her wet hair, coming down slow and savoring every blissful breath with her in my arms.

We stayed in that position until our heartbeats slowed from their frantic pace.

Chelsie finally poked her head up. "Wow."

A smile crested, lazy and satiated. "I concur." Blinking away the haze, I glanced over her shoulder, realizing Sam could have interrupted us at any moment.

Shit. Responsible parent fail.

Reaching across the couch, I grabbed the fleece blanket, draping it around her the best I could with one arm. A coy smile touched her lips as she took the blanket and wrapped herself up like a cocoon, lifting off my lap.

I instantly missed her warmth and envied the blanket that had replaced me.

She cleared her throat, sliding up next to me as I fumbled with my pants and zipper. "So... that happened," she said, her face pinkening in the tungsten light.

Her hair was wild, her cheeks glowing. She didn't seem to harbor any immediate regret. "Finally," I replied, the curve of my mouth twisting upward.

We sat in a reflective silence for a few minutes, the only noise around us being the soothing sounds of rainfall against the roof. I soaked up her presence, relishing in the feel of her warm body pressed against my side. This felt good.

This felt *right*.

"Want to go upstairs?"

Chelsie's voice penetrated my thoughts as I glanced at her. She was staring at me expectantly. "Bedroom?"

She ducked her head. "It might be more comfortable..."

I garnered the strength to pull myself up from the couch, hissing through my teeth as my body cussed me out for ignoring the doctor's orders of limited exertion. Chelsie was at my side right away, one hand clasping her blanket, and the other holding me steady. The journey up the staircase seemed painstakingly long compared to the usual trek, but mostly because all I could think about was being inside her again.

When we reached the bedroom, Chelsie turned to face me,

letting the blanket flutter from her grip. The moonlight brightened her ivory skin, and I couldn't help but stare in wonder. "You
have no idea how beautiful you are, do you?"

She replied by stepping forward and leaning up on her tiptoes
to plant a sweet kiss on my mouth. Reaching behind her back, she
unhooked her bra, dropping it to the floor beside her feet. "You
make me feel beautiful," she whispered against my lips.

I ushered her backward, walking her toward the bed and
climbing in beside her. "You just make me fucking feel."

Her hair splayed out around her on the bedsheets, her eyes
dancing with anticipation. She lifted one knee and cupped both
breasts in her palms, pulling a groan out of me as I leaned over her
to pepper kisses down her neck and chest.

"Make love to me."

Fuck.

I was insatiable—I couldn't get enough of her.

There was no reality in which I would *ever* get enough of her.

Chelsie curled up beside me, sweat-soaked and spent, after
I'd taken my time discovering every perfect inch of her body. Her
head was resting on my shoulder, her fingers drawing lazy designs
across my chest. I held her close, concentrating on the way her
skin felt against mine and burning it into my brain forever.

"We're, like... the perfect duet," I whispered, my hands
combing through her hair.

Chelsie's fingers paused on my chest. "Duet?"

I shrugged lightly. "I'm a music guy, so that's the first thing
that came to mind. You know, when you hear this killer duet and
you think, 'shit, they go so well together.' That's us... that's you
and me."

She considered my words, going silent as she laid sprawled
against me.

"Think we should get some shut-eye before the little man
finds his way in here?" I asked, giving her a gentle squeeze. "I
wish we could make this night last forever, but you know... dad
life."

She nodded into my chest. "I know." Rolling off me, Chelsie
pulled the covers up to her chin. "Noah?"

A pang of worry washed over me when she said my name.

The tone, the pitch—something in her voice had changed. The mood shifted ever so slightly. I braced myself for what she might say. "Yeah?"

She reached her hand out and rested it along my cheek, her eyes wide and expressive. "Sam is so lucky to have you," she murmured, her eyes shimmering in the milky moonglow.

I kissed her hand. "He's lucky to have you, too. We both are."

She smiled, but it didn't quite reach her eyes. "Goodnight, Noah."

"Goodnight." I watched as she rolled over to face away from me, burying herself beneath the blankets.

As I drifted off, I could have sworn I heard the faint sound of muffled cries. But I was so consumed with exhaustion, I was unsure of anything at that point, so I blamed it on the howling wind outside my window and fell into a comfortable sleep.

When sunlight spilled inside the room the next morning, I stretched with a content smile and reached over to the other side of the bed. Memories swirled around me. I was eager to feel her warmth.

But when I opened my eyes, my bed was empty.

I was alone.

Frowning, I sat up with achy muscles and throbbing wounds, looking around the room in a sleep-filled daze.

That's when I spotted a note resting atop one of the pillows beside me. My stomach sank. It took a moment for me to work up the courage to read it, so I just let it sit there for a few minutes longer. I savored those final moments living in a reality where Chelsie was still mine because I knew...

I just fucking knew.

Finally, I plucked the piece of green construction paper off the pillow and sucked in a tremulous breath, running a hand through my hair. My eyes scanned over the note, front and back, with clenched teeth. I analyzed every word with careful scrutiny.

I studied the curve of her letters. I envisioned her voice in my mind, reading to me with thoughtful reflection. I imagined the tears in her eyes as she put the pen to paper.

I could still smell the ink.

She couldn't want this.

How could she want this?

A desperate growl escaped me, and I grabbed my cell phone off the nightstand and dialed her number.

Straight to voicemail.

All ten times.

My heart was shattering. My mind was racing. My stomach was sick, and I wanted to retch. I reread the note over and over for the next hour, until Sam came running into the bedroom, completely unaware that his father's world was falling apart.

I tried to make sense of it. I tore apart every letter, every syllable, every fucking dotted *I*—but it was no use.

It was senseless. Illogical.

Hopeless.

And yet... *it was.*

This was how the cards had fallen. Chelsie had made her choice, and it wasn't me.

It was never going to be me.

And I knew I would get through this, just like I always had. Sam needed me to be strong.

Sam needed me.

If only she'd known how much I needed her.

CHAPTER THIRTY-THREE

CHELSIE

Sleep fell away at the sound of giggles and Sunday morning cartoons. The mouth-watering aroma of homemade pancakes wafted through the air, causing me to sit up in bed with a dreamy sigh. I loved pancakes.

The sun was shining that morning, a gentle breeze floating in through the cracked window. I smiled when I spotted two love-birds perched on a nearby branch as I threw my legs over the side of the bed, enjoying the feel of the plush rug beneath my bare feet.

"Breakfast is ready!"

I leaped up and put a robe on over my nightgown. Nothing got me out of bed faster than pancakes.

"Good morning. I thought you'd never wake up."

Entering the kitchen, a coy grin lit up my face. "I was tired. Someone kept me up late last night." I winked at the handsome man with a spatula in his hand.

"I cleared the table for you, Chelsie!"

My grin brightened as I strolled over to the kitchen table decorated with butter, syrup, and fresh fruit. "You did a great job, Sam."

Noah wandered up behind me and smacked my backside before whirling me around to plant a kiss on my lips. "I missed you."

"It's only been six hours, you nut," I teased, wrapping my arms around his neck and accosting him with kisses.

He grinned. "That's six hours of missing you."

"Eww, gross." Sam contorted his face into a mask of horror at the display of affection. "Growed-ups are yucky."

We chuckled as I moved toward the table to take my seat.

That's when I heard the distinct sound of music paying in the distance. My nose crinkled. "Are you playing... U2?"

Noah looked at me like I'd grown a second head. "I'm not playing any music, Combs. Why do you always think U2 is playing?"

I frowned, panic sluicing me. "I – I swear I hear it. Can't you hear it?" The music grew louder, and I ran into Noah's arms, shaking him as hard as I could. "Why can't you hear it?"

"There's no music. You need to wake up. It's a beautiful day."

My hands cupped my ears as I shook my head. "No, no, no..."

"... *It's a beautiful day...*"

Shooting up in bed, beads of sweat dripped down the sides of my face. My thoughts were disjointed, my breaths unsteady. It took a few moments for me to gather my bearings as I blinked, my vision blurred and hazy with sleep.

Inhaling deeply, I reached for my phone sitting on my nightstand and turned off the alarm clock, which was playing *Beautiful Day* by U2.

1112 days.

It had been 1112 days since I packed my entire life into a suitcase and drove twelve-hundred miles to south Florida.

Well... not my *entire* life.

I rubbed the sleep from my eyes and tossed my phone onto the bed covers.

I really hated that dream.

My cat, Misty, hopped onto the bed and nuzzled close, allowing me to take comfort in the one familiar thing I still had in my life.

Not that my life was bad—it was just different. So many things had changed.

I had changed.

And, well... that had been the whole point.

I often flashed back to that last night with Noah.

It had been the best night of my life.

It had also been the most soul-crushing.

That night led me on a journey of self-discovery and healing, prompting me to leave everything behind and start all over. I'd needed to mend a lot of things—mostly, myself, but also my relationship with my parents. I recalled leaving a note for Lisa, grabbing my cat, then hopping in my car and driving eighteen hours straight to St. Petersburg, Florida. I'd called my mother on the way down, hysterical and scared.

During my volatile relationship with Ian, I'd shut them out when they'd only tried to help me. I'd been so dependent on my abuser, so beyond repair, I had cast out everything truly good in my life. Even after I'd left him, I hadn't had the courage to make amends.

I'd been cowardly, mortified, and lost.

I'd eventually realized that, while I had removed the immediate threat in my life—Ian—I hadn't ever tackled the real, soul-deep problem.

Myself.

A steady paycheck, a tiny apartment, and proclaimed independence had only been a shiny exterior to the damage still hiding within, rotting me from the inside out.

"I'm coming home, mama," I had sobbed, silently praying for my parents to accept me back into their lives.

My mother had broken down into tears on the other end of the line. "I've been waiting years to hear you say that."

That was where my journey to healing had begun—on a little beach house on the gulf shores outside of town. It wasn't an easy transition. There had been many sleepless nights. There had been times where I'd cried so hard, I'd made myself physically sick.

There were plenty of moments where I had broken down and dialed Noah's phone number, only to quickly hang up.

But then the days started getting a little brighter, the nights a little easier. I'd begun looking for work as a cocktail waitress, only to run into a person who would forever change my life: Elsa Cunningham.

She was a counselor, a speaker, and a voice for victims of domestic violence.

She was hope.

And hope was something I'd desperately needed.

Elsa had taken me under her wing, helping me heal all my broken parts. She'd helped me move past the dark cloud that was Ian Masterson and put my life back together, starting with myself.

"A healthy soul plays the biggest role," Elsa had told me. "You will never find true happiness when you're full of self-loathing. Find happiness within yourself, then you can find happiness with another."

I had used those words to fuel me. Even though I had tried to hide from the media, there was no escaping the infamous name I'd made for myself back in the Freeze Frame days. At first, it had felt like a curse that would follow me around indefinitely.

Until one day, I'd decided to use my notoriety to my advantage.

With Elsa's help, I'd created a foundation for domestic abuse survivors called *Chelsie's Calling*.

I helped heal the broken and damaged souls, much like Elsa had helped me. Within two years, we had raised the funds to build a sanctuary in nearby Safety Harbor. The sanctuary was created to take in women for healing retreats, consisting of one-on-one counseling sessions, group therapy, meditation, spa treatments, yoga, and overall self-care.

I had truly found my purpose.

My mission had caught on quickly, and soon I was appearing on talk shows, podcasts, and even *Ellen*. I had used my fame for the greater good, and it was inspiring.

Eventually, I'd started bringing in enough income to leave my parents' house and rent an apartment down the street from the sanctuary. One of my greatest joys was sitting on my balcony with a cup of tea and chatting with my mother each morning.

I had turned my life around.

I no longer felt toxic to myself and to those around me. I no longer filled my mind with poisonous, self-sabotaging thoughts— no, I genuinely loved myself. I loved my new life, my work, my family and friends. I'd made a large and loyal social circle filled with positive and motivating people. Along with Elsa, my dear friends, Maggie, Anne, Thomas, and Jon were all an important part of my happiness.

Jon had asked me out on a date one afternoon a few months back. He was cute and charming with sandy hair and freckles on his cheeks. He had stopped me one day outside the sanctuary where he worked as a counselor. "Chelsie, wait up! I wanted to see if you'd like to grab coffee with me after work."

My nose had crinkled. We'd always gotten together after work with our group of friends. "You mean, a different kind of coffee from the kind we usually get?"

He'd ducked his head with a timid smile. "I mean, just you and me. Without the crew."

My heart rate had picked up. The thought of dating anyone hadn't dared crossed my mind. "Oh... I – I see," I'd stuttered, feeling flustered and unsure. "That's sweet of you to ask, but I'm sort of unavailable."

"We can do tomorrow," he'd said, eager and anxious.

"I'm sorry, Jon. I meant... I'm *unavailable*. You know, emotionally."

My friends knew about my past life in New York. They had watched my relationship with Devon Sawyer unfold and fall apart on national news. They knew about Ian and the attack. They knew about my deep-rooted emotional trauma.

But they didn't know about Noah Hayes.

They knew he existed, of course, but I had never talked about our unexpected friendship, profound connection, or whirlwind romance that had been cut short.

They didn't know I fell in love with him.

I often wondered if Noah still thought about me. I'd kept tabs on him through the media and various social outlets—he was a proclaimed solo artist now. His arm had fully healed, and he'd picked up playing guitar again. Noah never went back to Freeze Frame and the band had eventually dissolved, the remaining members going off to pursue their own creative outlets. None of them had created anything worthwhile, except for Noah.

Noah Hayes was the country's most promising rising star.

He'd released a hit single called *Aria* about a year after I'd left town.

I knew the song was about me.

I'd spent many nights crying myself to sleep while the song played on repeat, haunting my bedroom with old memories and a painful echo of what could have been. Noah's lyrics and the sound of his voice cut through me like a hot knife. It had felt like he was speaking directly to me.

God, it hurt.

It hurt more than I ever thought possible.

And the thing that hurt the most?

Noah Hayes was married now.

He had tied the knot with Beth Jessup six months ago. They had a baby together named Jeremiah, making Sam a big brother.

All of it hurt.

But I had to believe it'd been the right thing to do for everyone's sake, while making a conscious effort each morning to remind myself of my wonderful life. I'd made my choice; we were both happy. It was for the best.

Even though I still loved him.

I knew I always would. I had no desire to date or get married, or to fall in love with someone else.

Noah would forever have my heart.

My back-up alarm began to go off, startling me from the solemn memories as I frantically turned it off.

It was time for work. Luckily, my job was only a five-minute bike ride away, which was one of its many perks.

Making my way out of bed, I headed toward the bathroom to turn on the shower. As I pulled a fresh towel out of my hall closet, my phone vibrated on the bathroom sink. I ignored it and continued to fetch a washcloth and a new bar of soap.

It buzzed again.

"Fine, I'll bite," I muttered, closing the closet door and walking back into the bathroom.

Two missed calls from Lisa.

I had made amends with Lisa a few months after I'd left. We'd had an epic four-hour phone conversation and our friendship was restored. While we hadn't seen each other in person since I'd left, we talked regularly via text and video chats.

A frown claimed me when Lisa's name lit up the screen for a third time. I answered quickly. "Lisa? What's up?"

"Hey," Lisa replied on the other end. "Did you see the news?"

A ball of anxiety twisted inside my stomach. "No, I just woke up. Why? What happened?"

"Chels..." She hesitated, letting out a long breath into the receiver. "It's Devon."

"Devon?" I asked in bewilderment. "What about Devon?"

She fell silent on the other end, as if she were afraid to tell me.

"Lisa, what happened?"

"I'm so sorry, Chelsie..." she croaked out. "He's dead."

I froze, my blood running cold. I could feel the color leaving my face as nausea crept into my throat. "Wh-what?"

"They found him in his condo early this morning. The media is saying it was a drug overdose, but no one knows for sure yet."

How could this be real?

I hadn't spoken to Devon in years, but the news shook me to my core. Once upon a time, I had cared for Devon Sawyer. I'd created a life with him; I'd seen a future with him.

Now he's gone.

"Oh my God... I don't know what to say," I choked, bile rising in my chest.

"I'm sorry I had to be the messenger," Lisa said, her tone sober. "I didn't want you to see it on the news first."

"I appreciate you calling me. I just... I can't believe it."

Lisa paused. "Chels, do you need me to come down to stay with you? I don't want you to go through this alone."

I forced a smile. "Thank you, but I'll be okay. I'm not alone at all."

"Well, I'll let you get to work," she replied with a sigh. "I'm so sorry."

I was about to say my goodbyes when a thought popped into my head. "Hey... can you let me know if there's a service or something?"

"You would come to New York?"

A bundle of nerves bubbled in my gut. "Yes... I think I'd like to be there."

"I'll definitely keep you posted, then."

"Thanks, Lis," I replied. "Love you."

Setting the phone back down on the bathroom sink, my old life flashed through my mind, buried memories clawing their way to the surface. I recalled all the sweet moments I'd shared with Devon, from our very first coffee date, to our bonding session over pot stickers at one of the band's practices. I remembered the way I had felt when I'd picked up the phone that fateful day and heard Devon's voice on the other line. I couldn't believe he had called me after I'd stormed out of their V.I.P. suite.

It was a lifetime ago—I'd been a completely different person then. Frightened, insecure, and ridden with self-hatred. I'd be lying if I said those same feelings weren't inching their way back into my psyche as I stared at the cell phone in my palm.

I had always felt responsible for Devon's foray into drugs.

I shook my head, inhaling a long, calming breath.

It wasn't my fault.

None of it was my fault.

The days proceeded on like a bad dream. Reporters had started coming out of the woodwork, asking for an interview and wanting to know how I felt about Devon's death.

Horrible. Sick. Sad.

That's how any normal person would feel about the death of someone they cared about. I'd tried to avoid the cameras and media frenzy, burying myself in my work and relationships—afternoon shopping trips with my mother, fishing with my father, quiet lunches with Elsa and Maggie.

I appreciated the busy schedule; it kept my mind off things.

My phone buzzed one morning as I strolled into work.

"Good morning, Chelsie," Anne greeted as she ran a basket of spa towels down to the laundry room.

I smiled at my friend before reaching into my pocket for my phone. It was a text from Lisa.

Lisa: *The service is tomorrow at three o'clock. Can you make it?*

My breath caught. That was in less than thirty-six hours. I still had to research flight times, transportation, hotel...

Was it even realistic?

Should I leave the past in the past?

Anne stalled in her tracks after noticing the worried look on my face. "You okay, girl? You look like you've seen a ghost."

I glanced up, distracted. "Huh? Oh, sorry. I – I just found out that Devon's service is tomorrow. I wanted to be there, but I'm not sure I can swing it."

Elsa poked her head out of her office. "Chelsie, go home and book your flight. We'll see you when you get back."

I folded my lips between my teeth. My hand was trembling, so I put my phone back into my pocket. "I don't know..."

"You need closure, Chels," Anne spoke up. "You need this. You'll always have this cloud hanging over you if you don't go. Say your goodbyes, girlfriend."

"She's right," Elsa agreed, leaning against the doorframe. "Closure is necessary for healing. Take all the time you need."

Forcing a faint smile, I sucked in a breath.

It was settled, then.

I was headed back to New York City.

CHAPTER THIRTY-FOUR

CHELSIE

It was a foggy, damp day in New York City. It felt as if the entire city was mourning the loss of Devon Sawyer.

I pulled my sweater tighter, no longer used to the chilly, northern air. I felt out of place as I hailed a cab, dodging the busy pedestrians on their cell phones and cursing as I stepped into a puddle. There was so much noise. The smell of street-stand hot dogs filled the air and car horns blared as I hurried down the bustling sidewalk.

It was a short drive to the funeral home.

Too short. I didn't feel prepared.

When the cab pulled up to the brick building, I almost told the driver to bring me back to the hotel. My heart was beating rapidly, and my stomach had twisted with nerves and anxiety.

I pressed on, though. I'd made it this far, and I needed to see it through.

"Thank you," I said to the driver, handing him his cash and stepping out onto the sidewalk in black sandals.

There were people everywhere; family, friends, fans. It took my breath away.

Moving a few hesitant steps forward, my eyes darted left and right, unsure of who I might recognize.

Would Julia be there? We hadn't spoken since I'd left town almost three years ago.

Miles? Tad?

Noah?

My stomach churned.

I can't do this.

"Chelsie!"

I stopped in my tracks, recognizing the voice.

Lisa.

We eagerly embraced as I fought back tears. It had been a long time since I'd laid eyes on my dear friend. Lisa's red curls smelled like baby powder, tickling my nose as we hugged.

"I'm so glad you came," she whispered against my ear.

I let the emotions run through me, not wanting to fight my feelings. "God, it's good to see you," I replied, pulling back and wiping the fallen tears from my cheeks.

We stared at each other, taking one another in and studying how much we had changed.

"You cut your hair," Lisa noticed, sniffling back her own tears. "It looks really cute."

I raised a hand to my shoulder-length bob. My bangs had grown out, and I'd wanted something with less maintenance. "Oh, thanks. I'm still getting used to it."

"It suits you," Lisa smiled.

I pushed a few rebellious strands of hair behind my ear. "And look at you. You're in law school. I'm so proud of you."

Lisa nodded with excitement. "It's going really well. I'm so glad I decided to finally go for it. No more waiting tables," she said.

My mind wandered to Julia. "Do you still talk to Julia? I texted her after I left, but I haven't spoken to her since."

"Julia moved to California about six months after you moved to Florida. She sent me a Facebook message. According to her Instagram, she's dating some D-list actor and living as a socialite near Los Angeles."

I wrinkled my nose. "That sounds like Julia."

"Yep." Lisa seemed to catch sight of something out of the corner of her eye. She bit her lip, fidgeting with the hem of her shirt. "I just spotted Miles," she said to me.

My head jerked in the same direction. Sure enough, Miles

stood at the entrance of the funeral home with a mystery woman by his side. Tad was standing beside him.

Lisa had dumped Miles immediately after finding out he'd been cheating on her. As far as I knew, that was the last time they had spoken.

"Are you going to be okay?" I wondered, extending my arm and resting a comforting hand on Lisa's shoulder.

She straightened her posture and cleared her throat. "Of course. It's just a little awkward, you know?"

I nodded, understanding.

"Are you going to talk to Noah?"

Just the sound of Noah's name had my belly doing flip-flops. Lisa was the only person I had told about our last night together. "Um... I'm not sure. I don't know if that's a good idea."

She grabbed my hand and gave it a squeeze. "Well, if you change your mind, he's right over there."

I paled.

My eyes followed the direction of Lisa's finger, my mouth going dry. My heart was pounding so hard, I thought it might crack a rib. Lisa squeezed my hand even tighter, sensing my ever-growing panic. "I can't do this, Lis. I can't be here. It's too much."

"You *can* do this," she assured me. "Walk inside. Say your goodbyes to Devon. Make peace with everything. Then... go back to your beautiful life."

I nodded, trying to concentrate on my breaths, my gaze falling back to Noah. Beth was by his side, her hands clutching a baby stroller. A young boy, maybe three years old, was running circles around them as they chatted with unfamiliar visitors.

Then there was Sam.

He had grown so much. He was impossibly tall, his hair now shaggy, curling behind his ears. I wondered if he would remember me.

"Let's go inside, okay?" Lisa said, nudging my side. "I'm right here with you."

"Yeah... okay." I kept my eyes facing forward as we passed Noah and his family. All I could do was hope he didn't recognize me.

When we were safely inside, we waited in line to pay our

respects to Devon. It was a closed casket, and I was grateful for that—seeing my ex-boyfriend lying in a coffin would be too much to bear. Just knowing he was in there was enough to make my stomach sour.

When I was next to proceed, I pressed my hand on top of the mahogany coffin and bowed my head. "I'm sorry, Devon. I'm sorry for how everything ended between us." Hot tears pooled in my eyes. When I blinked, they fell down my face and landed on the shiny wood. "We shared some special moments together, and I'll always appreciate everything you did for me before we..." I trailed off, lost for words. "I'm a healthier person now. I wish we could have made amends... I wish I could have helped fix you. Wherever you go, I hope you keep making music."

I stepped away with a strangled breath. A combination of remorse and peace washed over me as I spoke my final goodbyes.

Closure.

Spinning around, I allowed a woman to access the snack table, almost bumping into someone else. "Oh, excuse me..." When I glanced up, I froze.

Noah stood before me, his eyes burning into mine.

I felt dizzy as the room spun. It was suddenly too hot—I couldn't catch my breath. I reached over to hold myself steady against something, but there was nothing there. As I nearly lost my balance, Noah quickly moved in to pull me back to my feet.

"You okay?"

That voice.

His voice.

I'd heard it on the radio, but this was different.

He was here. He was *real*.

My Noah.

His hand was still lingering on my elbow as I regained my footing, and it was the first time we had touched in almost three years. The physical contact sent me mentally spiraling for a moment. My entire universe felt off-kilter.

Reeling in my emotions, I let out the breath I had been holding for the last thirty seconds. "Noah."

His name sounded foreign on my tongue, like a lost and forgotten language. Sacred; a thing of beauty.

Something that should remain entombed.

Noah released his hold on my arm, his movements slow and lazy, as if he were reluctant to let go. "I saw you walk in. I didn't want to bother you, I just..." He scratched the back of his neck, his features unreadable. His green eyes used to tell so many tales. "I'm sorry, I probably should have left you alone."

I glanced over at Lisa who had finished paying her respects. She was sipping lemonade in the corner, giving us our space. My eyes fell back to Noah. "It's okay. I'm not staying long."

He slipped his hands into his pockets, the sleeves of his black button-down rolled up to his elbows. A tattoo of a guitar with various dates encompassing it had been newly etched into the fleshy side of his arm. "I can't believe he's gone."

Gone. That word was so final, so conclusive. I wondered if Noah had felt a similar chill in his bones when he'd realized that I was gone.

I folded my sweater across my royal blue dress and looked down at the floor. "Me, too. I think I'm still processing everything."

"Chelsie?"

My attention jerked to the right as the young, innocent voice registered.

Sam. He approached us with wide eyes and remnants of donuts on his face.

"Sam... you remember me?" I wondered.

He was seven years old now, in second grade. He likely had epic birthday parties with his friends and video game marathons with his father. His dinosaur pajamas had probably been replaced with superhero or *Minecraft* designs.

I pondered if he still had his Buzz Lightyear nightlight, or if that had also been replaced—or possibly, removed completely. Maybe Sam wasn't afraid of the dark anymore.

Sam stood beside his father with a dumbfounded look on his face. "Of course, I remember you. Why did you leave?"

Oh God.

How could I possibly put into words why I'd left?

What explanation would ever make sense to a little boy?

I had to stop trying to fix everyone else and finally fix myself.

I refused to drag you and your father down my toxic path.
You deserved a motherly figure who wasn't broken.
You deserved so much more than the person I used to be.

I knew I couldn't say any of those things.

I lowered myself to one knee until I was at his level, his face curious and expectant. "Sam... I couldn't stay. I hope you can forgive me," I said to him. My gaze was fixed on Sam, but my words were meant for them both.

Sam blinked a few times before nodding his head, as if contemplating his response. "We're learning about forgiveness in school," he told me. "I will definitely forgive you, Miss Chelsie."

Miss Chelsie.

I replied with a watery smile, rising back to my feet, knowing that a simple explanation and apology had been the way to go. My only hope was that Sam would carry that forgiveness with him through adulthood. "That means a lot to me," I replied. "Thank you."

Sam looked up at his father. "Do you forgive her, too? You were really sad when she left. You wrote a lot of songs. I think you should forgive her, Dad."

It felt like the air had been sucked out of the room. Noah closed his eyes and appeared to be grinding his teeth together. His shoulders were tense, and I had to resist the urge to lay a quieting hand against his arm. I interlocked my fingers together as a physical reminder to keep my hands to myself.

"Sam, why don't you go find Beth and your brothers? I'll be out in a minute," Noah advised.

Sam waved at me as he bounced away, unaware of the unresolved tension he was leaving behind. I held a hand up in goodbye.

"Sorry," Noah apologized. He hesitated a moment before saying, "I need to get back to my wife."

Wife.

The word stung.

I was happy for Noah and Beth, but there was still a subtle bite lingering just beneath the surface. I'd wanted Noah to move on and find peace, but when he had... well, it prickled.

Beth was bubbly, self-confident, and stable—all the things I was not back then. She seemed to bring out the best in Noah, even all those years ago, acting as a light in his life when I had been a black hole.

As much as it hurt, I had to believe this was exactly the way the story was destined to play out. Maybe it wasn't the ending I had originally planned or hoped for, but it was the right ending. It was the necessary ending for all of us.

"I completely understand," I said, wringing my hands together.

Noah studied me for another moment, almost as if he were questioning my presence. He narrowed his eyes, his brow furrowed and contemplative.

Then he cleared his throat, glanced at his shoes, and walked away.

I tried to regain my composure. I hadn't realized my legs were quivering beneath my weight until I tried to move.

As I began to trek back over to Lisa, who was awkwardly making small talk with a stranger in the corner of the room, I felt a strong hand squeeze my upper arm. I whipped my head around, surprised to find Noah standing in front of me again.

"How long are you in town?" he asked. His face was still unreflective as to what he might be feeling.

I, on the other hand, was an open book, clearly flustered and shaken. I chewed on my bottom lip as I often did when I was nervous. "Um... I leave tomorrow morning," I told him.

Noah nodded, my response sinking in. "Have a drink with me tonight."

"What?"

"Ernie's. Can you meet me at seven?"

My voice stumbled for words. "You're... married."

Noah shook his head, his gold wedding band catching the light as he ran a hand through chestnut hair. "No, I don't mean it like that. I just want to talk," he explained. "Beth knows."

Beth knows?

His wife knew he wanted to take his ex-lover out for a drink, and she was okay with that?

"Noah, I don't think that's a good idea. I feel like maybe we should keep the past in the past."

"Damnit, Combs, you owe me this." Noah glanced around the room, checking to see if anyone had heard him. He pinched the bridge of his nose and leaned in closer. "Please. I just want to talk. But this is not the place."

The sound of my last name on his tongue made my stomach flutter. My hands felt clammy as I squeezed them together, my normally disciplined thoughts running rampant through my brain. I wondered what we could possibly say to each other that would change anything.

Maybe that wasn't the point, though.

Maybe Noah just needed closure.

Maybe we both did.

And maybe, someday, I could fall asleep at night and not be drawn back into a world of Sunday morning pancakes and a perpetual vision of what might have been.

"Okay," I said softly. "I'll see you at seven."

Noah seemed taken aback, as if he'd already resigned himself to a rejection. "Good. Thanks."

Then he was gone, the familiar scent of his sandalwood cologne lingering behind.

I jumped when a hand tapped my shoulder, spinning to find Lisa standing there with a look of empathy on her face.

"Are you ready to go?" she asked.

I nodded. "Yeah... I'm ready."

We made our way out of the funeral home and back into the chilly New York air. The sun had begun to peek through gray clouds, and I chuckled to myself at the symbolism. Noah had returned to his family and circle of friends outside the doors, his hand gently rubbing Beth's back as she fumbled with a blanket inside the stroller. I spotted two tiny feet poking out and wiggling furiously, trying to break free from their confinement.

Beth looked up at that moment, catching my eye.

We both seemed to freeze for an instant, both of us equally unprepared for such a correspondence.

She was extraordinarily pretty. Her features were so delicate, one would be unable to imagine her angry or enraged. She was the epitome of grace and composure. Becoming a mother of three boys had not aged her one bit—there was not a single wrinkle to be seen on her slender face. Her eyes were auburn, matching the freckles on the bridge of her nose. There was no animosity behind her gaze. There was no look of superiority or arrogance.

There was only acceptance.

I smiled, as if to give my blessing.

As if to say, *"I'm happy for you both."*

Beth offered a friendly nod before returning her attention to the stroller.

Closure.

CHAPTER THIRTY-FIVE

CHELSIE

Seven o'clock lingered at the forefront of my mind. I attempted to occupy myself by calling my mother, sending some e-mails for work, showering—*twice*—and watching HGTV reruns on the hotel room television.

Nothing seemed to work.

The pit of ever-growing fretfulness continued to churn in my belly as the clock ticked down to that fateful hour.

When six-thirty rolled around, I checked my appearance in the mirror before heading down to the hotel lobby. I hadn't bothered to get glammed up— this wasn't a date. This was the final part of my healing process.

I combed my hair behind my ears and pressed my lips together, savoring the feel of the moist lip gloss.

I looked different, in the very best way.

Despite the circumstances, there was a light in my eyes that hadn't been there before. I wondered if Noah would notice it.

Would he recognize my newfound self-worth? Would he appreciate it?

Maybe Noah had been attracted to my darkness. Maybe my demons had pulled him in.

But if Noah was drawn to broken souls, he wouldn't have married Beth. She was the opposite of damaged... she was pure light.

Noah had likely been captivated by the version of myself that was yet to come. He had seen my potential, unaware that *he* would be the sacrifice I'd needed to make in order to get there.

Taking a deep breath, I popped a pair of dangly, turquoise earrings into my ears, straightened out my yellow blouse, and reached for my purse.

It was time.

It was a short ride over to the bar. I stared out the window as the familiar part of town came into view, my stomach fluttering with nerves at the memories connected to the brick buildings, light posts, and cracked sidewalks.

"Here we are, Miss."

I blinked through a swallow. The sign to Ernie's Pub flickered before me, tearing down my resolve. I had a physical reaction to it. My palms grew clammy, and my mouth felt like desert sand. It took a fierce pep-talk to force my feet out of the vehicle.

When the driver pulled away, I saw him.

He was standing outside the door, leaning against the distressed brick and puffing on a cigarette. There must have been an unseen force between us because Noah lifted his head at that moment, our eyes locking in a familiar hold.

An ancient swarm of butterflies came to life inside me, tickling parts of me that had been sealed shut. I wondered if he felt it, too.

Noah tossed his cigarette to the ground and tucked his hands into his pockets as he approached me. "You came."

"You thought I wouldn't?"

He studied me long and hard, and I had to lower my gaze under his scrutiny. I wondered what he was searching for.

As my eyes landed on a fire hydrant in front of the pub, the hair on the back of my neck stood up. We were standing in the exact spot Noah had collapsed on that fateful winter's night after taking two bullets from a madman. It was the same place I had cradled him in my arms, blood pooling all around us. I could still see it stained into the cracks and crevices of the cement pavement. It lived there now—an eternal reminder of my troubled past.

No matter what happened between us, we would forever be a part of these city streets.

"Should we grab a table?"

His voice interrupted my thoughts. "Sure."

It was all I could muster.

The pub was empty for a Thursday night. A few locals glanced up as we made our way to the back of the room. Everything felt so familiar, and yet... it felt like an entirely different life.

We took our seats across from each other as I folded my hands in front of me. I was biting my lip again, my eyes floating everywhere but him. A waitress stopped by the table and filled our glasses with ice water.

I chugged it.

Noah ordered a beer while we sat in silence for a few more minutes.

"Shit, Chelsie... I don't even know where to begin," he muttered, sighing as he scratched his head. "How are you?"

I blinked at the question. It was such an ordinary thing to ask, considering our very unordinary circumstances. "I'm good," I replied. "I'm really good."

"I saw you on *Ellen*. It's a great thing you've started."

I couldn't help but smile at the sentiment. "It's crazy how it all came together. I knew I needed to change my life, but I had no idea how big everything would become."

Noah flinched slightly.

He had been the biggest part of that change.

I brought the glass of water to my lips as the waitress returned with the beer, deciding to change the subject. "How is Rosa?"

A renewed twinkle sparkled in his eyes as he sipped the draft beer. "She's doing great. She flew back home to Mexico shortly after I made a full recovery. We still get postcards from her."

"She went back to Mexico?" Joy swept through me. "I can't believe it."

"Yeah," he nodded. "She reunited with an old flame and everything. She, uh... thanked you in one of the postcards."

I was certain a look of astonishment danced across my face. "Really?"

"I actually brought it with me." Noah reached into his wallet, pulling out a faded, folded-up postcard. "I thought maybe you'd want to have it."

He handed it to me, and I began to read:

> *Dearest muchacha,*
> *You were right. Mi Paco was waiting for me after all these years.*
> *Bendice su alma. El amor es el amor: "love is love." It will always*
> *be waiting.*
> *Wise words, señorita. My heart says gracias.*
> *Rosa y Paco*

There was a small polaroid photo attached of Rosa and Paco sitting by the ocean.

I didn't know I was crying until my tears seeped onto the postcard and caused the ink to run. I wiped at my cheeks with the sleeve of my blouse. "Sorry for the waterworks," I said with a sniffle. "I'm just so happy for her."

Rosa must not have realized I'd left town if she sent Noah this postcard. She was probably unaware I had abandoned my own advice and given up on my one chance at love.

The thought felt like a blade to my already bleeding heart; a silent betrayal.

"She's an amazing woman. I'm glad she's happy," Noah said from across the table. He was studying me again. He looked to be searching for the perfect words as his eyes scanned my face. "You look good."

I swallowed, placing my hands in my lap. My nails were biting into the heels of my palms. "I feel good," I replied softly.

It was the truth. I hoped so hard that Noah could see it, too. Maybe he would understand why I *had* to leave.

"You didn't say goodbye."

I gasped, recoiling at his words.

Oh, it hurt.

I knew it was coming, but it still hurt.

A new wave of tears threatened as I glanced up at the ceiling. "I am so sorry, Noah."

He leaned forward, his elbows on the table. "You just left." His words were hard and sober, straining with emotion. "You left

in the middle of the night with no goodbye, after we had just..."
Glancing away, his voice trailed off. "I tried calling you for
months. I tried finding you."

Sorrow seized his expression, and I wanted to reach for him.
My first instinct was still to comfort him. "I know," I
acknowledged.

"You broke my fucking heart, Combs."

I closed my eyes as the tears fell.

I *did* know.

I knew all too well because it had shattered my own heart into
a million fractured bits. Despite the wonderful life I had made for
myself, my heart would never be the same. Noah would always be
a missing piece.

There was no redemption without sacrifice.

Noah was staring at me like he was looking at a ghost. Regret
and melancholy shimmered in his eyes beneath the bar lights,
causing me to feel frazzled. My thoughts turned muddy. The air
felt scarce as the room closed in on me.

It had been so long since I'd seen him look at me like that.

"I – I have to go," I blurted without thinking.

He gaped at me, incredulous. "Are you serious?"

Yes. No.

I don't know.

I grabbed my purse and rose from the booth, unable to spare
him a final glance. I moved through the bar and pushed open the
main doors, nearly choking when the cold air invaded my lungs.
Even though I'd grown strong over the years, I knew that Noah
was my weak link.

I needed more time.

Walking briskly down the sidewalk, something caught my eye
on the right.

An alley.

The alley.

I stalled in my tracks, backpedaling until I stood facing the
opening. It was dark and wet while cars passed by at the opposite
end. Gulping, I knew I should walk the other way and leave New
York for good, but an invisible pull was dragging me into that

alleyway. My feet took on a mind of their own, and I found myself trudging through the gravel and rocks.

Stopping a quarter of the way in, I let the memories spill into every vein, every pore, every crack.

That's when I felt him.

He was standing behind me, maybe a foot away, silent and waiting.

I turned around to face him.

I needed to *truly* face him.

"It was the only way, Noah." My voice strained, my emotions running high. I wouldn't hold back this time. I needed to spill my guts to him, and if it had to be in this alleyway, then so be it. "It was the only way you'd let me go."

Noah stood perfectly still, his body shrouded in shadow. "You're right," he said. "I would have fought for you. I would have fought hard."

"That's exactly why it had to be like that. I wasn't healthy—I was broken, lost, and on a road to self-destruction. I needed to get out of New York. I needed to fix myself."

"And I just fucking needed *you*." Buried anger bubbled to the surface. "I never saw you as broken or damaged. You were perfect in my eyes."

Noah approached me in the darkness, his features coming into view by the light of a streetlamp. Tears spilled from my eyes as I absorbed his words. I didn't care if he saw me cry. I needed to feel everything, no matter how ugly it might be.

"I wasn't perfect," I croaked out. "But I never went looking for perfection; I went looking for peace. And I found it, Noah. I'm happy and healing. I finally feel like I've found my place in the world. I have... purpose."

"Why couldn't I have been a part of that peace? That purpose?"

His voice cracked with despair, and I almost buckled under the weight of his words.

"You never even gave us a chance," he continued. "I could have helped you. We could have gotten through anything together."

I shook my head adamantly, my fists balled-up at my sides.

"You're wrong... I would have dragged you down with me, and you deserved so much more than that. Sam deserved more."

"You have no right to decide what my son and I deserve. You were selfish."

My eyes rounded, my skin growing hot from his accusation. "I was anything *but* selfish," I argued. "The pain nearly *killed* me. I gave up the greatest thing in my life to protect yours. You would have drowned, Noah. You might not see it, but I do. Look at everything that had happened up to that point—your broken friendship with Devon, your departure from the band, your tarnished media image... your life almost taken from you!" I stopped to catch my breath, my chest heaving with heated conviction. "Now, look around you. You have a beautiful wife and three amazing children. You have a thriving solo career. You're *happy*. You're successful," I told him. "Don't you see? Don't you understand?"

Noah faltered for a moment to process my words before taking a long stride toward me. He reached out his hands and cupped my face, grazing his thumbs over my jaw. "I loved the hell out of you," he said. "That was enough for me."

I stared at him in awe.

And then I crumbled.

Unrelenting sobs poured out of me as Noah pulled me to him, crushing me to his chest. He hugged me fiercely, one arm around my back, his opposite hand knotted in my hair. I cried in his arms, my body shaking with years of stored-up grief and still-open wounds. "I'm so sorry," I said, weeping into the crook of his shoulder as I clutched him. His t-shirt was balled-up between my fists, and I could feel his heart drumming its heavy beats beneath his ribcage.

I felt closer to him than ever before. My mind wasn't racing with toxic thoughts. I wasn't worrying about hurting him. I wasn't overwrought with the stress of what could go wrong, and I wasn't overanalyzing every aspect of our relationship.

I was simply releasing.

Healing.

"Shh, it's okay," Noah whispered, his tone softening with

concession. He rested his cheek against the top of my head while his fingers stroked my hair. "It's okay."

We stood in the alleyway, clinging to each other for a long time, and when I pulled back, I gazed up at him with a sense of absolution. "I'll always love you, Noah. I'll always be rooting for you. But... I have no regrets. I see you now, so happy and fulfilled, and it would be impossible to regret the man standing in front of me."

Noah moved his hands to my neck and pulled me in one more time, placing a tender kiss against my forehead. "I'm rooting for you, too."

We held each other a while longer, old memories passing through us both, the hum of the streetlamp the background music for our dance of reprieve.

And when the chill of the autumn night got the better of us, we headed back into the pub for one last drink together. We sipped on whiskey and shared stories of our abundant lives. Noah spoke of Beth with the same sparkle in his eyes that had once been reserved for me. It made my heart clench with grief, but it also soothed me in a way. It solidified what I had known all along —*I had done the right thing.*

When last-call was announced, we finished our stories and whiskey and exited the pub.

As we stood in that familiar and painful spot on the sidewalk, we made new memories there. A memory of goodbye.

A *real* goodbye—the one I had taken from Noah all those years ago.

I hugged him tight, burning the scent of his skin into the marrow of my bones. This was the end of our song. This was our final note.

But the beautiful thing about songs was that they never really died. Months, years, even decades would go by, and that song would still play.

Songs were never lost; they were never truly over.

A song lived on forever.

EPILOGUE
NOAH

I stepped through my front door, dropping my keys to the entry table. They clinked against the glass surface, and I hoped I hadn't woken Beth or the boys.

The house was dark and quiet as I descended the staircase, my footsteps as heavy as my heart. New photos adorned the walls, a constant reminder of the beautiful life I had made for myself. As I traipsed into the bedroom with tired feet, I used the flashlight on my phone to light my path. Beth lied curled up in our bed, wrapped tightly in the sheets and blankets, and I couldn't help but smile at how peaceful she looked.

Peeling off my jacket, my eyes were drawn to the small drawer of my nightstand. I hesitated before approaching the side of the bed and sitting down, feeling the mattress sink beneath my weight.

I carefully opened the drawer, glancing at Beth as the hinges creaked in the quiet room. She stirred for a moment, then fell still.

Reaching inside the bedside drawer, I pulled out a familiar piece of green construction paper. I pressed it between my fingertips, memorizing the feel of its coarse and pulpy texture.

Then I turned my cell phone toward the paper and watched it light up. My breath hitched as my eyes read over the words that had stolen a piece of my heart many years ago.

Dear Noah,

I'm not sure how I'm supposed to fit everything I want to say into one letter, but I'll try. You've probably noticed by now that I'm gone. I know if I tried to tell you this in person, you would convince me to stay, and I would give in. I'm weak when it comes to you. I suppose we are all weak when it comes to love.

And please know, I do love you. I love you so much I'm sitting here sobbing as I write this, second-guessing myself with every stroke of my pen. But I need to do this. I can't be with you, Noah. I can't be with anyone right now. I'm broken, and I don't want to hurt you.

I know that sounds contradictory because I'm hurting you with this letter. But that's not what I mean. I'm talking about the dark, ugly kind of hurt. I can't possibly make you happy if I can't even make myself happy. I know you probably can't see it yet because you're consumed with anger and emotion. But I promise... one day you'll understand. One day you'll see why I needed to do this. And only then, when you're exquisitely happy and your life is full of beautiful things, you will thank me.

You said we were a duet, and I wish I could be your second half. I wish I could be a part of your perfect duet.

But I'm an aria. I am meant to fly alone.

I wish so many wonderful things for you. I hope you find love again and continue to make music. I hope all your dreams come true. I hope one day, when the anger has subsided and you are lying in bed with the woman you love, you will read this letter again. I hope you'll read it in a new light and see how everything is exactly as it should be.

Thank you for everything you've done for me. Thank you for believing in me when I couldn't. Thank you for all the nights you stayed up with me as I bared my soul to you. Thank you for the movie dates, the homemade pancakes, the laughs over whiskey, and everything in between. Thank you for Sam.

I love you, Noah. No matter what happens, you will always be the only song in my heart.

You will be my aria.

Love, Chelsie

I stared at the green piece of paper for a long time before tucking it back into the drawer of my nightstand and running a hand over my face. Visions of Chelsie flickered through my mind as I sat there in the darkness for what felt like a lifetime.

Pulling at the covers and climbing into bed, I scooted over to the opposite side where Beth was sleeping and tugged her close, nuzzling my face against her hair. She instinctively inched herself against me and squeezed my hand as she fell back into a quiet sleep.

The truth was, I *was* happy—exquisitely happy.

I loved Beth. I loved my life.

Maybe Chelsie had been right all along.

When I closed my eyes, exhaustion overtook me, and I drifted off to a familiar place in my dreams.

It was there that I found her.

She was sitting at my kitchen table, shoveling pancakes into her mouth and laughing with Sam.

"Easy there, tiger," I said with a wink.

Chelsie stood from her chair and strolled over to me, her silk robe trailing languidly behind her. "I can't help it. You know I love your pancakes."

"And you know I love you."

I kissed her mouth, almost tasting the sticky, sweet syrup on her lips.

"Noah, our song is playing. Will you dance with me?"

Pausing for a moment, I tried to hear the music. "I don't hear anything," I murmured.

She grinned. "I do."

And so we danced in my kitchen to a silent song, holding each other close and moving our bodies together in perfect rhythm.

Chelsie laughed, her blonde hair cascading all around her as I spun her in a graceful circle. She looked up at me then, her emerald eyes gleaming with unparalleled joy.

I always said I could get lost in those eyes.

And in my dreams, I did.

To Be Continued...

Their story continues with Coda, the final installment of this duet.
Keep reading to get a glimpse into Chelsie and Noah's second chance romance.

CODA

CHAPTER ONE

NOAH

I hated New York City.

It was vapid and uninspiring. I didn't feel like I was either of those things, and yet, here I was—one of them.

Clutching the newest iPhone in my hand, I rummaged through the pockets of my overpriced jeans for the keys to my Corvette.

Damn.

Sometimes it made me laugh. Sometimes it made me teeter on the verge of a mental breakdown.

I propped my sunglasses over my eyes as the sun singed the tops of the skyline buildings. I was in a hurry, as usual. Rushing was simply a way of life in this city. My recording session had run late, and Beth was waiting for me to relieve her of parental duties so she could get to a showing. Sam had a baseball game; Caden had karate. Dinner would likely be McDonald's Happy Meals as we raced home to squeeze in homework, baths, and bedtime stories.

I glanced at the time on my phone, picking up my pace as I turned into the parking garage. "Shit," I muttered.

Late as fuck.

"Noah Hayes?"

My name echoed into the sea of sports cars and luxury SUVs. Pausing, I slipped my sunglasses back onto my head as I pivoted toward the voice.

Sometimes I really loathed the sound of my own name. I tried to hide my sour expression as I faced the pair of teenagers who had cornered me.

"We love you, Noah! Can we get your autograph?"

The brunette snapped her bubblegum, while the blonde held out a gel-tipped pen, along with her forearm.

I forced my smile to stay put as the muscles in my jaw twitched with rebellion. "Sure."

"I'm Sara," said the brunette.

"I'm Chelsea," the blonde added.

I faltered, my hand freezing mid-reach for the pen. The familiar name sucked a breath out of me, and my tongue felt like a wad of cotton balls in my mouth.

The blonde jabbed the pen into my hand and continued to wave her arm in front of my face. "I don't have any paper with me. You can sign right here."

I blinked at the young girl in a crop top and high-waist leggings. "Yeah. Okay," I murmured, managing to scribble my signature onto the arms of both girls. "Thanks for listening to my music."

Thanks for making me ridiculously later, my brain silently added.

"Thanks! Toodles!" The sound of bubblegum popping and sticky sneakers could be heard as they skipped down the sidewalk.

I sighed, tossing my car keys into the air and catching them with my opposite hand. I fidgeted in place for another moment, scratching the back of my neck, my mouth still stale and parched.

It had been three years since I'd heard that name.

My phone buzzed inside my pocket as I scrambled to fetch it.

Beth: *You on the way yet?*

Shit. Late.

Typing out a hurried reply, I jogged the rest of the way to my car. I knew Beth had to be frazzled, even though she'd never show it. Beth didn't get angry. She didn't get flustered or stressed out, and it was one of the many things I admired about my wife. It was one of the many things that made her an exceptional mother to our three boys.

Beth had earned her real estate license one year ago. She'd quickly made a name for herself with her poise, knowledge, and friendly demeanor. Her colleagues respected her, and her client base was growing. I was proud as hell. She'd had her eye on the Prager estate for weeks when a call finally came through for a showing. It was a two-million-dollar property with a six-figure commission.

Granted, we didn't *need* the money. I was an acclaimed solo musician; an international star.

No... it wasn't about the money. Beth was a self-sufficient woman who prided herself on her personal successes and financial contributions. She'd been a single mother right out of the gate —she clung to her independence, and I loved watching her shine.

I hopped into my car and dialed her number as I sped out of the parking garage. Her soft voice sounded through the Bluetooth.

"Hey," she said.

A smile was evident in her tone. "I'm sorry I'm running late. My session ran over."

"It's okay, Noah. I get it."

She always *got* it. "Hey... let's take a trip soon. Just the two of us. I've been thinking about it."

Beth was silent for a moment. "Are you sure? You have your tour coming up in the UK. And who would watch the boys?"

"We can sort out the details. We always do," I insisted. "Our schedules have been crazy lately. I feel like we only see each other in passing."

It was the truth. In between my song writing, practices, promotional events, and Beth's real estate commitments, we'd been living as strangers for the past few months. Throw three boys into the mix, all with different needs, and I was desperate for some one-on-one time with my wife.

"Well..." Beth hesitated through the speaker. "If you really think we can pull it off, I'd love to."

I grinned as I weaved through the city's heavy traffic. "Yeah?

Well, shit. Let's start planning tonight. I was thinking Bali or Aruba."

"Oh, that sounds wonderful." She paused again. "I miss you."

"I miss you, too." Snatching my cigarettes off the passenger seat, I searched for a lighter as I sped through a yellow light. "I'll be home soon."

I made good time as I careened into the driveway, thanks to equal parts road rage and a V8 engine. Three happy faces greeted me at the door, mellowing me out instantly.

"Daddy!" Jeremiah was quick to plow through his two brothers and smash his nose against the screen. "Daddy's home!"

Sam unlocked the door and held it open as I breezed up the walkway. "Hey, Dad. I'm going to be late for baseball."

"Nah." I scooped Jeremiah into my arms and gave Caden's hair a firm tousle. "You know how I drive. We'll have time to spare."

"If we survive," Sam said with a laugh.

"Noah?"

Beth made her way down the staircase in a black pantsuit, her hair pulled back into a tight ponytail. Her face lit up when she spotted me in the entryway.

"Go sell a damn house," I smiled, meeting her halfway across the living room and kissing her forehead.

Her eyes twinkled with adoration as she stood momentarily entranced. "Right. The house. Gotta go." Beth snatched her purse off a wall hook and flung it over her shoulder. She popped her earrings in as Jeremiah tugged at her pant leg. "You're sure you're okay with the activities? I know it's a lot."

"I'm basically Super Dad," I shrugged. "You know this."

Caden jumped on me then, hanging from my upper arm like a monkey.

Beth giggled under her breath and smoothed out the fabric of her pantsuit. "All right, then. I should be home before you. Want me to whip up some dinner?"

I shook my head as I tossed the six-year-old over my shoulder. Caden screeched in frantic delight, pummeling his tiny fists into my back. "I'll pick something up on the way home. You should relax. Enjoy an hour or two without four obnoxious boys demanding things." I shot her a wink as I leaned in for another kiss.

"Are you even real?" Beth joked as she pulled away. She slipped on her pointed heels and gave me a final glance. Her chocolate eyes were still sparkling. "I can't wait to talk tonight."

I discreetly smacked her butt as she walked by. "It's a date," I concurred.

"Be good for your father," Beth ordered our three boys as she headed to the front door, her eyes still lingering on me. "He may look tough, but you know he's just a big softie on the inside."

My glare was mostly teasing. "You'll pay for that outright lie."

"Looking forward to it," she said with a smirk. "See you all tonight. Good luck at your game, Sam."

"Bye!" Caden yelled, jumping up and down.

"We're so late," Sam complained.

"Mommy!" Jeremiah crumbled into a fit of tears as Beth disappeared out the door.

I blinked, nearly blacking out for a moment. Then I jumped into Dad-mode and picked my son back up. "Get your shoes on, kiddos. Time to go."

Sam grabbed his catcher's mitt and backpack, while simultaneously fending off punches in the arm from Caden. Jeremiah continued to wail in my arms, his hands reaching desperately for the door.

Blacking out actually sounded kind of appealing.

Sucking in a deep breath, I reminded myself of the Super Dad title. And thirty seconds later, I'd managed to pile all three boys into the SUV until we were on our way to Sam's baseball game, dropping Caden off at karate on the way. My arm hung out the window, a cigarette dangling in between my fingertips. I always chain-smoked under pressure.

When the *Baby Shark* song began playing on repeat in the backseat, I sucked the sweet nicotine into my lungs with ardent voracity.

I definitely always chain-smoked during *Baby Shark*.

"Soccer!" Jeremiah pointed an eager finger at the playing field as we pulled into the parking lot. He clapped his hands with anticipation, bouncing in his seat. "Sammy play!"

"It's baseball, buddy," I murmured through the cigarette. I ground it out on the cement once we parked, helping the boys out of the car.

"Bye, Dad," Sam called out, running toward his coach.

"Break a leg, Sammy," I yelled back.

Jeremiah looked up at me, his eyes wide with concern. His little hand wrapped around my index finger. "Sammy don't want a boo-boo."

I chuckled as I carried Jeremiah up to the stands, nodding my head in greeting to the parents as we passed. I was used to the curious stares and starstruck gawking. Beth was normally the parent in charge of extracurricular activities, so my presence always came with plenty of gossipy whispers and scrutiny.

Climbing to the top row of benches, I took a seat next to a couple who lived on our street—Darla and Ken Nivens. Their son, Harrison, rode the school bus with Sam, and the two boys had become good friends.

"Howdy," Ken said, holding his hand out to me as I approached.

I attempted to keep my grip on the squirming three-year-old, who was in the process of making an impressive escape. Shifting the child's weight into my opposite arm, I returned the handshake. "Hey, Ken. Don't mind my unruly accessory." I turned my attention to the raven-haired woman with impeccably drawn-on eyebrows. She was pressed up against Ken, her blood red talons digging into his thigh. "Darla," I acknowledged.

"We've all been there, Noah," she said sweetly. "I can't say I miss that phase."

It was difficult to envision Darla Nivens with any maternal instincts. While the couple had always been kind to our family, they oozed old money and entitlement.

I took a seat beside Ken as Jeremiah slithered from my grasp and began running through the bleachers. The benches rattled from the weight of his Mickey Mouse sandals stampeding back and forth. I ran a hand over my face, exhaustion and mild embarrassment settling in, as I tried to hide behind my sunglasses and stoic visage.

The Nivens managed to rope me into idle chitchat as they discussed charity functions, their upcoming neighborhood barbecue, and the PTO board. Honestly, I'd rather throw myself face-first into a barbed wire fence than hear about why Lori McGibbons was removed from the bake sale, but I played the part of a dutiful father with school spirit.

"You just can't trust a woman who uses wheat flour in her vegan apple muffins," Darla said with a haughty chuckle. "Beth understands. She is such a gem, Noah."

I pretended to act engaged with my trademark "nod and smile" routine, but the mention of Beth had me digging out my phone to see if she'd sent me any updates on the showing.

Beth: *I'm here. Just waiting on the client. I love you!*

I grinned as I responded.

Me: *Love you, too. Bali awaits.*

The three wiggling dots showed that Beth was typing. I waited for her reply, certain she was typing out her reasons on why Aruba would be a better choice, but the three dots disappeared. After another minute passed, I slipped the phone back into my pocket just as Jeremiah heaved himself onto my lap with a concerning amount of force. My breath hitched at the sudden blow, and I cursed my body for not being used to the continuous abuse by now. I didn't recall Sam being such a monster—but, then again, I was in my thirties now. I was no spring chicken.

Glancing at my phone again, I noticed it was almost time to run out and pick up Caden from karate. "All right, buddy. Let's go get big brother."

"No! I staying here." Jeremiah stomped his little foot against the metal bleachers and crossed his arms in defiance. "I watch Sammy play soccer."

I pressed my lips together, preparing for a scene. "Sorry, bud. We need to pick up Caden. We'll come right back."

"No!"

There must be a hole I could crawl into somewhere around here.

"Jeremiah..." I reached for my son, but he was too quick. He bolted in the other direction, garnering glances from the other parents. "Shit."

"Why don't you leave him here with us?" Darla offered.

Her features barely moved through her countless plastic surgeries, but I was almost certain she was smiling fondly at me. "That's not necessary, but I appreciate the offer," I replied. "I'll only be gone twenty minutes."

Jeremiah made his way back to our group and hopped up onto the bench next to Darla. "Hi, I'm Amiah!" he chirped.

Chuckling, I plucked my car keys from my front pocket. "We're still working on his name," I explained. I turned my attention to Jeremiah, who was swinging his legs back and forth with enthusiasm. "Okay, kiddo, let's go. You can have ice cream after dinner if you're a good boy."

"Yay!" Jeremiah jumped down and grabbed my hand, dragging me to the parking lot.

It was a ten-minute drive to the karate studio, and Caden ran into my arms with giddy glee when he spotted us.

"Hey, Dad!"

"Hey, bud. Ready to go?"

Caden nodded and waved goodbye to his teacher, and after another ten minutes passed, we were back at the baseball game.

I looked into the backseat and noticed both boys were sound asleep. Leaning back, I reveled in the rare moment of silence. While I debated waking the boys and continuing my unremarkable conversation with the Nivens, the thought hurt me on a physical level. So, I decided to take advantage of my unexpected free time and get some writing in.

Sean, my business and PR manager, was eager to get a new song out by summer, and I had been feeling uninspired. He had followed me over from Freeze Frame to my solo career and had become a good friend throughout the tumultuous journey.

I pulled a notepad out of my glove compartment and scribbled down a few lines that had been floating through my mind. My hand tapped against my knee as I hummed under my breath. The sound of the ball game could be heard outside my window, and I peered out every now and then to watch Sam. A sense of pride washed over me as Sam high-fived one of his teammates.

He'd grown so much over the past ten years. *Ten years.* It was surreal to even think about. I had been a father for a decade. And even more unbelievably, I hadn't royally botched it up.

Sam was a good kid, maintaining good grades in school and accumulating a large circle of friends. I felt like I'd done a pretty good job.

Luckily, I'd had Beth to help along the way.

Instinctively, I pulled out my phone to check my messages, but there was still nothing. I was hopeful the showing was going well and there may be an offer on the table.

After an hour had gone by and I felt relaxed and recharged, I decided to wake up the boys and watch the end of Sam's game from the stands. We traipsed back up the bleachers and sat down to watch the final minutes, celebrating the big win for Sam's team. Caden cheered from his seat, waving his fist in the air. I clapped and whistled.

Jeremiah sobbed hysterically because his goldfish crackers spilled onto the ground.

"That's our cue," I sighed.

Darla Nivens squeezed my shoulder as Sam and Harrison joined us on the bleachers. "It was great catching up, Noah. Let's do a dinner party sometime."

"A dinner party sounds..." I searched for an appropriate adjective. *Nauseating? Painful? Terrible?* "Excellent," I opted for. "Text Beth about it. She's in charge of me."

Ken slapped me on the back with a hearty roar of laughter. "You got that right," he said. "Thank God for the female species. Sometimes I wonder if I'd put my pants on the right way without my wife."

I forced a smile. "Enjoy your evening," I said, gathering my three sons. "Let's head home, boys. Who wants McDonald's?"

As I pulled into the driveway, a sinking feeling rumbled in the pit of my stomach. The house looked dark—Beth's car was nowhere to be seen.

"I want the Minion toy!" Caden bellowed from the backseat.

"Mine!" Jeremiah shouted back.

"Dad, Jeremiah won't trade with me!"

Turning off the engine, I sat in perplexed silence, checking my phone again for the hundredth time. My last two messages to Beth had not been read. I thought maybe her phone had died—she was awful about charging it, content with living in a technology-free world. She only used her phone for work and to keep in contact with me.

But she's still not home.

Worry raced through me.

"Dad?" Sam's concerned voice echoed through the vehicle. "What's wrong?"

I shook my head, unbuckling my seatbelt as the two younger boys continued to bicker over their Happy Meal toys. "Let's head inside," I said.

I carried Jeremiah, while Caden and Sam trailed behind, and when I twisted the house key into the lock, I realized my hand was trembling.

Something was wrong.

The front door opened to darkness. The lights were still turned off and an eerie silence greeted us, the only sound being the leaky kitchen faucet and my thundering heartbeats.

"Dad... where's Beth?" Sam asked, tossing his baseball gear to the floor and flipping on the entry light. "She said she would be home before us."

"Mama!" Jeremiah cried. "Where Mama?"

I set my son down, running two sweaty palms over my face. "It's okay. She's probably just running late."

It had been hours.

She should have been home *hours* ago.

I pulled out my phone to call her, but there was no answer. I tried three times.

Voicemail. Voicemail. Voicemail.

Maybe she stopped to pick up dinner. Maybe she ran to the

grocery store. Maybe her car had stalled on the way home. "Boys, why don't you bring your dinner to the table and eat up," I told them. "I'm going to have Chrissy come over to play with you."

"Yay!" Jeremiah ran to the kitchen table at full force, his French fries spilling out of the paper bag along the way.

Chrissy was the high school student who lived next door. She was our date-night babysitter.

I was thrilled to see her standing in the doorway five minutes later.

"Hi, Mr. Hayes," Chrissy said with a beaming smile. She flipped her sandy hair over her shoulder and giggled when Caden came dashing into her arms. "Hey, little fella. Is that a Minion toy?"

"Mine!" Jeremiah yelled, joining us in the living room and reaching for the toy.

I snatched my car keys back up. "Thanks for coming over so quick," I said to the bubbly teen. "I just need to run out. Hopefully I won't be long."

"It's all good, Mr. Hayes. I brought my homework just in case." Chrissy held up her backpack for effect. "Take your time."

Offering a strained smile, I glanced at Sam, who was sitting on the couch with a sullen expression. "Take care of your brothers, okay, Sammy?"

Sam continued to look straight ahead. "Can I come with you?"

"I'd rather you stay here. I'll be home soon."

Sam crossed his arms and leaned back against the sofa cushions. "She left, didn't she?" he muttered. His voice was wounded. "They always leave."

My muscles locked, and my next breath lodged in the back of my throat. I blinked slowly, grinding my teeth together, my own harrowing memories sweeping through me. "No, Sam. Beth would never leave you. She loves you."

"Yeah," he whispered. "That's what they all say."

I watched as my son rose from the couch and stormed over to the staircase, his feet pounding each step with defiance.

"I'll go get the plates out for their Happy Meals," Chrissy

said, breaking through the sudden bout of tension. "I hope everything is okay, Mr. Hayes."

A sigh left me, and I nodded my thanks.

Pulling up the address to the Prager estate, I noted it was only a few miles east. I decided I would drive the same route and be on the lookout for any stalled cars or accidents along the way. Beth couldn't be far.

I drove uncharacteristically slowly, my eyes roaming over both sides of the road. Cars honked and swerved around me as the inconvenienced drivers flipped me off. Every car horn and flashing light put me on edge as I continued to call Beth's cell phone over and over, until I turned onto Prager Court. The estate loomed in front of me, all six-thousand square feet of it casting its eerie shadows onto the cul-de-sac.

My bones froze with ice when I spotted Beth's Tesla sitting dormant in the driveway.

Fear bubbled in my gut. Bile burned my chest, then climbed into my throat. I swallowed it down and threw the car in park, kicking open the driver's side door, leaving my keys in the ignition, and racing toward the front of the estate. "Beth!" I pounded on the door with furious fists, peering through the narrow glass window to the right. It was dark inside. There was no sign of life.

I twisted the doorknob, surprised when the door creaked open. Panic coursed through my veins as I stepped inside. Something was wrong... I could *feel* it.

"Beth?" My voice echoed through the sky-high ceilings and endless rooms. I flipped on a light switch and was greeted by a sleek lion statue staring back at me. "Beth?" I called again.

Silence.

My lungs squeezed as I swallowed giant gulps of air, tasting my own fear on my tongue. I had to force my legs to move because my shoes felt glued the marble tile in the entryway.

I took a hesitant step forward. Then another.

And another.

Th-thump. Th-thump. Th-thump.

The resounding lub-dubs of my heartbeat were deafening against the excruciating silence of the sprawling home. The walls laughed at me with their gaudy floral wallpaper. The shadows watched as I traipsed from room to room. "Beth..."

Fucking answer me!

When I made my way into the kitchen, my eyes landed on a bloody handprint smeared across the granite island countertop.

"No... fuck..." I glanced up and saw a similar bloodstain wrapped around the doorframe of an adjoining room. My body teetered between shutting down completely and running full speed into the room ahead. I lowered my gaze, discovering a trail of blood staining the hardwood floor. My stomach lurched. I'd never been more terrified in my entire life. "Beth."

She didn't answer.

When I finally gave my limbs permission to move, I stumbled forward, slipping on the streaks of blood, my shoes squeaking in protest. I caught my balance as I entered the adjacent room, my hand landing on the bloody palm print.

That's when I saw her.

Her legs were peeking out from behind a wooden dining table. A chair was tipped over beside her, one of her high-heeled shoes lying crooked near her ankle. Her cell phone had fallen out of her hand, the screen cracked and peppered in blood spatter.

I couldn't process it. I couldn't even breathe.

My wife was lying in a pool of blood, her favorite pantsuit torn from knife holes and saturated with bloodstains.

I don't remember moving, but I suddenly found myself kneeling beside the lifeless body of the woman I loved, cradling her limp hand against my face. A guttural sound escaped me, something wretched, and it seeped into the laughing walls and burned itself into the very bones of the sterile house. Anyone who entered would feel its pain.

My pain.

The shadows continued to watch as I pulled Beth into my arms and buried my face into her blood-soaked hair. She was cold. She was still.

She was gone.

And nothing would ever be the same...

CODA
CHAPTER TWO

CHELSIE

I was sitting in my office entering patient information when Anne came barging through the door. Her dark brown bob bounced as she hopped up and down on both feet, her stare frantic. "Chels, you need to come see!"

Glancing up from my laptop, I frowned, my reading glasses perched on the bridge of my nose. "Is everything okay?"

"Just... trust me. Hurry!"

Anne waved her arm in a melodramatic fashion, her chestnut eyes begging me to follow. I pulled my bottom lip between my teeth, my gaze shifting between the glowing computer screen and my anxious friend. It must be serious, so I stood from the rolling chair and adjusted the straps of my mustard-colored tank top. "Okay, I'm coming."

"In the lobby." Anne motioned me out the door, her sundress twirling at her knees.

I followed the perky brunette out of the office, and we headed toward the main entrance. It was a busy Thursday. There were deadlines, multiple new patients joining the sanctuary the following week, and payroll was due in three hours. Employees rushed past us as we sauntered down the hallway, and I wondered what the commotion was all about. "Anne, what's going on?"

Anne reached for my wrist, dragging me the rest of the way. "You need to see this."

As we rounded the corner, a grand sight came into view.

Jon was down on one knee with a shell-shocked Maggie standing before him. Her hand was clasped over her mouth.

Well, I'll be damned.

"...having said that, I would love nothing more than for you to become my wife. Will you marry me, Maggie Mills?"

"Yes!"

Jon leaped to his feet, and the newly engaged couple collided into each other's arms with an emotional hug. There was an uproar of applause from the curious onlookers. I clapped my hands together, a smile creeping onto my lips. I was happy for my friends. They had been dating for one year, sharing the kind of love that one might see in a sweet romance novel or on the Hallmark Channel. There were picnics under the willow tree during lunch breaks, stolen kisses in the halls, and fresh flowers delivered as a special surprise at least twice a month.

I was happy for them. Truly.

I was also a little bit envious.

How could two people love each other so effortlessly? Where was the pain and heartache? Where were the dramatic exits and fiery words? How did they make it look so... *easy?*

I had taken Jon up on his offer for a coffee date one afternoon. It was a few weeks after I'd returned from New York after Devon's wake. He had been persistent, but in a charming way, and I felt ready to take a chance on a new relationship. At the very least, I was ready to open my mind to the possibility.

There had been pleasant small talk and a few laughs, and Jon was nothing short of a gentleman. I decided to go on a few dates with him to test the waters. It was nice. Jon was nice. Jon was everything I wanted in a man. He was passionate about helping people, and he was the best listener. He was good-looking in a quirky way with crystal blue eyes and a lanky frame, but... he had one prominent flaw.

Jon was not Noah.

There had been one evening where I'd let him kiss me. It was my first kiss in over three years, and I recalled sitting on his leather loveseat with sweaty palms and a racing heart. My insides were pitched with nerves and anxiety.

The kiss had been awkward, a mess of wavering hands and cowardly tongues. Jon had tasted like church on Sunday morning.

When he'd tried to take our blundering make-out session to the next level, I'd panicked. "I – I'm so sorry, Jon. I don't think I can do this."

Jon had pulled back, licking his lips and catching his breath. "Did I do something wrong?"

"I guess I'm just not ready yet. It's nothing you did," I had told him.

It's simply who you are. Or... who you aren't.

So, things went back to our semi-normal routine. Jon would duck his head with bashful accord as we crossed paths at work. Eventually, Maggie had taken an interest in the counselor, and I'd suggested they go on a date together.

"I couldn't do that, Chelsie. That goes against girl code," Maggie had insisted.

"Nonsense," I'd said dismissively. "Jon and I were never serious. You two would make a cute couple."

Fast forward one year, and here they were. Jon and Maggie were engaged.

It was bittersweet.

"Gosh, they are sweeter than the homemade brownies in the break room," Anne said, clapping her hands and waving her fist in the air with a 'whoop.' "You made a good call hooking those two up."

My lips thinned. I suppose I had.

I suppose I was far better at organizing happy endings for other people than I was for myself. "They're perfect for each other," I murmured.

Thomas, one of the swim instructors, snuck up behind me and squeezed my shoulders. I startled as I spun around to face him. "You scared me," I scolded, a ghost of a smile toying at my lips. Thomas was the poster boy for "tall, dark and handsome."

He had black hair and tanned skin, along with a dreamy British accent that the female employees swooned over.

"Sorry, love. Didn't mean to make you miffed."

He flashed his pearly whites in my direction as I twirled a golden strand of hair around my index finger. Consider me one of those female employees. "It's fine. You're fine."

You're fine? Wow.

Thomas shoved his hands into his pockets, the muscles in his arms flexing beneath his polyester t-shirt. He nodded his head at the two lovebirds, who were still embracing and whispering into each other's ears. "It's a tad dodgy, don't you think?"

My nose crinkled when I glanced at Maggie and Jon, who seemed blissfully in love. "How do you mean?"

"Oh, you know. Only a nutter would propose after a sodding year, am I right? It takes me a year to decide if I even want a second date."

Chuckling under my breath, I shrugged. "It takes me a year to decide if I even want a first date."

Thomas' dark brown eyes flickered with playful flirtation. "Six years, to be precise."

I blinked, my cheeks flooding with heat.

"You're a curious bird, Miss Combs," he said with a wink. "You must know I fancy you by now."

My heated cheeks began to swelter. I raised a hand to my chest, as if to hide the rosy flush crawling up to my neck. "Oh..." Thomas had always been flirtatious with me. There was a friendly chemistry between us since day one.

But, I had closed my mind off to the idea of men, and Thomas knew that.

Everyone knew that.

"Sod it," Thomas said. He sniffed, teetering on the balls of his feet. "Go out with me."

"Oh," I repeated through a gulp. My mind shut down as I dug my fingernails into my collarbone. I chewed on my bottom lip, my eyes looking anywhere but at Thomas. "I – I don't know. I'm not good at the dating thing."

"Bloody hell, woman. You're far too smashing to die single. Let me take you out on a proper date."

Smashing.

Thomas was the opposite of Jon in every way. Confident, sexy, tenacious. I felt my resolve begin to weaken beneath his steely gaze, and I was certain he wouldn't take no for an answer. That intrigued me a little. "Okay," I agreed. "One date."

Thomas grinned as he ran his fingers through jet black hair. "All right, love. Tonight, then. Dinner at Mackenzie's at eight o'clock? Unless you'd rather get pissed and snog instead."

My eyebrows wrinkled into a frown of confusion. His laughter swirled around me. "I'm not sure what that means, but I like food. Dinner sounds good."

Thomas reached out and took my hand with a delicate grip. He kissed my knuckles, and his warm breath made my insides flutter. The sensation felt foreign.

"Looking forward to it, love," he whispered.

His touch lingered for a moment before he dropped my hand and turned away, whistling to himself as he ambled down the long hall. My eyes burned into his retreating back, my mind buzzing with both uncertainty and titillation.

"Well, would you look at that." Elsa approached beside me with her arms folded across her chest. A knowing smile pulled at her lips as she addressed me with a cocked eyebrow. "That only took over half a decade."

I couldn't help my eyeroll. "Any commentary or "I told you so" remarks will not be permitted. Thank you and good day." I glanced at my friend and mentor, and we shared a laugh.

Elsa reached down, giving my hand a tender squeeze. "You did the right thing. You need this," she assured me.

I appreciated the sentiment, but I still felt gravely unsure. "I hope you're right. I have no idea what I'm doing."

"Nobody does," Elsa said, shooing away my concerns with a flick of her wrist. "No one has any clue. I've been married three times and I still haven't figured it out."

I studied the woman on my right. Her strawberry blonde hair looked more golden under the fluorescent lights. She had aged a bit over the last six years; the lines and sunspots on her skin told thousands of stories. Her crow's feet became more pronounced when she smiled, sipping on a mug of iced tea in her hand. The ice cubes made a clinking sound as they danced against the glass.

Elsa was in her early forties. She was more of a sister to me than a friend, really.

She was there for me at the start of my new journey in south Florida. She was there when Devon died and I came back from New York a grieving, emotional mess.

I had stayed at Elsa's house that first night back, and she'd held my hair back as I ugly cried into a throw pillow and a pint of butter pecan ice cream. I'd had one dark and frightening moment in which I'd regretted everything—I'd regretted my sacrifice.

I'd regretted abandoning Noah and Sam. I'd regretted how things ended with Devon. I'd regretted giving up the one thing I had ever really wanted... *real love.*

I'd regretted falling in love in the first place.

"What if I made a mistake?" I had sobbed. My tears had mixed with the frozen dessert melting in my lap. "What if I just ran because I was scared? What have I done, Elsa?"

Elsa had combed back my damp hair with soothing fingers. "We both know you didn't run. You did a hard thing for the greater good of your well-being. Don't you dare second-guess yourself. That will only take you back to where you started... then it would all *truly* be for nothing."

I had sniffled against Elsa's shoulder. "Maybe I handled it all wrong. Maybe I was selfish."

Elsa had grabbed me by the shoulders and stared deep into my wounded eyes. "There is no part of you that is selfish. You're the least selfish person I know."

Oh, Elsa. Her words were always wise and astute. She knew exactly what to say.

And so, the dark cloud passed, and I remembered that everything was exactly the way it should be. Elsa reminded me of my accomplishments and bravery. She reminded me of how my decision had opened new doors and paved the way to the ultimate self-discovery. She reminded me of all the lives I'd changed through my sanctuary.

I was happy. Noah was happy. Sam was happy.

Life was good.

There was no room for regret.

I stood in the middle of the lobby, my gaze settling back on Thomas. He was chatting with a patient, his hands telling an elaborate tale. I was looking forward to the tales he would tell me on our dinner date.

"You'll have fun tonight," Elsa said, as if reading my mind. "Thomas is a good man. He's waited a long time to ask you out."

I sighed. "I'm sure he was petrified of me. The only two men I ever actually dated are dead. And the third man, who I almost dated, almost died at the hands of one of my dead exes." I paused, blinking. "I think I just wrote myself into a reality show."

Elsa chugged the rest of her tea. "This tea does not contain nearly enough alcohol to help me process all of that."

Anne was listening in on our conversation. She waved her hands into the air with dramatic animation. "I can see it now: Chelsie Combs—the black widow with a heart of gold. Loves cats and *Citizen Kane*."

I supposed I had to laugh at my plight. It was better than crying. "Poor Thomas," I mused, my shoulders sagging with defeat. "He doesn't stand a chance."

"Oh, stop. You're going to have a great time," Elsa said. "Why don't you head out now and get a head start? I'll finish payroll."

I stared at her, slack-jawed. "I still have—"

"I'll take care of it." Elsa smiled. "Go rest up and have fun tonight. I will be turning my phone off silent mode as I await all of the juicy details."

"Are you sure? I—"

"Go!" Elsa and Anne both shouted in unison.

I grinned through the bundle of nerves in my belly. "Okay... thank you. I'll see you guys tomorrow."

As I breezed through the lobby a few minutes later, there was a new skip in my step. I glanced over at Jon and Maggie, who were sitting by the fountain feature, huddled in close and making moon-eyes at each other. A smile crested on my mouth.

Maybe there was hope for me, after all.

I sauntered into Mackenzie's that evening feeling equally intimidated and excited about my date with Thomas.

Mackenzie's was a laidback restaurant with a bar and big screen TVs. It was busy and boisterous, and it had two pool tables in the far corner. It was full of distractions, which made it a prime first date location. I didn't need to worry about fancy dinner etiquette or awkward silences.

A Freeze Frame song was playing as I pushed through the double doors, causing me to pause in my tracks. I closed my eyes for a moment, soaking in the memories before casting them aside.

"Bloody hell."

Thomas appeared in front of me looking extraordinarily handsome in a cerulean button-down and crisp jeans. I beamed up at him as I entered. "Hey, you."

"You look... smashing," he said. His eyes were drinking me in like I was a high-end liquor. "I'm the luckiest bloke in the room right now."

I blushed beneath his gaze. I felt particularly pretty in a black cocktail dress with off-the-shoulder sleeves and a low neckline, my hair in curls, my face painted. It had been years since I'd dressed up for any occasion.

"Shall we take a seat?" Thomas offered, extending his hand to a nearby table.

Nodding, I clutched my purse tightly between nervous fingers, then glanced down at it when I saw my phone light up from inside. Lisa's name was flashing across the screen.

I'd have to call her back later.

We slid into opposite sides of a booth as menus were set in front of us. I lifted the menu to my face, more to hide behind the plastic pages than to actually read through the dinner selections. Food was the last thing on my mind while my belly churned with nerves.

"Do you fancy this place?" Thomas asked.

I lowered the menu slightly, peering over the top as I cleared my throat. "This is my first time here, actually. I'm not exactly a social butterfly."

Thomas' laugh was gritty and sensual. "I don't suppose you are. I like that about you. You're... refreshing."

"Or boring, in some cultures," I cringed.

"Rubbish. You're a breath of fresh air, love. Once you stop hiding behind your tormented past and that bloody menu, you'll see what I see. What everyone sees, really."

I almost choked on a breath.

"I see what Sam sees. And Devon. And probably every person you cross paths with. I'll never understand how you don't see it, too."

Noah's words slammed into me like a sucker-punch to the gut as I set the menu down on the table. I picked at the peeling plastic, trying to collect my thoughts. A heavy silence settled in.

"Is it something I said, love?"

My head popped up as I swallowed back the penitent residue on my tongue. "Not at all. That was quite the compliment. Thank you."

He smiled. "Drinks?"

"I'd love that."

When the waitress approached, Thomas ordered our beverages. "A rum and Coke for the lady, please. I'll take a whiskey on the rocks. Be a love and fetch us that flowerin' onion appetizer as well."

I ran my tongue along my teeth.

Whiskey. Did it have to be whiskey?

It had been six years. Six goddamn years, and I still reeked of Noah Hayes.

He was haunting me.

My purse began to vibrate as the waitress set our drinks in front of us. Lisa was calling again. I turned my phone to silent mode and reached for my cocktail. Maybe a solid buzz would kill my nerves, right along with any trace of Noah Hayes.

"So, what exactly brought you to Florida?" Thomas asked as his gaze roamed over the dinner menu. "We've worked side by side for six years, and I'm realizing I don't know a lick about you."

His eyes twinkled as he paused. "Aside from playing remarkably hard to get."

I ducked my head, my cheeks pinkening. "I just needed a change," I said. "A fresh start. My parents were in Florida."

"Go on," he encouraged.

I clutched the cold glass in my hand and sipped on the straw. The cocktail was sweet as it slid down my throat, providing me with a bout of liquid courage. "Well..."

Hesitation suddenly seized me. Something made me stop mid-sentence. Swallowing, I stood from the booth, my drink still gripped tightly in my hand.

That name.

His name.

"What is it?" Thomas asked in bewilderment.

I hardly heard him. My eyes landed on one of the televisions above the bar, and I moved toward it, as if the newscaster on the screen had full control over my body. I felt hypnotized. Possessed. I drowned out the clamor of music and laughter, only hearing the "Breaking News" report that flashed across the TV.

"A tragedy occurred tonight here in Jericho, New York. Beth Hayes, wife of acclaimed solo artist Noah Hayes, was found murdered in the home of one of her real estate properties earlier this evening. She was allegedly found after she failed to return home after the showing of this property on Prager Court."

A female reporter stood in front of a sprawling estate as red and blue police lights flashed around her. A helicopter loomed over-head in the distance.

"This story is still developing as authorities try to piece together what happened in the early evening hours of Thursday night. The police advise the public to come forward with any information that may lead to an arrest in this case. I'm Jasmine Delgado, reporting live from ABC7 – New York."

The glass slipped from my hand and hit the floor, shattering into a thousand pieces.

Much like my heart.

Two strong arms were suddenly around my waist, catching me. I hadn't even realized I was falling until my limp body was being propped back up and guided toward a bar stool. I sat down in a daze, muddled voices swimming in my ears as Thomas' concerned face came into view.

"Bloody hell, Chelsie. Are you all right?"

No. I was not all right.

Worried patrons swarmed me.

"Can we get a sodding glass of water over here?" Thomas ordered to the bartender. He turned his attention back to me. "Talk to me, love."

I couldn't speak. I could only stare up at the television screen as pictures of Noah and Beth reflected back at me. My vision blurred with hot tears. My skin prickled with insurmountable dread. My wildly beating heart was in my throat.

I felt sick. Dizzy.

Darkness was closing in.

Noah.

I had a feeling that nothing would ever be the same...

ACKNOWLEDGMENTS

In 2009, I began to create the little world of Chelsie and Noah. They were only seedlings at the time, pushing through the dirt, waiting to bloom. Luckily, they were patient, as it took an entire decade to write this book. After stopping and starting too many times (becoming a mother was quite time-consuming, I discovered), I committed to finishing their story late summer of 2019. I have my husband to thank for the push.

This leads me to my first acknowledgement. However, it's less of an acknowledgement and more of a grand outpouring of gratitude. Jake Hartmann, I could not have finished this book without your love, support, and ongoing encouragement. I know love stories are not "your thing," and you are not at all my target audience, but you read every chapter I sent you. You brainstormed with me, gave me your unbiased input, and even inspired storylines. You gave me uninterrupted time to write, helped me with the formatting and the techy aspects that are far beyond my interest, and created (and re-created, two years later) my book covers.

Thank you for always believing in me, even when—no, *especially* when—I struggle to believe in myself. I love you.

Much love to Nicole Vaughn for being the gorgeous model on my original cover. Our photoshoot day will always hold a special place in my heart. I'm so happy to have you in my life.

Big shoutout to my editors and original beta readers: Chelley St Clair, Amanda Jesse, Ruth Dowling Coffman, Kate Aley, Molly Nicole, Megan Rusek, Danielle Grobe, Laurie Romano, Megan Lick, Deana Birch, Trisha Roon, Kelly Anderson-Kole, and LuAnn Meinheit Moon. This story would not have evolved or become the best version it could be without all of you. Thank you so much for your feedback and your willingness to offer critique and suggestions.

Special thanks to Kristina Mahr, fellow author and inspiration, for being the first to read my hot mess of a first draft. I am absolutely tickled you were able to see its potential. I appreciate all your invaluable advice as I navigate through the unknown world of publishing.

Thank you to my family for accompanying me on my debut journey into the writing world: my children, Willow, Liam, and Violet, my father, Keith Lindquist, and his wife, Cynthia, and my "second parents," Marlene and Scott Bowers.

And, always and forever, to my late mother, Theresa Lindquist. I miss your wise words and encouragement. I miss your warmth and laughter. I miss *you*.

You celebrated my terrible poems and silly stories from a very young age.

I wish you were here to celebrate with me now.

ALSO BY JENNIFER HARTMANN

Still Beating

Lotus

The Wrong Heart

June First

Claws and Feathers

Co-Writes

The Thorns Remain

Entropy

CONNECT

If you enjoyed this story and would like to chat more about it,
check out the Aria/Coda Discussion Group on Facebook!
And feel free to join my reader's group:
Queen of Harts: Jennifer Hartmann's Reader Group
Follow me:
Instagram: @author.jenniferhartmann
Facebook: @jenhartmannauthor
Twitter: @authorjhartmann
TikTok: @jenniferhartmannauthor

No pressure, but my heart explodes when I see a nice review.
Leave your thoughts on Amazon, Goodreads, and Bookbub!

www.jenniferhartmannauthor.com

ABOUT THE AUTHOR

Hartmann resides in northern Illinois with her devoted husband, Jake, and three children, Willow, Liam, and Violet. When she is not writing angsty love stories, she is likely thinking about writing them. She enjoys sunsets (because mornings are hard), bike riding, traveling anywhere out of Illinois, binging Buffy the Vampire Slayer reruns, and that time of day when coffee gets replaced by wine. She is excellent at making puns and finding inappropriate humor in mundane situations. She loves tacos. She also really, really wants to pet your dog. *Xoxo.*

CPSIA information can be obtained
at www.ICGtesting.com
Printed in the USA
BVHW042044020423
661637BV00001B/11

9 798823 116640